THE CORNERS

BUILDING THE CIRCLE - BOOK 4

MAGGIE M LILY

This is a work of fiction. Names, characters, events, and incidents are the products of the author's imagination. Any resemblance to actual persons, living or dead, or actual events is purely coincidental. Certain long-standing institutions, agencies, and public offices are mentioned, but the characters and situations involved are wholly imaginary.

Cover design by Melony Paradise of Paradise Cover Design

Standard Print Paperback ISBN: 978-1-7353887-6-2
Large Print Paperback ISBN: 978-1-7353887-7-9

Thank you, Julie, for your sage advice and guidance on everything from character names to cover images.

PROLOGUE

Wednesday night, Ellie Hapner sat bolt upright in bed, head pounding with energy.

Too much energy.

Matilda had too much energy.

Getting her bearings, Ellie realized it wasn't just too much energy. Matilda had a disastrous amount of energy.

"CHARLIE!"

"Uh?"

"Charlie, wake up!"

"Time is it?" Charlie muttered.

"Three thirteen a.m. WAKE UP!"

Charlie groaned. "Ells, wha—? Oh. Whoa. Ugh. Are you going to be sick? I might be sick. Have you heard from Matty?"

"She texted last night, saying they were in Dallas for a family thing," Ellie snapped.

"I'm sure she's fine, Ellie."

"How are you sure of that? I'm not sure of that. This is a 'gone nuclear' level of energy, Charlie."

"Maybe call Eric? He might know more."

"Charlie, Gay Boy never knows more than me. Give it up. Why are you placating?"

"Because I can't think straight. Now that I'm awake, my skin is trying to fly off my body," Charlie muttered, scratching his arms as he tumbled out of bed. "I need to run."

"I'm calling her."

Charlie's eyebrows shot up. "What will you say if she answers? 'Hey Matty, just calling to make sure no one sucked away your life.' Something like that? What will you do if she doesn't answer?"

"Anyone could have sent that text, Charlie. If she doesn't answer… I don't know. I'll call Jake. If she answers, I'll tell her I had a nasty dream or something. I don't know," Ellie snapped, diving for her phone.

"Here's an idea: Let's sit her down and explain. That way, she knows," Charlie said, heavy on the snark. This was a long-standing point of contention for Charles and Eleanor.

"Charlie, again. I told you. I tried that in college. Often. She looked at me like I was nuts. Shit was awkward. Let's not go back to that. She'll figure it out. Creepy fucking Sam will figure his shit out."

"Again, Ells, if we talk to her together, I can show—"

"Charlie, we can't show-and-tell; she's not here. FUCK. She's not answering. Something bad is happening. I know something bad is happening."

"Ellie, calm down. Call Jake."

"Jake's not answering, either," Ellie panted, waiting for the tone to leave a voice mail. "FUCK A DUCK! Call me back, Jacob!"

Ellie started pacing the bedroom.

"I can't believe you left that voicemail. I love you so much. I'm going for a run. Call Eric. I'll be back in twenty minutes."

MIRANDA TIP-TOED out of the guest bathroom on silent feet, stepping past the master bedroom where her husband slept. Out of range of Lawrence, she took a deep, calming breath.

The fern in the front foyer needed water; the cactus in the kitchen window needed to be rotated. Otherwise, the house was peaceful.

On the back porch, Miranda smiled, basking in the bright, hot July morning sun. It felt glorious after the artificial air conditioning.

The damp grass in her small backyard was cool underfoot. She didn't sit. Lawrence would be mad if he found her sitting in the grass again. But she wiggled the toes on her bare feet and said good morning to the earth beneath her.

This was Miranda's favorite part of the day. The house was quiet. The anxiety and loneliness that plagued her were absent, leaving calm contentment in their place. She could sense the earth and its joy at her presence. Gravity gently pulled at her, making her safe.

As she did every morning, she searched through the world for her loved ones. Her parents were still asleep in their house. Her brother was at the office while his wife lay in bed.

At last, Miranda searched for her older sister. Finding Matilda was always a challenge. She lived in a high-rise, far removed from contact with the earth.

But this morning, Matilda was on a ground floor, somewhere in the southern United States for the second day in a row.

Matty didn't mention traveling. I wonder if we're still getting together on Friday. I'll call her later, Miranda decided.

With the check on her loved ones complete, Miranda focused on the earth around her. There was an animal den in the park across the street. Maybe bunnies. She'd watch for the park caretaker before he mowed the grass.

Her planter box garden was doing well. If it didn't rain in the next day or two, she'd water the soil. The roses in the front—

"MIRANDA!" Lawrence bellowed from the kitchen.

"LINDA," a voice called. "Linnnndaaaa. It's time to wake up."

It was a happy dream. As a little girl, maybe five years old, she was visiting her mother's older sister. They sat around a bonfire and ate toasted marshmallows on long sticks.

As she swam back to wakefulness, Linda wasn't sure if it was a dream or a memory. The warm fire was bright, though. Peace washed over her from the remembered sensations.

She never got the chance to take Ree camping. Lucy would show him how to toast marshmallows. Lucy would love Ree and keep him safe. *Thank God for Lucy.*

Linda resigned herself to never seeing her son again. Still, she trusted Ree's life would be as joyful as possible with her best friend and adopted sister. Ree would have a better childhood than Linda or Lucy.

We had each other when no one else wanted us, though. We made our way together. If that's not family, I don't know what is.

Mental force slammed against Linda's brain while she was adrift in sleepy reflection. Sometimes, if they caught her at just the right moment, her mind was open enough to take before she was alert enough to fight. Today wasn't one of those days.

"Why do you keep fighting?" he asked. "You'll lose. You'll get tired and be forced to let go. We all know it'll happen. Just let me help. We can let you out of the cage, Linda."

"Fuck you," she breathed.

"No, I want to understand. Why are you fighting this?" His voice sounded concerned. Compassionate.

This one always pretended to care. He asked questions, concerned for Linda's wellbeing. It made the violent invasion of her mind that much worse. She didn't bother answering. She wouldn't allow a mental binding to persist.

"Linda, why? You don't need to stay in this basement. Just let me bind with you. Accept it. Binding to me is better than David. You can get out of the cage. I hate seeing you like this. Please stop suffering this way. Let the binding hold. Let it be. There's no use to this, no point to it," he pleaded.

She spit in his face. His mental attack flinched back in surprise and revulsion.

"That was uncalled for," he said, voice frosty.

She smiled, mental walls now firmly in place, ready for a siege.

"Why? Why are you doing this to yourself?" he demanded.

Linda's smile turned toward a grimace as the pressure built behind her eyes. "I'm hoping you fuck up and kill me by accident. You can't take my bindings, John."

"WHAT A WEIRD FUCKING WEEK," Jake groaned, dragging himself toward wakefulness. Matilda was still asleep, resting against him in a booth. Trellis siblings and significant others slumbered in clumps and clusters throughout Clyde and Ava's restaurant.

"It's only Wednesday, man," Will murmured from the booth behind him. "Your head going to explode?"

"Yup. And not from the whiskey. Everyone else still out?" Jake whispered.

"Hennessy was awake an hour ago then crashed again. Any idea what time it is? I can't see the bar clock from this angle, and my phone's in my pocket," Will muttered.

"You been sittin' on your phone all fucking night? It's 5:42 a.m." Jake's chuckle was quiet as he noticed missed calls from Ellie.

"Who am I going to call? Everyone I talk to is here. I didn't want to shuffle around and wake Pip. Sun's coming up. Can you feel it?"

There was a pause. "Yeah. Yeah, I can. Will, why can I feel the sun coming up?" Jake asked, just a hint of worry to his voice.

"No idea, man. Can feel gravity pulling on me, too, if I think about it."

"Holy. Fuck."

JULY

1

Adaline giggled. "Quit touching! It tickles when they move."

"I know. That's why I keep touching them." Sam laughed, running his fingers over the wildflower garden marked on Addy's back. Without his touch, the markings looked like a typical tattoo. But, as Sam's fingers drifted across her skin, the flowers swayed, caught in a light breeze.

The Walker and Mistress Life stood in a patch of tall grass in the middle of their clearing outside of Dallas, surrounded by blooming plants and scurrying creatures. The scent of fresh flowers and damp earth mingled with the energy of love, uplifting all life within the vibrant space.

"We should go back to the restaurant. See how everyone is doing," Addy offered reluctantly.

"When the wildflowers sway, is it time for sex?"

"Isn't it always time for sex?" Adaline asked.

"You *can* read my mind!"

"Children, now is not the time for sex." Evelyn chuckled from the perimeter of the clearing, just past the tree line. "It's sunrise. It's time to talk."

"Boo," James chided her. "They're good kids. They did what we wanted them to do. We can come back later."

Evelyn rolled her eyes while they walked toward the center of the clearing to be closer to Samuel and Adaline. "They weren't thinking sexy thoughts. We should talk to them before they go back to everyone else."

Evelyn ran her fingers through the wild grass, inhaling deeply, a slight smile reflecting in her violet eyes.

James heaved a put-upon sigh, untouched by the loving energy around him. "Fine. How do you feel, Sam? Why are you glaring at me?"

"Did you know about the cold?" Sam demanded. "I knew it would do something. But not that."

"What cold? What happened?" Watching Evelyn revel in the positive energy amused James.

Sam continued to glare.

"We've discussed this. You're better at Walking than me," James said, flippant, still watching Evelyn. "What happened? I didn't look. I couldn't see you taking the name, so there was no point in looking."

"After we took the names, the cold took Adaline." Sam's voice vibrated with anger. "You could have warned me about that! It could have hurt her…more than it did."

"What the fuck are you talking about? What cold?" James grunted, now paying full attention.

Sam glared harder. "The cold. The emotional distance. The coldness. When Walking."

Evelyn's voice was full of wonder. "The indifference? Adaline got whacked with indifference? What was *that* like?"

"I didn't feel anything. I-I tried to take his power," Addy stammered, eyes filling with tears.

James snorted, looking at Sam. "That's interesting. You're still tightly bound in accordance. How did you keep your energy and keep the accordance?"

"I took her through time with me. It hurt her. Why didn't you warn us?" Sam snapped.

"Took her through time? You shared the thoughts with her?" James asked.

"No, I took her through time. I took her with me," Sam clarified, confused by James's confusion.

James's face dropped into a grumpy scowl. "I don't know what that means, Sam."

"I took her with me. Like I brought Matilda back with me when she fell into time."

Evelyn's mouth dropped open. "Lady Light fell into time?"

"You pulled Adaline through time? Not just sharing the thoughts, but pulled her with you in time?" James ran a hand through his hair, bewildered.

"Yes. You should have warned us, James! It hurt her. I didn't realize the cold was part of the energy that could be shared. I wasn't paying attention to it while I was waking up!" Sam yelled.

"Uh, I didn't know, Sam," James soothed.

"You two are in uncharted territory on the accordance front. Anyway, don't be afraid of the indifference. 'The cold.' So dramatic. It's an emotional switch. It serves a purpose. Use it to maintain sanity." James was moving away from Evelyn as he spoke, trying to be inconspicuous about getting out of arm's reach.

Evelyn's body posture screamed of unhappiness, shoulders rigid with anger in the middle of the love clearing. "James," she warned.

"That's not what we're here about," James blurted. "How do you feel?"

"Too much energy," Adaline murmured.

Evelyn nodded in understanding. "I can feel the energy radiating from you both. It's gigantic. We didn't know it would do that."

Sam's face was a question mark.

"The accordance you two have is absurd." James scrunched up his face in disgust. "Do you share brain space now? Yeesh. Anyway, don't worry about it, Adaline. It changes. It'll shrink as you two get less lovey-dovey."

Evelyn scowled at James again. "Stop that! I don't want them to be less lovey-dovey. They're adorable like this. Quit saying that shit. There's too much rampant energy here. You'll fuck it up!"

Sam's lips quirked at the corners.

"Don't look at me like that, Samuel." Evelyn shared her scowl with both men. "We didn't do this phase—"

"Oh, yes, we did!" James argued, offended.

"No, we didn't. We had a lustful decade of rampant sex," Evelyn corrected. "Then we got bored and became more like snarky siblings."

"We didn't get bored. You tried to kill me," James mumbled.

"You started it. Don't be a jackass. You picked a fight and lost. Not my fault," Evelyn shot back. "Anyway. Yeah, there's a lot of shared power. It'll settle down once you use it. What's with the flower garden and the compass markings? Are they part of the accordance?"

Sam shook his head. "We planned to ask you. You're Mother Life and Father Time now. You're supposed to know things."

Evelyn glowered at him.

"It doesn't feel like the accordance mark. It moves like the accordance, but it feels different," Adaline added.

"We didn't have that, even when I allowed accordance. Josiah and Madrid didn't, either." Evelyn shrugged. "Sometimes the energy does interesting things on its own. Other than the power overload, you feel okay? Reasonably like yourselves?"

"Who else would we feel like?" Adaline's face furrowed in confusion.

"Oh," Samuel said, gaze unfocused.

"Did he just—?" Evelyn stammered.

"Yeah." James laughed. "He did."

Sam's voice was distant. "I understand. I see them. No, that didn't happen to us, Evelyn. We're fine."

Adaline looked at Sam. He shrugged.

"There was a pair before James and Evelyn who didn't transition well. She lost control and started the Black Death. We're fine. Still us."

James's gaze turned suspicious. "You'd say that even if you weren't fine, though. If you were out of control, would you know it?"

Still staring at Sam, Evelyn smacked James. "Stop it."

There was a lengthy pause. Sam eventually broke it. "Why are you staring at me?"

"She's scared," Adaline whispered. "She fears you. Fears us."

"I told her we use time differently. She's never seen it before." James grinned. "She'll be fine."

Sam's brow furrowed in concern. "I didn't mean to scare you, Evelyn. It's fine. I'm still me."

James let out a quiet, mocking chuckle. "At some point, we'll Walk together, so you understand. I don't step in and out of it like that. It's difficult for me to use time. I don't pinpoint focus. But Josiah taught me how to do it, and he was terrible at it. There were benefits to leaving you both to play with your energy on your own, without our guidance."

Evelyn shook her head. "Time will tell."

"I just did. I just told you," James teased with a grin, trying to ease her tension.

An eye-roll later, Evelyn was back on point. "What are you two going to do with yourselves? What's next?"

Sam blinked. "Isn't that what you're supposed to tell us?"

James smirked. "You're not double-oh-nine. We won't send you out on missions."

"Nine?" Sam asked.

"Like the spy guy," James said, disappointed that Sam didn't get the reference.

Sam grinned. "It's seven. James Bond is double-oh-seven."

Evelyn pulled a smug smile across her face, distracted from her fear. "I've told you that more than once, dumb ass. It's more fun for me when you're stupid around others. It highlights how much you don't listen to me to your own detriment."

"What are we supposed to do?" Adaline tried to stay on topic.

"Dump energy into the world. You have enough of it, even without that giant circle of yours. We talked about this." Evelyn sighed.

James shrugged. "This is why I was so surprised that you struggled with the decision, Sam. You were already healing things. The extra energy, pairing, and circle just make it easier."

"Go build out the rest of your circle and start dumping energy into the world. It'll go faster and easier as the circle fills out. The energy spreads more evenly with more people. Evie and I will focus on cleaning up now. Maybe build out a circle of our own."

"Meh." Evelyn shrugged. "You keep talking about that. I don't know how you think that will work. We don't have Pillars, James. Did you and Micah kiss and make up? Is he going to stand with us? We need at least a few Pillars. I wouldn't want to share energy with most of the other outcast Pillars."

James glowered at her. "Micah wouldn't drink my beer."

That reminded Sam of a question. "How is Micah still roaming around with his power after giving up his name? How does that happen? I thought the energy had to be recycled over time."

"Micah was the Pillar of Hate. Do you ever see the world running short on hate? Do you think life would suffer if there was less of it?" James challenged.

Sam nodded. "Matilda is right. It is annoying when someone answers a question with a question."

"The vibrant Lady Light is quite something. I can't believe she fell into time. Lots of power packed into that little curvy body," James said with a smile that leaned toward a leer.

Sam glared at him again.

"What?" James asked, looking innocent.

Sam continued to glare.

"She's into the Anchor? Really? But he's a dumb ass." James's face fell.

Evelyn smacked him again. "Anyway. Pick up Ava's old circle. You need more bodies now. You won't be able to close another circle like yesterday. Don't try it. You'll scorch people. There's too much power with just the two of you, let alone with the Pillars.

"The circle in Chicago is one of the largest in the country and also one of the strongest. It's an excellent home base to start with. You can build outward from there."

Evelyn shifted her focus as Addy's terror rolled through the clearing, overwhelming the sense of love. "Being in a populated area is different. But you'll be fine now. You can't stay in this clearing in the middle of nowhere, Mistress Life. The Anchor will be there with you. It's easier to move the energy with him. He'll help more than this field ever did."

Sam looked skeptical. "How would Jake help? He's stuffed full of Matty's energy. I was plenty out of balance with him around."

Evelyn patted Sam's arm with a condescending smirk. Her world was back in order with Sam's power tucked away and his ignorance showing. "You were thirty years out of balance. If he hadn't stayed with you for so long, the clock would have ticked on midnight years ago."

"I thought the organic circle thing balanced us all?" Sam asked, undisturbed by Evelyn's tone.

"It does. Jake's the only one who cycles energy out of the circle, though. The rest of you just keep dumping more energy into it. Your parents can only absorb so much. Your organic circle would crumble if he disappeared from it for any length of time." Evelyn glared at James again.

"They don't *need* the organic circle. It's a nice-to-have," James mumbled.

Samuel, as The Walker, stared at James, eyes glowing.

At fifteen seconds, the silent staring became uncomfortable.

At thirty seconds, James squirmed. "I won't bother him. I'm teasing."

"You are lying," Samuel warned, voice loaded with power. "They are mine. You will not disturb their balance, James."

"Oh, shut up. I'll leave him be. She'll get bored with him eventually, anyway."

"What do you need from us?" Sam asked Evelyn, all signs of the Walker's power gone.

Evelyn blinked several times, processing the rapid change. "Nothing, really. We needed to make sure you were both sane and warn you that you need more people in your circle."

"Are you able to stand in our circle?" Adaline inquired.

"I don't know," James admitted after a few seconds, surprised by her question. "Josiah was very stingy with his circle. We could not talk to their pillars directly. Given that you're on cooking duty and we're on clean-up duty, I'm not sure what would happen if we all stood together. That might be a good question for the thief."

Sam nodded. "I'll ask him."

"Are we able to share accordance with you?" Adaline asked.

Evelyn and James both rocked back in shock.

"Addy," Evelyn muttered, voice subdued. "Accordance is uncommon, even between a pair. James Walked through the past to look for it. We don't think it's ever been shared to the level you and Sam have."

"The largest mark I could find went to the Walker's elbow," James murmured, looking at his feet.

Evelyn sighed. "Josiah and Madrid had none. I shared a negligible amount with James in the beginning."

"There is so much energy—more energy between Sam and me than I imagined in the entire world. And then we each have more of our own. It scares me. I think it may be hard to cycle it. You have no circle—limited energy. I would not mind sharing with you," Adaline explained.

"I don't know that it's possible, Addy. And I don't know that it'd be advisable. I do not have Samuel's aversion to the indifference," James confessed. "Power is intoxicating, even when you don't intend harm."

Adaline nodded, eyes downcast.

"Do you feel the binding to me, Sam?" James's voice was somber.

Sam nodded. "I can find you if we need you."

"WHAT WERE THOSE WORDS, ADALINE?" Sam inquired as they walked through the forest, back toward the restaurant.

She jumped at Sam's sudden break in the silence.

"You said words on Monday. About guilt and blame," he muttered, eyes going unfocused for a second. "'Guilt and blame do not belong between us.' That's what you said. It's still true."

"You Walk easily now," Adaline murmured, astonished.

"It's hard to *not* Walk now. It pulls at me. I can't turn it off anymore." Sam's voice was muffled with concern as he watched where they walked through the forest.

"Life is everywhere for me now, even more than before. It's like that?" she asked.

Sam shook his head. "I don't know. When they asked how we felt, you asked something about how else we would feel. I didn't even think about it. I Walked to the place and time. It pulled me directly to the answer to your question. I asked what your words were. It pulled me to the words. I didn't mean to do it. It's distracting."

Silence fell between them again as her feelings of shame flowed through their link.

"Addy—" Sam started.

"Stop, Sam. It's not okay. There are no words to make it okay."

"It's over, Adaline. Shame and guilt have no purpose."

Adaline sighed. "I might have destroyed us. A minute of quiet in my mind, where there is always noise and distraction, could have destroyed things. It's not a lesson I will forget."

Sam stopped walking and turned to face her. "What lesson did you learn?"

Addy's shoulders drooped, damp violet eyes focused on the ground. Her black hair hung loose, partially hiding her face.

"I am not trustworthy with that power," she whispered. "I am not immune to it."

As Sam's anger rolled through their binding, Adaline flinched, snapping her gaze to his.

"You've missed the larger point. We don't stand alone, Addy. When you were lost, I found you. You told me you'd remind me of who I am. Is it so bad that you might also need that help? Am I the only one allowed to need help?"

After a moment, she nodded in acknowledgment.

Sam continued. "It seems things are mutable between us. We can shift and change. Our connection can shift and change. I nearly destroyed it last night. We rebuilt it quickly enough. It is broader and more robust now—more energy.

"The only change to come from last night is a healthy fear of the cold. Or the indifference. Whatever. I thought it was a character trait. We learned that it's not. That lesson is well-learned. Everything else? Meh. Shit happens."

Adaline burst out laughing.

"We are here now. Let's be happy." Sam grinned, repeating Adaline's own words back to her.

She smiled up at him, the last few tears dripping down her cheeks.

SAM PULLED on the restaurant back door only to find it locked.

"Really?"

"Hunters," Adaline reminded him.

"Oh!" There was a touch of panic in his voice.

"They're fine. Everyone's here. Sleeping mostly. The Anchor and Fear are awake. Ask one of them—"

Without warning, Sam and Adaline appeared in the center of the restaurant.

"I forgot about that," she admitted. "We didn't need to walk from the clearing."

Sam gave a sheepish smile. "We needed to talk."

"How is everyone?" Sam whispered to William.

"Why can I feel gravity, Sam?" Will's tone was flat as he glared at his brother.

"Uh, I don't know," Sam admitted, surprised. "I don't feel— Oh. Yes, I do. I don't know."

"The sun?"

Sam shrugged. "I don't know much more than you. How is everyone?"

"My head feels like it'll explode any minute. Jake's, too."

"Hurts to have my eyes open," Jake mumbled. "I think I'm getting some of Jess's shit. How do I make that stop?"

"I don't know," Sam said again, looking at Adaline. She shook her head. "We don't know."

"Can you get those two assholes who knew what the fuck they were doing to straighten this shit out?" Jake bitched.

"We just talked to them. They said we need a bigger circle with more bodies. We need to go back to Chicago."

Jake squinted his eyes open at his little brother as Matty stirred. "Great. Zap us home. Let's do that before I puke."

"Oh my God," Matty moaned, trying to focus her eyes. "My head."

Noah shifted around, two booths over.

"I want to die. I can't move. I'd puke, but I'd have to move to do that," he croaked, voice hoarse and tight. "Why is the room fucking spinning? Why are you people breathing so fucking loud? Why do I feel like I'm on fire? Sam, this is absolutely your fault. I just fucking know it. You're a giant fucking pain in the ass. You are my least favorite brother until the end of time."

"It was all fun and games when you were just horny, but now that shit's gotten real..." Jake laughed.

"Fuck you, too, whatever the fuck weird thing you are." Noah sighed. "Can we just sit quietly?"

"Matty?" Jake whispered, concerned when she put her head down on the booth table.

"I'll take that as a 'no.' I hate the world." Noah groaned.

"Every inch of me hurts." She sighed. "I'm fine. My chest is tight. I can feel the sun."

"How are you doing, Sam?" Jake asked, eyes still closed as he ran his hand through Matilda's mussed fiery curls.

Sam snorted, breaking out in a full grin. "I've never felt better."

Noah glared at him.

Sam's pale blue eyes shone with health and happiness. His normally gray, ashen skin had vibrancy.

Sam looked like the young man he was, rather than the exhausted, drawn, sickly wretch he'd been for most of his life.

"Fucking thirty-year-old virgin finally had fucking sex, and now we're all fucked up," Noah mumbled under his breath. He paused at Adaline's touch on his forehead.

"Addy, he's a whiner. Don't!" Sam's voice was sad.

"Oh, sweet mother of God. That is so much better. I love you, Adaline." Noah groaned, smiling up at her. "You are an angel. A violet-eyed, beautiful angel-woman-girl. I will love you forever."

Adaline slapped him on the forehead.

"What did you do?" Noah rubbed his forehead.

"I took the excess. You were severely overloaded," Adaline whispered, words laced with power.

"She took the extra energy because you're a crybaby," Sam bitched, the echo in his voice making his displeasure known.

Jake leaned away from Addy as she approached him. "Does it hurt you?"

She shrugged. "Used to it."

"I'll be fine." Jake grunted.

Addy looked surprised.

"It sucks, but not enough for me to hurt you. It's fine."

"Jake, she wants to know if she can touch you to build the link for you to hear her without words." Sam's unhappiness continued to spread throughout the room.

"Don't be pissed off because she wants to talk to people other than you, jackass," Jake said, glaring at Sam.

"I'm not pissed off because she wants to talk to you, idiot. I'm pissed off because she's planning for the inability to speak again. She's planning to be severely overloaded and in a fuckton of pain. Again."

"Give Noah back his shit! He'll be fine. He's a great big sissy," Jake barked, causing the others to stir.

Addy raised her eyebrows, hand hovering over Jake's in a question.

"Yes, of course, you can talk to me." He nodded.

Adaline grinned at him, sharing joy. Jake couldn't help but smile back.

Adaline's eyes dropped to Matty.

"I'm fine. Just feel strange," Matilda muttered. "It's not so bad I can't function."

Adaline nodded. *"You could burn off the excess, Matilda, as fire. Outside or in the fireplace."*

"How do I do that?" Matty asked, intrigued.

"I don't know. I don't have fire. Sam?" Addy broadcast.

"I've never done it on purpose. We can try together, Matty," Sam offered.

Will started talking before Adaline even finished turning toward him. "It's a headache for me. I'm fine. Give me Noah's energy when you give me the link for talking, Adaline."

She shook her head, gesturing at Emma before touching Will's hand.

"She may need your help with the little ones. I'm fine for now," Adaline broadcast.

"But no more words? Already? There was no pain earlier," Sam lamented.

"I don't want to make a mistake. I went so long without talking, Sam. This is more natural for me. It will be fine once the energy is balanced again. The pain is not bad," Adaline responded.

"Jake, try sucking the power from her like you did in the circle," Will suggested.

"I can't," Jake said.

"Why?" Will asked.

"I don't know. There's no more room. I just can't. I know I can't."

A banging on the door drowned out the sound of Ava, Clyde, Jess, and Blake coming down the backstairs.

"You gotta be kidding me," Will growled as he peeked out the window. Gently shifting Emma, he walked over to open the door. "I thought you left yesterday."

"No, I told you I'd chase off the hunters." Micah grinned.

"What do you want?" Will groaned. "Please be less chipper and loud. It makes me want to punch you in the head."

Micah snorted. "Go for it, He-Man."

"What. Do. You. Want?" Will repeated.

"I can tell you how to balance some of the energy. But if you don't want to know, I'll leave." Micah shrugged, eyebrows raised.

"Well, you can come in for that."

Will moved out of the doorway.

2

Micah's laughter drifted across the room. "You all look at least as bad as I thought you would. Except for Lust over there. Why's he fine?"

"Because he's a sissy," William growled, glaring at Noah.

"Mistress, Walker," Micah greeted Sam and Adaline with a formal bow. "May the balance of life be joyful and prosperous during your times."

"It's still 'Sam,' if you don't mind," Sam requested. "The formality seems misplaced unless we're at odds. We are not at odds, Micah. Not yet, at least."

Micah's eyebrows shot up in surprise. "I have no desire to be at odds with you. Are we to be at odds?"

"I hope not," Sam responded with sincerity.

After nodding in acceptance, Micah looked at Adaline and then turned to glare at Noah.

"Don't bother," Will muttered.

"Where are the others?" Micah asked. "Madam Sight will need help until a circle can balance things. She's blind right now."

"Yeah." Jess groaned, coming down the back stairs, holding onto her husband's shoulders.

Micah nodded. "It may be best to cover your eyes until the circle is closed. I know it doesn't help the sensation, but it will help the glare."

"Why do you know this? It's more now; it's feeling, too. But why do you know this?" Jess asked.

"This is why Madam Sight doesn't hang out in this crowd. Too much energy." Micah sat with Jess at the closest table, ignoring her question while taking her hand. "I'll take as much of the excess as I can. It's the only thing that helps without a circle."

"Why is the organic circle gone?" Jess sighed in relief as Ava wrapped her eyes in an ace bandage, and Micah pulled away energy.

"Maybe because Jake is overloaded," Sam suggested. "Evelyn said he holds the organic circle. And Jake, you are never to Walk with James. Never. There is not a valid reason to Walk with him. Ever. Understand? He means you harm."

Micah snorted, tossing *I told you so* looks to both Sam and Jake.

"What the fuck did I do to him?" Jake grumbled, head laying on the booth table.

"You romanced Lady Light." Micah grinned. "It's not you. It's her."

"Me?" Matilda sounded appalled. "I want nothing to do with the weird French potato dude. Fuck that."

"Where are the others?" Micah asked again, still laughing. "The young ones should stay upstairs if they can. This might upset them."

"Well, that's ominous," Adrian murmured from the corner booth where he and Lucy slept. "I'll go check how they're doing upstairs. Clyde, could I trouble you for some coffee?"

"Already brewing, Adrian. Emma, do you want tea? Decaf?" Clyde offered.

"Water would be wonderful, thank you. Why do I feel the sun? Get out of the way, Will. I might puke on you." Emma ran for the bathroom, hand over her mouth.

"Where is Joy?" Micah inquired. "Peace?"

"I'm here," Luke called, climbing upright from lying in the back corner on the floor. "I'm fine, though. Overloaded but not sick. Why is everyone sick?"

"Where is Joy?" Micah snapped, ignoring Luke.

"I'm here," Ethan murmured, coming down the back stairs. "I slept on the floor upstairs."

Micah nodded a greeting. "Chaos is with you, Peace?"

"I'm right here." The eye-roll was audible in Matthew's voice as he walked over to shake Beth and Hennessy awake.

"Oh, God. My head," Beth grumbled, jumping over Hennessy, running for the bathroom.

Micah winced. "Loyalty, are you well? Able to function?"

"I guess," Hennessy mumbled. "What do you need me to do?"

Micah's eyes flashed with sadness.

"Nothing, Hennessy." Micah's voice lacked the firm command it held. "I was trying to gauge if you need help with the pain. Hope and Love will be fine if they can move. You are all coherent enough for this."

"You all right?" Will noticed Micah's subdued voice.

Micah smiled. Not his typical toothy grin, but a smile. "I'm fine, Will. It's awkward to see the pure traits displayed. The Pillars rarely make it this far uncorrupted, as far as I have seen. And I've seen a lot of Pillars."

Jess squeezed his hand. Micah started, having lost track of the fact that he was holding Jess's hand.

"Thank you for helping me now, for helping us all yesterday. You need not be so alone, Micah," Jess offered.

Micah's slight smile fell. "I am not of your flock, Jess. Don't worry about me. Mistress?"

Adaline stood before Micah, holding out her hand.

"She'd like to form a binding so you can hear her mental communication," Sam explained.

Ava began pouring coffee as Hank and Darla came down the stairs.

Micah stared warily at Adaline.

Addy's sadness wafted through the room with her sigh. "By my power, just the ability to receive my thoughts. No more."

"I don't doubt your honesty, Adaline. I doubt the wisdom of being bound to me, no matter how lightly," Micah explained, taking her hand. "You will break this binding when I leave today."

Samuel chuckled, eyes glowing as he coasted through time. "You will not die at the mercy of a hunter, Micah. You're not a threat to her."

"Oddly, Walker, that makes me hopeful. If you know that, it means I will die one day." Micah chuckled.

"Well, aren't you sunshine and happiness this morning?" Will joked. "What the fuck, man? You didn't seem suicidal yesterday."

Micah's lips twitched up. "Tell me, Fear. How does one die when time will not take them and they are near-indestructible?"

Will snorted in disbelief.

"There are a few of us who broke from our circles before the pairs died. I know of two who are even older than me. I don't recommend the experience. I don't regret it, but I don't recommend it."

"Good morning," Micah continued, nodding to Hank and Darla. "Are you both well? Ava and Clyde seem fine. Are you?"

Darla smiled, giving him the same peck of a good morning cheek kiss she greeted all her family and friends with. "I feel fine. Not much sleep, but fine."

She didn't seem to notice Micah's baffled look or William's snort of laughter.

"How are you, kids?" she asked, making a lap of the room. "No more bleeding from the head, right? Where are Beth and Emma?"

"Puking," Noah blurted.

Darla looked both startled and hopeful.

"Beth is overloaded, not pregnant," Adaline broadcast as she touched Hank's hand.

"Well, damn," Darla muttered, hearing Adaline after the good morning kiss.

"Hearing you like that is not much different from hearing your voice, Adaline. I expected it to be different. I don't know why," Hank admitted. "Why aren't you talking, though? I thought we worked that out yesterday?"

"Noah's a sissy," Will bitched.

Adaline rolled her eyes at Will. *"Leave him be. Fleeting emotions offer no protection from pain. Fear will overcome pain when life depends on it. Anger, too. It is not so with lust."*

"Huh. I guess I never thought of it that way," Will acknowledged. "He's still a sissy. Horniness is a lame super-power."

"Pfft. Works out great for me." Noah laughed. "Not my fault you're whipped."

"Oh, Noah. You do not understand what you're missing, man." Will laughed back at his little brother.

"Lust is never particularly bright or strong." Micah grinned. "He or she is always in it for a good time. I would not underestimate Noah's ability to distract or taunt, though. How are you, Ethan? You're upright, at least."

Ethan nodded, sitting down across from Noah with his eyes closed.

"Clyde, do you have ginger ale?" Beth croaked, coming out of the bathroom to sit at the bar. "I feel so nasty."

"Oh, Beth," Darla sighed, running her hand over her daughter's head.

"The others?" Micah inquired as Adrian walked back into the room.

"They're coming. We're going home today? Did I hear that right?"

"I think so," Sam responded. "We saw James and Evelyn this morning. We need more people in the circle. They said to go home to Ava's circle."

Sam turned at the sound of a grunt as Greggory and Nora walked into the room, followed by Ben and Jared.

"I hold that circle, not Ava. I wonder why they called it your circle, rather than mine or Luke's." Greggory nodded his thanks as Ava handed him a cup of coffee.

Adaline held out a hand to Greggory and Nora. They each took it without question.

"Will the children stay upstairs?" Micah asked.

"The kids are all still sleeping." Adrian reached for his coffee.

"What do you expect us to do, Micah?" Sam frowned. "James and Evelyn were very clear about not trying to stand another circle as we did yesterday."

"No," Micah agreed. "There's nowhere for the energy to go. I'm not suggesting a circle. They must take their names. They have power and are bound to you, but they can't work with it like this. Taking the names will help. Closing a circle will finish it."

"Why am I fine? I'm overloaded, but not sick." Luke's brow furrowed in confusion. "Maybe I'm not the..."

"What?" Matthew asked.

Luke groaned, smacking himself in the forehead. "I took the name yesterday. When Gregg, Ben, Nora, and Jared got here. I introduced myself as the Peace Pillar. My eyes felt like they would explode out of my head, then my nose popped."

Micah's expression was doubtful. "I've never known a Pillar to take the name before the Center. Your power is bound to your pair."

"I'm pretty sure I did," Luke disagreed.

"Good morning," Ben took Adaline's offered hand without hesitation.

"What's this?" Jared didn't move as Adaline extended her hand.

After a frown at Sam's lack of explanation, Jake explained. "She'd like to share her thoughts, Jared. She's having trouble speaking aloud again."

"Addy—" Samuel warned, voice heavy.

"No, thank you." Jared turned his back on her.

"Jared?" Nora asked, confused.

"I don't want to be bound to them." Jared shrugged.

Adaline looked at Ava. Ava looked at Nora. Nora looked at Ben. Ben looked at Greggory.

"You were all feisty to claim the circle a minute ago. It's all yours, Gregg," Ava said, voice snarky and sad at the same time.

Greggory blew out a heavy sigh as he held a hand out to Jared.

"I'm out of here." Jared ignored the offered hand as he headed for the door.

"Stop." Greggory's voice rang with controlled power. He kicked a chair at Jared. "Sit. Let's chat."

Against his will, Jared moved back into the room and sat in the offered chair.

Greggory's lips twitched up as most of the eyes in the room turned toward him in shock. "Don't look so surprised. I may not be a Pillar, but I am strong and have had a lifetime of experience. Every one of you, Ava included, uses raw power to compensate for lack of precision. I am not so wasteful."

"Jared," he continued, voice chilled. "Why would you opt out of sharing this energy? They intend to take Harbor, and I have no objections to giving our circle to them."

"I understand." Jared nodded, voice flat.

Greggory blinked. "You'll be bound to them before long. What's the problem?"

Jared shook his head. "No, I won't. I'll break from the circle. It's fine; I've thought about it. I won't be a part of this. I'll head home. My flight leaves in two hours. I assume you have no more questions? I'd like to take our rental car back with me."

"Do you want to—" Ben started.

"Nope. No need to discuss it, Ben. Be well," Jared called over his shoulder on the way out of the door.

"What just happened?" Nora asked, stunned, as the restaurant door closed behind Jared.

Greggory's face was blank as he turned to Matthew.

"Yeah, I noticed it, too. Last night, after Matilda," Matthew acknowledged.

Sam frowned, turning toward Matty. "What about you?"

"Noticed what?" Ava and Ben asked together.

Greggory dropped his face into his hands, rubbing his eyes. "I got a hint. I wouldn't have noticed it if I wasn't paying close attention. I haven't seen it in a circle."

A sea of confused faces turned toward Matthew.

"What the fuck do you think he's talking to me about?" Matthew barked. "There is an early crack of madness in him or a severe crack that has always been part of his fundamental nature. Either way, he'd break easily and be irreparable. That's why I said I couldn't have used him to demonstrate last night."

Sam narrowed his eyes at his younger brother. "What did you demonstrate last night? What happened to Matilda?"

"I can see that kind of thing," Jess admitted, ignoring Sam. "He always looks pea-soup green with envy and hate. My whole life, every time he visited, nothing but swirling pea-soup, toad green. He flickered twice last night. There was fear of Matthew. And then, when Hank was taking bets, a flash of raw, angry, red rage before he turned back to a toad. I couldn't see the madness in him yesterday. But no one else is consistent with emotions like that."

Jess shrugged into the silence, unaware of the glances going on around her. "I always thought he was envious of Mom's power or envious of Dad's love. Before this visit, I only saw him for an hour at a time."

Sam turned to Matilda. "Why won't they tell me what happened? What were we betting on?"

WILL JUMPED up as Emma exited the bathroom. "What can I do?"

"Nothing. Just sick," she whispered, looking pale and exhausted. "Feels like my skin will fly off my body."

"Taking the names is easy," Micah began.

"Great! Tell us what the fuck to do," William demanded, pushing a chair up behind Emma.

Micah grinned at Emma.

Her lips turned up in response. "Don't laugh at him. It's fine."

"Whipped!" Noah faux-coughed into his hand.

No one made eye contact until Darla burst out laughing.

"Oh, fuck you all," Will bitched at the room full of chortling family. "Can we get on with this?"

"This is easy. You know what you are. Take your name with caution. It will affect how your power manifests. Matthew, decide if you're 'Chaos' or 'Madness.' There is a difference, just as there is a difference between terror and fear, rage and anger," Micah counseled.

"Once you declare yourself with intent and purpose, the name is yours."

"Are they all going to bleed again? I'll get the paper towels now. That was a mess," Ava joked, trying to break up the heavy trailing silence.

Micah shrugged. "I have no idea. It's an odd circle, and they are the most tightly coupled pair I've ever seen."

Ava's teasing smile fell away. "Should we go outside for this?"

Micah shrugged again.

"I am Peace," Luke declared, without preamble. "Yeah, I did this yesterday. No change."

"Joy," Ethan announced, the word loaded with energy. He sighed, taking a deep breath and blinking fast before closing his eyes again.

"Better?" Noah asked.

Ethan nodded. "Jarring. But much better."

Matthew groaned from the booth behind them, putting his head down on the table. "Better, but dizzy."

"I didn't catch it!" Noah complained. "What name did you take?"

Luke frowned across the table at Matthew. "He didn't say it out loud. I didn't hear it, either."

Matthew smiled.

Luke frowned at his favorite brother.

"BE WELL, all. I hope to see you again." Micah stood to leave.

Darla frowned. "You're going?"

"Yes." Micah's tone was indifferent as he avoided Darla's eyes. "I've done what I can. You'll be fine."

"You will not take your name? Stand with us?" Sam's surprise was written on his face.

Micah shook his head. "James asked, too. I will not. I turned from this path eons ago, Walker."

Sam smiled. "I know."

"I'll not stand with you." Micah glared at him. "You'll find Hatred elsewhere."

"We will." Sam nodded in agreement. "Be well, Micah."

The door opened as Micah approached it. Micah nodded in thanks as the newcomer held the door for him to exit.

"Good morning," Sheriff Jack said, entering the restaurant.

Ava frowned, reacting to the drawn expression on Jack's face. "Good morning. What's wrong? What's happened?"

Jack exhaled hard, his relief palpable. "Are you all okay? Are you in trouble? Is there something I can do?"

Ava looked confused.

"The restaurant was closed last night. Clyde called around, saying trouble might be on the way. This morning, we've found six bodies at bizarre places around the outskirts of town. I feared I would find you next."

"Six people?" Ava breathed, appalled.

Jack nodded. "Looks like natural causes. Heart attacks or aneurysms, probably. We'll run tests, but they weren't in fights or injured as far as we can tell.

"I was afraid I'd be finding you or Jess or Addy next, Ava," Jack admitted. "Are you in trouble? What's wrong, Jess? What happened to your eyes?"

"I have a terrible migraine, Jack. Like I used to get as a kid, remember?" Jess's voice was quiet. "Mom covered my eyes to make me less light sensitive. Who died?"

"No one from around here, no one from town. Only two seem to have real identification, the rest appear to be fraudulent. We're running fingerprints. What happened? How can we help?" Jack asked.

Ava shook her head. "I don't know."

"Ava, what happened?" Jack demanded.

"I had nothing to do with it, Jack." Ava's expression was startled.

Jack frowned. "I'm not accusing you of anything. I'm trying to help."

Clyde shook his head. "We were here last night, Jack. We all stayed together, expecting trouble that never got here."

"Is there anything we should look for? Anything we should *not* look for? Who are these people?" Jack asked.

Ava shook her head, eyes filling with tears.

"Christ, Ava! I know you wouldn't go off murdering people. That's not what I'm asking. That's not what I'm suggesting. I'm trying to understand so I can wrap things up quickly."

"I don't know who they are or what you'll find in the autopsies, Jack." Ava shook her head. "We were all here last night. If they were at odd places on the outskirts of town, our protection wards might have blocked them. There is nothing in the wards that would harm anyone, but they would stop someone from getting closer."

"Like the tornado?" Jack tried to understand.

Ava nodded. "If that's what happened, they're not good people. You'll probably find information through the fingerprints."

"We'll see what comes back," Jack agreed, still unhappy.

"Thanks, Jack." Tears leaked down Ava's face.

"We planned to go home today," Sam murmured into the awkward silence.

"Safe travels." Jack nodded.

"You don't need us to stay?" Sam inquired.

"No. I'm investigating deaths, not homicides. I do not suspect you of wrongdoing, and I'm not accusing you of anything. Even if I was, I would not attempt to hold you here, Mr. Trellis."

Sam flinched at the formal name, dropping his eyes. "Oh."

"Thank you for your help with Delilah Wecker, Mr. Trellis. We're hoping for the best for her, and we're grateful you've provided this opportunity for inpatient treatment and rehabilitation." Tense and formal, Jack sounded like he was reading from a notecard.

Sam's eyes flicked to Adrian.

"There's a great center in Dallas. No need to go any further. It was just a phone call," Adrian murmured. "Word travels fast, though."

Jack nodded. "Thank you. Both of you. All of you. The Weckers called me yesterday after they got the call, asking for help to verify that it was legitimate. We did some quick research. It didn't take long. Del packed herself into the car with her dad within ten minutes."

"I lost track of talking to you about that on Monday," Ava muttered to Sam.

"I heard the conversation," Sam muttered back, not looking at the sheriff. "Adrian's the one to ask about that stuff. I don't do much with it. I asked him yesterday."

Adrian let out a brief chuckle in the strained room. "He pays for it all, but he's also easily embarrassed, Sheriff. Do you need anything from us before we go home?"

"No, Dr. Trellis. Safe travels." Jack's voice was respectful. He was uneasy about making the rich people uneasy.

"Sheriff, my patients don't even call me Dr. Trellis. There's no need for formality. I'm Adrian. Clyde, Ava, Adaline, Jess, and her family will probably come with us."

Jack's eyes snapped to Ava and Clyde, looking for signs of distress. "You've been here almost twenty years, never traveled."

Ava sighed. Jack never asked questions, even when things got strange. His concern for their safety tore at Ava's heart. "I have family in Chicago. It's a good time to visit." It wasn't a lie, and Ava hoped it would help ease Jack's worry.

"You'll be okay?" Jack scrubbed his hand through his hair, unsure of what to do.

Clyde nodded, understanding Ava's discomfort. "It'll help Adaline."

Jack nodded, no more information needed.

3

"Addy, can you show us how to burn off the energy?" Matty inquired.

"I don't have fire or light, Matty. I don't know more than you do," Addy broadcast.

"Gee, if only there was someone here who knew how to work with fire," Nora deadpanned, holding a handful of flame out to Matilda.

"Oh!" Matty clapped. "Show me!"

Nora glanced at Greggory. "They're so clueless, it's painful and a little scary."

He nodded in agreement. "They also don't seem to understand that we've been doing this for a long time."

"It never even occurred to me to ask," Adrian admitted. "Greggory uses life energy, like Ava, right?"

Gregg gave a brief laugh. "Ava uses energy like me, Adrian. She wasn't much older than Ree when she started learning from me."

"Because that's an important distinction," Nora said with an eye-roll. "I use elemental fire and a negligible amount of earth."

"Elemental fire is the same as Matty, right?" Jake asked.

Nora shook her head. "No. I have control of the power, heat, and light of fire, so far as it reaches. Light wielders are a little different and

Lady Light even more so. Most light wielders don't have a ton of power. Their gifts lean more toward subtlety: moving shadows, glares, and changing other ways we can perceive light.

"When she learns how to channel it, Matilda will have power akin to the sun. Everything of fire, all of light and heat. As you saw yesterday, she can tap into other types of energy with minor effort," Nora finished.

"And Ben?" Will asked.

Ben looked at Ava and Lucas, who both shrugged.

"Might as well show them." Lucas grinned.

"I'm skilled in mental energies and life," Ben broadcast to the room.

"Wow, no need to bind like Adaline?" Will asked, surprised.

Ben's lips turned up a bit as he glanced at Lucas again, who shrugged.

"I am bound to Adaline, and Adaline is bound to you. I can use Adaline's binding to communicate with you without contact. Depending on the mind and the thought patterns, I can even affect behaviors and notice inconsistencies," Ben explained.

Noah opened his mouth to say something as Will turned to glower at him.

"Do not make a Kevin Bacon analogy."

"But it is! It's like six degrees of Kevin Bacon," Noah objected without pause.

"Well, the quality of connection deteriorates as you get further down the line. If I were to use Addy's binding to Ava and then Ava's binding to the good Sheriff Jack, my abilities would be diminished."

Sam was nodding along, looking at Adaline. "We found Jonah like this on Monday? You are bound to me, I touched the grandmother, and then the grandmother's connection to the boy? We jumped like that?"

Adaline shook her head. *"You took us to him, Sam. I was along for the ride, not involved. You pulled the binding forward and followed it after you named her."*

"Named her?" Gregg and Nora blurted at the same time.

"When June hesitated to answer his question, Sam named her,"

Ava confirmed. "Didn't even pause. Didn't have to look for the name. It flowed out of his mouth in one smooth phrase."

Greggory, Nora, and Ben turned toward Sam with mouths agape, stares wavering between shock and horror.

"Please stop staring at me like that," Sam whispered. "Sometimes, I know things when I touch someone. Not always, but sometimes."

"How many pillars will stand in your circle, Sam?" Greggory demanded, trying to startle an answer from him.

"Thirty-two," Adaline broadcast.

"I don't know," Sam admitted, laughing at Addy.

Adaline shrugged. "I felt that yesterday. It will be a large circle and shift often. Lots of visitors."

Greggory shrugged after an extended pause. "Well, okay."

The entire room full of people stared at him.

"What?" he asked.

"What does that mean?" Jake asked back.

Greggory grinned. "I don't know everything."

"Comparatively, you do," Beth pointed out. "What were you expecting?"

Greggory shrugged again. "Traditionally, the Mistress names people, and the Walker holds the circle's shape. But he's naming people, and she knows about the circle. Either they're different or the legends are wrong. We've seen both possibilities be true in the last twenty-four hours."

"William?" Adaline asked, watching him stare at Ben.

"Sorry," William muttered, looking down at his hands.

"What's wrong?" Adaline responded.

Will looked around the room. "Am I the only one who caught that? Ben just said he could control people's minds, and you all got side-tracked."

Ben snorted. "Not to that extent, Will. I can't make you do something you don't want to do. But I make a great counselor and friend because I can feel when a mind gets pulled off course. I can point it out. That's why I asked to speak with Jared. And he knows it. Something is not right there."

Luke grinned at Will. "That's freaking you out, isn't it?"

"Absolutely," Will said as Adrian nodded in agreement.

That startled Ben. "Why? I mean you no harm."

"I believe that's true," Will said. "But I'm not over here playing with peace and joy, Luke. A nudge from me in the wrong direction and people will die. Yes, the thought of anyone influencing me without my knowledge is terrifying, and I'm adult enough to admit it."

Ben rocked back in his chair, thinking.

Will's face scrunched up. "What the fuck?"

"I don't think I can influence you much, Will. Even if we had a stronger link. Your mind is not the type that drifts toward suggestions," Ben said.

"Did you just try to make me wave to Matilda?" Will asked, incredulous.

"Yep," Ben said. "It's not something you'd fight doing, so I thought we'd see if you'd do it. On the other hand..."

Noah blew a kiss to Emma.

William's glare was icy.

"I can mess with him." Ben laughed.

"What the fuck?" Noah muttered. "Not awesome. Matty! I understand your pain."

"Not even close," she snapped back.

"What can Jared do?" Matthew asked, trying to change the subject.

Nora shook her head. "He has some elemental earth and a bit of love."

"A bit," Jess noted. "Like, unless you were in a circle, sharing energy with all power forward, looking for it, you would miss the love part."

"He wasn't always that way," Ava added. "He was a much warmer person when we were younger."

"Even when I joined the circle," Luke agreed. "He hasn't been happy for a while."

"This is fascinating, but the plane will be ready in about three hours. I thought that'd be fine for everyone?" Hank asked.

"Are we going to close the restaurant?" Clyde asked Ava. "What do we do with all this food?"

"I'll call Father Dominic now," Ava offered. "But we'll freeze the butter. Gotta keep the priorities straight."

"Agreed." Clyde nodded. "Maybe take it with us?"

Ava's lips turned up into a quiet, brief smile for her husband.

"Blake, get some paper and a pen. I'll tell you what to pack," Jess said. "You'll have to do it. I can't see."

"We should talk about this, babe," Blake muttered.

"Talk about what?" The surprise was obvious in Jess's voice.

Sam's head snapped up. "Oh."

Hank looked at him with raised eyebrows.

Sam turned to Blake. "I need a talented carpenter."

It was Blake's turn to be confused.

Sam talked fast. "You'll argue with Jess about losing your job if you don't show up tomorrow. Please don't argue about that. I need a carpenter or general contractor; I have houses and hotels everywhere. Maybe you could teach me?"

"Say no, Blake," William jumped in before Blake could answer.

Jake laughed with the rest of the Trellis clan. "Trust us. 'No, I will not *attempt* to teach you handyman skills,' is the correct answer."

"It might be better now," Sam said, voice hopeful. "I slept for two nights in a row."

"No, Sam," Adrian disagreed. "No. You are capable of so many things. Home repair is not one of them. Say no, Blake! Job, yes. He's a great boss. Teaching, no. Play it safe. Trust us. You'll risk your digits trying to teach him to use a hammer."

"That was one time!" Sam objected.

Luke cleared his throat over choked laughter.

"Okay, two times. But the second time—"

"Say no, Blake!" Will yelled over Sam.

"ADDY SHOWED you how to pull the sight forward yesterday, right?" Nora asked, standing around the outside fire pit with Matilda, Adaline, Sam, and Jake.

Matilda's mouth pursed with frustration. "Yeah, but I couldn't do it when I tried."

Nora nodded. "Perfectly fine. It takes a while to get the hang of it. Fire is easier. For me, at least."

Matty nodded.

"Let's start with instinct. Matilda, light a fire in the fire pit," Nora directed.

"How?" Matty looked puzzled.

"Just light it."

"But how?"

"Do it. Don't worry about how."

"I can't do it if I don't know how."

"Yes, you can," Nora disagreed. "Don't think about it."

"But how do I do it?"

"Use your colors," Sam answered.

"Sam, please—" Matty groaned.

"No, really. Use your colors!"

"Please stop saying that. It makes me nuts."

"Don't be a coward!" Sam argued.

"Sam, I'm not a coward! How could you say that?"

"You are. You won't even try."

"I am not!" Matilda yelled.

"Yes, you are!" Sam yelled back.

"Matilda, light the fire," Nora interjected.

The fire pit burst into flames.

"Oh!" Matilda cheered for herself before the fire burned out. "Oh."

Jake laughed. "Aww, sad little fire."

Nora's eyes turned to slits. "Jacob, light the fire."

"I can't light the fire," Jake disagreed.

"Sure, you can," Nora said, grinning with Adaline and Sam as Matilda looked on smugly.

"WHY CAN'T WE ALL WALK?" Noah whined. "James brought us all back here yesterday. You can bring us all to Chicago!"

Sam sighed. "Anyway, we'll meet you—"

"No! Come on, Sam!" Noah nagged.

"Noah, on Monday, I tried to talk to Ethan like Adaline broadcasts thoughts and accidentally Walked to the center of Mom's dining room table. Do you really want me to learn how to drag people with me with *all* our family in tow?" Sam challenged.

"Well, fine. Just take me, then! No one cares if I'm lost for a while," Noah offered.

"Holy fuck!" Jess fell out of her chair, laughing uncontrollably.

Ethan tried to choke back a startled laugh but lost it when Jess tipped over.

Darla fixed Sam with an icy glare. "You *stood* on my table?"

"Oh. Damn," Sam mumbled as Adaline giggled with Ethan and Jess. "I didn't mean to tell you that. I cleaned the table. It was an accident."

"I can't breathe. Ohmygod!" Jess choked out.

"What's so funny?" Hank asked.

Sam shrugged. "They wanted to Walk with me. I told them no. I'd take Noah first because it'd be fine if I lost him for a while."

Everyone looked at Noah.

He nodded. "It's true. It's my role as his unattached younger brother. He gets to test fun shit on me. But I'm not Lucas. Don't make my brain explode. That shit looked like it hurt. The closest younger brother differs from the *youngest* younger brother. So I'm Walking to Chicago!"

"No, Noah. Let's try it on a smaller scale, first," Sam disagreed.

"Sam! Come on!" Noah bitched.

"Oh, shit. My sides hurt," Jess gasped as she landed back in her chair.

"Adaline and I will meet you in Oak Park around five o'clock tonight, Dad. Where is the circle meeting?" Sam asked Nora.

"I own farmland outside Rockford. We close large circles there. More space to spread out," Nora explained.

"I let everyone know we'd meet there for a seven-thirty circle," Ben offered. "Not everyone can make it. But we should have forty people besides us."

"Wow. How many people are in Harbor?" Jess asked.

"Seventy-three active people, including Nora, Ben, and me. Not counting Jared," Gregg answered quietly as Nora touched his arm.

"It's shrunk," Ava said, sad.

Gregg nodded. "And more today."

4

"Can we go now?" Luke asked again. "Everyone else is here. Sam will find us. Let's go!"

"Lucas, I don't think you've sat down since we got home," Hank observed.

Luke nodded. "Yeah! That's because we should go!"

"It's not five o'clock yet," Adrian murmured. "We'll be obnoxiously early, Luke."

"It's fine. I can just go. I know where I'm going. I can just meet you there."

"Lucas, did you miss your circle?" Gregg teased.

"Gah. Yes! Let's go!" Luke urged.

"You walk around in a circle pretty much constantly. Chill the fuck out," Jess snapped, rubbing her temples.

"It's not the same. Why can't we go now?" Luke nagged.

"This is hilarious," Jake muttered to William.

"What?" Luke asked.

Jake grinned, no longer hiding his amusement. "I have never seen you this antsy before. You're always calm. The whole peace thing made perfect sense to me until this moment."

"Yeah, Luke. Roll that peace crap out and calm down," Will suggested.

"Bah. Ignore them, Luke," Ava sympathized, smiling.

"Can I ignore them in the car? Because it'll be easier after we leave," Luke pestered. "How did you stand this for thirty-five years, Ava?"

Ava's smile turned melancholy. "It gets easier. You forget. The energy forgets. I was too busy being victimized to admit that it was lonely."

Greggory shifted uncomfortably.

"The circle was fun and all, but I don't get wigging out like this," Ethan commented.

"No! That wasn't a circle. Well. It was a circle. But it's not the same. It was a bunch of energy we already knew. Not the same," Luke objected.

"You'll see, Ethan," Nora promised. "The more people and combinations of energy, the better a circle feels. There's a reason we call it 'standing' a circle. It takes on a personality when there are more people involved. Standing a circle with family differs from doing it with a larger group. Once you're part of a larger group, part of a larger circle, it's tough to adjust to life without it. Ava is actually the only person I've known who stayed sane and stayed out of a larger circle for as long as she has."

"No," Ava disagreed. "My mother and aunt are roaming around perfectly fine."

Nora dropped an icy glare on Ava. "I would not call them human or sane."

Ben nodded in agreement. "I've known them since they were girls. They were never particularly well-balanced. Amazingly, you and Claire are lovely human beings."

"Oh!" Hank exclaimed. "I forgot about Claire. Is she coming tonight?"

"I'm sure she will." Ben smiled. "You forgot about the person who started all this crap? I haven't talked to her directly, so she doesn't know *you're* coming. Someone might want to call her."

Luke grinned. "Please don't! I want to see her face. She'll lose her cool. Have you talked to her, Ava?"

Ava laughed. "I haven't. I'm with you—more fun like this."

"Hello?" Sam called, coming in the back door.

Jake's eyes narrowed. "Is that my Goonies t-shirt?"

"It is. I didn't have much at the lake house after showering. I didn't want to wear a button-down," Sam admitted.

Ava looked at Adaline. "I think that's your sundress, right? Did you shower at home?"

Addy shook her head. *"I took some clothes from home to the lake house."*

"Go to your apartment to get clothes! You can zap yourself anywhere you want. Don't steal my clothes. I can't believe you're wearing it anyway. It has a design on it!" Jake bitched.

"Let's Walk to your apartment and get a fresh shirt, Sam. I'll go with you and pick out clothes. That way, you won't look like a dumbass. Jake will cry if you spill something on that shirt."

"Oh, would you shut the fuck up?" Jake snapped.

"Jacob!" Darla snapped back. "There are children in this house. You will not speak like that."

"I'm not going to my apartment," Sam said. "This is fine for now."

"You people are lame. No fucking fun at all!" Noah bitched.

"Noah Michael Trellis, what did I *just* say?" Darla scolded.

"Great, now I'm in trouble—" Noah complained.

"Please shut up!" Jake said, smacking Noah upside the head.

"Hey!" Noah yelled.

"You three morons are adults! We should not be having this conversation. Grow up!" Darla bellowed.

There was an awkward silence. No one looked at anyone else for fear of laughing at Darla.

"My apartment is in the middle of the city. Too loud for Adaline. Your t-shirt was sitting in my house. Possession is nine-tenths of the law, jackass," Sam replied sanctimoniously.

Jake shook his head in disbelief before looking at Noah.

Noah stuck his tongue out, pulling a face that made Matty crack up.

Jake glared at Sam. "I'm rubber, you're glue—"

"Ugh. Let's go!" Luke yelled.

SAM AND ADALINE rode in the SUV with Luke, Matthew, Noah, and Ethan.

As their mental link rolled and shifted with her anxiety, Sam held Adaline's hand. She stared out the car window, trying to narrow her area of perception.

"There are so many people," Adaline shared with Sam.

"Yes, more here. Is it painful?"

"Loud. You don't hear it? Sense it?"

"This is all I've known, Addy. Smaller towns feel different, but I don't think I could describe the difference. This is normal to me." Sam shrugged.

A few miles later, she flinched as a car cut them off.

"We'll go back to the clearing tonight," Sam offered.

Adaline shook her head. *"Evelyn is right. Areas with large populations need energy. I can't hide in the clearing forever. I will adjust."*

"Not forever," Sam agreed aloud. "But we can take this in stages. We can go back and forth. Why be more uncomfortable than necessary?"

After considering his words, Addy nodded in agreement. *"We'll decide after the circle."*

"I dislike that you two mind-meld without us," Noah complained. "I don't know what that conversation was, but you didn't want me to be a part of it."

Addy smiled to herself. *"He's ridiculous. Loud. He feels strongly about everything."*

"You have no idea." Sam laughed.

"He might be my favorite brother," Addy admitted.

Sam shook his head. *"Too soon to call it. Don't limit your options."*

After breaking free of the Chicago rush hour traffic, Luke put the gas pedal down.

"You know, I'd like to arrive with all my bits intact," Matthew commented.

"Whatever," Luke griped. "You do speedy healing. Ethan, Noah, and I will be in trouble if we get in an accident. You, Sam, and Addy will be fine."

"Great, you recognize this. Why are we going ninety-three miles per hour?" Matthew inquired.

"Because I want to get there," Luke muttered.

"It's six-fifteen, Luke. I thought the circle thing didn't start till seven-thirty tonight," Ethan pointed out.

"People are always early. Just shut up. You'll see. There is no 'fashionably late.'"

BY THE TIME Luke pulled into the grass alongside other large SUVs, there were already fifteen cars parked at the farmhouse.

"Why aren't we parking in the driveway?" Ethan inquired.

"Because we can all walk unaided on uneven ground," Luke answered. "We leave the driveway for those that can't."

Ethan paused, surprised.

"All kinds of people in this circle: super young in strollers, elderly in wheelchairs, everything in between. This is a social gathering at which Matilda will be comfortable," Luke said, his annoyance at the delay clear.

As they approached the house, the sounds of people laughing and talking greeted them. About ten feet from the front door, they heard a shriek before the house went silent.

"LUCAS!" a woman's voice yelled as the front door banged open. In a blink, a woman had launched herself off the porch into Luke's arms, wrapping her legs around his waist and almost knocking him to the ground.

Fuck, Luke thought. *I should have gone to see her. I shouldn't have left her. Fuck.*

"Talise, I need to breathe. Next time, a slight pause would help. I need some warning before trying to catch you," Luke gasped out.

"Never do that again!" she cried, burying her face in his chest. "It's been horrible."

The cheer drained from Luke's voice. "I'm sorry, Tali. I'm so sorry." Luke kissed the side of her head. "I'm back now."

"What are you doing?" Matthew asked as Luke tried to shift Talise's clothing.

"Tali, I can't find your skin to help. You have like eight layers on. Take off your gloves," Luke directed.

Without moving her head, she dropped onto her own feet and pulled off a pair of elbow-length evening gloves that tucked under her long-sleeve turtleneck shirt. Wrapping her arms around his waist, she tucked her bare hands under Luke's t-shirt, gasping in relief.

Luke could feel her pull on his energy, desperate for the calm it brought.

"Better?" he murmured.

She nodded then shook her head, still crying.

"I'm back now. I'm staying. I'm so sorry," Luke murmured again.

Another sob broke from her.

I'm a giant, selfish fucking asshole, Luke cursed at himself again, running his hand down the back of her head. "Do you want to meet some of my brothers?"

She shook her head.

"Can we go inside so everyone else can meet my brothers?"

She shook her head again. Luke laughed.

"It seems you've grown a Talise-shaped lump since I last saw you an hour ago, Luke." Nora laughed.

"It launched itself out of nowhere in a surprise attack," Luke agreed. He felt, rather than heard, Talise laugh.

"You know we were following you, right?" Will asked, annoyed. "We had a whole discussion about how we were following you. You just jetted off without warning."

Luke rolled his eyes, knowing Will couldn't see him. "You had Nora with you. You were fine."

Luke looked back over his shoulder. The last carload of his family was walking up the path with Ben. Gregg's carload was almost to their group.

"Oh my God, that's Ava!" someone yelled from the porch.

"Sorry for the late notice and off-night circle, everyone. We've been collecting lost sheep and finding a whole new flock. Let's go inside," Greggory called.

As the crowd moved toward the house, Sam waited, watching Lucy.

When she finally glanced at him, she nodded. "This is the farm. Linda's aunt's farm."

"Linda?" Nora asked, shocked. "This has been my family's farm for generations. It was my sister's farm until she died several years ago. How do you know Linda?"

"How do you know Linda?" Sam asked back.

Nora's brow furrowed. "She's my niece. I haven't seen her in years, maybe fifteen years. She went to live with her father and his family after my younger sister died."

Lucy's mouth hung open in shock. "Linda is Ree's mom. We were in foster care together."

Nora blinked several times, trying to process the connection.

"Let's go inside," Gregg said again.

"Tali, we have to walk now," Luke coached.

There was no response.

"Hey, you awake? Did you pull too much juice?"

A small chuckle vibrated against his neck.

"You'll make me pick you up, won't you?" Luke teased.

First one hand, then the other, moved from being folded under the hem of Luke's shirt to being tucked into the collar of the shirt, still touching his skin. In one fluid motion, she jumped straight upward in place, wrapping long legs around his waist again.

"So, that's a yes." Luke laughed.

Too thin, Luke thought as he climbed the porch steps and walked through the front door. *I am a selfish dick.*

Her head banged against his. "Stop it."

"I'm so sorry, Tali," he whispered back.

"Circle will help," she whispered. "I'll be better after."

"You will be completely better before tonight is over," Luke promised.

"Well, it's about fucking time," a gravelly voice called to Luke. "Welcome home, Lucas. Don't ever fucking do that again. Longest couple of weeks of my life, and that's saying something."

"Yeah, yeah. I'm aware. Selfish asshole. Hi, Mike. Hi, everyone," Luke called back. "We'll do hugs later."

The crowd of about twenty people laughed. It was only then that Luke noticed Ava passing among them, hugging and weeping in turns. His family, with Jess and Adaline, looked a little lost.

"We can do introductions," Luke offered.

"More people are coming. Let's wait," Nora disagreed. "Lucy, how do you know this place? How did Ree come to be with you?"

Lucy flinched. Sam quirked a slight smile.

"Weird fucking deja vu, Sam. Don't do that," Lucy scolded.

"I didn't do it deliberately if that makes it better." Sam laughed.

"That makes it a little worse," Lucy disagreed.

"Lucy?" Nora hissed, getting angry.

"Oh. Uh, sorry, Nora," Lucy responded, surprised by her tone of voice. "Linda and I ran away from foster care together. Linda thought her aunt would understand and help us. But when we got here, your sister wouldn't let us stay. She kept babbling about me belonging to the violet-eyed girl. So, we left."

"When? When were you here?" Nora demanded.

"Uh…" Lucy looked at Adrian, confused by Nora's abruptness.

Sam reached out to grab Nora's hand. She started at his touch and backed away a bit as his eyes unfocused.

"Lucy?" Sam asked, eyes still unfocused.

"Eight years ago? I was fifteen. That's about right," she answered as more people came in the front door to join the watching crowd.

"Oh, Luke's home," someone called, followed by someone else crying out Ava's name.

Sam shook his head. "I can't see precisely, Nora. It was about two weeks before they came for her. The girls didn't lead them here."

Nora frowned at Sam. "That's not why I was asking."

"I know. But you wondered," he said.

"What's happening?" Lucy asked.

Nora shook her head, looking back at Lucy. "Drainers murdered my sisters. Got about as much power as it takes to draw a small circle in total. Not even hold the circle, just draw it. There was no point in killing them. No big gain. They did it because they could. My sisters were defenseless. Uncircled. The same hunters took both sisters." Nora's voice was icy. "I'm hoping to come across those hunters one day."

Murmurs of sympathy broke out around the room. The circle knew Nora's sisters.

William's eyebrows lifted with a glance at Adrian, who nodded in agreement.

"Micah has a point," Adrian acknowledged. "I didn't disagree with him."

William snorted. "You wanted to. Can't save everyone, Adrian, especially when they don't want to be saved."

More people came in the front door.

"Yeesh, standing room only," someone complained, followed by, "Hey, Luke!"

Ben chuckled. "We're only expecting two more, Gregg. Why don't we introduce the circle first to give the stragglers a chance to get here?"

Going around the room, Greggory introduced thirty-six members of the Harbor circle before getting back to the woman wrapped around Luke.

"Luke, put her down. I can't believe you're still standing like that. But put her down," Gregg directed. "I'm curious."

Luke dropped his arms. Talise didn't move, arms and legs still wrapped around Luke. "I'm just standing here. I have little to do with this."

"Tali, let go," Gregg commanded. "I think some here might help you."

When she didn't respond, Luke poked her in the side, eliciting a squeak.

One hand untucked itself from Luke's collar and followed his arm down to grab his hand with a white-knuckled grip. Legs dropped back to the ground, supporting their owner on her own two feet. As the other hand moved from Luke's neck to dangle at her side, her shoulders sagged.

"Turn," Gregg coached. "Say hello. This is Luke's family."

The woman turned and picked up her face, red and splotchy from her tears. Long mahogany-colored hair was back in a tight bun, with a few strands flying free. Her bloodshot amber eyes glanced over the crowd. She gave a small nod of greeting.

"Oh!" Sam exclaimed. "Talise. Oh. Wait."

He looked around the room, confused. "You're…not where I expected you to be. I didn't know you were here. This isn't where I thought we'd be."

"Ugh, I hate this," Jess complained, unwrapping her eyes. "Something's wrong with her; I can't see what it is with my eyes wrapped."

Talise's face flamed red as she glared at Jess.

"She calls me Puking Peace," Luke muttered. Talise let out a surprised chuckle. "Don't take it personally."

"Holy fuck," Jess exclaimed, getting her eyes opened at last. "Who did that?"

Greggory nodded, unsurprised. "This is Talise. She has elemental water and powerful life energy—"

"Oh, God," Ava gasped.

"It gets worse," Gregg said. "An ignorant, unskilled person tied her mind when she was young."

"Ya think?" Jess interjected. "That's worse than William cutting his binding to Emma."

"We've been trying to unravel it for years without success," Gregg finished.

Sam nodded. "I didn't think she'd be where she is. I can take out the tie—"

"No!" Luke objected. "Absolutely not."

Sam frowned at him.

"No. You'll burn it out with fire and then leave her in a heaping pile of snotty, bloody pain," Luke explained.

Sam rolled his eyes. "You gotta let that go. We were in a hurry."

"Fuck you! I'll never let that go," Luke said, startling laughter from most people in the room. Mild-mannered and calm, he wasn't one to swear with gusto.

The front door opened then closed behind Claire. She gave a squeak of surprise then grinned at Ava.

"You're home!" Claire exclaimed, walking over to hug Ava and Jess. "Luke, why is everyone here?"

"Anything you want to tell us, Claire? Anything to share with the group? Something you've been keeping to yourself for a decade?" Nora laughed.

Claire gave a brief snort of laughter. "More like two or three decades. By the way, Luke has siblings with energy. One of them has so much power, it makes my eyes feel like they'll explode. But you look better, Sam!"

Sam smiled and nodded. "Hi, Claire. I feel better."

Greggory smiled at the crowd, trying to convey that all was well. Tense energy flowed through the room after the reminder of Nora's sisters. Now, it was downright fearful after Sam recognized Talise. It would get worse before it got better. "Let's go form the circle. We'll finish introductions and explain."

5

"Where's Jared?" someone asked as they walked to the field behind the house.

Greggory nodded as he came to a stop in the middle of the group. "Jared has decided to break from the circle."

"Are we trading Luke and Ava for Jared? Because that's an upgrade," someone else called, releasing a bit of the group's tension with a laugh.

"Well," Greggory's smile was sad, "not exactly. I made my intention to hand Harbor to Luke's family known, and Jared decided not to participate."

The crowd went silent again, uneasy gazes swiveled toward the Trellis family.

"All is well," Gregg soothed. "I am not leaving the circle. Only stepping from the center."

"Luke? You're going to hold the center?" someone called.

Surprised, Luke frowned. "Did you all know I was tied? Why didn't anyone tell me?"

A guilty pause wafted through the group.

"You clearly didn't want to know. Holy fuck, I've never known anyone more afraid of their own power. The tie is gone now?" the same person asked, forcing a laugh.

Luke snorted. "Wait till you meet my brothers, Jim. Yeah, it's completely gone. And, no, I'm not going to hold the center. I will stand as a pillar, though."

"A pillar?" a dark-haired woman standing with Nora asked. "Like a pillar, pillar? Walker and Mistress pillar?"

Greggory grinned and nodded. "You're going to love this, Monica. For a lot of reasons. I'm still downright giddy.

"First, tonight we welcome home one who has been lost to us for too long. Ava, cast out for reasons too ugly and wrong to discuss, is back with us. While I'm sure you've all heard of Ava, I don't think it's common knowledge that her elder daughter, Jessica, accesses all-sight."

There were surprised mutterings around the circle.

"Elder daughter?" Claire asked, confused.

Ava hugged her cousin again without a response.

"We also welcome home Luke. Luke, what is your name?" Greggory asked.

Luke nodded, looking at the grass, suddenly shy. "I am Lucas, Peace. The Pillar of Peace. 'Lord Peace' still sounds too holy and pretentious, so let's not go with that one."

There was a little squeak of surprise from the crowd.

"Oh, good. Someone else saw that power flare-up, too. I'm not completely out of whack," Jess muttered to herself, making Ava choke back a laugh.

"Luke's family will join us. Hank and Darla Trellis have nine children, of which Luke is the second youngest. You have all heard me prattle on about my scholarly pursuits related to the Walker and Mistress. They stand among us tonight."

"Oh shit!" Claire burst out. "Sam. That makes so much sense."

Sam rolled his eyes, smiling. "Now she tells me."

The crowd backed further away from Sam, who looked around in confusion before his face fell.

"Ugh," William groaned. "Uh, Gregg. Already overloaded, man. Please?"

"Oh, stop it!" Claire chided the group. "I've known him for his entire life. He's very kind and only sometimes scary. Obviously, this is not a scary time. You'll know it when you see it."

"Thanks?" Sam asked.

Claire gave a sheepish little smile. "It's true."

As the terror rolling off the group was palpable, Greggory winced in sympathy for Will.

"William stands as Lord Terror with his wife, Emma, Lady Love," Greggory picked up the introductions. "And yes, she is Emma Gracen."

He continued as murmurs of interest broke out. "Adrian, the Pillar of Rage, and Lucy, Lady Wind. Jacob, the Anchor and his fiancé, Matilda, Lady Light."

"Holy shit," Monica exclaimed. "All of them? The whole family?"

Gregg nodded, continuing the introductions. "Ethan, Pillar of Joy. Noah, who we will never call Lord Lust, just on general principle."

"No fucking fun," Noah muttered as the crowd gave a startled laugh.

"Matthew, Lord Chaos. Bethany, Lady Hope, stands with Hennessy, Pillar of Loyalty."

Greggory looked to Sam, who shrugged.

"Finally, Samuel, the Walker, and," Gregg paused as Sam shifted Adaline out from where she was hiding behind him. "Adaline, Mistress Life, and Ava's younger daughter."

"Ava!" Claire gasped.

"I couldn't tell, Claire. I just couldn't," Ava explained quickly. "It was to keep her safe. It took Sam forever to find her."

Claire's face scrunched up in the setting sun as she thought about it. "Ah, shit. I should have outed Sam years ago."

"I should have come home when I couldn't close a circle with her," Ava admitted.

"Hey, speaking of circles," Jake interjected, "how about we do that shit before I start fucking puking?"

"Agreed," Will muttered.

"AH!" Noah flinched, grabbing his head, as Adaline snapped the circle closed around them.

Holy fuck, I can feel every person in this field. I can feel their energy brushing against my skin, Noah realized.

A glance around the circle showed his family also reacting to the circle in some way. William was downright scowling. In the center, Sam was fidgeting unhappily.

"That tie has to go. That's not where you belong," Sam muttered to Talise.

She glanced at Luke, who shrugged, squeezing the hand he was still holding.

That is one hot brunette hanging onto Luke for dear life, Noah chuckled to himself, watching her out of the corner of his eye.

"Circle's closed," Ava yelled. "Offload, Addy. Let's get the show on the road."

Adaline smiled at her mom, letting a small amount of energy out into the circle, causing it to flare with brilliant white light.

Nora nodded at the gasps of surprise around her. "That's a small drop. A very tiny drop. Most of you probably see the circle already. It will be visible and likely tangible by the time we do a lap. Please understand there is a lot of power here. The circle will feel different."

Umm, "probably" see the circle? It's full daylight in this field with the circle's radiance, Noah mentally corrected, scratching the bare skin of his arms as a headache started settling in and his neck tensed. *This is so fucking odd!*

Bodies shifted uneasily around the field as people tried to adjust to a new reality.

"Turns out some of the legends were complete crap. The ones related to the raw amount of power were accurate, though." Gregg nodded in agreement with Nora.

By the time Jake's turn came, the circle was glowing with a rainbow of colors inside a wall of heatless flame.

"I can't hoover this up, Ava. No room," Jake apologized.

Ava laughed. "Push what you have out, Jake. The circle is fine. It won't collapse with this many people."

Jake's eyebrows shot up. "Really? All of it? I can just push it out?"

Adaline nodded, answering quietly. "It's fine, Jake."

Without any apparent effort, Jake pushed out a fountain of energy that contained every color imaginable. The wall of the circle blew skyward, but it stayed closed.

"I still don't know how you walk around with all that power tucked away." Jess laughed as the crowd shifted with giddy, nervous energy.

"Can we get a move on?" Noah asked. "I'm going to puke if I don't blackout like a moron. Do I have to wait my turn? What happens if I just unload now?"

Gregg's lips turned up. "Remember this the next time you tease Luke about being in a rush to get to the circle. Go ahead and try, Noah. The circle might let you go out of turn."

Noah tried to push energy out, similar to the circle with his family in Dallas. Nothing happened.

"For fuck's sake. Really? Single file? I'm standing on the other side next time. How come we didn't have to go in order in Dallas? I feel like a little kid waiting for my turn to go down the slide!"

The people around him laughed at his impatience.

"The circle in Dallas was family, Noah. Your energies are naturally intertwined and well established. This circle is just getting acquainted, one at a time. Calm down and pay attention to what's happening," Nora suggested. "You'll learn a lot about the people around you."

Doing as he was told, Noah took a few deep breaths and nodded. "Fine."

There was a man in a wheelchair on the other side of the circle that was in a crushing amount of pain, but he remained hopeful that the new energy would help. While the pain was obvious in his power, it was the hope that shone through, as if Noah, himself, was hopeful for the man. Then Noah realized he *was* hopeful that the circle and energy would help. The man's hope triggered Noah's own compassionate response.

Next to Beth, a young baby in a stroller mewed happily. The

emotion flowed through the circle, but it was flat, more like looking at a picture of happiness than experiencing happiness. The baby's happiness made Noah smile in the same way that baby giggles triggered joy. But it didn't come with the same depth of response as the man in the wheelchair.

The guy in the wheelchair shared energy mixed with his emotions. The baby shared pure emotion. There's a difference.

As the energy looped around the circle, closer to Noah, his antsy feeling increased. He could feel heartbeats and breaths from the people around him. He began to pick out the sensation of each type of energy, every kind of emotion, and its source.

This is fucking awesome! It makes my skin crawl, but I've never been this tuned into other people. I can feel them all, and I can feel how my energy responds.

A man standing four people away from him was nauseous with stress and worry over his wife's depression. His wife was anxious and embarrassed about her husband losing his job and not having health care. The teenager standing with them feared that their lives were about to change for the worse.

I wonder if Sam is catching all this. Are we going to end up hiring these people?

The woman standing next to Noah was frustrated and lonely. Her partner was pissed off that she was sharing the loneliness for everyone to feel. Their relationship wasn't as bright as the married couple, but their emotions were coming through without issue.

Finally, at his turn, Noah tried to push out his lusty energy. Nothing happened. The circle seemed to reject the power offered. Noah paused, unsure of what to do. Then, without any effort on his part, the circle ripped his confusion from him. With it went his humor, love for his family, and the uneasy feelings related to his energy that he had been trying to ignore.

"What the fuck?" he asked, louder than intended.

Greggory smiled at him. "It's not possible to hide from the circle, Noah. It will take anything genuine you offer and also anything it feels you need to release. We can talk about those uneasy feelings later if you'd like."

Noah's eyes narrowed. "It didn't do that in Dallas."

"No," Greggory agreed. "It didn't. The circle in Dallas was extremely powerful but in limited ways. Fewer bodies and fewer types of energy. Again, the more people, the more types of energy, the more personality the circle has. You'll get used to it. Often, the circle will pull things from you that you didn't realize were bothering you."

As the person on the other side of him took his turn, Noah realized that he did feel better. Lighter. His mind was more focused. He was calmer.

But his mind continued to turn over the uneasy feelings about his energy that he'd been working so hard to ignore.

BEFORE THE SECOND lap of the circle, Gregg frowned at Sam. "Did you let your energy go? I didn't feel it. You don't seem to be standing with us."

Sam realized "standing" was the correct term. The circle stood, like a home, around them. The strands of different energies wove together, with the center's power as a foundation, the corners as load-bearing walls, and the pillars as the frame.

With just pillars and a few additional people, the circle in Dallas was a framed house under construction. It stood in three dimensions but with no detail. The larger group of people with a broader variety of energies made the circle stand alive with color and detail.

Sam shook his head. "I'm fine."

Greggory's frown deepened. "That's not how this works, Sam. Addy, you, too. You have to be a part of it for the circle to be whole. You can't dip a toe in like this."

"Dip a toe?" Monica asked, watching the wall of power shift around them.

"I'm serious," Greggory said. "Offload it or break my circle and get out."

Sam quirked a disbelieving smile. "Remember how I didn't want to be standing here?"

"I do," Gregg replied, voice flat. "But you're standing there. You chose to be standing there. Either take the center in truth or leave it."

The Walker's anger flared up, replacing Sam's nervous fear.

"You forget your place," Samuel growled, all humor gone from his voice.

The circle seemed to react to the emotion, slapping him with the combined energy of those standing with him but taking nothing from Sam.

Greggory grinned, happy with the reaction. "No, I don't. You forget yours. You can't be afraid of it, Sam. You can't fear the energy. You are what you are; there is nothing wrong with it. Go!"

Without warning, Adaline dumped the power of their shared connection into the circle, knocking Sam and herself to the ground as the circle exploded and then flamed out.

"I didn't do that," Jake yelled. "What happened? Did it collapse?"

"No, the circle is still closed," Jess said. "It's just not physically visible anymore. What did you do, Addy? I saw it flare out from you."

"I pushed it out," Adaline whispered.

"Out where?" Ava asked.

Adaline looked at her mom with a blank expression. "Out. Like when I was small."

"I didn't understand it then, either, Adaline. Out where?" Ava asked again.

"She pushed it to other circles. Other people. Out from us." Sam shrugged. "Other people who are bound to those here, and the bindings that relate to them and so on. She pushed it throughout the world like we're meant to do. You don't feel it?"

Ava blinked, mouth hanging open.

"That's why the circle needed more people? So you could push the energy further?" Sam asked Addy.

Adaline nodded. "One of the reasons. More people to make it close, but also more people to share the energy. I can't push energy at all if I can't get the circle closed."

Ava shook her head in bewilderment as Hank and Darla laughed in sympathy. "I don't know why I asked. Never mind."

"One day, we'll go house shopping with Sam," Hank promised Ava. "Please believe me when I say I understand that look."

"Samuel, we're waiting," Greggory yelled.

Sam tried to release the energy again. For the third time, the circle wouldn't accept what he offered.

Am I going to have to admit that the circle won't take my energy? I don't understand what's happening. What am I supposed to do?

Feeling his panic, Adaline squeezed his hand, offering peace through their binding.

"You are not alone, love. We will figure it out," she soothed, sharing the thought.

In response, Sam shared the depth of his love for her and his gratitude for her in his life.

The circle swayed around them, glowing with energy again. This time, it radiated the color of deep purple love.

Hopeful, Sam tried to push his love for Adaline out to the larger group. Nothing happened.

Maybe it won't let me contribute because Talise is in the wrong place? Sam guessed.

"It's not the right shape. Talise is not where she's supposed to be," Sam complained while climbing back to his feet.

"Yes, we all quake in fear of the whiny Walker," Jess teased as others broke out in small, startled chuckles. "Go, Sam! The circle is standing, even if it's a bit lopsided."

Determined to find a solution, Sam walked toward Talise.

"Ah! No! Nope! You take that energy back to the middle," Luke scolded. "You're not doing that. Adaline will do it."

"It only hurts for a second," Sam argued. "Then it'll be fine."

"No, Sam! Go. Back away," Luke yelled, tucking Talise behind his back protectively. "Bad, Sam. Bad!"

The circle erupted in disbelieving laughter.

Sam closed his eyes, savoring the feeling of the energy tingling merrily against his skin.

Well, maybe something is happening?

"Luke," someone muttered. "That's the Walker. Don't do that."

"Oh, shut it. He's my brother. He only hurts me when he means to," Luke snapped back as the circle broke out in laughter again.

The circle welcomed the humor as energy danced against Sam's mind again.

Then it clicked. *The circle won't welcome me because these people are terrified.* The circle stood, but it was rigid around him.

Sam paused, thinking for a minute before turning to William. "Why won't you let Blake teach me handyman stuff? You know I love that!"

"No, Sam," Will barked.

"Will, I'm better now. I've slept and ever—"

"Sam, you went to pound a nail in and broke my hand. No!" Will cut him off.

"You heal super-fast! You're a dick for wearing that cast for weeks." Sam laughed, realizing only then that Will played up the injury.

After the laughter died down a bit, Sam continued. "I won't do that again. My aim will be better. I can see straight now!"

"No, Sam. No," Adrian said, backing up Will.

"Why do you two always have to stick together?" Sam whined.

"Because we're right," Will responded immediately as the circle continued to laugh.

"I can do home repairs!"

"No, son. No, you cannot," Hank disagreed, watching the faces around him relax. "You've tried your best. It's not one of your many skills—no home repairs, no fishing. No."

"But—"

"Sam, you almost took my eye out trying to use an electric screwdriver," Luke added. He could feel the circle's energy shifting toward something more light-hearted and welcoming and wondered if Sam was doing it intentionally.

"The fishing thing was not my fault," Sam disagreed.

"You whacked me upside the head with your fishing rod, knocking me off the boat while trying to cast out four feet in front of you," Matthew said with a straight face.

"You shouldn't have been standing there," Sam argued.

"I was six feet behind you, man. For the dude with control over space, your depth perception sucks," Matthew argued back.

That made Adaline burst into giggles of joy, lifting the entire circle with her happiness.

"I was close," Sam said to her with a little smile.

"Sam, we Walked to the top of the neighbor's garage." She grinned.

Ethan's laughter flowed through the circle, spreading additional joy. "That's why you came in through the back door today? I was afraid to ask. You jackass! Did the neighbors see you?"

Sam shrugged at his brother's laughter then tried to release his energy. He offered the circle the truth of his feelings: shame, fear, and sorrow. The circle accepted those emotions and washed them away as if they didn't exist. Instead, the circle pulled and retained the silvery-purple energy of familial love and acceptance from him.

Well, that was unexpected, Sam thought, unsure what to do. For lack of a better option, he answered Ethan.

"I don't think the neighbors saw, but that yappy dog in the yard behind Mom and Dad is afraid of me now."

When Sam faced him again, Greggory nodded and grinned in approval. "The circle has to accept you as you truly are. Sorrow, fear, and shame are not you, Sam. They'll adjust, and so will you."

Sam's return smile was sad.

6

Talise was unsure what to do after the circle finished. Soon, Luke would tell her to let go, and all the emotions would wash back into her.

"We won't let Sam break that tie. You don't need to be afraid," one of Luke's brothers said quietly as they walked back toward the house. She knew he was the oldest but couldn't remember his name.

In Talise's experience, there was usually a good reason to be afraid when people told her not to be scared. She squeezed Luke's hand. He glanced over at her.

"He's not breaking that tie, Will," Luke muttered. "I'm serious. No."

William. That's his name. William, walking with his wife, Talise recalled.

"I know," Will agreed. "So she doesn't need to be afraid."

Luke's lips turned up into what Talise considered his non-smile. He wasn't happy but couldn't bring himself to make others aware of it.

"Will, I know you're not going to understand this, but this level of terror is fairly normal for her and has nothing to do with Sam," Luke explained.

"Tali, I can't feel my fingers," he continued as she white-knuckled his hand again.

"Are you any better after the circle?" Luke asked her.

"I am," she said. "But I still don't want to let go."

"This is going to be super awkward when I go to the bathroom." Luke gave her a teasing side-eyed glare.

She tried to smile.

"I'm back now. I'm not going to leave the circle again," he reassured her.

She nodded.

Luke's genuine smile peeked out. "Still not letting go?"

"Nope," she said, unrepentant. "Can I scarf a sandwich or something before you make me let go?"

"You have trouble eating? Like Sam?" Will asked.

Luke made a so-so gesture with his free hand. "Correct me if I'm wrong, Tali, but you don't taste emotions, right?"

She shook her head. "Which one is Sam?"

She knew Sam was a brother but couldn't place him.

William's eyebrows shot up as Luke nodded at him.

I guess I should know who Sam is, Talise sighed to herself.

"Sam is walking at the very back of the crowd with the violet-eyed woman. She's Addy. Before we leave, we're going to see if she can take the tie out," Luke said, patient as always.

"It won't come out, Luke. Even Greggory has tried," Talise said, resigned.

"We'll see," Luke muttered, gently squeezing her hand again.

The crowd cleared out quickly as people rushed home to get ready for work the following day. Within twenty minutes, just Talise, her parents, Luke, his family, Greggory, Ben, Nora, and two women Talise couldn't place were left.

Talise wanted to ask who the two women were but didn't want to offend anyone. She should probably know who they were by now.

The blond-haired woman must have felt Talise's gaze on her. She turned, smiling.

"Hi, Talise," she said. "I'm Ava. Can I touch your hand? I'd like to feel the tie."

Talise's anxiety doubled. She shot a panicked look to Luke, who smiled back. "You don't have to let go of me. Ava's not going to hurt you. She's like Gregg. She'll keep her emotions and energy to herself. She just wants to feel the tie a little bit better."

Ava smiled again, reaching for Talise's hand.

After a minute, the woman shifted.

What is her name? She just said it, Talise wondered.

"My name is Ava, Talise. You forgot because I was touching the tie in your mind. It's fine."

Talise looked around, lost for a moment. They were sitting in the living room at the farmhouse. She looked over to Luke, next to her.

Ava's anger bled into Talise's awareness, breaking through Luke's calm energy. *Is she mad at me? Did I do something?*

"There's no edge to it," Ava muttered. "Do you know who did it, and has that person been tied in a similar fashion?"

Oh, not mad at me. Mad for me.

One of the men Talise didn't know started laughing. "Holy hell, Ava. That's awfully punitive for your tastes, isn't it? You were mildly miffed at Luke's tie."

"WILLIAM, don't ever compare the two ties again," Ava said with a flat glare. "Luke's power was tied, neatly and carefully in a way that did him no harm whatsoever. It was originally in his best interest."

"Storytime!" Ben said quickly before William could respond. "There's a fundamental difference between what happened to Talise and what we did to Luke that won't make sense unless you have context."

At the general nods of agreement around the room, Ben started his story.

"Once upon a time, a lost and confused teenage Lucas found his way to a circle. He had no control over his energy or understanding of how it worked. His mind was disturbed by the things he could sense. He was a danger to himself and needed help to find control.

"On a near-identical timeline, though she's two years younger, Talise awoke one morning screaming in terror. Her energy had roared forward while she slept, manifesting as a miserable marriage of elemental water and life."

"Why? Why is that miserable?" Hank asked, curious, with a concerned glance at Talise. "You alluded to that before. I don't understand."

"Elemental water energy means she can sense things around her. She doesn't have to see behind her to know that someone is standing there," Ava explained. "The life energy means that she's also picking up emotions and traits from the same radius she's getting physical awareness from. If Matthew stubs his toe while standing near her like he is, Talise will feel that pain. If Noah gets pissed off that no one will call him Lord Lust, she's going to feel that angst. Just like Will feels fear and Adrian feels another person's anger.

"And, while Will senses someone else's fear, he's able to *do* something with it. Water doesn't have that type of effect. It's awareness, not control," Ava continued, looking a bit sick. "Ben is saying that Talise can feel the presence, movement, and emotional state of everything around her, constantly. She can't do anything with the sensory input, either. She's just stuck with the constant bombardment of other people's actions and feelings."

The room was silent for a moment in the wake of Ava's explanation.

"How come my anger is 'angst,' but Adrian gets to be Lord Rage?" Noah bitched, startling laughs out of Tali's parents.

"Addy, you're like that, too, right?" Ethan asked.

Adaline shook her head, not offering any detail.

After a pause, Ethan asked, "What's different for you?"

"I feel life everywhere. In this room, at home, on the other side of the world. Everywhere. More than emotion. Energy and intentions. Sometimes thoughts, too," she replied.

"You have some control, as well, correct?" Ben asked. "You can turn it off or focus it?"

"Tune it out. Turn it down. Not turn it off," Sam answered for her. "But she can focus it. Join minds. Share experiences."

"Control other minds?" Will asked.

Without making eye contact, Adaline gave her head a single nod.

"I don't think she tried that until Monday," Sam offered. "When we helped Jonah, she used my body."

"I couldn't touch him," Adaline whispered. "I burned him. If Sam didn't let me do what we did, the boy would have died."

William gave a slow nod. "At least I know. With all the other weird shit we've seen, I figured someone, somewhere, must have the ability to take control of others. Maybe you could try with me later, so I know what it feels like?"

Adaline nodded again.

"Back to Tali," Ben continued after a pause. "She can tell us what each and every one of us is feeling right now. She can also tell us, without looking, where each person is and exactly how they're positioned."

Tali's face scrunched up. "You don't want me to do that, though, right?"

Ben smiled. "No. We'll do party tricks another night."

"She can't turn it off, turn it down, or control it as far as we can tell. To Ava's point, it's a constant onslaught of other people's emotions and movements—highly distracting at the best of times. Horrific for a thirteen-year-old girl."

Talise gave a nervous little smile as everyone turned to stare at her.

"So, Talise woke up one morning with a ton of out of control power," Ben picked up his story. "Unlike Luke, Talise grew up in a circle. Her parents, Mike and Monica, knew exactly what happened."

Mike grunted. "We didn't know how much power there was. Neither of us could see it. She is hazy in our sight."

"Can you see the tie? Have you seen what happened?" Jess demanded, still offended by the visual representation.

"No, Madam Sight. And I don't think I want to see it," Monica said with deference.

Jess nodded.

Ben continued. "So, they called the center of their circle for help. The center realized that Talise's power was out of control and too large to stay within their circle.

"Here's where the story takes a turn. Luke came to us. I am very skilled with mental energies, as is Nora. Before the pillars and pair surfaced, Greggory was arguably the most empowered person on the planet. He certainly was, and probably still is, the most trained and skilled life wielder.

"We tied Luke, and we knew exactly what we were doing. It was done with precision and care, knowing that it would come out one day. Once Luke had control, he could have pulled the tie out on his own. We assumed he'd recognize it over time and deal with it when he was ready. But Luke was decidedly uncomfortable with his energy. So, Gregg siphoned away what he could. Nora, Jared, and I poked and prodded at the tie, trying to draw his attention to it. Again, we never intended the tie to stay in place as long as it did. We always intended for it to come out. Talise was not as lucky."

Luke glared at Sam.

"We didn't have time," Sam mumbled defensively.

Mike frowned, not understanding the exchange. "It never occurred to us that Mark would attempt to do something he didn't know or understand. He led our circles my entire life. He was a trusted member of our family."

"It took us a couple of days to figure out that she wasn't herself and then a while longer to realize it wasn't the energy causing problems," Monica continued.

"What kind of problems do you have, Talise?" Darla asked, not wanting to talk about Tali like she wasn't there.

Tali's mouth opened and closed before she glanced at Luke, flushing red.

Luke shook his head at Darla. "It doesn't matter, Mom. The tie's coming out."

Darla looked at Monica, wanting to understand.

Recognizing another concerned mother, Monica explained. "The tie doesn't restrict her power. It restricts her mind. Her memory. She has almost no short-term memory. She can't remember the circle we had a half-hour ago, and she doesn't know your names right now. After a good night of sleep, she'll probably recall everything tomorrow."

Adrian's mouth dropped open in surprise. "Short-term memory loss is a byproduct of brain trauma, but perfect recall later is...strange."

Mike continued. "We called Mark and told him the tie had to come out. He fessed up that he didn't know how to take it out. Things didn't go the way he expected when he was doing it. We had no idea what to do. For lack of a better option, we saw doctors and specialists. They couldn't repair the damage and asked a lot of questions about how she was still functioning. Things got uncomfortable, fast."

"Eventually, Mark sent them here," Greggory jumped in. "He kept hoping the tie would break on its own. When it didn't, and when the medical route was no help, he knew he'd made a mess of things. They flew in to visit, thinking we'd poke it once or twice and it would unravel. It didn't. When we couldn't pull it out quickly, Mike and Monica decided it would be best if they moved here so we could work on it over time."

"We haven't had much success," Ben admitted, a small smile lurking around the corners of his mouth. "But Luke's here, so she's happy."

"I'm not sorry. He's so calm. He mutes everything." Tali grinned, patting Luke's hand. "Don't ever do that again, ass!"

Luke rolled his eyes at her before turning to Adaline. "Take it out! Enough storytime."

Adaline frowned, moving closer. "I don't think I can, Luke. I've been looking at it. There's no edge to it, nowhere to unwind it."

"I can!" Sam said.

"No!" Luke and Will yelled in unison.

"Addy, maybe if you touched her, you could see it better?" Luke almost begged.

Adaline opened her mouth to respond.

"I can do this!" Sam yelled.

"No, Sam, that was terrible. The worst couple of days of my life. No!" Luke yelled back.

"It's just—"

"No!" Will said. "No, I'm not watching her head erupt with blood. No, Sam!"

"But, I can—" Sam began.

"No! Addy—" Luke cut him off.

"HI, TALISE." Luke's brother with pale eyes smiled, squatting down in front of her. "Just hold still for a second."

No one else moved. Luke didn't finish his sentence. The other man sitting with the pretty woman was halfway shifted forward like he was going to stand up from the couch.

"They're fine," he reassured her. "Just a sec. This part is going to hurt, but then Addy will fix it. They're going to move again, and it's going to hurt in three-two-one..."

White-hot searing pain exploded behind Talise's eyes, but it was gone almost before it fully registered. The last thing Talise remembered before sleep was the panicked, enraged expression on Luke's face.

"THERE. ALL DONE," Sam said, pleased with himself.

"What?" Mike said, jumping to his feet.

"What the fuck did you just do?" William roared.

Sam looked around, puzzled by the alarmed faces. "I fixed it. It's gone."

Monica's mouth dropped open as she dove to touch Talise's head. "I don't feel it. It's gone. It's *gone*?"

"I'm going to beat you fucking senseless. Don't you ever do that again," Will bellowed, lunging for Sam.

Sam scooted out of the way quickly. "What the fuck? Why are you mad? You guys were all like 'Be the Walker,' and now that I'm the Walker and I do Walker things, you're mad!"

"I'm not mad because you're the Walker. I'm mad because you locked me down. Come here. I'll put you in a body cast and see how you like it," Will growled, circling Sam.

"William," Darla snapped. "Not now. We don't need to put on a show. Berate him later."

"I'm going to fucking beat him later," Will muttered under his breath, still tracking Sam's path around the room.

"She's fine!" Sam yelled. "You all threw a fit for nothing. We were just upsetting her more. We were going to spend more time arguing than it took me to fix it."

"Sam," Luke ground out. "Why is she fine?"

Sam stepped back, startled by the rage on Luke's face.

"What? What do you mean?" Sam asked, sounding less sure of himself.

"Why is she fine? Why isn't her nose spraying blood everywhere? WHY DID MY FUCKING HEAD EXPLODE?" Luke bellowed.

Sam looked around the room again, lost.

"Don't look at me," Darla murmured. "You're on your own with that one, Mr. Walker."

Ava dropped her head, shaking with laughter.

Watching Ava, Nora couldn't keep a straight face and broke down in her own choked laughter.

"You're laughing at me, aren't you?" Luke asked, voice terse.

"Nope. No," Nora objected, still choking back laughter. "We are not laughing at you, Luke. We're laughing at Sam and his utter confusion. Big scary Walker, terrified of his little brother."

Sam looked around the room, still looking for support. "He doesn't get mad. I didn't think he'd be mad at me. Maybe a little annoyed, but not mad."

"You made his head explode, Sam! There was blood coming out of his fucking eye sockets!" Matthew yelled, mad on Luke's behalf.

"I told you!" Sam yelled at Luke. "We were in a hurry! But you're fine now!"

Luke blew out a disgusted sigh, glancing at Monica and Mike then turning to Addy. "It's really gone?"

"Gone," Adaline confirmed.

"She needs to sleep for a while for it to heal. Probably off and on for a couple of days. Then it will be better. By Monday, she'll be healed. Physically, at least. There was no edge to it, Luke. It had to be like that," Addy tried to explain.

"Mine had an edge, Adaline. He could have just unraveled it," Luke bit out.

"Are you really mad at me?" Sam asked Luke as the room broke out in another round of choked laughter.

RATHER THAN GO to the clearing in Texas, Addy asked to spend the night at the lake house in Michigan.

"It's still remote," she admitted, looking out the wall of windows in the living room onto the black night above the black water. She sat on the cream-colored couch, bouncing a bit on the firm cushion. "But there's a roof. And furniture. I like it here."

Sam smiled for her, but it didn't reach his eyes. "It's one of my favorite houses, too. We come here for some holidays. Are you hungry?"

She shook her head. "Tired, though. Sleep in a bed sounds like a fantasy come to life. Like hot water, when we were here earlier."

That brought Sam up short. "I guess I didn't consider the lack of plumbing in the woods. You didn't go home for showers? You were always clean and well-groomed in the dreamscape. You were no different when I finally got to you on Monday."

Addy shook her head. "I didn't go to the restaurant. Not in years before you came. Mama brought me soap, things to clean with, clothes, and food. There's a river about a mile and a half south of the clearing. It flows into a little pool that I used. Mama made sure to only bring me natural things that wouldn't hurt the fish or pollute the water. I think she made my soap herself. It smelled of mint and rosemary and felt like love."

"Thinking of you so alone for so long hurts my heart," Sam admitted. "I feel so stupid in retrospect. I don't know how many times you told me to just come to you."

"Will we talk of the people tonight?" she asked, changing topics.

"The circle?"

Adaline nodded.

"There's not much to say. They're afraid of me. It is what it is," Sam said, monotone.

"Did you feel their surprise when they recognized your energy as love?" she asked. "After you made them laugh at you and before you turned to Greggory. Did you feel it?"

Sam shook his head. "I don't feel others as clearly as you do."

Adaline patted the couch next to her, waiting for Sam to settle in before she spoke again.

"Walk back and watch for it," she suggested. "They are afraid but curious, too. Some of them are already interested."

"I'm fine, Adaline. I'll get used to it," Sam offered.

"I hope not. I think you will not be tender-hearted Sam if you expect fear. No. Will you look?"

"You're doing better with words," he tried to change the subject.

"I will wait here," she said, undeterred.

Sam sighed, pulling power into himself.

Adaline was right, of course. When his energy flared with pale purple love, there was shock on most faces. He watched Ava closely as a small smile danced in her eyes, and joy flowed from her. Three days ago, Ava thought Sam would torture Adaline. Tonight, she stood the circle with happy excitement, watching them.

Back with Addy, Sam nodded in acceptance.

"Luke was angry with me," Sam whispered.

Adaline nodded.

"I made William afraid."

She nodded again.

The silence sat heavily between them.

Adaline smacked Sam upside the head with a couch throw pillow.

She grinned when he turned to her with a startled expression. "That does not make you a monster. Luke feared for his Talise then was reminded of his own pain. William fears losing control of himself more than anything else. It needed to be done. I could not have done it."

"I should have just argued with them until they let me do it," Sam said, remorseful.

"No," she replied.

"No?"

"No. That is not who you are. Talise was terrified and confused. You knew how to fix it. The arguing would have just made her more afraid. It might have been easier for Will if you argued, but it would have been worse for Luke when he had to give in and far worse for Talise after all the arguing," Addy said, quiet and serious.

"For being alone so long, you understand people well," Sam complimented after considering her words.

Addy tipped her head from side to side in a so-so gesture. "Some things, I understand very well. You, I understand most of all. With your family, I understand from their feelings, not so much from their thoughts. Outside of your family and mine, I am not as confident. Talise is Water?"

Sam nodded. "If she chooses to be, yes. I don't see her clearly. I couldn't see Matilda or Lucy, either. But I knew who they were when I saw them. They were where they should have been. I didn't expect Talise to be here with Luke. I thought she'd be somewhere else."

"Where?"

"It doesn't matter. She's here. She is Luke's match?"

"There is love between them," Addy confirmed.

As Sam nodded, he smacked her with a couch pillow.

"What?" Addy giggled, trying to fake outrage.

"Revenge." Sam smiled at her laughter.

Addy sighed, touching his face. "A smile, but no joy. I am sorry they were afraid, Sam. They will learn who you are. It won't take long."

"It will be hard for a while, but they will adjust. I will, too. It'll be fine," Sam agreed.

"Sam?"

"Hmm?" He smiled as he read the energy in their binding.

"What direction is the compass pointing?" Addy laughed.

Sam grinned, leaning over to kiss her as she rolled them off the couch.

"You know what's good for this?" Sam asked.

"Hmm?"

"A bed," he muttered against her mouth.

"Bah," she muttered back, getting real laughter from him.

AUGUST

7

Thursday morning, Noah woke up alone before the sun was up, without plans for the day.

I have no idea what to do with myself, he realized. *We're off work for the rest of the week.*

Over the last couple of days, Noah had been thinking back over his adult life and his bed partners. He was no longer sure how much of his sex life was his own decision making. It wasn't that Noah felt like he always needed someone new in his life. That was just how things seemed to work out.

When things were dull, he'd make a new friend. When things got busy again, he'd move on, fully aware that his friend was just as ready to call it done. Lust burned bright and fast. There wasn't much to do or say with someone who shared nothing but sex with you.

In retrospect, he should have recognized the lust thing earlier in life. From puberty onward, he could sense people's attraction to him. He thought he had been reading body language and behavior. He didn't focus on the intuition until the visit to Dallas last week. Now, when he paid attention, he could pinpoint other people's interest pushing against his senses.

Noah was good-looking. He could admit that without sounding

like a jerk because he recognized "good-looking" didn't mean "supermodel." Light brown hair, dark brown eyes, muscular without being bulky. No one would run away in fright at the sight of him.

But, thinking over the last few years of girlfriends, he began to wonder why some of them would be interested in him.

Maybe the money? Maybe Sam's money pulled in the women?

That didn't add up. The parade of women in and out of his life started before the money showed up.

Charisma? I'm fun.

He looked around his bare apartment and bland decor.

No, I'm not. I'm a smartass. And a flirt.

Nearing twenty-eight years old, Noah realized he had no life outside of work, no close friends outside of his family, no hobbies, and no responsibilities.

There is absolutely no substance to my life when I'm not making new "friends."

For lack of a better option, he headed for a shower and then for the office.

NOAH WAS the first person on the forty-third floor that morning. He had to search to find the light switches. After getting everything powered up and coffee brewing, he headed for his office.

His desk was clean, exactly as he left it last week. Logging into his laptop, he had over two thousand emails waiting for him.

"Fuck my life," he muttered aloud as he sorted the emails by name and started deleting the ones from people he didn't like.

"What are you doing here? I thought you were out all week," Jen said, walking in with a grin.

Noah glanced up, giving her a small smile. "Hi. We got home yesterday afternoon."

"Everything went okay? Hank said some kind of emergency? I dodged calls like mad all week."

Jen was the executive assistant and receptionist for the Trellis family. There were additional personal assistants for Hank, Will, and Adrian, who had more contact with people outside the organization. But Jen kept everyone in line. Her sweet face, blond hair, and blue eyes were deceiving. She didn't take crap from anyone.

"We're good. Sam met someone and went over the edge, as only Sam can," Noah said lightly. It wasn't exactly a lie. Friends and coworkers would wonder how Adaline appeared in their lives without some sort of story.

"Met someone? Like, *someone* someone?" Jen asked, mouth agape.

"Yup."

"Wow. Holy shit!"

"I know."

"Noah, if you were to classify this person's gender..." Jen began fishing for details.

"She's a tiny little sprite of a woman-girl. Maybe five-four, doesn't wear shoes, and has, honest to God, violet eyes. About Beth's age."

"Violet?" Jen's face went blank.

"Purple," Noah confirmed.

"Like, so blue they're almost purple, right?"

"No. Like, lavender eyes and black hair."

"That can't be, Noah."

"Wait till you see. Jen? You okay?"

Her gaze was unfocused as she stared out the office window.

"Huh? Yeah. Sorry. Just thought of something. Anyway, that's crazy. Good for him. He's happy?"

"He's Sam."

She rolled her eyes. "Does she sleep?"

"She does! And he's sleeping more, too."

"Well, you called that one. I guess he did just need more sex in his life." Jen's laugh was brittle.

Noah wrinkled his face. "You're not going to go all mushy, pining away for Sam, are you?"

"You're the only Trellis for me," she said, sotto voice, grinning again. "What are you doing here so early, anyway? You never beat me into the office. How long did it take you to find the light switches?"

"I'm not answering that."

"Why are you here early?" she asked again.

"Couldn't sleep," he admitted. "What happened around here this week?"

"We were sad and lonely without you, and we made a mess in Jake's office. Gary wanted to leave an old pizza on the pool table so we could watch Jake freak out. I didn't allow it because I thought you'd be gone all week. Old pizza would have been funny. Moldy pizza would be nasty."

"How come no one ever comes in here to hang out? I feel like I'm not one of the cool kids," Noah said, looking around his office.

"Noah, you have two guest chairs and a basket of tennis balls in here. Your office is lame. Even you think your office is lame. You're never in here if there's anyone else around to talk with."

"Maybe I should get a foosball table," he muttered.

"Do you play foosball?" she asked, surprised.

"No, but other people might." His tone was hopeful.

"What's with you?"

"What do you mean?"

"You're...melancholy. Very un-Noah-like. Don't like Sam's woman?"

"I love Sam's woman. I like Sam's woman more than I like Sam. And that's saying something."

Jen's eyebrows shot up. "Crushing on Sam's woman?"

Noah snorted. "She's not my type."

"She's not breathing?" Jen asked, faux-serious, eyes wide.

Noah's lips turned up into an almost smile.

"So, what's with you? You've not mentioned a new lady. You've not made jokes about Sam getting laid. You even passed up the opportunity to make a crack about the pool table. What's wrong?"

"Meh."

"Meh?"

Noah nodded.

8

When Talise opened her eyes on Thursday morning, she was confused.

I was at the farmhouse for a circle in the evening. It's daylight now. What happened? she wondered.

Confusion was part of her worldview, so she paused to sift over the memories from the previous day.

Ben called, asking Talise and her parents to come to an off-night circle. Cycling energy helped Talise contain her abilities; they never missed a circle.

Luke is back. She smiled to herself. *With his entire family.* William, Adrian, Jake, Ethan, Sam, Noah, Matthew, and Beth. Hank, Darla, Emma, Lucy, Matilda, Adaline, Hennessy…*Hennessy? Is that right?*

"This part is going to hurt, but then Addy will fix it. They're going to move again, and it's going to hurt in three-two-one…" Sam had said.

Luke's brother was trying to break the tie. There was no breaking the tie. She'd given up on that long ago. But, as she thought about it, she felt…odd. Focused.

She thought back over the night again, realizing she was missing pieces.

They had gone to the farmhouse. She recognized Luke as he

approached the house. There were introductions. Something about pillars. They were in the field. There was a circle, but Greggory wasn't holding the center.

Talise jumped out of her bed, ran to her desk, and wrote a note to herself. "Today is Thursday. It's 7:13 a.m., and I want scrambled eggs for breakfast."

She folded the paper, leaving it on her desk as she headed for the bathroom. This was an often-repeated test. She spent most of a decade trying to improve her memory. She'd leave herself a note then see how long she could remember what she wrote to herself.

"I feel life everywhere. In this room, at home, on the other side of the world. Everywhere," Adaline had explained the night before.

Yeesh. I feel you on that one, Adaline, Talise thought as she got in the shower. But Sam had said she could mute it, too. *That'd be nice.*

There was something tacky in Talise's ears. *Is that blood?*

She dried off, thinking about her day. It was Thursday. No circle. No dance classes. She'd spend the day dancing in her garage studio.

It's Thursday, and I want scrambled eggs for breakfast.

After combing out her long hair, Talise headed back to her room to get dressed. She glanced at the clock. 7:41. *I wrote that note at 7:13. Not bad.*

Her best record at her little test was about fifty-two minutes. Her worst was less than seven minutes.

Talise could feel her dad, up and moving around in the kitchen. *He's usually gone by now. What's he doing home?*

After getting dressed for a day around the house, Talise looked around her bedroom with a sigh. Her walls were covered with notes and memory cues. Some things, she just knew: reading, writing, math. Other things were a struggle. Situational things that changed were a struggle. There were notes on her door:

Are the lights turned off?

Is there a candle burning?

Is the window closed?

Where are my shoes?

Is my phone charged?

"Today is Thursday, and I want scrambled eggs for breakfast," she muttered aloud to herself. The clock on her nightstand showed 8:03.

Rapidly approaching a new personal best!

Her condition was odd. She'd forget what was written on the piece of paper any time now but recall it without pause later today or tomorrow. Medicine had no explanation for this. The specialists had accused her of playacting at first. But when the tests came back with abnormal results, they'd asked a lot of questions for which there was no answer.

"I'm so sorry, Tali," Luke had whispered.

She continued to think over what she could recall from the previous day.

"You will be completely better before tonight is over."

"William, Adrian, Jake, Ethan, Sam, Noah, Matthew, and Beth," Talise whispered, fighting off a wave of dizziness.

It was unusual for her to recall a full list of things, like the names of Luke's siblings. The long-term memory was selective about what it retained. But Luke was her friend. Her only friend, really. She'd work to remember his family.

"This part is going to hurt, but then Addy will fix it. They're going to move again, and it's going to hurt in three-two-one..."

It was suddenly hard to breathe.

"Today is Thursday, and I want scrambled eggs for breakfast."

"This part is going to hurt, but then Addy will fix it..."

As if in a dream, Talise wandered down the hall to her dad in the kitchen.

"Today is Thursday, and I want scrambled eggs for breakfast," she mumbled, eyes wide, handing him the note.

The clock on the wall said it was 8:41.

Tears leaked down her father's face as he kissed her forehead. "I'll make scrambled eggs. We'll let your mom sleep for a little bit. It was a crazy night."

THE NEIGHBORS WERE HAVING sex at two-thirty on a Saturday afternoon. Talise could feel their movements. He was way more into it than she was.

"Talise, are you listening?" her mom asked.

"I am. I'll stay here if you don't mind."

"I do mind. We haven't gone anywhere or seen anyone since Wednesday! The tie has been gone for a couple of days, Tali. It's time to be out among people again."

Talise pressed her lips together, considering how to respond. "Mom, people that know us, that knew me...before. They're going to stare and ask questions and be curious. I can't do that yet."

"Talise Marie Ayers, you've been hiding for years. It's time to go out and do things. You're better. It's fixed. We need to get on with life," Monica insisted.

"I'm not ready to be stared at. I'm still adjusting, Mom."

"This is a good thing, Tali! A good thing happened! You have your mind back, your life back!"

"I'm going to go dance for a while."

"Tali! Don't walk away yet. Wait," her mom yelled at her back. "It's just dinner with the neighbors! Barbecue. You can do a barbecue!"

9

Sunday morning, Hank took Jess and Ava on a tour of the empty houses Sam owned around the city while Darla went through her Sunday cooking rituals. Blake and Clyde opted to stay with Claire and spend the day tossing the girls around a swimming pool.

"This is ridiculous." Jess laughed, walking into a luxury home in the western suburbs.

"It's on an acre lot, so not as much room as the restaurant, but you wouldn't be crowded," Hank replied, stoic. "There are five bedrooms and six baths in this one, I think."

"Why does he own so many furnished houses in the same city?" Ava asked. She laughed a little harder after seeing each successive house.

Hank shook his head again. "I told you. He has this weird compulsion."

"Yeah, but why would he buy this giant house in the middle of suburban soccer mom living?" Ava asked, still laughing. "I don't understand why he'd spend money on this house, even knowing he's never running out of money! There are two houses here: this one and the one next door, and then nothing else on the street!"

"Oh, Ava. That's funny. He didn't spend money to buy this house." Hank's smile was unusually sarcastic.

"Someone gave him a house?" Jess asked.

"No. He spent money to build this subdivision, so he could build this house and let it sit empty."

After Ava blinked at him a few times, Hank continued.

"This subdivision was a field. We were out here, meeting work contacts, about three years ago. He started yelling for Will to pull the car over. Sam walked out into the middle of the field and yelled something like, 'This is good space. I'll build houses here. Let's go talk to the farmer!'"

"Then what happened?" Jess laughed.

Hank looked around. "What do you think happened?"

"He bought the land and what? How'd the empty street subdivision happen?" Jess asked.

"He bought the land, petitioned the ordinance committees to let him build houses, found a community planner, and put together a home-building company," Hank summarized.

"That doesn't just happen, Hank," Jess argued. "Blake has been trying to get approval to build a house on an existing odd-shaped lot for two years. In a town that adores us. And he's still working on it."

"Jess, think about what you're saying. This is what he does!" Hank laughed with frustration. "I used to think he did it just to bug me, but now I'm sure there's some kind of rhyme or reason to it.

"We were breaking ground on this house about a year after he bought the land. The house has been vacant for eighteen months. Someone comes to clean up the yard, treat for pests, dust the furniture, and wash the floors. Otherwise, empty. Just like the six other houses we've already looked at," Hank finished.

"Well, I love this house. It's gorgeous," Jess said as she finished touring the rooms. "It makes my home look like a shack. The girls' bedrooms are even already decorated. Far and away, this is my favorite. The schools are acceptable?"

"They are now some of the best schools in the country." Hank nodded.

"We'll live here." Jess grinned. "With just the people next door for neighbors."

"I am absolutely certain Sam would be delighted to buy other property if this doesn't suit you, Jess. He's probably buying other property right now. You can go shopping for your own house, too. You can also just stay in Texas. There's no rush to make a decision," Hank clarified.

"No," Ava said. "We discussed it with Clyde and Blake. We'll move with Adaline, move to the circle. For now. Clyde doesn't want to sell the restaurant right away, but we own it outright and just pay taxes on it. We can 'retire' if we're careful."

Jess smiled at Hank's concern. "Blake asked if he could burn our house down on general principle."

Hank looked horrified.

"It's old. The plumbing needs work. He's a carpenter. He hates plumbing and electrical work," Jess explained. "Truth be told, he's delighted to be out of his shitty job, too. His boss doesn't have any problem cutting corners to save a buck. It makes Blake uncomfortable."

Hank shrugged. "If he decides to come work with us, it won't be a problem."

"Pretty sure he's counting on that job connection," Jess muttered. "Not sure how else we'd get started up here."

Hank's brow furrowed in confusion. "Let's have this conversation with Sam."

"Yeah, agreed. You don't want to vouch for anything on his behalf." Jess nodded.

Hank frowned at her, shifting his weight on his feet.

"There's one more house, right?" Ava asked.

Hank nodded.

"Let's go take a look!" Ava grinned.

Hank sighed.

"What?" Jess asked.

Hank opened and closed his mouth twice before words came out. "It's the four-bedroom ranch next door."

Jess burst out laughing. "That is fucking creepy."

Nodding, Hank continued. "He owns all eleven empty lots. Four more on this side of the street, going from this house on the corner, down to the cul-de-sac where Sam insisted there had to be a single three-acre lot. It was the only major hiccup with the zoning and planning—he demanded that giant space stay one single lot. Then six more lots on the other side of the street."

Hank shook his head.

"What?" Jess asked, not understanding Hank's furrowed brow.

Hank sighed. "One each for Will, Adrian, Jake, Ethan, Noah, Matthew, Luke, Darla and me, and one big lot for Adaline so she has more space. I don't know who the other lots are for."

Ava's mouth dropped open. "You think?"

"I didn't get it when he built two houses and left the other lots. He refused to sell."

Hank stood quiet and alone as Ava and Jess walked through the rooms again, making mental notes. When they got back to Hank in the kitchen, he was still frowning.

"What's wrong?" Ava asked.

"It's a long commute to the office. I wonder if we're moving the office." Hank scratched his head. "I don't know. We'll ask him."

"He probably just didn't think about the commute. I mean, this was years ago, right?" Jess asked.

"Jess, do you believe he actively thinks about any of this? I've asked him eighty-five times why he was saving these lots. He didn't know. He just said he had to keep them." Hank shook his head again.

"Maybe he didn't want to explain it?" Ava suggested. "He doesn't care about commuting. He Walks."

Hank snorted. "My teleporting problem child. Who knows?"

SUNDAY AFTERNOON, Noah pulled up in his parents' driveway at the same time as Will and Emma.

"Hey, Pip! This time last week, I didn't know you. It's been a weird fucking week," Noah called, walking toward his eldest brother. "Four brothers married or on their way to being married in a week."

Will winced. "Been married for years, man. Don't get me in trouble again."

Noah grinned. "It's my job as your younger, better-looking brother."

"Don't make me hurt you." William's eyes narrowed. "Have you seen Sam since Wednesday? He hasn't been at his apartment, and he's not answering his phone."

"He left his phone in the car Wednesday night," Noah said, walking toward the house with them. "Jake has it. You looking for him?"

Emma made a face. "He wants to move. He doesn't think his house is adequate for a family."

Noah nodded in agreement. "Makes sense."

"See!" Will said. "I'm not wrong!"

Emma rolled her eyes. "Hi, Roscoe. Oh, who's a good boy? You're a good boy. Here, belly rubs. Now, sit pretty."

"Freaky," Noah muttered as the family dog did precisely as directed before tucking his head along Emma's leg.

"Hi," Darla yelled from the big room. "Everyone's early today."

"We must not have spent the requisite amount of time together this week," Noah joked, glancing around the room. Adrian, Lucy, Ree, Hank, Darla, Ethan, Matthew, Jake, Matty, and Luke were already gathered. "Where's the chosen one?"

There was a pause as everyone in the room processed Noah's words.

Matthew smacked his own forehead. "Noah, Let's not start calling him that. I have to draw the line at that. It makes me feel icky."

"Too far?"

"Too far," Matthew agreed.

"Fine. Where's the problem child?" Noah asked. "Has anyone seen them?"

"Nope," Luke said, voice flat.

"Still pissed off?" Noah asked.

Luke glared at him.

"Yeah, totally," Noah agreed. "Where's the hot brunette?"

Luke lifted his eyebrows, confused.

Darla scowled at Noah. "Stop that."

Noah rolled his eyes, messing with Ree's hair before flopping on the couch next to Emma. "No one understands me, Pip."

"Poor you," she replied without expression.

"Poor me," Noah agreed.

Darla swiveled her gaze back to Luke. "Luke?"

"Hmm?"

"Where's Talise?" Darla asked, all innocence.

"Oh, that's bullshit!" Noah bitched.

Darla cleared her throat.

Noah looked at Jake. "No 'bullshit?'"

Jake shook his head.

"Where are we drawing the kid-safe language line?" Noah asked, looking for clarification.

Jake shrugged.

Noah started laughing. "Are you just going to stay silent as much as possible?"

Jake nodded as Matilda shook with silent laughter.

"Luke?" Darla asked again, not getting distracted.

"Hmm?" Luke asked, also full of innocence.

"Lucas," Darla snapped.

Luke was startled. "I don't know. She's doing Tali things? Probably singing or dancing."

"Why isn't she here for dinner?" Darla asked.

"I don't know. I haven't talked to her. I didn't know you invited her," Luke said.

Darla cleared her throat as Hank tried to hide his smile. "I didn't invite her, Lucas. Why didn't *you* invite her?"

"Oh!" Luke exclaimed.

Darla's face fell.

"Pushed it too far, man. She wasn't sure if you were messing with her until the end there," Matthew muttered.

"Should have downplayed that a little more, huh?" Luke muttered back as everyone laughed.

Darla was not pleased as Hennessy and Bethany made their way into the room.

"What's Mom mad about?" Beth asked, taking the seat Noah vacated on the couch for her.

"Luke didn't invite the hot brunette to dinner," Noah summarized, rolling around with Roscoe.

"Noah!" Darla barked.

"What?" he asked, unperturbed.

Will was grinning. "Don't talk about your future sister-in-law like that, man. It's weird."

"Whatever, she's super f—" Noah paused, looking at Ree. "She's stunning. Also, when she jumped straight upwards to wrap her legs around his waist? Do you know how much strength it takes to do that?"

"Noah," Luke said quietly. "Do not. I repeat. Do *not* go there with her. She cannot do that."

"I'm pretty sure she can, but—"

"Noah." Luke's voice lost all emotion. The air vibrated with angry energy. "We will have problems if you cause her pain or embarrassment. Do you understand?"

"Holy sh—" Noah paused again. "Holy cow. That's not what I was going to say. I was going to say she can, but not with me. I'm not going to hit on your would-be girlfriend."

"Oh, fuck you!" Jake yelled.

Matilda bent over at the waist, laughing hysterically. "Twenty-two minutes, forty-two seconds!"

"Go, right now," Darla barked.

"Sorry, Ree," Jake mumbled as he walked out of the room.

"I can't breathe," Matilda choked out as tears dripped down her face.

"Where's he going?" Will asked.

Darla glared at her eldest son. "He's having a time out."

"Ohmigod," Emma choked out, laughing with Matty and Lucy.

"Please tell me he's sitting in a chair, facing a corner, thinking about what he's done." Will laughed.

"He's doing chores," Darla said, ignoring the laughter. "I won't have that language around little ears."

"Oh, man. I have to see this." Noah jumped up, pulling his phone out of his pocket.

From the big room, the family could hear Noah walking through the dining room, around the corner, into the kitchen. The sound of loud laughter rolled through the house as the camera shutter sounded from Noah's phone.

Noah walked back into the big room, hunched at the waist, laughing. "He's wearing Mom's fucking apron while he washes pots."

"Go, right now," Darla barked again. "You're drying. I'm not kidding about this. Go."

BY THE TIME lasagna was served, the table's occupants had grown considerably, but Sam and Adaline were still missing. In addition to the Trellis family, the table also included Greggory, Nora, Ben, Ava, Clyde, Jess, Blake, Mia, and Meg.

"Can someone mind-beam them and tell them dinner has been served, and they're officially late?" Hank asked, annoyed.

"Sam just said they're doing something and will be here soon. And they have a surprise," Ethan said. "Mom, lasagna? Really?"

"Don't judge. It makes me happy." Darla smiled.

"Field greens and lemon wedges," Will taunted, hoping to get a reaction from Jake. "That's never going to stop being funny now that it's a joke rather than reality. Thank God for Carrots."

Matty grinned at William.

"How come he's allowed to call you 'Carrots,' but when I do it, I get the glare?" Noah complained.

"She likes me more than she likes you," Will said with a shrug.

"It's a term of endearment from him. It's a condescending nickname from you," Matilda clarified.

"Hgrh," Noah grunted, not wanting to get into trouble. "So, did we ever figure out why Luke's girlfriend isn't here? Did I miss that?"

Greggory, Ben, and Nora dropped their heads towards their plates as one, trying to hide grins.

"Talise is not my girlfriend," Luke objected quietly.

"Yet," Jess stage-whispered to Blake, causing little bursts of stifled laughter. "Puking Peace has a lady!"

"You're not dating her? Really? Sticking with that?" William asked.

"Yup," Luke said to his dinner plate.

Noah stretched his arms out in front of himself, cracking his knuckles. "Ah. I got this one, Will. Challenge accepted!"

"What did I tell you?" Luke said, voice chilly.

Noah pasted a look of innocence on his face. "Luke, I would *never* hurt such a lovely creature. No. No. You misunderstand. Talise is absolutely gorgeous. I intend to woo her, win her love, and gain her heart."

Luke's gaze snapped to Greggory and Nora.

Gregg adopted Noah's innocent tone. "I'm not sure what you want me to say, Lucas. She's a single, attractive woman, now in good health and mental state. She's entitled to some romance after such a hard road, don't you think?"

Luke blew out a disgusted breath before leaving the table to take his plate in the kitchen. After giving Darla a kiss goodbye, he was out the door.

"Six months," Darla said, pleased. "Five of you will be married off within six months."

"How are you counting that? Matty and I are the only ones engaged," Jake pointed out.

"You and Matty, Sam and Adaline, Adrian and Lucy." She paused to glare at both of them, daring them to disagree.

They both shrugged.

"Beth and Hennessy." She paused again.

"I've asked her. Twice. She says Jake and Matty have to plan their engagement party first," Hennessy muttered.

Darla rolled her eyes and then glared at Matilda. "He asked for Hank's permission almost a week ago. You're killing me, Matty!"

"Yeesh. I'll get on that. Sorry, I didn't know we were blocking!" Matty said defensively.

"And then Luke and Talise. They were so cute!" Darla gave a little clap.

"They're not dating yet," Hank reminded her.

Jess snorted. "Oh, please. Those amber and silver bindings of friendship and familial love are so bright they could glow in the dark. It's a small step from here."

"It's perfect. Then it's just Matthew, Ethan, and that one." Darla made a flippant gesture at Noah.

William glared at Hennessy.

"What? We've discussed this!"

William continued to glare.

"Oh, fuck you!" Hennessy bitched. There was a pause. "Ah, shit. Sorry, kids. I'm an asshole."

"Yes!" William cheered. "I knew he'd do it."

"Jessup," Darla said, startled.

Hennessy shrugged. "Figured I'd get my money's worth. Am I washing dishes now or after dinner?"

Darla grinned. "You get a pass this time for making me laugh. Kids, we don't talk like that, right?"

There was a chorus of "Yes, Mom" mixed with "Yes, Grandma Darla" that made Darla grin.

"This is fabulous! I should have done this years ago." Darla clapped again, delighted with herself.

HALFWAY THROUGH DINNER, the back door opened and slammed closed, followed by little mewing sounds.

"What is that?" Hank asked, getting up.

Before he made it around the table, Sam ran into the room, vibrating with happiness.

"How are you still eating? I thought you'd be done by now! We found them! Come here! You have to see them!" Sam ran out of the room without another word.

After sharing confused glances, the family filed out of the dining room and back into the big room, where Sam and Adaline were surrounded by six mewing, barking baby puppies.

"Puppies!" Hank yelled, excited. He sat down next to Sam, reaching to scratch ears.

"Ah, shit," Darla muttered, making Jake glare at her.

"Aunt Lucy!" Ree hopped up and down.

Lucy grinned. "Go see."

"Mom, can we go see?" Mia begged Jess.

Jess sighed, resigned. "Of course."

"Sam?" Will asked.

"Hmm?"

"Why do you have a box of puppies?"

"Oh! Adaline felt them this morning. Someone threw them out of a moving car. When she felt them hit the pavement, we went right away. So now we have puppies!"

"Where were they that you felt them so clearly?" Ava said, frowning. "Not by your clearing, right? No one would do this by us."

Adaline shook her head. "Somewhere in the middle. I don't know. I was waiting for puppies. Sam wants a puppy. These are good puppies. Strong and protective, but not aggressive."

Sam grinned. "I think we were in Oklahoma. Addy healed them up no problem, but they're still babies. They shouldn't be separated yet. We'll keep them with us at the lake house for a few weeks. But who wants a puppy?"

"Sign me up!" Adrian laughed.

"Mom, please?" Meg begged, gently hugging the puppy in her lap. "Please? We'll take care of her! We can teach her tricks!"

"Yeah, I knew that was coming." Jess glared at Adaline.

Addy grinned.

"Will?" Sam asked.

Emma snorted, crouching down to see which puppy walked to her. "Absolutely. There's my good boy. Sit nice."

"Can I have a puppy?" Nora asked in a small voice.

Sam grinned at her. "Of course."

"Addy and I will keep one. So there's one left," Sam taunted Hank.

Darla rolled her eyes. "Sam, you know he's already named that puppy."

"Who's my good Glinda? Huh? Who's a good girl?" Hank muttered to the puppy in his lap. "Why do they have to go to the lake house? No, they should stay here. Our yard is fenced. Roscoe is here to show them the ropes."

"A few weeks?" Addy whispered. "They can't eat solids yet. They're only about three weeks old. Easier with me than with you."

"Well, Glinda can stay here, so you have one less to worry about. We can bottle feed her."

"No, Hank," Darla objected.

"But—"

"No."

Hank looked genuinely sad.

"I'll bring them to visit every day," Addy offered.

Hank grinned. "I'm getting a puppy!"

10

"Hi, Dad," Sam said, answering his cellphone at ten o'clock on Monday morning.

"Where are you right now?" Hank's voice was terse.

"I'm at the lake house. Addy likes it here."

"I'm glad she likes it there, but why aren't you at work?" Hank asked.

Sam paused, confused. "I told you. I don't want to do that anymore."

"You can't just stop," Hank disagreed.

"Why?"

"Samuel. This is your company. You own half the shares of this company," Hank ground out.

"You can have them. I'm done with that now," Sam said, pleased to resolve the problem.

There was an extended pause.

"I'll talk to you later, Dad. We're going to have breakfast."

"Samuel. Come here."

"Huh?"

"Come here. Right now. I'm in my office."

"Oh. I made french toast, though."

"Bring. It. With. You."

Sam frowned. "Are you mad at me?"

"Samuel James Trellis. Come here. Right now."

"Don't be mad. Why is everyone mad at me lately?"

"SAM!"

The phone shifted. "Addy, I can't stay for breakfast. I'm in trouble. I don't know what I did."

There was a murmuring response.

"Addy says I should eat first. Then I'll go to Adrian's house and come to the office from there. I'm not sure I can get the floors of the office building right. Adrian only has two floors."

Hank took a deep breath. "That's fine. I'll see you in thirty minutes."

"More like an hour?" Sam hedged.

"Forty-five minutes," Hank muttered, rubbing his temples as he hung up.

"I DON'T THINK anyone will even notice, Dad," Sam objected for the third time. "I'm weird. No one expects me to do any actual work."

Hank closed his eyes, trying to stay calm. Lunchtime had come and gone on Monday afternoon while he and Sam had the same circular conversation.

"Sam, this company is too big, too much a part of the global economy, for you to just walk away. You need to be a part of your company, son. You don't need to run it—"

Sam snorted. "I've never actually run this company!"

"I know." Hank nodded in agreement. "But you've always been involved. People invest in our products because you tell them the product will succeed."

"That's crap! No one knows who I am. No one cares. I'm not saying we should close the company. I'm just saying I'm not going to come here anymore," Sam said in his most reasonable voice.

Hank rubbed his temples again, taking a calming breath. "Samuel.

Do you want to move the company? Out to the suburbs? By where the big lot is? What if we moved out that way?"

"Oh! Did Jess like the house? Did Ava like theirs? Are they going to move into them?" Sam asked, excited.

"Yeah, Sam. Yeah, they liked the houses. Yes, they're going to move there. So, you and Addy can put a house on the big lot, and we'll move the company to the suburbs—"

"Dad, everyone's life is structured around the office being here. We can't just up and move and expect everyone to like it. That doesn't sound like a good idea. We should take a poll," Sam said, face scrunched up.

"Sam, the people who work here need you to keep on working here, at least part-time. This is a huge company. You can't just walk away from it without throwing things into a tailspin," Hank said.

"Tailspin?" Sam asked, his eyes going vacant for a second before glowing with a touch of white light.

"Sam?" Hank asked.

"Sec," Sam muttered.

Hank looked around his office, waiting, hoping no one walked in while Sam was adrift in time.

Sam shifted in his chair, blinking his eyes, then nodded.

Hank took another deep breath. "So, you can't—"

"I understand what you mean; I have to stay involved. But I don't want to come here all the time. We should all do other stuff, maybe take turns being here," Sam murmured, subdued.

"What happened?" Hank asked, morbidly curious.

Sam looked at his hands, shifting uncomfortably.

"It's just me, Sam."

Sam shrugged, not meeting Hank's eyes. "Tailspin. Wrong direction. Not good. I didn't think it'd matter. I didn't look to make sure. I should have looked. I would have done the wrong thing. I would have been selfish and done the wrong thing."

Hank gathered his thoughts for a few seconds. "You're going to be wrong sometimes, Sam. We're all wrong sometimes. But you came here and had this conversation with me. You listened to my words, even when you thought I was wrong. You still listened."

Sam nodded.

"We'll be in trouble if you stop listening. Until then, you're not in this alone. We'll help."

Sam shifted in his seat again. "Are you afraid of me, Dad?"

Hank burst out in big, rolling waves of genuine laughter. "I'm going to tell your mother you asked me that. She'll laugh herself silly."

Sam's eyebrows hiked up. "You didn't answer the question."

Hank sat back in his chair, the smile still lurking in his eyes and around the edges of his mouth. "When we were in Dallas, Ethan made an important distinction. The power is scary. Some of the things you can do are scary. You—Sam—are not scary. I haven't lost track of that. I suggest you don't, either, son."

Sam nodded, not meeting his dad's eyes.

"Topic change," Hank declared. "You have to talk to Addy's family about money."

"What? Why?" Sam was horrified.

"Because they don't seem to understand about the money. You need to talk to them about it," Hank said.

"What don't they understand? What's not to understand?" Sam was panicked. "There's money. They should spend it."

"That's what they don't understand. Ava said something about shuttering the restaurant and living frugally in retirement. Jess said something about Blake banking on your job hookup. Otherwise, they're not sure how they'd get started up here."

Sam's mouth dropped open. "I'm not talking to them about that! You do it."

"I'm not doing it! It's your money, you talk to them," Hank disagreed.

"Dad, I can't talk about that! No. I'll give you all the money. You can do it."

"No, Sam. There's no conflict of interest here. You have to do this," Hank insisted.

"Well, I'm not doing it. That's just too awkward for words. No! I'm not good at that stuff," Sam refused.

"They're your future wife's family! You should talk to them about this," Hank pressed.

"No! They're family. I can't talk to them about this. You didn't make me talk to Beth or Luke or Hennessy about this. No! This is worse than having to work!"

"I'm not doing it. It's too weird coming from me. Too much like pity," Hank decided.

"Tell Mom to do it!" Sam suggested, hopeful.

"I asked her yesterday. She refused," Hank harpooned the hope.

"I'm not doing it," Sam declared.

"I'm not, either. And someone has to talk to them."

"HELLO? Hello? Can you hear me? Oh, this silly thing. There. Hello, can you hear me? Is this Ava?"

Ava frowned at her cellphone. She thought maybe one of the Trellis family was calling, so she answered the unknown number as she was sitting down to lunch with Claire. "Yes, this is Ava. Who is this, please?"

"Oh, hi, Ava! My name is Martha. Martha Washington. I work with your son-in-law. Future son-in-law. Well, no. I work for him. Well, that's not right, either. I work for Adrian. But Sam asked so nicely, so I thought I'd just give you a call to chat.

"I just can't wait to meet your daughter, oh my goodness! All the boys getting matched up at once! I bet she's sweet as pie, right? He's such a good boy. All those boys are good. Except for maybe Noah, but you know there's no accounting for taste. But Sam's so sweet. Adrian's still my favorite, but Sam's a good one, too. Oh boy! My granddaughter should be so lucky..."

11

Harbor's circle met on Monday nights at seven o'clock. By general agreement, the circle would meet at the farmhouse until the energy leveled out.

Ava and Jess were waiting when Hank and Darla arrived.

"Are you kidding me?" Ava demanded.

"I didn't do it," Hank said immediately. "It wasn't my idea."

"What? What's going on?" Darla asked, suspicious.

"Your son had his senior citizen, rambling, babbling assistant call to tell me that we should spend his money." Ava glared at Hank.

"Martha called you?" Darla was startled. "Adrian's assistant?"

"Yes!"

Knowing Ava's irritation was legitimate, Darla did her best not to laugh. "Oh, Hank."

"Too awkward! No!" Hank insisted.

Darla rolled her eyes. "Ava, you have to understand. Sam is incredibly embarrassed about the money. He's never been comfortable talking about it under any circumstances. He knows that you have... reservations about him. He didn't want you to feel even more uncomfortable," Darla explained.

"That makes perfect sense. The part which baffles me is that Hank didn't mention it when we were looking at houses. He could have just told me what Sam intended!"

They were gathering an audience of onlookers.

Hank shifted around uncomfortably. "Well, I mean, Addy is his... whatever she is. It just felt like it should come from him. And I didn't want you to be uncomfortable. And we haven't known each other long, but you know..."

Ava stared, mouth agape.

Darla shrugged, doing her own little nervous shuffle. "We don't make many new friends. It's hard. With the money. It makes having normal friends difficult."

Ava's anger deflated like a balloon. "That's so sweet and so obnoxious all at the same time. I thought it was a crank call. I couldn't figure out what the hell she was talking about for a solid ten minutes! By the time I got it, she had to hang up to go to the bathroom. Claire laughed until she was dizzy."

"Classic Sam move. One for the record books. Painfully awkward, but good-natured," Claire announced to the room full of observers.

Hank looked around, blushing as people started muttering.

"I'm still not clear on what we're talking about here. He's giving us the house?" Jess asked.

"No, Jess. I mean, yes, of course, the house. He built those houses for you; he just didn't know it at the time. But, in general, he intends to give you a chunk of his wealth and shares in the company, akin to what the rest of us have. You're family, after all."

"Hey, Luke, what the fuck? Your family's rich?" someone yelled as Luke walked in the front door.

Luke looked around, shrugged, then nodded. "No little ears. Yeah, Dan, filthy fucking rich. Did you need something?"

The room broke out in startled laughter at Luke's language and grin. It took a minute for his words to settle in.

Then Ava was hugging Darla and Hank together.

"I'm still going to give him grief," Ava teased with a little grin.

People were staring at Noah, Matthew, and Ethan as they followed Luke through the farmhouse door. On Wednesday, these people seemed fine, like ordinary people. Tonight, they looked more like sharks. Noah could spot the singletons by their glances and toothy smiles.

"Fuck my life," Ethan muttered.

Noah grunted. They were aligned.

The front door opened and closed again behind them. Turning, Noah spotted the hot brunette's parents…without the hot brunette. Luke's face dropped into his "I'm concerned" expression.

After pausing for a minute to talk to her parents, Luke was gone looking for Talise. In effect, Noah, Matthew, and Ethan were left standing alone in a room full of unknown people who were interested in their power and money.

"Do you see anyone?" Matthew muttered from behind Noah.

"Mom and Dad are in the back with Ava and Jess," Ethan responded, stepping to the side so Matthew could lead the way through the crowd. Much like William, people got out of Matthew's way without thinking about it. Noah and Ethan just followed in his wake.

"Hi, boys," Darla said, accepting the obligatory kisses. "Where's Luke? I thought he was riding out with you?"

"He went to check on the hot brunette," Noah said.

Darla's smack to the back of Noah's head was pure reflex. "Stop it. We're in public. Don't make a scene. These people don't know we're nuts yet."

"They've met Sam," Matthew disagreed.

Darla did a side-to-side head wobble that meant, "Maybe."

"He was glowing on Wednesday night. Literally glowing," Matthew continued.

"I think that actually helps. They're wary of him. They don't realize he's…how he is yet," Darla responded.

"There's someone in the back corner wearing a giant fish pin. I don't think these people judge," Ethan muttered.

Ava burst out laughing. "He's been wearing that pin for as long as I remember. Go ask him about it. He'll tell you a story."

"Would I like the story?" Ethan asked.

"No. No, not at all. It's about how he caught a fish, started cutting its head off, and then the fish jumped out of the boat, escaping his frying pan in the process. It's a pin for the one that got away," Ava explained, laughing to herself at the memory.

Noah blinked. "I really hope the fish is not a metaphor for a lover."

Ava's grin fell. "I didn't consider that. He does go into pretty graphic detail. But a lover would not fit the descriptions of..."

Noah stared at her.

Jess started giggling. Ava flushed bright red. "Oh. I'm sure it's not. It can't be. It's not."

Noah let the silence rest for a few heartbeats.

"I'm ninety-five percent sure it's not a metaphor. But he did tell me the story when I was ten years old," Ava admitted.

She turned to Ethan. "Go ask him about the pin. See what he says."

"Absolutely not," Ethan said, shaking with laughter.

Ava glared at Noah. "You're ruining my childhood."

"What's ruining your childhood?" Claire asked, joining the group.

"Did George ever tell you the story about the pin?"

"The story about his ex-wife who left him for another man?" Claire asked.

"No, the fish pin!" Ava insisted, turning redder.

Claire stared at her cousin. "Bless your heart. What other pin could I possibly be referring to? That pin is eight inches wide. You can't miss it."

"Yeah, he told me... Never mind," Ava barked out as she turned around and stomped in the other direction, disturbed.

"Well, that made the ride out here worth it," Noah admitted as Jess, Matthew, and Ethan laughed. He dodged Darla's follow-up head smack.

"So, where is Luke?" Hank asked again, looking at Matthew.

Matthew rolled his eyes, still laughing. "I'm pretty sure Noah had it right. He left us right after we got in the door. Talise's parents came in without her."

"Is everything—?" Darla stopped talking as the room went uncomfortably silent. The only noise came from people shuffling around in a hurry.

Noah could see William's head by the front door. The entire crowd backed away from where Will was standing. Glancing to the side, Will ruffled someone's dark hair. It had to be Sam.

"Don't worry about it, Midas." Will forced a laugh.

Oh, fuck. Poor Sam. Will should have gotten this job. This wouldn't bother him, Noah thought.

"Hey, Ma, you're right! They don't yet realize Sam's a ninny!" Noah called, startling laughter from several people.

"Don't ruin it!" Ethan answered on queue in an equally loud voice. "Once they start talking to him about houses, the cat's out of the bag. Let him be a badass with those tats for a little bit longer."

"Yeah, yeah. Terrifying fucking Walker. Holy fuck, it's crowded in here," William grumbled, pulling Emma behind him. Jake, Matty, Sam, Adaline, Adrian, and Lucy followed in their wake.

"Pip!" Noah yelled. "You're still super-hot. When are you going to get all preggo with those babies?" More shocked laughter broke through the tension.

Will was trying to glare, but it wasn't working. Emma was grinning at Noah. He'd never admit it, but Emma's smile made Noah's chest lighter. She was the perfect opposite to spend eternity with solemn, scary William.

"Sorry. We dropped Ree off with Clyde and Blake. Traffic took longer than we thought it would. Are we waiting for more people? Beth and Hennessy?" Lucy asked, looking around the crowded room.

"There has to be close to a hundred people in here," Jess muttered.

Ava nodded. "Large turnout. Guessing most of these people aren't regulars. I saw Beth earlier in the kitchen. They're here somewhere. I think they came out early to help Nora get set up. I haven't seen Gregg or Nora, so I don't know if we need to wait."

"Adaline and Matilda hate this crowd," Sam muttered, not making eye contact with anyone. "We should start making our way to the field. Addy, can you feel Gregg?"

She nodded.

"Let's start making our way out there, everyone. We're only missing two or three people," Greggory's voice called from the other end of the house. "If you all show up next week, we're gathering in the barn. This is crazy."

Sam and Adaline managed to fall to the back of the crowd as they were leaving the house. When Noah and Ethan slowed to walk with them, Sam shook his head. "Luke and Talise will be here in a second. We're right behind you."

TALISE SAT in the back of her parents' SUV, working herself into an anxiety attack. She was about to stand a circle, wholly herself, for the first time in almost a decade. These people didn't know her as anything but the vacant-eyed ditz who couldn't remember anything.

It wouldn't be so bad, except she remembered people laughing at her. Now, the delayed embarrassment hit home all at once.

Luke would be in there. Luke would help. He didn't laugh at her. Even when she was at her worst, Luke didn't laugh. When things were terrible, when nothing would stay in her mind, Luke would sing with her to help her stay calm. Even when her mind wouldn't work, she could remember the music, could feel the music inside herself when someone helped her get started. The words came naturally without thought. Luke understood about music, he played music, too.

As the weekend progressed, a backlog of relief, fear, and anger hit home. So many lost years slammed into her. Stomach-wrenching terror dropped her to her knees a couple of times over the last few days. What if her mind reverted to what it was?

Talise's parents were frustrated. They wanted everything to be normal. She was better now; the vacant stare was gone. They wanted to call people and go places. Places where people knew them. Near people who knew her as she was before last week.

She knew she had to face that soon, but she'd feel better in a few more days. More adapted to the way life was now. She'd be less focused on the before and after of her situation. She would be less inclined to think of things as "then" and "now."

The passenger side back door to the SUV opened, startling Talise. Luke got in the car and closed the door. She hadn't felt him coming, too absorbed in her thoughts.

"So, where are we going? Are we escaping?" There was a real Lucas smile in his voice. She didn't need to look at him to see it.

Talise tried to smile, tried to make words come out of her mouth. She didn't know what to say. It was all mixed up inside, and she couldn't find the right of it. Couldn't find words, even for Luke, who always listened.

He quirked an eyebrow at her, holding his hand out, offering his energy. She grabbed his hand like an addict with a long-awaited fix. Peace washed over her, lifting the emotional flotsam from her mind.

She almost moaned in relief.

"Better?" he asked.

Talise nodded, taking large gulping breaths of air as the anxiety dissipated.

"How are you? How do you feel?" Luke asked, voice quiet. Calm. Soothing.

"There's so much. Everywhere. All the time. It just keeps rolling in; I can't make it stop. Before, it was different. I couldn't put my thoughts together. It wasn't as bad because I was always distracted. Now, I don't know how to make it stop."

"Okay."

"Okay?" she asked, surprised by the simple answer.

"Yup. Your mind was in bits and pieces for years. I'm guessing it's going to take more than a handful of days to feel right."

Talise nodded slowly in agreement.

"When Sam broke my tie, it was better and worse. I had my full mind the whole time, but I had no idea the tie was there. I didn't know what to do with the energy. I felt betrayed and alone. Scared. Even now.

"I don't want to go in there," she whispered. "They laughed at me. I made a fool of myself. I embarrassed my parents. I don't want to face them."

Luke sighed. "Want to go for ice cream?"

Startled, Talise laughed.

Luke grinned. "I won't make you go in there right now. Fuck, no. I don't think they were laughing at you, though, Tali. Your situation terrified most of them.

"There were times in the circle where power channeled directly through you, avoiding the center completely. There were times when you were singing or dancing that the real you peeked out at us. You were a very potent reminder of what could happen when playing with imperfect energy. It was hard to watch. Easier to laugh at the situation than think of the possible side effects that threaten us all," Luke explained.

She blew out a frustrated sigh. "I don't know how to act now."

"Then don't act. Just respond. It's fine if things go sideways. You're among friends."

She shot him a skeptical glare.

Luke chuckled a bit. "How about this? Sam will be upset if anyone upsets you. He's very protective of his people, and that includes you."

"He doesn't know me at all."

"No, he doesn't. But he knows you're important to me, and he still thinks I'm mad at him, so we'll go with that." Luke squeezed her hand. "What's it going to be? Circle or ice cream?"

AS THEY GOT out of the hot SUV, Luke wondered if she knew how different she looked. The spark of focused intelligence in her eyes changed her appearance drastically. She had the same long, dark hair, the same beautiful face, the same slender, muscular body. But Noah had it right. Talise was gorgeous. Luke hadn't noticed before, hadn't thought of her in those terms.

"What are you thinking? Your shock is very…loud," Talise asked.

"Hmm." Luke's smile was shy. "I was thinking that you're several orders of magnitude more beautiful like this, even if you are struggling. I need to contain my emotional noise better if I don't want to be embarrassed. I don't think I can lie without you knowing."

She flushed pink and dropped her eyes. "I didn't mean to intrude or embarrass—"

"I know. I don't mind. Are you up for meeting my family?"

Talise smiled. "It's the only reason I got out of the car. I need to thank your brother."

"Bah! I bet he doesn't even know what he did."

The house was empty when they walked in the front door, so they passed directly through to the back door and yard. They could see the tail end of a line of people moving to the field.

"How are you?" Sam's quiet voice came from directly behind them, startling Luke. Tali didn't flinch or react. She knew he was there.

"Don't do that," Luke bitched.

Adaline smiled at him. Luke smiled back. Addy had the type of smile that made other people smile.

"I'm sorry. I didn't mean to startle you," Sam said, instantly contrite. "Are you still mad at me? Tali's okay, right?"

Everyone looked at Talise. She had a baffled expression on her face, staring at Sam, head tilted, focused on something no one else could see.

"Talise?" Luke asked.

She glared at Luke. "Tell him you're not mad. He's devastated at the thought of you being mad. He looks calm, but he's panicked. Stop it."

It was Luke's turn to glare. "Sam, you are such a pain in the ass. You're the only person on the planet who could make me feel guilty after *you* burned a hole in *my* head. No, I'm not mad. I'm annoyed, but not mad."

Sam looked at Talise, then Adaline, fidgeting with his hands. Looking back to Luke, he finally spoke. "I'm so sorry, Luke. I'm sorry I hurt you. I knew it would hurt, and I did it anyway. I had to do it. I wasn't even sure what I was doing, but I knew I had to do it. I didn't think you'd be so angry at me. I don't want you to hate me."

Luke rolled his eyes. "For fuck's sake, Sam. I don't hate you. If I had to choose between the scorched brain and losing a brother, I'd take the scorched brain without remorse. It was annoying that you zapped Talise's tie without the exploding brain, though. And don't tell me we didn't have time. It took you like a second."

"But I don't have the energy to heal! I would have helped you heal if I could, but I don't have that type of power. And I couldn't make you sleep because you had to help Adrian and Will. There was no other way to do it quickly enough to help them. I'm so sorry," Sam said again.

"Ugh. You are such an asshole. I feel like I accidentally kicked a puppy. Didn't you get the memo? You're supposed to be this legendary badass who smites without remorse. Get it together, man," Luke scolded.

Sam's mouth opened and closed. He was at a loss for words, unsure how to explain.

"Lucas," Adaline chided. "It's one thing for everyone else to think that of him. It's a whole other story for his family to feel that way."

Luke pulled a face at Addy, making her laugh. "Tali, this is my brother, Sam. That's Adaline."

WITHOUT WARNING, Sam turned to Talise and hugged her, touching the bare skin of her face and neck as he pulled her close. He said something, but she couldn't make out the words as his entire emotional profile slammed into her.

"NO! Sam, FUCK!" Lucas yelled as Talise fell to the ground, gasping for air. Sam's emotional cocktail of self-loathing, fear, love, grief, and sadness swallowed her mind.

"Oh, shit!" Sam yelled, dropping down next to her, looking for a way to help. "What just happened? What did I do?"

Luke was digging in the layers of her clothes, trying to find her skin. Finally, getting hands on her midriff, he pushed peaceful energy into her as fast as he could.

"Don't touch. No touching. No skin contact. Especially from you. You're a hot mess!" Luke yelled. "Now I'm mad at you again!"

"I didn't know!" Sam yelled back. "How—"

As she stepped over both men, Adaline smacked the back of their heads, rolling her eyes. She sat on the ground, pulling Talise's head into her lap. Luke could feel the waves of peace, love, and joy flowing from Adaline, through Talise, and into him.

Talise blinked her eyes several times.

"Oh, that's nice." She sounded intoxicated.

Luke grinned at Adaline. "She's drinking from the firehose of peace."

Adaline grinned back. "I don't want her to fall asleep. They're waiting for us in the circle. Talise, are you back to us?"

"Hi," Tali mumbled with a little giggle.

"I'm sorry, Talise! I don't know what I did," Sam apologized, making her laugh again.

"S'ok. This is so nice," she muttered.

"Sam, you can't touch her. Don't touch her skin." Luke tried to sound calm.

"You touch her," Sam complained, confused.

"I am Peace, Sam! When I touch her, she gets a shot of emotional calm. You're the freak show, angsty Walker. She got stuck in your emotional backwash while standing four feet away from you. When you touch her, you force your emotions into her senses in high definition. It confuses everything. That's why she wears like three layers of clothes and gloves in the middle of the fucking summer!"

Luke helped Talise sit upright as Adaline climbed back to her feet.

"Better?" he asked.

Talise turned to him with a smiley, stoned look on her face. "I'm great. Let's do this circle."

"Why are you smiling?" Luke demanded, glaring at Adaline.

Adaline put on an affronted face. "I'm not smiling. I'm working hard at not-smiling."

Luke took a calming breath. "Fine. Why are you not-smiling?"

"Why not just touch her forehead, Luke? Why did you go digging for her tummy?"

Talise started a bit as the question sunk in, but she didn't say anything.

Luke chewed on his bottom lip. "Sorry, Tali. It just always seems to work better like that. Like it's a surface area thing."

Sam was turning his lips into a frown to keep from smiling. "I watched you drop Adrian and William at the same time from fifteen feet away."

Lucas kept walking in stoic silence.

"When we were at the fundraiser with Matty, you—" Sam started.

"Shut up, Sam."

They walked in silence for three paces.

"Are you mad?"

"Shut up, Sam."

12

At long last, Noah could see Sam and Adaline walking toward the field with Luke and Talise. *Hot brunette. Hot brunette. Hot brunette. Have to keep that up. It makes Luke batshit crazy.*

Noah smiled to himself. Like calling dibs on Matty, Noah intended to needle Lucas until he admitted there were feelings there. This would be easier than Jake. There was no shrew of a girlfriend in the way.

Glancing over again, Noah got a good look at Talise as she walked, hand in hand, with his youngest brother. Head held straight, shoulders level, she moved with a dancer's grace.

Did Luke say she was a dancer? I think he said she danced, right? Noah wondered.

Talise's eyes shifted to take in the entire circle. When her gaze landed on him, the breath whooshed out of Noah's chest. The sweet, vacant look was gone. In its place, understanding and intelligence lurked. The people around Noah shifted, noticing the change, too.

I hope Micah finds whoever fucked up her head.

The thought startled Noah. He wasn't much for vengeance or anger. Too stressful.

But holy fuck. I understand the impulse now.

Looking away, Noah saw Jess, directly across from him. She was watching him, eyebrows lifted in surprise. He shrugged. Talise wasn't the most beautiful woman he'd ever seen, but she was the most alluring. No sense pretending otherwise.

Plus, it'll irritate Luke.

Sam and Adaline walked the line of the circle, closing it with their combined energy. As they moved to the middle, Sam kept frowning at Talise.

"Sam?" Gregg asked.

Walking straight into Talise's personal space, Samuel paused just short of touching her. "What is your name?" he asked, words vibrating with power that shook the circle around them.

Fear flowed through the circle. Voices muttered all around Noah about the evil Walker.

Morons, Noah thought, scornful.

Talise didn't respond. She just stared at Sam, looking lost.

"Do you know who you are?" Samuel tried again, eyes glowing with power.

Talise flinched like he slapped her.

Probably not the best question for someone recovering from memory issues, Sam. Without realizing it, Noah was glaring at the back of Samuel's head.

"Yes. I am Talise Marie Ayers," she responded. Unless Noah was mistaken, there was a "fuck you" embedded in her tone. It made him smile. Looking over, he saw Luke frowning at Sam.

"That's not what I meant," Sam said, all signs of power gone as he walked back to Addy. "If you don't know yet, it's fine. The circle will stay lopsided."

Adaline effortlessly dumped a fuck ton of calm, peace, and joy into the circle. The woman on the other side of the circle staring at Noah moaned.

Fuck my life, Noah thought. *These people are assholes.*

Ethan dumped patience and loneliness in it, causing most of the singletons to focus on him. As Ethan glanced around the circle, noticing the stares, Noah saw his face fall into his resigned expression. Ethan typically saved that face for Sam. He must have been frustrated.

Luke hit the circle with excitement and happiness, surprising everyone. Then Talise's energy flowed through the circle in a giant tidal wave of emotions so intertwined and complex, Noah had trouble parsing them. Fear, joy, anger, resignation, affection, confusion, something that might have been stubbornness, and something lighter. Cool. Fresh. Pure.

Noah rocked back in surprise. Talise was like Matilda and Lucy. The amount of power, the way it moved, the feel of it...Talise was a corner. Not entirely sure why the corners were important, Noah recognized that Sam was looking for Talise to take the name of Water. Someone needed to tell her.

Luke will tell her, Noah thought. *This is not my problem.*

Matilda blew up the circle, literally. It exploded in a giant ball of flame around them. Jake sucked all the energy back in and then pushed it out as something else that Noah couldn't identify.

"Jake!" Ava exclaimed. "That was amazing!"

"Huh?"

"You made it all pure life energy! That was amazing!" Ava said again.

"Oh. I meant to take the fire, but then there was too much fire, so I pushed the energy back out," he explained.

Nora was scrubbing her hands across her face. Greggory's mouth was hanging open. Ben looked calm and interested, the same as always.

Noah chuckled to himself. *Heh. Yeah. We have no idea what the fuck we're doing. Sorry to all you people who know what you're doing.*

Lucy's energy managed to call down actual lightning, scaring everyone.

"Oops," she muttered, going red.

Sam smiled. "Wind. Clouds. Thunder. Lightning. That's going to be fun when you're mad at Adrian."

Stifled laughter sounded from around the circle.

Yeah, see, you fucking idiots. It's just Sam, Noah thought. *He's nowhere near as scary as Will or Hennessy. It's fine. Stop making him sad.*

Emma dumped nothing but pure love in the circle. Noah got the sense that she did it because she wanted to see if she could.

Sam snorted, looking at Noah as he dumped energy into the ring. "Feeling cynical?"

"Meh." Noah smiled.

"No lust?"

"Nah." Noah shrugged.

Sam shrugged back.

Two more laps of the circle later, Adaline was pushing the energy out into the world. As people were laughing, walking back toward the house, Noah ended up directly behind Talise and Luke.

"Well, hello gorgeous," Noah purred, jogging to catch up.

Luke glared at him.

HA! This is going to be so easy! Noah grinned at his little brother. "Introduce me."

"Go away," Luke muttered.

"Lucas, how rude! Hi, Talise. I'm Luke's older, better-looking brother, Noah."

Luke's glare turned glacially cold. "Talise, this is my man-whore brother, Noah."

"Boo!" Noah yelled, startling the people around them. He got no reaction from Talise. Her eyes were narrowed, almost glaring at him. "I take it you're feeling better?"

She muttered something Noah didn't hear as they walked in the back door of the house.

"Luke! Thank you for fishing her out of the car." Talise's dad, Mike, walked up, smiling.

Luke smiled at Talise. "She got out on her own accord. I wanted to go for ice cream."

"What's with all the whispers about you being rich?" Mike asked.

Noah snorted. Luke and Mike glared at him. Talise didn't respond at all, didn't even glance at him.

Well, that doesn't work at all for me, Hot Brunette. We have to be friends, at least. I can't bait Luke if you don't like me.

THE CROWD of people and their mix of emotions was making Talise ill. She wanted out of the room, out of the house. Being in a group was much harder now that she understood what was going on around her.

Still reeling from Sam's touch, she was trying to shut down her senses. It didn't seem to be working. This other brother had powerful emotions. He caused intense emotions all around him. Especially from women.

Go away. Please go away. Go away. I'm sorry. I know I should be talking with you, but if I open my mouth, I'm going to puke, Talise chanted at Noah in her head.

She looked up into his dark eyes and watched his mouth move as he tried to talk to her. When her eyes met his, a wave of possessive lust slammed through Talise's brain, startling her.

Please go away. I can't talk to you.

Her perception switched to slow motion as she continued to process the avalanche of his emotions. Talise wondered if she was going to blackout. His lips were still moving. He was moving closer to her, a smile in his eyes.

Talise tried to lock her senses down again. She had no control at all. She tried to unfocus her brain. She couldn't do that anymore, either.

His hand was moving. Luke's brother's hand was moving toward her. He was going to touch her. Touch her face.

Breathtaking terror of another emotional deluge rolled through Talise. She couldn't do that again. No. He wouldn't touch her. Luke would stop him. Or she'd get it together enough to tell him to stop.

Luke was focused on her dad. Talise's mouth wasn't opening. She couldn't breathe. His hand was getting closer. Closer. Closer. Closer.

Oh God. No! Talise thought as she swiftly lifted her knee, kicking Noah in between the legs.

Then she was gone, out the back door, running through the yard, into the field.

"WHAT?" Noah whimpered, dropping to his knees. "What just happened?"

"Noah! What the fuck!" Luke yelled.

Mike's eyes were huge with rage. "What did you do to her?"

"What did I do to her?" Noah breathed, unable to catch his breath. "Are you fucking kidding? I asked why she wears so many layers of clothes, then she kicked me!"

Adaline was standing next to him now, mouth hanging open in shock. Jess was behind her, laughing.

"Fuck you, too, Jess!" Noah groaned, trying not to puke.

As Adaline touched his face, the pain eased.

"Addy, I really do love you with my whole heart," Noah breathed.

She smacked him in the forehead again.

"I swear I didn't do anything!" Noah objected as the rest of his family was getting close enough to hear. "Not a damn thing! Luke, I will absolutely kick you in the nads if you don't stop laughing right now."

"Nope." Luke laughed, heading out the back door after Talise.

"What the fuck is wrong with her?" Noah bitched.

"CAN I HELP?" Sam asked, standing behind Talise as she dry-heaved in the field.

She jumped, turning to scowl at him.

"He wouldn't have hurt you," Sam said. "I'm sorry. I didn't see it happening until it was almost happening. You're not where I expected you to be. I can't find you easily."

Talise looked up at him, trying to convey both *I have no idea what you're talking about* as well as *Please go away* as her stomach heaved again.

"Addy said she'll be here to help as soon as Noah is back on his feet. I'm sorry. I think I could help you, but I don't want to make it worse again," Sam muttered, eyes on the ground.

"Tali!" Luke was calling her name from the yard.

"We're here," Sam called back to him.

"Sam! What happened? Tali, oh fuck," Luke said, dropping to the ground behind her, pulling her down into his lap. One of his hands went across her forehead, the other on the bare skin of her neck.

Talise was gagging for air as her stomach suddenly stopped rolling. Then Adaline was there, offering her hand as well.

"Where'd you come from?" Tali whispered to her.

Adaline grinned. "I followed Sam. Shh, don't tell anyone."

"You can do it, too? That's bullshit!" Luke complained. "What happened, Tali?"

"He was going to touch me. I panicked. Too much. Too many. Too much," she choked out.

Sam's voice was confused. "He was going to touch your shirt."

Talise shook her head. "No, he was going to touch me. His hand was reaching for me. He was talking, but I couldn't hear him. He has very loud emotions."

Adaline nodded in agreement.

Sam shook his head. "No. He was asking why you wore so many layers and if your outer layer was cotton. He was reaching to touch the shoulder of your shirt. I saw that clearly."

Talise blinked. "Oh."

Luke started to laugh again.

"I-I kicked him hard. Don't laugh. It's not funny. He shouldn't have been trying to touch me, though!" Talise objected.

"Tali, this is funny on many levels that you don't yet understand," Luke said, laughing hard enough to shake Talise in his lap.

"He wasn't going to touch me?" Talise asked Sam, horrified.

"No," Sam said, frowning. "Now everything's jumbled. I don't know where you go."

"Oh, no," Talise breathed.

"Fucking hilarious," Luke said. "Don't worry about it, Tali. He'll get over it."

Sam pressed his lips together, decidedly unhappy.

"DON'T TOUCH HER. Don't ever touch her," Luke said for the fourth time in the car on the way back to the city.

"I heard you the first three fucking times!" Noah growled. "I *didn't* touch her. I wasn't going to touch her! Holy fuck!"

"She thought you were going to touch her. She saw your hand moving toward her and thought you were going to touch her. She panicked. Sorry." Luke laughed, unapologetic, while keeping his eyes on the road.

"Stop laughing," Noah bitched to Ethan and Matthew in the back seat.

"This is going to be funny for a while, man," Matthew disagreed.

"She's nuts!" Noah argued. "Number one, I wasn't going to touch her. Darla would lose her mind if I didn't keep my hands to myself."

The car went quiet as the brothers nodded in agreement.

"Number two, I was talking to her! I asked her about her shirt and all the fucking layers. Find another hot brunette, Luke. I'm not teasing you about this one. She's got the crazy eyes."

"Noah, she is perfectly sane. Stop being an asshat. You caught her at a bad moment," Matthew objected, still laughing.

"Whatever! She attacked me," Noah bitched. "I hate you all for laughing. Adaline is the only sibling I like right now. The rest of you people suck. It wasn't funny."

"Oh my God," Ethan exploded. "It was so funny. I thought you were going to puke for a second."

"Well, let me kick you in the junk and see how you like it! Also, why is she so fucking strong?" Noah continued to bitch.

"She's a dancer. Ballet, for the most part. She's strong. Good muscle control," Luke said, laughing hard again.

"I hate you all."

"TONIGHT WAS BETTER," Adaline said as they walked into their bedroom at the lake house.

Sam nodded.

"They're more interested than afraid now," she said.

He nodded again.

"*Sam?*" she asked through their link, trying to remind him that she could feel his unease.

"It's wrong. It's all wrong now. I thought she was just in the wrong place before, but now I don't know. I can't find her. It'd be easier if I could touch her, but that hurts her. I keep looking, but I can't find her anywhere close to now, and I can't find her anywhere other than where I thought she'd be when I look further out," Sam babbled.

"Talise?" Adaline asked, eyebrows raised.

Sam's nod was somehow confused.

"You don't know what's going to happen to her?" Adaline asked.

"No. I don't know what's going to happen to everyone. But, usually, things feel fine. This is all wrong. It feels all wrong. We're somewhere we shouldn't be!" He spat the words out in frustration.

Adaline frowned at him.

"If you weren't here with me, I'd swear I was lost in time. This is what being lost feels like. But we're not lost, and it's all wrong."

"Where is she supposed to be, Sam?" Adaline asked, trying to work through it.

"I don't know!"

Adaline sighed. "Where did you think she would be?"

He didn't answer, lost in his own thoughts.

"Where is she when you look further out?" Adaline tried again.

"Huh?" Sam asked, eyes flickering with power.

"Where is she in the future?"

"I don't think it will happen now, so it doesn't matter," Sam said, collapsing on the bed. "I can't find her anywhere other than where I thought she'd be. I can't find her standing with Luke, and I can't touch her to look closer."

"You didn't answer my question."

"I know. I'm sorry. Sometimes saying things out loud causes everything to shift, so I try not to do that."

Adaline sighed again. "You're approaching this from the wrong angle."

"What do you mean?"

"Can you find Luke standing with her?"

Sam's face went blank. "I love you."

Adaline's lips twitched up. "I know."

13

"Just leave him here tonight, Lucy. He's really out. Exhausted from all the little girl playtime." Jess laughed, watching Ree in the sleeping kid pile with Mia and Meg. His face was painted with makeup. He was wearing one of Mia's dresses over his clothes.

"Mia insisted," Blake muttered from behind them. "I think she's claimed Ree as her future spouse. Might want to discuss the downside of pre-arranged marriages with her."

"You can do that!" Jess objected quietly.

"I tried. She told me I don't understand girls." Blake laughed.

"He has treatment in the morning," Lucy said, voice regretful. "I hate to wake him, but we have to go back to the city tonight. I'm going to see if I can switch his days to Monday and Wednesday instead of Tuesday and Thursday."

Adrian walked past, scooping Ree up in his arms. "We'll bring the dress back on our next visit."

Ree didn't stir as Adrian buckled him into the booster seat in the car.

LINDA TRIED to open her eyes as she was dumped on the cement floor of her basement cell.

"Round 382," John muttered. "Linda, stop doing this. Just leave the binding there. He's not going to kill you. It's not going to happen. You're torturing yourself."

"Fff ooo," she slurred. The right side of her face was beaten and swollen. Her jaw was broken. She couldn't feel her legs.

"Yeah. I know. You hate me. Fine. Hate me all you want. But stop this. He's not going to kill the kid! Your kid isn't part of this," John explained again. "That's not what he's after. Just leave it be. There's no point in doing this. He's going to win. I can't watch..."

Linda lost some time.

14

Sam woke suddenly on Tuesday morning to a wave of Adaline's confusion and fear. She was gone from the bed next to him. Jumping out of bed, he went in search of her, calling for her throughout the house. She wasn't there. Searching through the mental binding, he realized she was down by the lake with the puppies.

"What's wrong?" he asked, moving quickly to hug her and wipe away tears.

Grabbing hold, Adaline buried her head into his chest and sobbed.

"Addy?" Sam muttered, running a hand down the back of her head, trying to offer comfort. It was early; the sun was just starting to lighten the sky to the east.

Through their link, she showed him the fire from her dream. The vision sucked the air out of Sam's chest and knocked him to the ground. He pulled her down with him, wrapping himself around her as she cried.

"I'm sorry," he murmured. "I'm sorry. You shouldn't have that dream. I didn't want you to get that. I haven't had dreams since I found you. I'm sorry. I didn't know you had them. Why didn't you tell me?"

"I didn't have them before last night. I slept fine for most of the night. I woke up when the moon was still up, checked on the puppies, and then came back to bed. When I drifted back off to sleep, the house was burning."

"Addy, I'm sorry. We should limit the accordance. You shouldn't have the dreams. We need to restrict it, so you don't have them," Sam insisted, even as Addy violently shook her head.

"I've been up for a while. Maybe an hour or so. The puppies and I came outside, and I felt better. But then I had to go back inside. I don't want to be inside anymore, Sam."

"You don't want to go into the house because of the fire dream?" Sam asked.

Adaline shook her head. *"I don't know what to do, Sam! I don't know how to do this!"*

"Do what?" Sam asked, searching the binding for more information.

"I don't know how to be in the house! I can't work any of the stuff," Adaline confessed aloud. "I like it here. I like being here with you. But I don't belong here. I don't know how to do this! I can't be anywhere now!"

Sam blinked.

"I can't cook, I don't know how to work the stove, I don't know how the dish cleaner works, and I don't know how to use the clothes washer. I don't belong here," she mumbled.

Sam grinned at her. He couldn't help it.

A spike of her anger shot through their binding.

"I know how to do those things. Maybe I'm not a good cook; it depends on who you ask. I can show you. Do you want to learn?" he asked.

"You shouldn't have to teach me. I should know," Adaline whispered.

Sam laughed. "Really?"

Adaline shot him a confused, hurt look.

"Addy, you've taught me so much about what we are, our energy, and how to use it. I can show you how to load and work the dish-washer if you really want to know. Or I can do it. I'm a modern man with a healthy fear of my mother. Darla would knock the stuffing out of me if she heard me talk about 'women's work.' They're chores." Sam shrugged. "We can do them together. They're not worth being upset about."

"I don't know what to say to people. When they try to talk to me. I don't know what to say back. They tried talking to us last night. The people from the circle. They wanted to talk with me. I didn't know what to do," Addy shared, exasperated.

"I know. I felt your fear. It was fine, though. When I started talking, they ran away." Sam made a face at her. "Spooky Walker. They probably think I terrorize you."

Adaline made a face back at him. "I should know—"

"Adaline! Please cut yourself some slack. Before last week, you hadn't spoken or shared thoughts with anyone but me in a decade. You're doing amazingly well. A-MAZ-ING," Sam insisted. "If it's overwhelming now and you want to go back to the clearing for a while, we can do that. I'm happy if you're happy. But getting upset about not working the washing machine and not being great at small talk is not a good use of energy."

Addy sighed, shifting to wrap her arms and legs around Sam. "I do not want to hurt the accordance. They are just dreams."

Sam nodded.

She was quiet for a while, thinking. Sam could feel the thoughts churning but couldn't focus enough to understand them.

"Did you go to school?" she finally asked.

Sam rocked back to see her face. "I did. You didn't?"

"I could not. Mama taught me how to read and do numbers. I have not read in a long time. I can't do it anymore."

Sam nodded. "I'll teach you that, too. I like to read. Were you considered home-schooled, then? How did that work?"

"I don't know. The town understood that I could not, so I didn't go. I don't think anyone minded, just like they understood that I didn't want to talk. So, I didn't talk. They did things with me that I liked instead," Adaline explained.

"That whole town loves you," Sam murmured.

"I love them, too," she said simply. "I don't want to leave them. I know that we can't stay there, but I don't want to leave them without energy."

"So we'll go back regularly? I can buy a house there!" Sam grinned.

Her lips turned up. "I think they will teach me how to do things if I ask. Cook and clean."

Sam laughed. "I can teach you. Darla or Ava or Jess or any of my siblings can teach you, too. But if you want to learn from your friends at home, share that with them, I understand that."

"Friends?" Addy asked.

"Friends," Sam agreed. "They are non-family members who you love and value."

"I know what the word means, Sam. I just didn't think about it like that before," Addy mumbled.

They were quiet, watching the sky lighten with the rising sun.

"What was school like?" Adaline asked, wistful.

"Miserable," Sam admitted.

Addy leaned back to look at Sam's face, surprised. "You went even though it was miserable?"

"I did. Hank and Darla insisted. It was...hard. Too many people. Unstructured minds. I didn't know how to put time away yet, so it kept branching before me. I'd answer questions before they were asked. If I touched someone, I'd find their thread in the web or their wildflower in the garden and start following it. I'd be too distracted to have a conversation."

Sam was silent for a few heartbeats before continuing.

"My head kept bleeding. My ears and nose bled most nights. I woke up screaming from the nightmares. They thought something was wrong with my brain. I was in a special classroom for a long time.

"One of the special education administrators told Hank and Darla to let me do independent study so I could move at a faster pace and be done with school earlier. They said no. I needed to be able to have conversations and social interactions. Independent study wouldn't help that happen."

"Hank and Darla are wise," Addy interrupted. "It is painful to figure out now."

"When I was about ten, the administrator convinced them to let me skip a grade, so I'd be in a class with Ethan. That helped me a lot. I could focus better because I would just pay attention to Ethan. From then on, I followed Ethan through school. We were fine.

"By the time high school was over, I was done with the school experience. But Hank and Darla said they'd fund my first work project if I finished a college degree. I chose a university that allowed the 'independent study' model and rolled through the content as quickly as possible."

Sam shrugged. "I don't regret the education, but I don't know that I benefited from the classroom. Ava was right to spare you that pain. It was horrible when I was young. Until I was with Ethan, being at school was absolutely miserable. They tried to put me in a mainstream classroom for third grade. The teacher had a mental breakdown during the second week of classes. She screamed and raved that I could read minds."

He stopped talking again as he ran fingers through her hair.

"You had more friends than me, Addy, no matter how you communicated that friendship. I didn't have friends other than my family until college, and then only a few." Sam's voice was subdued with reflection.

Wrapped up in his own thoughts, Sam didn't notice the puppy sneaking up behind him until it nibbled his side. "Oy! This is Uncle Jake's t-shirt. I'll never hear the end of it if you put a hole in it."

Sam could feel Adaline's amusement in their link.

"Feel better?" Sam asked.

"I'll adapt, I guess."

"We don't have to stay here, love. But you are awake now. I think the clearing might be lonely, all day, every day," Sam counseled.

"We cannot be there," Addy agreed.

"Why do you keep saying it like that?" Sam asked, confused. "We shouldn't isolate ourselves there, but we can go back if it helps."

"No."

"Why?" Sam asked.

"No, Sam. We cannot. We will stay here, with our circle."

"Addy?"

"I'm hungry," she said aloud.

"Toast? Eggs and bacon? Cereal?" he asked, allowing the distraction.

LATER THAT AFTERNOON, Adaline took a nap in the living room, buried in little warm puppies. Once Sam was sure she was asleep, he Walked to their clearing in Texas.

Their energy was gone. The flowers and grass had died; the critters had scurried back into the forest.

Sam could feel and taste the foulness of a hunter who had taken lives. Someone had made it to their clearing, took their energy, and desecrated their space.

ADALINE WOKE from her nap to Samuel's anger.

"When did the wards fall?" he asked, voice rich with energy and rage.

She blinked.

"I saw it. When did it happen?"

"Last night. I think it's how the fire dream came to me. After the circle, when we were still at the farmhouse, the inner ward fell without any of the other wards being disturbed. I thought it just fell on its own. That happens sometimes. But when I woke from the dreams, I knew the energy was gone from the clearing. I don't know how it happened. I haven't gone to look."

He nodded. "Do you know who did it?"

"No." Tears dripped down Adaline's face.

The power drained from Sam's eyes. "You could have told me why you were upset this morning, Addy. I don't know how to feel about you hiding it, lying about it."

Adaline frowned in confusion. "I did tell you why I was upset this morning. Someone was going to take that energy eventually. I knew it when we left the clearing. Evelyn even said it."

"I didn't understand when Evelyn said it. I thought she was making fun of us," Sam admitted. "But you could have told me this morning."

"Sam, I wasn't upset about the clearing this morning," Adaline insisted.

"Addy," Sam said, voice terse.

"I would tell you if I was. I figured we'd talk about it later."

He watched her as he searched their binding for insight.

She shook her head. "Sam, I don't belong anywhere. That clearing is no longer mine. This house is not mine. We are far from most of the people I know and love. I don't know how to be here yet. I'm lost. I like it here. I love you. But I'm lost right now. Everything has changed. For the better, but it is all different."

Sam paused, thinking, then closed his eyes.

"Sam?"

He smacked himself in the forehead.

Adaline touched his face.

"Hank told me what to do. He told me yesterday. I should have shown you yesterday."

"What's wrong?" she asked.

"Nothing at all. Can you feel Ava or Jess? Can you ask them where they are? If they're at one of their houses?" Sam asked.

After a pause, she nodded. "Jess says they're measuring rooms. When did Jess get a house? How did I miss that?"

Sam's mouth opened and closed. "It's easier to show you than explain. Where are your shoes? Would you ask her if we can visit?"

JESS WAS STANDING in the living room, waiting for them, when they appeared. Getting a running start, she tackled Sam down to the couch, kissing his cheeks.

"I CAN'T BELIEVE THIS HOUSE! I CAN'T BELIEVE YOU DID THIS!"

"Uh, hi Jess," Sam said, bewildered.

"Ha! Hi, Sam. Hi, Addy. She said she was going to do that. I didn't believe her." Blake laughed as he walked out of the hallway to the downstairs bedrooms.

"I didn't get to talk to you last night! You showed up right before the circle, and then Noah got kicked, and I was laughing. Then you were gone!" Jess yelled.

"I'm sorry, Addy was—" Sam started.

"Never apologize for anything ever again!" Jess demanded.

Sam blinked. "That seems highly unrealistic."

"I cannot believe this house! How did you know? No. Don't answer that. But I still can't believe this!" she rambled.

Glancing at Blake, Sam's expression begged for clarification.

"She's excited," Blake said with a grin. "But this house is amazing. You're really going to let us live here?"

Still confused, Sam nodded. "Of course. It's for you. I just didn't know it until Hank mentioned it yesterday. Ava and Clyde will live next door?"

"Yes!" Jess yelled. "It's perfect! The girls are over there right now. Are we all going to live here? That's what Hank thought."

"We can if we want to," Sam said, tentative. "I wanted to show Addy the big lot."

Jess turned to see her little sister glancing around the house, eyeing the windows, pausing at certain spots.

"Yup!" Jess called to her. "It's even more obvious in your space."

Adaline turned, startled. "I don't have a space."

"Well, you could. We could. I mean, if you want to be here, we can be here. We can build a house here. There's a big piece of land down the street that we can live on," Sam babbled, nervous.

"You own this?" Addy asked, pleased.

Sam nodded. "This house, and the one next door. They're for Jess, Blake, the girls, and your parents. I own all the land on this street. Hank mentioned it yesterday; I didn't catch it. Now, I understand."

"What do you understand?" she asked.

"You don't belong at the clearing anymore, and you don't belong at the lake house. It's because we should be here," Sam explained.

"Sam, do you know what this land is?" Adaline asked, head tilted, interested.

"Home?" Sam asked.

"It's a power sink! The land is a power sink," Jess cheered.

Sam shook his head in confusion.

"The land! The way the houses are positioned. Even where the light comes in. It all helps energy move smoothly. It's easier to pull energy here, and it's easier to cycle energy. Mom just about lost her mind when she noticed," Jess explained. "The restaurant is positioned on a tiny sink. It helped Addy when we were small."

Sam looked at Adaline.

"Do you feel it?" Addy asked.

Sam shook his head. "No. I don't know what she means. I like it here, though. I've always liked it here."

"So intuitive." Adaline grinned.

"It's more pronounced as you walk down the street, too. That big lot is the center of it!" Jess laughed.

"Show me?" Adaline asked Sam.

"I CANNOT BELIEVE YOU DID THIS!" Ava yelled as Addy and Sam came in the front door a few minutes later with Jess and Blake.

"Please don't jump on me," Sam begged.

Ava laughed. "Did you know you did this? How did you find this? How did you know?"

"I didn't," Sam said. "We were driving by one day."

"Hank told us," Ava said. "We spent a lot of time and money looking for the tiny sink that the restaurant is on. They're difficult to find."

"What is it?" Sam asked, hoping for a better explanation.

Ava smiled. "Sam."

He sighed, knowing that his ignorance was showing again.

"A sink is a natural place of power in the world. It's a space that just naturally maintains healthy energy. It will pull energy from someone overloaded and push it to someone who needs it. If you add wards to it, even tiny sinks like the one at the restaurant are helpful. Most of the sinks in the world are covered with churches, sacred spaces, and other monuments. I can't believe you found one in the middle of a cornfield!" Ava laughed.

"It's easier here?" he asked Adaline.

She nodded, smiling.

"We'll live here," Sam said, glad to see her smile. "We'll figure out what kind of house we want and get it built."

Adaline kissed his lips briefly.

"I want to go fix the clearing. That's ours," he decided. "Can we do different wards or something to keep others out?"

"We'll go in the morning," Adaline agreed. "I don't know how to make better wards, but we'll figure it out."

Sam nodded.

"What's wrong with the clearing?" Ava asked.

"Mama, is there anyone within our ward lines at home who would not like our energy?" Addy asked, not answering the question.

15

"This ward line is all about keeping energy away from the building," Adaline explained, standing at a line of energy that circled about twenty yards out from the restaurant at daybreak on Wednesday.

"We need one of these wards around the clearing?" Sam asked.

She nodded. "A person who has stolen energy to sustain another life cannot cross here. We'll do this one at the clearing, too. But I want to place the ones around the restaurant and town first," she continued.

He nodded. "It's for the best."

"That bad?" Addy asked, frowning.

Sam didn't respond.

After a few seconds, Addy continued explaining the wards. "We also don't want big blasts of energy to make it through the line. If a circle blows outward on us, this line keeps the restaurant and the people in it safe."

"Can you see it?" Addy asked him.

"Nope. I can feel it, though."

"Can you see it if you look with energy?" Addy asked.

"I don't know how."

"Watch," she muttered, showing him how to pull the energy into his vision through their link.

"I see. What is this layer?"

"I think it's time," Addy said. "I'm not sure. What happens when you touch it?"

"It's not time. That's something else. Oh. I see. It's time in this place," Sam continued to mutter.

"Oh," Addy whispered, surprised. "I have that, too. Now that you showed me, I see it. It's not time?"

"No. It's just time *here*. The other time is much larger."

"*What is the other Time?*" she asked mentally.

"This," Sam said. "Can you feel it now that I pushed it to the link?"

Addy shivered. "I don't have that one. It makes me feel wrong."

Sam shrugged.

"Can you add space to this? So energy spreads across the entire ward, even if the energy only hits a single point?" Adaline asked.

"Hmm. I'm not as good with space. I'm better with the time part. Let's see. This is the part of my energy that Walks. If I tie it with the part of the ward that absorbs, maybe? Try it. Throw some power at it," Sam suggested.

They both hit the ward with energy at the same time. The ward collapsed.

"I see. Put your part back. I know where that space part goes now," Sam said.

"THE SECOND WARD line will stop a person who has stolen energy to sustain their own life. It also fosters health and goodwill for those within the ward," Addy explained.

"Why not just stack the hunter-related wards at the furthest line?" Sam asked. "Why layer like this?"

"The layers offer more protection than just one thick ward. A hunter would have to fight for each line, rather than one big one. It gives us more warning that danger is coming. Also, a line with that much purpose would be dangerous. The energy and focus are better divided."

THE THIRD WARD line ran around the outskirts of the town.

"This line will stop a person who has stolen energy for selfish purposes. It also brings peace and joy for those within the ward," Addy said.

"Why not health and goodwill at this one, too? Wouldn't that help more people?" Sam asked.

"Yes, it would. But, to bring health, you need to have a deep understanding of the life you're healing. That's hard to do with a diverse group of creatures. It's harder to do with more people, especially from a distance. And I'm going to change it."

"How?" Sam asked, surprised.

"I want it to share love, but love will not stand like peace or joy," Adaline said. "It must burn for love."

"You need fire?" Sam asked.

Adaline nodded. "I need the energy of fire but would rather it not burn. Like the fires when we were children."

"You have that," Sam said.

"Fire belongs to you," Adaline insisted.

Sam smiled. "You probably have that power if you look for it."

There was a pause before Addy met his eyes in surprise.

By the time they were done, the ward line glimmered with purple fire that did not burn, sharing Adaline's love with those who shared friendship with her. A hundred years after the flames were no longer visible, crossing the line caused one to remember all the best parts of life.

"IT WASN'T BURNT like this yesterday," Sam said as they walked through the clearing of scorched, dead plant life. "Is someone still drawing the energy from here?"

"No, I don't think so," Addy whispered, eyes filled with tears. "The land is trying to cleanse itself. It feels wrong here."

Sam nodded. "I felt that yesterday. How do we fix it?"

"Wait," Addy said, eyes going vacant.

Sam watched her for a minute before sitting in the dead grass to wait.

A few minutes later, she blinked rapidly, sitting down next to him.

"What do we do?" Sam asked.

"Let's go back to the restaurant," Adaline answered. "He said he will come quickly."

"MISTRESS. WALKER. WHY AM I HERE?" Micah asked an hour later.

Sam's head tipped to the side. "Where did you come from? How did you get here?"

Micah grinned at him, not answering.

"The wards have changed," he eventually noted to Adaline.

She nodded.

"You won't continue here?" Micah asked.

Adaline shook her head.

Micah's eyebrows lifted. "Chicago?"

"The suburbs," Sam said. "Where do you live?"

"Why am I here?" Micah asked again. "I told you to break that binding after I left last week."

"I know." Adaline sighed. "I didn't."

Micah's lips twitched as he fought off a smile. "What do you need from me?"

"Will you help us learn to Walk with others?" Adaline asked. "There is something I want you to see. I don't know how to fix it, but I thought that you might."

Ten minutes and six attempts later, Adaline stood in the clearing with Micah and Sam.

Micah's shoulders drooped as his gaze traveled the clearing.

"This was your space?" he asked Adaline.

She nodded. "For many years. And our circle was here last week."

Micah nodded. "They didn't just take the energy. They took life here. They left their foulness here, drained people here."

"How do we fix it?" she asked.

"Don't. Leave it for now," Micah advised. "Any energy you dump here will be siphoned off for a while yet. What they did leaves a binding to the place. They expected you to come back to fix it."

Sam frowned. "How can I find who did this?"

"You don't."

Sam's eyebrows lifted. "It can't be done?"

"I didn't say that. I said *you* don't find them. I like you as you are: bright, shiny, and uncorrupted. I'll find them. I'll let you know when you can restore the space."

There was a pause as Sam processed the words. His eyes went unfocused as he looked through time.

"Will you take your name?" Samuel asked.

Micah paused, considering how to answer.

"I will not stand as Hate again, Walker," Micah said with quiet resolve.

"I know. Will you take your name?" Samuel asked again.

Micah rocked back in surprise. "I don't know what name I'd take if not Hate. And I left this path a long time ago."

Sam nodded, power gone. "Not yet, then."

16

Noah was in the office early again on Wednesday morning after another restless night. He left a box of bakery cupcakes on Jen's desk on his way to his office.

There was a plant on his desk and a painting on a wall, new additions from his weekend of wandering a north-side street fair.

"Hello, plant. I should name you. What's your name?"

"Hi, Noah. My name is Fern," he answered himself, speaking in a falsetto voice.

"Fern? You're not a fern. Too leafy to be a fern," he continued the fake conversation.

"I enjoy being contrary and lack imagination, just like you."

"You're an asshole, Fern," he bitched.

"Did you just call your plant an asshole?" Jen asked from the doorway.

"My answer to that is going to depend on how long you've been standing there," Noah said, straight-faced.

"I'll grant that you are contrary, but the plant conversation proves you have imagination," she replied. "Are these cupcakes a bribe? What are you buttering me up for? I'm not helping you rearrange Will's office furniture again. He's still mad at me."

"No, he's not," Noah disagreed. "He loves you."

"True, but let's not do that again. What do you want?"

"Nothing," Noah replied, turning to his laptop. "Just thought you might like them."

"All right, enough of this, dipshit. What's wrong?" she demanded.

Noah frowned at her.

"Don't look at me like that. I dislike Morose Noah. Where's Cheerful Noah?" she asked. "You've been mopey since Dallas. What's going on?"

He shrugged, not meeting her eyes.

"I'm going to pull your boy-band hair if you don't start talking," she threatened.

"Don't be mean."

"Don't be an idiot."

"You know, you do work for me," he replied.

She snorted. "Who are you, and what have you done with our Noah?"

"Shuddup."

"Spill it!"

"There's nothing to spill. Honestly, I just realized I'm not a terribly interesting person while in Dallas. I don't have much of a life. It was a rude awakening."

Jen's eyes narrowed as she considered his words.

"Stop looking at me like that," he complained.

"So, Adrian has a girlfriend, Jake has a Matilda, and Sam has a girlfriend. You're getting antsy about not being tied down. Do I have that right?"

"Not exactly," he disagreed.

"What, then?"

"I don't have a life. My hobby is sex with random women—no friends outside of my family and this office. Nothing," he finally spat out.

"And?" she asked.

He shrugged.

"Try words with that shrug."

"Feels like there should be more," he admitted.

"Aww, our Noah's growing up. It's annoying. Stop it." She grinned.

"I'm serious," he muttered, frowning.

"Me, too. I hate this. Stop it. You're a great person, Noah. If you're done being a man-whore, stop sleeping around and try having an actual girlfriend for once. If you want a hobby, get a hobby. But don't stop being you. There's nothing wrong with you. The world is dimmer when you're serious and sad."

Noah shifted uncomfortably in his chair.

"You're in this far. Might as well finish spilling your guts," Jen coached.

"Monday night, we were at a social thing with some friends of the family. Luke has a soon-to-be-girlfriend that I was going to troll him about, but she got scared and kicked me in the junk," Noah said, almost too quick to understand.

Jen's face went blank. "She was scared…of you?"

Noah nodded.

Jen grinned.

"It's not funny."

"Noah, you're a pathetic sissy. How could anyone be afraid of you?"

"Thanks?"

"You're welcome. You know this about yourself. I don't understand how anyone can be afraid of you."

"She literally ran away."

"How bad do you feel?"

"Absolutely terrible!"

"You're a lover, not a fighter." Jen laughed.

"I know!"

"Let me guess. She kicked you, but you apologized."

"Well, no. I disappeared before she resurfaced. She was scared! I didn't want to make it worse. But I would have apologized. I will apologize the next time I see her."

"What did Luke say?" Jen asked.

"Told me to stay away from her," Noah muttered guiltily, looking at his desk.

"Ah, now we're to the root cause of Sad Noah. Luke won't play along, and his girlfriend's scared of you."

He gave a halfhearted shrug. "She's gorgeous, and he acted like I had intentionally scared her. My brother thinks I'm that big of an asshole. I just thought he knew me better than that."

"He was probably upset for her. What did you do that scared her?"

He shook his head. "It was a misunderstanding—my fault. I didn't catch that she was upset and dealing with other shit. One hundred percent my fault. I just hate that I scared someone that much."

Jen nodded. "Apologize. You'll feel better. Stop sleeping around, get a girlfriend. I'm tired of Sad Noah. I want Snarky Noah back."

"Thanks," he said, smiling.

"I'm going to send you a bill for my life coach services."

"Sounds good," he agreed, grinning. "Cupcakes will only get me so far in life."

"I want a parking spot."

"Huh?" he asked, startled. "How do you not have a parking spot? You manage the building parking spots."

"No, not a parking spot here. A parking spot in my condo garage. They just added new ones. They're twenty-five thousand dollars each, and I don't want to take out a mortgage for a parking spot. Buy me a parking spot, Noah," Jen demanded.

"It shall be so," he agreed, laughing. "Do you even have a car for it?"

"Nope," she said. "I'm going to tell Hank that you guys are buying me a car for my birthday."

"I like it," he agreed, nodding.

"Do we need to discuss anything else before I go do actual work?"

"Does my boy-band hair look bad?" he asked.

REE HAD an appointment with Dr. Garaff late Wednesday morning.

"You look good, Ree! No fever, not sick. How do you feel?" Dr. Garaff asked.

"Just tired, not sick," Ree agreed, eyes drooping.

Dr. Garaff nodded. "We'll keep going. If you want to change days to Monday and Wednesday, that's fine with me."

Lucy shifted uncomfortably in the chair next to where Adrian was standing in the tiny exam room. She was about to make him mad.

"Are we sure the diagnosis is correct?" The words came out quickly, as if that would make them less silly.

Adrian went still next to her. "Lucy. The tests are conclusive. We've talked about this."

After an uncomfortable silence, Lucy started rambling at Adrian. "It's just, nothing seems to work. He's not getting better or worse, and he's tired all the time. I've read up on this, too. With all the complications and failed treatment, Henry shouldn't be doing this well, but he's doing fine. What if she's right? It's worth asking."

"This is why I got mad when she said it, Lucy. I didn't want her to confuse you like this," Adrian responded, disgust clear in his voice.

Dr. Garaff's eyebrows lifted. "What if who is right about what?"

Lucy and Adrian both shifted uncomfortably, avoiding eye contact.

"Out with it," Dr. Garaff barked.

Adrian sighed. "A family friend is into some unconventional life energy stuff. Last week, she insisted Ree didn't have leukemia. We had words."

"What does she think is wrong?" Dr. Garaff asked, curious.

Adrian's eyes snapped up. "Gretta—"

"I taught you better than this," Dr. Garaff cut him off.

"I'm not saying his case is typical," Adrian said. "I'm trying to avoid false hope and confusion."

Dr. Garaff actually snorted. "Hope is never a bad thing, Adrian. Sometimes, it's the only thing that keeps us going. What does she think is wrong? What does she want to change?"

"She didn't know what was wrong," Lucy admitted. "She doesn't want to change anything. She just 'shared energy' with him. He seemed better afterward."

Dr. Garaff looked at Ree.

"Grandma Ava makes me feel good," he said with a shrug.

"She doesn't give you strange food or medicine? Doesn't put pastes or anything on your skin?" the doctor asked.

"Nope," Ree popped the P. "We just hold hands for a little bit."

Dr. Garaff shrugged. "Okay."

Adrian grunted in displeasure.

"Look at this one." Dr. Garaff laughed at Adrian. "So sure he knows everything. We *practice* medicine, Adrian. I'm not going to pretend like I know everything there is to know. Not too long ago, in terms of humanity's existence, people were burned alive for suggesting the Earth was round. Who knows what they'll think of us one hundred or five hundred years from now?"

Turning to Lucy, she continued. "Ree's diagnosis is conclusive, like Adrian said. I don't see any harm in holding hands with Grandma Ava in addition to continuing treatment, though. I wouldn't suggest stopping treatment. I wouldn't suggest trying more exotic drugs or ingestible substances to 'help.' Let's talk about it first, at least."

"I'm not suggesting Ava's energy is a bad thing. I'll even agree that he seems better with it. I don't want to confuse things, though. Ree, you need this treatment. We need to stay on this course and not get sidetracked," Adrian said, trying to not sound defensive.

"I agree with that. I'm not suggesting otherwise," Lucy said, not trying to hide her defensiveness.

Adrian nodded. "I didn't say that Ava should stop her stuff. I just said it was a conclusive diagnosis."

Dr. Garaff rolled her eyes. "I'll leave you two to not-argue on your own. Treatment on Monday, Ree. I'll see you all in two weeks."

LUCY AND ADRIAN WERE SILENT, walking back to the car with Ree between them. The security team followed at a discreet distance.

"You could have talked to me about that," Adrian muttered, getting into the car.

Lucy paused. "I know."

"Why didn't you?" he asked.

"I wanted to ask Dr. Garaff," she replied. "You got upset with Ava over it."

Adrian stared out the windshield for a second before starting the car.

"Are you hungry, Henry?" Adrian asked.

"Tired," Ree responded.

By the time they pulled into Lucy's driveway, and the security team gave the all-clear to enter the house, Ree was zonked out. Adrian carried him into the house and to bed.

Walking back out to the main living area, Adrian found Lucy with her head stuck in the fridge, digging for leftovers.

"Do you want me to go?" Adrian asked, voice somber.

"What!" Lucy whacked her head, trying to get out of the fridge quickly.

"If you don't want me here, I'll go," he said, looking at his feet. "I'll visit him. I won't disappear again. But I don't have to stay if you don't want me here."

"Adrian, I want you to be here. I told you that you were moving in. Why would you think otherwise? Do you not want to be here?" she asked.

"Of course I want to be here, Lucy," Adrian grumbled, frustrated. "But I don't want you to be afraid of me. If you're afraid of making me mad, this isn't going to work."

Lucy's face scrunched up. "What the hell are you talking about?"

"You didn't talk to me about the Ava thing because you didn't want to make me mad!"

"I didn't talk to you about the Ava thing because I already knew your opinion on it. I asked Dr. Garaff because I wanted *her* opinion on it," Lucy disagreed. "There was no sense telling you I was going to ask, knowing you thought it was bullshit."

"You can talk to me about things," Adrian insisted.

"I know, Adrian. I wasn't insinuating that I can't talk to you!" she argued.

Adrian blew out a frustrated sigh as he sat at the table.

Lucy sat next to him after a minute. "I know I can talk to you. And I knew asking her would upset you. I was going to ask no matter what you said, Adrian. Not because I don't trust you or because I think you're wrong. Ree is the absolute center of my world. I'm going to ask every damn question, and I'm not sorry about that."

She paused, thinking.

"I'm not great at this relationship and family stuff. I'm sorry if I hurt you by asking her. I thought you'd be upset, not hurt. I'm doing the best I can right now. Two months ago, I lived in a shithole apartment, just about out of hope. Maybe I bungled this, I don't know. But, if I was afraid of you, I wouldn't have asked the question today."

That realization brought Adrian up short.

He nodded, reaching for her hand. Energy zinged between them, lifting the heavy silence. "It's hard to believe it's only been two months."

Lucy nodded back, eyes on the table. "Still mad at me?"

"Nope," he said. "Angry with me?"

"Depends."

"On what?" he asked.

"Did you eat all the pasta salad?"

WILLIAM WALKED into his house on Wednesday afternoon to the sound of female laughter. The sound of it eased the tightness in his chest.

"Hello, darling princess," he said, kissing Beth on the head as she tried, and failed, to smack him.

"Hello, queen of my heart," he said, giving Emma a kiss.

"Aww, we're so mushy!" Beth exclaimed.

"When are we moving?" Will asked, not responding to the taunt.

"Really?" Emma asked, exasperated.

"Did you think about it?" Will replied.

She sighed. "I really don't give a flying fuck where we live, William. There's enough room here for us for a while yet."

"Dad thinks we're moving to the suburbs," Will said, undeterred.

"Ech! Why?" Beth asked.

"Ava and Jess are moving into the cornfield houses," he explained.

Beth narrowed her eyes. "That's where all those empty lots are, isn't it? We're all going to live on the same block?"

"That's what Hank thinks," Will agreed.

Emma and Beth looked at each other.

"That would be hilarious. Can you imagine Mom trouncing Jake over language constantly?" Beth laughed.

"Where is this?" Emma asked.

"Just west of Naperville," Will answered. "Sam owns all the land with nothing else immediately around us. We can gate and secure it."

She rolled her eyes. "That's going to be less important over time."

Will shrugged. "Still doing it."

Beth snorted, "We're going to live in a compound. If people didn't think we were freaky before, they will now. We're upping the weirdness factor. Matthew and Ethan better hurry up and find partners."

"What about Noah?" Will asked, laughing.

"Oh, please." Beth chuckled. "He'll never run out of sex-kitten women, no matter how crazy we get."

"So why are you asking me about moving if you already know where we're going?" Emma asked, grinning.

"Well, we need to ask Sam if that's what he wanted, and he still isn't answering his phone. If it is, we need to build a house. It'd be good if we could get it done before winter hits," Will said, thinking.

"I have to go back to California next week for reshoots. I figured we'd pack up my crap while I'm there," Emma interrupted.

Will nodded.

"That's it?" Beth asked.

"Huh?" Will responded.

"We've been shooting the shit, waiting for you to get home. We thought backup would be helpful when you went all ballistic about her career," Beth admitted.

"Oh." Will ran his hand through his short hair, uncomfortable. "Hank yelled at me."

"I heard," Beth said.

"It was bad." Will blew out a sigh.

"I heard that, too."

Will nodded, not looking at his sister or his wife. "I've thought about it. I should let Pip live her own fucking life. If that happens with me, I'll count my lucky stars and blessings every last day of my life."

Emma grinned.

"And we're back to the mush," Beth muttered, standing up to leave.

EMMA LAUNCHED herself at her husband when he walked back into the house after walking Beth to her car.

"You're really going to pipe down about this?" she asked.

Will grinned. "Yeah, I think so. You're right. No one would bat an eye if we got together now. You've had every chance to walk away and haven't. So I'll accept the victory gracefully."

She snorted. "Gracefully? Seven years later?"

"Some things are timeless."

Really laughing, she kissed him. "This makes me extremely happy."

"That makes me happy."

"When we're in California next week, we should go see my parents. Tell them about the babies in person." She grinned.

"That sounds like a plan."

"We're having babies!" she squealed.

"Did that just sink in?" he asked.

"No," she laughed, "but now I feel like I can be happy about it."

The smile fell from William's face, replaced with a look of regret. "I'm sorry, Pip. I have only ever wanted you to be happy."

"I know," she whispered, kissing him. "Knowing that made it

easier for me to be patient while you got your head together. And it worked. Now we have forever together."

He quirked an eyebrow at her. "If Micah is to be believed, literally forever."

She rolled her eyes. "If Micah is to be believed, we're all going to play spouse swap. I can't see that happening. How about we just take things as they come?"

"That sounds like a good idea," he muttered, returning her kiss with dividends.

17

While walking to work on Thursday morning, Noah realized a woman was following him. This was not a rare occurrence.

How the fuck did I not realize the lust thing before now? he wondered for the thirty-eighth time since Jess spilled the beans.

I'm not even sure I brushed my hair this morning. I am wearing a wrinkled t-shirt and unfashionably worn jeans. What is this woman thinking?

He decided to ignore her. In days past, he would have struck up a flirty conversation, maybe gotten a phone number. She wasn't hiding the fact that she was following him. She paused when he did. This was an open invitation to make a pass. Now, knowing that it was an energy thing, he wasn't sure if this woman was really interested in him. And he wasn't sure he wanted anything to do with a woman that followed men around.

"Excuse me," a voice said behind him, "did you drop this?"

The woman was holding out a smartphone.

Ha! Not interested in me at all. Just trying to be a decent person, he thought, smiling at her.

"No, not mine. Thanks, though."

She pulled out a flirty little smirk. "I know. It's mine. I just couldn't think of a better way to start talking to a random guy walking down the street."

Well, fuck.

Noah smirked back. "What would you do if I said it was mine?"

"Call you a liar and walk away. I didn't offer to give it to you, after all. I just asked if it was yours." She grinned.

"Fair enough." He chuckled, starting to walk away.

"Hey, wait! You're not going to ask for the number that goes with this phone?" The smirky smile returned.

She was gorgeous, and she knew it: blond hair, blue eyes, great fake boobs, and four-inch heels with jeans.

Yeah, I'd already be naked with this woman if this happened two weeks ago, Noah acknowledged, giving himself a mental head slap. *So fucking stupid. How did I not recognize this?*

"No," he said, smiling. "Enjoy the rest of your day."

"Girlfriend?"

"Nope."

"Boyfriend?"

He gave a small smile, not bothering to respond.

"Wife?"

He shook his head. "You're gorgeous. Any other time, I'd be really into this. But I'm working through some things. Now's not a great time."

Assertive and maybe a bit aggressive. I'd be really into this…two weeks ago.

Her smile fell a little bit. She wasn't accustomed to rejection.

Stepping closer, she touched his bicep. "How about we work through it together?"

NOAH FLOPPED down in one of Jake's guest chairs in his office.

"What's with you?" Jake asked, lining up a shot on the pool table.

"Meh," Noah responded, glaring out the window.

"Want to play?"

"No. That's your vice and outlet. It just irritates the fuck out of the rest of us."

"Woo, someone's cranky. Time to make a new friend, man."

Jake's laughter stopped short at Noah's glare.

"What happened?" Jake asked, starting to get concerned. Noah was not known to be in a foul mood for more than three minutes at a time.

Noah blew out a gust of frustrated air.

When no words followed, Jake's concern increased. "Noah?"

"I don't know what I'm doing or why I'm doing it," Noah finally spat out.

"Huh?"

"All the women. All this time. Did I really *want* to be the flirty man-whore, or was the energy fucking with my head?"

"Does it matter? It's done now. You can't change it. If you don't like it, stop doing it," Jake replied.

Noah tipped his head back, staring at the drop ceiling. "I can feel it."

"Feel what?"

"When I pay attention, I can feel when people are attracted to me. Now that I'm aware of it, I don't know how the fuck I missed it."

Jake shrugged. "Will and Adrian said they can feel their shit in other people, too. It's probably the same for you."

"Yeah. Will feels fear. He knows it's not his fear because there's nothing around him that's triggering his own fear. Adrian knows it's not his anger because he's so fucking calm, always. They know it's the energy fucking with them. With me, how do I know if I'm really interested in someone? Even worse, how do I know if she's really interested in me?"

Jake gave a small nod. "Fair questions."

Noah was quiet for a moment, thinking about how to phrase the next part of his worry.

"I can hear your mind spinning all the way over here," Jake teased.

"There have been women that seemed baffled by their actions afterward. A couple of days together, then I break things off. There has been relief and confusion a few times. 'I don't know how we ended up here,' a few times."

"And?" Jake asked, eyebrows raised.

Noah's eyes were wet when he looked at his older brother.

"Stop, Noah. Just stop. Don't do this to yourself. I don't think there's any part of you, conscious or subconscious, that would hurt someone like that. If someone doesn't want to be with you, you have always left them alone and carried on the path of friendship or silly acquaintances. I have watched it happen, man.

"Maybe your mojo lowers inhibitions. You should probably figure out how to control the mojo if this bothers you," Jake advised.

"How do I figure that out?"

"Like I fucking know?" Jake asked back.

"HOW THE FUCK am I supposed to know?" Will asked, looking appalled at his two brothers.

Jake frowned. "I thought you could control the fear thing?"

"Yeah, and?" Will asked.

"Can't you explain how you do that?" Jake asked, brow furrowed.

"Let's try this. Explain how you feel things with your hands, Jake. How did you learn to touch something to feel and understand it?" Will asked.

"Uh, nerves in the skin transmit signals to the brain, the brain transforms the signals into a sensation? And I don't know? Something instinctual causes humans to reach and touch as infants," Jake suggested.

"How'd your nerves learn to transmit signals?" Will asked.

"Evolution? How the fuck do I know?" Jake asked, getting pissed.

"Yeah." Will grinned. "That's exactly how I feel about your dumbass question."

"Fell into that one," Jake muttered.

"So I'm screwed. And not in a fun way," Noah muttered, resigned.

"Good grief, you're both morons. I'm not the brother to ask about passive, positive abilities." William rolled his eyes, reaching for his phone.

"Hi, Will," Luke answered, sounding confused.

"What's wrong?" Will asked, immediately on alert.

"Why are you calling me?"

"What the fuck? I call you!" Will objected.

Luke didn't respond.

"I'm pretty sure I've called you before," Will hedged.

Luke remained silent.

"Whatever. Come to the office," Will instructed.

"I'm kind of in the middle of something," Luke said.

Will sighed. "Tell the hot brunette to take a chill pill unrelated to you and come help your brothers, jackass. See you in twenty."

Noah and Jake were both laughing as Will hung up, ignoring the fact that Luke was still talking.

"He'll be here in less than twenty minutes," Will promised, chuckling.

Jake snorted. "He's going to be pissed."

"Eh, he'll get over it. He's too afraid of me to not listen."

"I don't think he's actually afraid of you, man," Noah offered.

William stared at him.

"What?"

The stare continued.

"What'd I say?" Noah asked Jake.

Jake smacked himself in the forehead. "Holy fuck, man. What does Will's energy do again?"

"Oh," Noah muttered, frowning.

"Yeah," Will replied, still glaring.

"You're okay with him being afraid of you?" Noah asked.

"Not really. But it is what it is. The feeling is somewhat mutual," Will admitted, voice flat. "He loses track of the fact that he dropped both Adrian and me like sacks of potatoes, at the same time, from fifteen feet away. We joke about Puking Peace, but he might be scarier than the rest of us. Including Sam."

Noah snorted.

"I can make you afraid, Noah. I can make you hurt, and I can trigger fight or flight. Luke can send you off to peaceful sleep without you ever realizing anything is wrong. I'm not sure of this, but I'm guessing he can hold you there indefinitely, too."

"Why do you think that?" Jake asked, interested.

Will was silent for a couple seconds. "Because I can make you afraid for days on end with minimal effort."

"Wow," Jake said, suddenly uncomfortable.

"How'd you figure that out?" Noah asked.

Will blinked at him. "I fought a war, Noah."

"WHAT?" Luke bitched, walking in William's office eighteen minutes later. "You realize the walk from my place is roughly twenty-five minutes, right? I hauled ass. What's wrong?"

"Noah needs to turn the mojo off," Will said, grinning while Jake tried to hide a smile.

Luke glared at Noah.

Noah glared back. "Not my fault you ran here in a tizzy. I didn't call you."

Luke continued to glare.

"Are you going to help me?" Noah asked.

"Of course."

"Then why are you glaring at me?"

"Because I know you guys are laughing at me. I just don't know why." Luke glared at Jake.

"What the fuck are you glaring at me for? I didn't do it!" Jake protested.

"This is why I don't hang out with you guys. Matthew and Ethan don't do this," Luke bitched.

"Holy fuck. Shut up and help your brother," Will snapped.

Luke frowned at him.

"What?" Will demanded.

Luke's eyes narrowed. "Are you grumpy? Need a nap?"

Will's mouth went to a flat line.

"Yeah, thought so," Luke muttered. "Noah, what the fuck?"

Noah squirmed uncomfortably.

Luke rolled his eyes. "Do you want help? You're going to have to tell me what's wrong."

"I think women have been sleeping with me because of the lust thing," he muttered.

"Duh," Luke immediately replied. "You leak energy everywhere. Not as bad as Emma, but close."

"You gonna teach Pip this, too?" Will asked.

"Only if you're nice to me." Luke grinned.

Will sighed, shaking his head. "All assholes out of my office. Do this elsewhere. I already know how to work my shit."

"You don't want to know if there's a better way?" Luke asked, surprised.

"I'd love to," Will admitted. "But if you keep baiting me, I'm going to murder you. So, no."

Luke's lips twitched. "I'll be good."

After a pause, Noah snorted. "Group hug!"

Will threw a crystal desk decoration at his head.

"Hey! That would have hurt! Where'd that come from, anyway?"

"It's some stupid fucking award. I don't know. Let's get on with this," Will bitched.

"I learned to do this by controlling my sight first. Once you can do that, it's easier to find and recognize the energy. Start by closing your eyes. Imagine that pulling extra energy into your eyes lets you see more. Like moving a piece of paper for better focus..."

18

The door flew open as Luke approached Talise's parents' house on Thursday afternoon. Talise had herself wrapped around him before he made it to the stoop.

"Well, hello to you, too." He laughed.

"Hi," she muttered, head buried in the crook of his neck.

"I thought I'd check on you," he muttered back.

"Good."

He waited. When no more information was forthcoming, he asked, "And how are you?"

"Same," she whispered, dropping her legs back to the ground.

"When were you last out and about?" he asked.

She shifted uncomfortably.

"Not since the circle?"

"No," she responded.

"Ice cream?" he asked, smiling.

"I'll go put on more clothes," Talise whispered, stiff and scared.

"Tali, why not go like this? Shorts and a t-shirt. Give it a try?" he asked.

"If someone touches me—" she started.

Luke shook his head. "I'll be there. How about we try it? If Dairy Queen is crowded, we'll stay in the car."

She stared at his chest, unresponsive.

"Tali? Do you want to try it?" he asked.

"No," she admitted.

"Addy said she can shield herself. Do you remember that?" Luke asked.

Talise nodded.

"If she can shield, you probably can, too. But we won't know until we try."

"Luke, I went down hard on Monday after your brother touched me," she said, voice monotone.

"Yeah, but that was Sam. Sam is complex at the best of times. He's never been functionally normal. You can't judge based on that." Luke grinned at her.

Talise didn't meet his eyes.

"How about a walk, then? Just through the neighborhood?" he offered.

She nodded, accepting the compromise. "Come in. I'll find shoes."

"What is your mom cooking?" Luke asked, sniffing the air. "Smells beefy."

Talise shrugged. "She's in the kitchen. I'll be right back."

Luke chuckled to himself, watching her scamper down the hallway into an airborne leap then landing gracefully without sound at her bedroom doorway.

"Do that often?" he called.

"Yep!" She laughed.

"Oh, Luke! You scared me," Monica said, coming around the corner from the kitchen.

"I'm sorry, I was coming back to say hi before we went for a walk," he apologized. "I got distracted by the leaping."

Monica rolled her eyes. "Grand jeté. Get it right. She does it all the time. You're going for a walk?"

"She declined ice cream again. I'm beginning to think there's a severe lack of ice cream appreciation in her life."

Monica's smile didn't quite reach her eyes. "I'm glad she's going outside, that she's leaving the house and garage. Thank you for visiting."

"It's just a week today," Luke murmured, touching her hand, sharing a bit of peace. "Time will help."

"I hope," Monica said, blinking fast before Talise returned.

"TALI, this is what's known as sunlight. This is called a sidewalk, and what's we're doing is called walking. There's no running, scampering, or jumping involved."

She snickered.

"Was that an actual Talise giggle? Is that what I heard? I didn't know you did that!"

"Almost." She laughed. "It surprised me, too."

The smile on Luke's face turned sad. "The tie is gone, Talise. It's not coming back. You're not trapped in your mind anymore."

"I know," she murmured after a pause. "Just a little bit lost. So much changed suddenly."

Luke nodded. "Now you can decide what to do with your life. You don't have to stay tucked away in the house."

"Being around people is hard, Luke. I'll try it. I'll work on it. I'll work on shielding. But small steps, okay? Small steps so the missteps aren't quite so bad."

"You're talking about kicking Noah?" Luke grinned.

She nodded, looking at the sidewalk.

"I'm pretty sure he had it coming. Maybe not from you, but from someone. He'll get over it, Tali. He's resilient. Even more than me."

She didn't respond.

"Want to come to Sunday dinner? You can apologize," Luke offered.

She shook her head. "I think that would be hard."

"Probably," Luke agreed. "But my family is pretty great and utterly ridiculous. You'd be welcome, even if you're working through things. We just won't let Darla touch."

Talise thought about it as they crossed a street. "The Walker and Mistress would be there?"

Luke nodded. "Yep, Sam and Adaline will be there. They're people, Tali. And they've had their own trials. They wouldn't judge yours."

Talise gave him a disbelieving look. "Your billionaire Walker brother, with the power to see all of time and move through space, has trials. Yeah, right."

Luke gave a burst of surprised laughter. "Please say that to him!"

Talise's eyes flew wide open. "I didn't mean it to be disrespectful. I just don't think he'd understand the shit-show that is my thought process right now!"

Luke laughed at her expression. He couldn't help it. "Talise, you've felt the emotional cesspool that is Sam. You saw his despair at my anger. How could you *possibly* fear him? He's afraid *of me!* I am the least scary person on the planet."

"When he pulled energy and asked my name, he was terrifying. His eyes were glowing. His energy felt strange. Not like the rest of us. Scary," she admitted.

"Oh, fuck yeah. Sam can be scary when he pulls the power out. But he doesn't do that often. Usually, when he's looking for something like your name. He's certain you are not where you belong. It irks him."

Talise frowned. "Where does he think I belong?"

"I haven't asked. And I suggest that you don't ask, either. I'm unsure what would come out of his mouth. But my guess is that you can stand as the water pillar if you want to. Taking the name is part of being a pillar. I think that's what he was asking you on Monday," Luke explained.

"I have almost as much life energy as I do water energy, Luke. I'm not a strong primary power like you," Talise disagreed.

Luke shrugged. "It's my guess. I don't know. I can't imagine why else he'd be asking for your name, though. Give it some thought. He's going to ask again."

She nodded, still watching the sidewalk pass below their feet.

"Be prepared. He's probably going to ask seven hundred times," Luke admitted.

"Huh?"

"It's what he does. He gets stuck on stuff. Ninety percent of what he does is instinctual or power-driven. He just rolls with it. I still maintain he has no idea how he zapped the tie in your brain. He felt it, it was wrong, and he took it out. That's what he'd say if you asked. The circle gives him way too much credit by being afraid of him. Will is a lot scarier."

They walked in silence for half a block.

"So that's a pass on Sunday dinner?" Luke asked.

"Raincheck?" Tali whispered.

"Sure." He smiled.

When they were at risk of falling into an awkward silence, Luke squeezed the hand he was holding. "What's your grudge against ice cream? I feel like you lack an appreciation for dipped cones!"

"Matty, I'm home!" Jake called, walking into the apartment Thursday evening.

"One second. Let me finish this thought," she called back.

Jake smiled. They started each evening this way. For a quick second, he considered what life would be like now without her. He couldn't fathom it and didn't want to try.

"How was your day?" she asked, coming into the living room.

"Uneventful." He shrugged. "Sam didn't show. Hank was pissed off again. Other than that, not much going on. How about you?"

"I talked to your mother, then to Ellie, and then to Eric. We're going to meet at your parents' house early on Sunday afternoon to plan whatever it is we need to do for an engagement party."

Matilda pulled a face.

"You don't want an engagement party?" Jake asked.

"Not really. People are going to stare at us. But Darla says we have to either have an engagement party or a wedding, and I'm not having a big wedding," Matty declared.

"Agreed." Jake nodded. "So, party planning on Sunday? What I'm hearing is that I'm going to drink beer and watch sports with Hank. Ellie and Eric are staying for dinner, right? What about Charlie? Does he want to drink beer with us?"

"I don't know. I'll ask." Matilda grinned.

"Sounds good," Jake said, thinking about how to ask the next question.

"What?" Matilda asked, laughing at the pensive look on his face.

"Miranda couldn't make Sunday?" Jake asked, waiting for the fallout from mentioning Matty's family.

"Oh! I honestly didn't think about inviting her. You think I should?"

"She's been obnoxiously excited to see you every time you've met up with her. She'd probably be weepy happy to be included." Jake shrugged. "It's up to you."

"What do you want for dinner tonight?" she asked. "I didn't get around to cooking anything. What's wrong?"

Jake's face had the disgusted look of someone sucking on a lemon. "Maybe don't invite Miranda."

"Why?" Matty asked, surprised. "I thought it was a good idea."

"I don't want to drink beer and hang out with Larry. Please no," Jake whined.

Matilda grinned. "I'll suggest it as a girl outing."

"She's so sweet. Why, Matty? Why?" Jake continued to whine.

"Because she didn't meet a Trellis brother before she met Larry?" Matty grinned.

"She should come to dinner without the jackass and meet Matthew! That could work. Matthew's so nice. They could be nice people together," he enthused. "Darla would be delighted."

"She's married, Jake," Matty reminded him.

"I know, but it'd be a lot better if she wasn't. Then you could do sister things without the threat of Larry's company."

Matilda rolled her eyes.

"You know, I'd take pretty much anyone that's not an asshole. It doesn't need to be Matthew. The new husband can be lame. I can work with lame."

Jake paused, thinking.

"I really fucking hope they're divorced before the wedding. I am a little worried that Will would kill him over after-dinner drinks," Jake continued.

"Miranda doesn't say she's unhappy," Matty offered.

"Does she mention it at all? Does she say she's happy?" Jake asked.

"Nope. We talk about things other than our shared family and her home life. She likes Darla stories."

"Who doesn't? For fuck's sake, maybe Mom will get a hold of her and straighten it out," Jake muttered.

"Dinner?" Matty asked, changing the subject.

"Dinner. Then a sexy bath?"

"We've reached a sexy bath level of pouting and whining?"

"I feel gross after talking about Larry. A bath is definitely in order," Jake pretended to shiver.

19

"Jake, you will drive us everywhere for the rest of our lives," Ellie declared from the back seat of Jake's SUV on Sunday afternoon. "Cars are too expensive to keep in the city, and Lyft just isn't consistently this nice."

"That's fine," he agreed.

"Woo, that was easy. Feeling accommodating?" Ellie laughed.

Jake snorted. "There's no use in disagreeing until there's something to disagree about. I'll happily drive to my parents' house. I don't even mind driving for best friend shopping."

"Smart man," Charlie muttered from next to Jake.

"Oakbrook!" Eric squealed. "Black Amex and the Rich-People-Shopping-Mall! I'd prefer to be called Enrique from here on out. It sounds more interesting and wealthier."

"Eric, are you going to sniff my parents?" Jake asked, trying not to laugh.

"Abso-fucking-lutely!"

"That's tacky. I love it," Ellie agreed. "Matty's not turning red, though."

"Not even a little bit," Eric said, disappointed.

Matilda snorted. "Hank and Darla would find that hilarious. Go for it."

"She's more neurotic about her own family than your family, Jake. This isn't as much fun," Ellie complained.

"It's a two-for-one. Miranda will be there tonight," Matilda offered.

"I know." Ellie grinned. "I'm looking forward to taking the long-lost sister down about fifteen pegs."

Jake scrunched up his face. "Miranda's pretty fucking sweet and harmless, Ellie. Save the smackdown for Megan."

"Wait! The Anteater's coming? I'm not properly prepared for this. We need to stop for holy water," Ellie declared.

"She is not joining us. At least, I didn't invite her. And I don't think Miranda would have," Matilda clarified.

"We should crank call that bitch again," Ellie muttered.

Jake burst out laughing. "What?"

"Don't. Just don't ask. We were drunk and in college." Matty laughed.

Ellie chuckled to herself. "She was so fucking clueless. That was one of our better drunken college evenings. So simple, so funny."

Jake shook his head as Matty and Eric laughed with Ellie.

"I can't believe I missed the crazy college years. I need to hear this story," Jake muttered.

"Bah! We were much crazier singletons after college. You popped up at the opportune time," Ellie assured him.

"This is easily the largest driveway I've ever seen. What the fuck, man?" Charlie asked.

"I have eight siblings and a Hennessy, Charlie. Even with carpooling, that's a lot of cars," Jake said.

"Fair point. Am I going to end up eating at the kids' table? Should I jockey for good dinner seating?" Charlie asked.

"There is no kids' table," Jake responded. "You'll see. What's wrong, Eric?"

Eric was frowning, looking out the back window. "I feel like I'm being cheated. There was no security guard checking IDs, no gates or anything. This looks like...a house."

"Amazingly, this is a house," Matty snarked.

"Where does the butler live?" Eric asked. "And you better not tell me there's no butler."

Jake nodded. "Roscoe greets people at the door and runs the household."

Ellie's eyes were slits. "Isn't Roscoe the fat Rottweiler?"

"How about we get out of the car?" Matilda asked, grinning.

Eric, Ellie, and Charlie followed as Matilda and Jake led the way to the front door.

"Hello!" Jake called, throwing the door open.

"Roscoe!" Matty howled with the dog.

"That's bullshit," Eric muttered, walking in the door behind them.

"What are you looking at, Ellie?" Jake asked.

"I think there's a bird's nest in the porch roof," Ellie muttered.

"Maybe." Jake shrugged. "Are you two going to come in or stay on the doorstep all day?"

Ellie pulled a face.

"Jake, can we please come in?" Ellie asked, heavy on the sass.

"Please come in, Eleanor and Charles. Be my guest," Jake said in his best pompous jerk voice.

"I don't mind if I do," Ellie said, pulling out a southern drawl, grinning at Jake.

"Ugh. You two are ridiculous," Charlie muttered.

"He is the male version of her!" Matilda insisted. "Ellie, you okay?"

"Huh?"

"You look a little out of sorts," Matty said, frowning.

"Oh, just a little dizzy. Feel weird. Anyway, hi, Roscoe," Ellie muttered, bending to pet the dog.

"Hello!" Darla's voice called from the big room. A few seconds later, she came bustling around the corner to greet everyone.

"You're here! I'm so excited. Now, I've met Ellie and Eric, so this must be Charlie!" she exclaimed, liberally distributing kisses and hugs among the relative strangers.

"Roscoe, what are you doing? Get up," Jake called. "Sorry, Charlie.

I don't know why he's rolling around on your feet. He doesn't usually do that."

"Roscoe, go sit by Jake," Charlie said, shooing the dog off his shoes.

The dog jumped up and ran to Jake, sitting down next to Jake's leg while staring at Charlie.

"I think Emma's really starting to affect his manners. Meaning, he's getting manners." Jake laughed. "Where's Dad?"

"I'm coming," Hank yelled from the kitchen. "Almost done!"

"Dad's cooking?" Jake's eyebrows shot up.

"Skillet queso." Darla grinned.

"Oh, it's a good day." Jake grinned back. "What's for dinner?"

"Fajitas, rice, beans, guacamole, and all the trimmings," Darla answered.

Jake's look was affronted. "Are you slacking on Sunday dinner? That sounds dangerously close to a taco bar."

Darla smacked him upside the head. "You five, Miranda and maybe her husband, your dad and me, Will and Emma, Adrian, Lucy, Ree, Ethan, Noah, Matthew, Luke, hopefully Talise, Beth, Hennessy, Ava, Clyde, Jess, Blake, the girls, Gregg, Nora, and Ben. Maybe Claire and Tom. When we put the extension in the table, I get to streamline. I'm making twenty pounds of fajitas, Jake. You'll live. You need to get more chairs out of the garage."

"Holy cow!" Charlie laughed.

"None of the boys are light eaters. Adrian and William eat their body weight in protein if you let them, and Emma's not much better," Darla noted.

"I can't believe I'm going to meet Emma Gracen!" Eric yelled, jumping a little bit in place.

"Yes, she'll be here," Darla agreed, smiling. "More importantly, have you met my Ethan? Are you seeing anyone, Eric?"

Jake handed Matilda ten bucks.

Darla raised her eyebrows.

"I thought it'd take at least fifteen minutes in the big room before we got there. Matty bet within ten minutes before we made it to the couches," Jake muttered.

"Smart girl." Darla grinned, hugging Matty again. "We'll talk about that later, Eric. Ethan needs a nice boy in his life. Now, where's Miranda? Is her husband coming?"

"UGH!" Jake groaned.

"Stop it." Darla's look was flat. "She's your family. You'll live."

"He's an incredible asshat, Mom. You have no idea. Wait until you see. Your head is going to explode."

"They'll be here closer to dinner. They had brunch at my grandfather's house this morning," Matty said. "I tried, Jake. It was your idea."

Darla's face crumpled into an unhappy expression. "Your grandfather is sitting next to the bathrooms at the wedding. Who has brunch and doesn't invite all of the grandkids?"

"Assholes!" Jake yelled.

"I THOUGHT you guys were going to watch sports," Darla commented.

Hank frowned. "You want us to go away?"

"No, I'm just surprised you're doing this with us," Darla said as she handed Matty a third bundle of pamphlets for party spaces.

"Doesn't Sam have a house somewhere that we can use for this party?" Matty asked. "Does it have to be in a banquet space? It's like we're having a wedding reception before the wedding."

"Shut it," Ellie barked. "You will be a pretty-pretty princess for your engagement party, or we will have words!"

"Uh-huh." Eric nodded in agreement.

"I want you to get a wedding dress for the engagement party," Ellie threw in as an afterthought, startling a laugh from Hank.

"I love this idea!" Darla yelled.

"Not a chance in hell!" Matty yelled.

Darla glared at her future daughter-in-law. "You're no fun. I'd wear a wedding dress. Not a floofy one, but a wedding dress all the same. I didn't have a wedding dress. I might just get a wedding dress for this."

"Woo! Let's do that!" Ellie clapped. "Me, too! Me, too!"

"Deal!" Darla agreed, laughing.

"Matilda, you will get a wedding dress with us," Ellie declared.

"I will not."

"You will. You will do it for me," Ellie said, voice flat.

"I do a lot of stupid shit for you, but I won't be wearing a wedding dress to my engagement party, Eleanor," Matilda said, undeterred.

"Darla and I are wearing wedding dresses for your party. You will wear one, too."

"Nope, I won't," Matty said, starting to chuckle.

"Boo!" Ellie yelled. "Please, Matty? Please? It'd be amazing!"

"Nope."

Eric wrinkled his nose. "I don't wear dresses. I feel like I can't participate in this harassment."

"This just means that we need fancy suits or tuxedos, Eric. You'll see." Hank grinned.

"Ugh. Suit? No suit. It's our party," Jake objected. "No suits, no wedding dresses."

"Bullshit!" Hank disagreed. "This is my party. This is your mother's party. You're just the excuse. Shut it and be a good sport."

"Armani?" Eric breathed, afraid to give voice to the question.

Hank shrugged. "Sure. There are other suit labels you might like better. We'll look."

"I'm not wearing a suit unless all my brothers are wearing a suit. Good luck with that," Jake challenged.

"They will all wear suits," Hank agreed. "And I'm guessing your mother will get Beth in a wedding dress for this, too."

"I will. I can't wait. She said something about eloping the other day," Darla complained.

Hank glared at Darla.

"I'm not the one that said it. I don't know why you're glaring at me."

"I will discuss it with Hennessy. They will not be eloping," Hank growled, all signs of merriment gone. "Small wedding, fine. But I will be there when my daughter gets married."

Before the awkward silence could sit too long, the doorbell rang.

"Maybe Miranda got away early. I'll go!" Matty said, jumping up.

"Roscoe, stay," Charlie muttered. "Don't trip her."

"Emma does that, too! Look how nice he's sitting here." Hank laughed. "That dog listens to everyone who is not me. Glinda's going to be my good girl."

Charlie grinned. "He's a good boy. Who's Glinda?"

"Sam and Addy found a box of puppies. I'm getting a puppy." Hank's smile turned wistful. "She's a sweet little girl. She'll be here tonight. You can meet her!"

"I lied, not Miranda." Matty came back into the big room with Jess and Ava in tow.

"We're here for the planning party! Clyde and Blake will bring the girls later," Ava announced.

Jess came to a full stop in the doorway, glaring at Charlie, then Eric, and finally Ellie.

"Hi!" Jake smiled. "This is Sam's...girlfriend's mom and sister. Ava and Jess, these are Matty's closest friends, Ellie, Charlie, and Eric."

Jess didn't move.

"Jess? You okay?" Hank asked.

"What the fuck are you?" Jess blurted, eyes on Ellie.

"Excuse me?" Ellie asked, startled.

"What are you?" Jess repeated. "You're not normal. Any of you. Not a normal person in this room other than Hank and Darla. What are you? The loose energy is trying to sink into her, Mom. What the fuck are you?"

"Uh, Jess, they don't—" Matilda started, taken aback.

"Matilda," Charlie muttered, cutting her off. When she glanced over at him, he shook his head.

ELLIE COULDN'T BREATHE. Her chest wouldn't move.

Not like this. Oh God, not like this. She's going to freak out. What do I say? What do I do? Ellie's thoughts were morphing into a panicked babble.

She grabbed Charlie's hand, squeezing. After he flexed his fingers, Ellie realized her grip was white-knuckled.

"We should go! It's time to go. Come on, Charlie, let's go home!" Ellie said, jumping off the couch.

"Babe," Charlie murmured, "it's going to be fine. Breathe, Ellie."

"No. No, really. It's fine. Obviously, family time. We should go!"

Eric sighed, not moving as Ellie pulled on him.

"What's going on?" Matty asked, confusion and hurt plain on her face.

"You're a vampire," Ava whispered, eyes wide as she held Jess's hand.

"OH, SHUT THE FUCK UP! I am not a vampire," Ellie yelled, tears filling her eyes.

"What the fuck is going on?" Jake yelled back.

"Everyone needs to calm down. Everything's fine," Eric said. "Ava, no one is in danger. Please stop gathering energy. You're going to make Ellie sick."

All eyes turned to Eric.

"Ava," Eric tried again. "There is enough loose energy in this house to feed an entire nest of Siphons. She's not interested in you or yours. Please stop gathering your energy."

"Who are you people?" Ava said, voice cold and expression flat. "How are you in this house?"

There was a charged moment of silence.

"They're my friends. My oldest friends," Matilda whispered. "I don't understand what's going on."

"Everything's fine, Matilda," Eric soothed. "It's absolutely fine."

Ava's eyes narrowed.

Charlie's face scrunched up. "This isn't ideal."

"You think?" Eric snorted.

"What is happening?" Matilda muttered, looking at Ellie.

Eleanor shook her head.

"Ellie, the energy is better. She knows more about things now. It's time to explain," Charlie murmured.

Ellie glared at her husband, tears running down her face. "I want to go. Please, Charlie, can we go?"

"No, Ells. It's going to be fine. Breathe," Charlie soothed. "Matty, do you know what you are now?"

Matilda's mouth didn't move. She stared, eyes like saucers.

"She knows. They all know," Eric offered. "Fire? They're not thinking clearly, so it's hard to understand. But they know what a circle is now."

"Okay," Charlie said in the same calm voice. "That's great. That's perfect, actually. Eleanor, sit down. Breathe. Calm down. It's going to be fine. We're not leaving, babe. We're done with secrets."

Ellie dropped to the floor, burying her face in her hands, pulling her knees up protectively to her chest.

"I think that's as good as you're going to get, Charlie," Eric muttered.

"I'll take it," Glancing around the room, Charlie realized all eyes were on him, transfixed with horror, except for Matty.

Matilda's eyes were laser-focused on Ellie. She didn't react to Charlie's words at all.

"In college. Sophomore year. We were doing spa night, drinking," Matty whispered eventually. "I thought you were joking. I thought you were testing if I was gullible enough to believe you."

Charlie nodded. "My second year of law school, I ran into Eleanor and Matilda at a bar. I knew what she was immediately, Matty. I originally came over to help you, get you away from her. But, as I got closer, I could feel the energy flowing off you in waves.

"I figured you were some kind of empowered person being obtuse. It took a few minutes for me to realize you had no idea at all what you were, let alone what she was."

"I'm sorry, I'm having trouble reading between the lines," Jake objected. "I can't fucking believe this. What exactly are you, Ellie?"

Looking at her hands, Ellie opened and closed her mouth twice before she spoke. "I'm a Siphon. I pull energy from others and use it."

"Like a hunter?" Hank asked into the trailing silence.

"No, not really. I think they originally got the idea from us, but no. I have very little energy on my own. Hunters have their own energy. They're just selfish fucks that want more of it. Without other energy sources around me, I would be lethargic and sick for a while, then slip into something like a diabetic coma and eventually die."

"Other sources of energy?" Jake asked, voice lacking the warmth and love he usually allotted to Eleanor.

She nodded, not meeting his eyes.

"I need more detail than that," Jake responded.

Eleanor nodded again, staring at the floor in front of her. "It's exactly what you think it is, Jake. People like me feed on the energy generated by others. We're typically terrible, selfish beings. It's easier to generate negative energy in others, so we tend to trigger hate and sadness, then feast upon people's pain."

Charlie sighed. "Ellie is different."

Jake and Eleanor snorted in unison.

"Not originally," Ellie disagreed. "Before college, I was just like everyone else. The craving and need for energy are all-encompassing. Impossible to ignore.

"But then I went away to school. My assigned college roommate leaked power everywhere. Raw power. More power than I could handle. Ten minutes in her company every other week, and I had so much fucking power, I became a high-energy extrovert. Holy shit. The first day I met you, Matty, your angst-riddled energy was so thick in the fucking dorm hallway that I was flying high by the time I made it into our room. I thought my brother was going to lose his mind and hump your leg."

Ellie fell silent, staring at Matilda.

Matty stared at her hands, unwilling to meet anyone's eyes.

"I don't know how much you know, Matty. You are empowered and very strong. You know that, correct?" Charlie asked.

Matty cleared her throat. "Yes."

"Do you know what happens to empowered people who don't know how to cycle energy?" Charlie asked.

"They go insane," Matty whispered. "And then they die."

"Do you know when your power manifested?" he asked.

"No," Matty muttered.

"Within an hour or two of meeting you, it became clear that she was keeping you sane. I almost shit myself the first time Eric closed a circle with you, completely oblivious, sitting around chatting and drinking wine," Charlie said.

Ava's head swiveled to Eric.

He nodded. "I can hold a circle with her. I can hold a circle with you both, Ava. I've not met an empowered yet that I can't hold a circle with, so I'm guessing I can hold a circle with the other daughter you're thinking of, as well. I have a different type of energy."

When Matilda seemed unresponsive, Jake asked, "You're like Ellie?"

Eric chuckled. "No."

"Again, I'm going to need some detail," Jake said tersely.

Matty turned to Jake, dazed. "You haven't caught it? He's reading minds."

Eyebrows raised, Jake turned back to Eric.

"Correct. Good, Matty," Eric said softly. "You've known I do this since college. You've just never consciously acknowledged that I'm reading you. You tend to believe I just wait for the right opening to talk about important things, and you're not wrong. There's just a little more to it. That's all."

"You're reading our minds right now?" Jake asked.

Eric shrugged. "Sort of. It's akin to listening. I have to focus on doing it, but I can interpret thoughts and emotions. Not exactly read minds, but close. So, right now, I know Ava is trying to remember back to some of the histories and legends that she read as a girl. I cannot influence things directly, though. So it's a little bit different than the empowered man you're thinking of, Jake."

"Would you tell us if you could influence us?" Darla asked, frowning.

Eric grinned at her. "Yes, Darla. I absolutely would. I don't believe for a second anyone in this room would be an enemy. Matty is dear to me in a way few people are. Jake, too. I don't lie to my friends."

"But you hid this. For most of a decade," Matilda accused.

He shook his head. "No, Matty. We did not. Think back. We have tried to have this conversation with you at least a dozen times over the years. *At least* a dozen times. You just thought we were assholes. You weren't going to believe us until you could understand your own energy better."

Matilda stared off into space, thinking it over before nodding.

"The empowered people I know aren't great," Eric continued. "I almost brought you to them a couple of times, but then I thought of all the terrible shit empowereds do to each other. So, when you looked at us like we were nuts, we dropped it and just kept cycling energy away from you, trying to keep you healthy. It worked well, for the most part."

The room was silent and still.

"Huh," Jess grunted after a moment, looking at Ava. "You know who looks like him?"

Ava raised her eyebrows.

"Delilah Wecker."

A small gasp escaped Ava's mouth before she nodded. "That might make sense. Not mental illness, then? Why didn't you mention that she looked different before?"

Jess shrugged. "Very few people look like plain old boring humans. I thought maybe there was an empowered lurking somewhere in Max's family tree that made her colors more vivid. She's not as vivid as Eric."

"I'm sorry," Charlie interrupted. "Can we go back for a minute? Jess, what exactly are you doing that you know we're different?"

"I'm looking," Jess answered, providing no additional information, her expression shut down.

Charlie looked at Matty, hoping for clarification. Matilda didn't acknowledge the unspoken question.

"We'll come back to that. I'd like to understand that a little better," Charlie allowed.

"How do you fit in, Charlie?" Hank asked.

"Roscoe," Charlie said, "go to Hank, stand on the chair without touching him, and sniff his right ear."

"What the hell?" Hank exclaimed as the dog did exactly as instructed.

"I have animal magnetism. It's why Ellie and I do so well together." Charlie grinned.

Eric rolled his eyes. "So not the time, Charles."

Charlie laughed a little. "There are a fair number of people that have instinctive connections with animals in the world, but most are limited: one type of animal, one gender of an animal family.

"My sister can command male cats of all sizes from house cats to lions. She's a zookeeper. I have a cousin that controls birds. Don't piss her off. She'll dive-bomb your head.

"I am part of a tiny group of people that can command any mammal with brain functions less complex than humans. I can negotiate behavior with some elephants, though it's not the type of obedience you see with Roscoe. I have minimal connections with dolphins and whales. I cannot command humans at all, much to my dismay."

After a short pause, he asked, "Am I correct in understanding Emma Gracen has a similar ability?"

Matty opened her mouth to respond.

"Wait," Hank interrupted. "Ava? Jess? Thoughts?"

Ava shook her head. "I have no idea, Hank. Honestly. Our legends say Eric's kind died out centuries ago and that Siphons are vampires that will suck the life energy out of someone. But they also say Sam is the embodiment of death and destruction. I don't know anything at all about what Charlie is."

Ellie nodded along vigorously. "Siphons will absolutely suck the life energy out of someone. Absolutely. Don't hang out with them, except me. I don't need your life energy. My BFF is a blazing inferno of raw energy, and my husband loves me. Either one of those things is good enough to keep me stocked up. Both together? Well, I'm the 'life' of every fucking party."

"My energy makes you an extreme extrovert? I swallowed a dildo in front of thirty people because you got too much of my energy?" Matilda snorted.

"What?" Jess asked, startled.

"No, you swallowed a dildo in front of thirty people because I love you." Ellie grinned. "It's the same reason you're sitting next to Prince Fucking Charming right now. I'm going to have him a t-shirt made with the title and then send him the bill."

Matilda sighed then nodded with a sad smile.

"Please don't hate me," Ellie whispered, touching Matilda's arm from her place on the floor. "I would never hurt you."

"Does everyone in my life have secret superpowers?" Matilda asked. "Seriously. What the fuck? Am I a magnet for this shit?"

"Yup." Charlie laughed. "You are absolutely a magnet for anyone that can sense that kind of energy, Matty. Until today, you leaked it everywhere. At all times. In your fucking sleep. I have never felt anything like it. We've been scaring off the assholes for years."

Jake scrubbed his hand through his hair. "What the fuck?"

"OH MY GOD, you have no idea. Every user and abuser in a ten-mile radius, Jacob!" Ellie exploded. "What changed? Did you find a circle? Why are you better now? Not as leaky. And what the fuck with this powder keg of a house? I just about passed out from the spike of energy when we came inside."

"Yeah, sort of. I mean. Yeah, circle." Matty nodded, mind elsewhere.

"Matty, how are you?" Charlie asked, pulling her back to the conversation.

Matilda sighed again, looking around the room. "Charlie, I can light a fire with my mind. What the fuck do I know? Whatever. They have tried to tell me before. Honestly, Ava. They have. They've been my best friends for almost a decade. I don't believe they'd hurt us."

Charlie nudged his wife. "We can stop arguing about this now. I was right, you were wrong."

"Whoa, Charlie. Whoa. Those are words a smart husband never says. What are you thinking?" Hank looked horrified.

"It's the only thing we ever argue about! Holy shit. I woke up last

Wednesday, feeling like my skin was flying off my body. Ellie was freaking out about Matty's energy exploding. She started panic-calling them nonstop. We could have just had this conversation years ago," Charlie complained. "I get that Matty thought they were fucking with her in college. They screw with her a lot. But I could have done my beast-master thing as a party trick and put it to rest."

"That bitchfest feels like it's been stewing for a long time," Jess commented.

"He's repeated that bitchfest at least weekly for as long as I've known him." Ellie rolled her eyes. "You wouldn't have understood until you understood your own shit, Matty. We tried and tried."

Jake's eyes narrowed. "Was that the 'fuck a duck' voicemail?"

"Yep." Ellie laughed.

"You said you had a bad dream!"

"I lied. 'Someone's roasting Matty's brain' sounded too alarmist."

Jake nodded, giving her a small smile. "Touché. Ava? Jess? Are you going to stay?"

Ava shook her head in disbelief. "Shit just keeps getting weirder with you people. Whatever," she said, perching on a couch.

Jess shrugged.

"Jess, how do you know we're different?" Charlie asked again.

Jess looked at Ava, then Matty. Ava gave a half-hearted shrug; Matilda nodded.

"I have all-sight, Charlie. I see everything that makes a person who they are."

Eric's mouth dropped open. "Um, everything? True all-sight?"

"Down to the bones," Jess replied.

"Holy fuck," Eric muttered.

"I want to hear the dildo story!" Jess grinned, sensing good dirt on Matty.

"There's a video!" Eric clapped. "Where's my phone?"

"Nope, no. Nope. I draw the line there. We're not watching the dildo video with my parents," Jake declared.

"Oh, fair point. Sorry," Eric said, turning red and not looking at Hank and Darla.

"Who wants queso?" Darla asked into the awkward silence.

Eric burst out laughing. "I love that Hank and Darla are all 'whatever' about this. Mind readers and vampires? Whatever. Who wants queso? It's not an act, either. After Ava admitted she didn't know what to think, they lumped us back into the 'Matilda's family' mental pile."

Ellie punched Eric in the thigh from her spot on the floor. "YOU KNOW I HATE BEING CALLED THAT!"

Eric grinned. "Ow! Bitch. That's why I said it."

"Punch you in the dick next time," Ellie muttered.

"Did anyone explain the Little Ears policy?" Hank asked.

"No, I was going to let them find out on their own." Jake grinned.

"WHOA!" Eric shouted, interrupting Matilda mid-sentence when Sam and Adaline walked into the room with the pack of puppies following along.

Ellie scrunched up her face. "Holy fuck, Sam. How is it even worse now? Damn."

"Ellie, shh. Don't. Shh. He's the fucking Walker," Eric murmured, head bowed, trying to drag Ellie to her feet and away with him, behind the couches.

"What the fuck is wrong with you?" Ellie asked, shaking herself free of Eric. "He's a fucking nerdy billionaire. Go sniff him!"

Charlie gasped, dropping his eyes immediately. "Eleanor, this is not a good time to be abrasive or assertive."

She paused, looking at both men, and then glancing at Matilda. Matilda rolled her eyes.

"It's just Sam. Same guy, more energy," Matty explained.

"Ellie, do you know what the Walker is?" Eric muttered, head still bowed.

She shrugged, shaking her head.

Sam sighed. "My predecessors were destructive assholes. I'm still me—same nondestructive asshole you drank beer and trolled Matty's ex-boyfriend with."

"See? It's fine. What the fuck is wrong with you both?" Ellie asked, baffled by their behavior.

"Seriously," Matty said. "Give it a rest. The Walker shit is getting old. It's fine. That's Sam's...Adaline. This is Ellie, Charlie, and Eric."

"We can come back later if you need some time," Sam offered, eyes downcast in humiliation.

"No," Matty snarled. "You will not come back later. Charlie! Eric! NOW! Eyes up. Say hello. He's still Sam."

"Mistress," Eric greeted Adaline with a nod, avoiding looking at Sam. "Ava, I would not be able to hold a circle with your other daughter."

Adaline grinned at him, causing some of the tension in Eric's shoulders to relax. "Hi."

"I don't intend to harm anyone at all, especially family and friends. Please don't do this," Sam mumbled without looking at anyone. "There's no reason to be afraid of me."

"What's going on? What are you, Sam?" Ellie asked.

Sam snorted. "I'll tell you what I am if you tell me what you are."

WHEN LUCAS ENTERED the big room, Charlie was buried in puppies. Ellie and Eric were bickering with Matilda about fancy dresses.

"Hey, Luke!" Hank called. "Watch Charlie with the damn puppies! This is amazing."

Charlie glanced over at Luke, still laughing at the puppies, and then froze. His mouth dropped open as he stared at Luke.

"Hi, Charlie," Luke said, immediately uncomfortable. "Everything okay?"

When Charlie finally spoke, it was in a tone of reverence. "Greetings, Peacekeeper."

Luke's lips turned up into a half-smile. "That's a new one. What's going on?"

"How many of your children are empowered beings of legend?" Eric asked Darla, eyes wide.

Darla shrugged. "All of them. You get used to it."

Eric's eyes drifted back to Matilda. "Not fire. Lady Light?"

Matty grinned, nodding.

"Holy fuck," Charlie muttered.

"Where's Talise?" Darla demanded, ignoring the shock and awe.

Luke rolled his eye. "Raincheck."

"Don't you roll your eyes at me." Darla glared at her youngest son. "Go get chairs out of the garage with Jake."

"Make Sam do it. He can just do his teleporting thing," Luke responded.

Sam glared. "I'm not that good at it yet."

MIRANDA AND LAWRENCE were the last to arrive.

"I'm so sorry, I wanted to be here sooner, but then Lawrence got tied up and anyway. I'm sorry," Miranda rambled when Matty and Jake opened the front door.

"What's all this, Miranda?" Jake asked, giving her a little hug as he took the basket and Pyrex she was juggling out of her hands.

"I brought a dessert and some goodies from my garden. Do you think that's okay? Will your mom mind?"

"Are you kidding? Darla will be ecstatic. Larry, do you have anything I need to take?" Jake asked, eyeing Lawrence's empty hands.

"Ha! Jake, such a kidder. I really do go by 'Lawrence,' though," he boomed out, voice carrying through the house as the big room went silent.

"That's what you think!" Jake grinned at Miranda. "Come on in. Everyone's in the big room. Mom, where do you want this stuff?"

Darla came around the corner, out of the big room, grinning widely. "Come in! Hi, I'm Darla. Oh, isn't this just so sweet, look at all the produce! Thank you so much! Jake, that dish needs to go in the fridge. The basket goes on the kitchen island, please."

Matilda tried not to laugh at Darla's expression as Lawrence swaggered in front of the ladies, down the hall, and into the gathering room.

"I thought you were exaggerating," Darla muttered as Miranda followed in Lawrence's wake, head down, looking at her hands.

"Nope," Matty said.

They turned into the big room just in time to see the horrified look on Sam's face as Larry tried to greet him like an old friend.

Sam leaned away from him, tucking his hands behind his back.

"Don't touch me," he muttered, stepping away from Lawrence.

"Oh, Miranda! I had not put that together. Hi!" Sam greeted Miranda with a rare hug.

"Do you know each other?" Lawrence asked, brow wrinkled, looking between his wife and the eccentric billionaire.

"No," Sam said, stepping away from Lawrence and pulling Miranda with him toward the opposite end of the room.

Right after Matilda started introductions, Matthew wandered back into the big room. "The beer is officially restocked, you lazy jerks!"

"Matthew!" Miranda exclaimed, moving halfway across the room toward him before she realized what she was doing. She stopped in limbo between Sam and Matthew, her husband glaring at her from behind Matthew's shoulder.

"Randa! What the hell? How are you here?" Matthew did not pause in scooping her up into a foot-swinging hug.

"How am I—?" Miranda said, near tears. "Trellis. I-I didn't realize you were...I'm so sorry. You're Jake's brother?"

"We're all sorry about being Jake's brother," Noah snarked.

Luke and Ethan were the only ones to laugh. Everyone else was watching the scene unfolding before them.

Matthew was still hugging Miranda.

Matthew, who had never shown interest in anyone, never brought anyone home, seemed unwilling to let go of Matilda's little sister.

Looking around, Miranda flinched back at the sight of her husband's rage. Stepping away from Matthew, she smiled a nervous smile. "Matthew, this is Larry—Lawrence. Lawrence. He is my husband. Because we're married. That's what happens when you get married. You get a husband."

"Oh. My. Goodness. There's another one!" Eric stage-whispered, laughing with Ellie. "It's Matilda, eight years ago! I'm so excited we get to do this again! Do you think she knows how to bounce her boobs?"

That caught everyone off-guard, triggering laughter.

Miranda's face was beet red. "I'm sorry. I was surprised. Lawrence, Matthew was a teacher's aide working on his Master's degree when I was in college. I've told you about him before."

"Huh," Lawrence grunted, ignoring Matthew's offered handshake. "I don't remember. Must not have been important."

Just like that, everyone in the room hated Larry.

"Miranda, what's your name?" Sam asked.

Turning to blink at Sam, she said, "I am Earth."

Sam grinned, a genuine smile that touched his eyes as he hugged her again. "Yes, you are."

"MIRANDA," Lawrence barked, "don't start that bullshit. We agreed you'd never talk about that in public. Go sit down."

Well, that does it. I'm going to have to snap his mind like a twig, Matthew decided. It was one of the only times he could recall consciously wishing someone ill.

With a glance around the room, he realized his entire family knew exactly what he was thinking. Hank was holding his breath. Luke was already trying to move closer without seeming to move closer.

Matthew rolled his eyes at his younger brother. Luke's eyebrows hiked up.

Whatever, man. He's a nasty dick. A tiny little dick with a belly paunch and a bald spot he's trying to hide. Complete with a small little mushroom head and a foul smell.

Luke grinned. It wasn't the first time Matthew wondered if he could share thoughts with his youngest brother.

Sam scrunched up his face. "We'll talk about earth later," he whispered to Miranda.

As he led Miranda by the hand toward the crowd at the other end of the room, Sam turned to smirk at Matthew.

AS SOON AS they were backed out of the driveway, Jake started bouncing with joy. "It's perfect! Did you see his face?"

"Are you fucking kidding? Did you see *her* face? She introduced the shit-bag as 'Larry!' That was amazing." Matty clapped.

"Larry's days are numbered. We gotta make that happen. I'm going to razz Matthew all day tomorrow. She'll be filing for divorce before the week is over," Jake predicted.

"How did she end up with that asshole?" Eric asked. "She's so incredibly sweet. Not a negative thought in her head."

"I have no idea," Matty said, shaking her head.

The car was silent for a few minutes as the city lights flowed by outside the windows.

"Matty, do you want me to leave you alone?" Ellie whispered. "I would understand if you do. I really would."

After a thoughtful pause, Matilda responded. "No, Ells. I don't want you to go away. I'm glad you're in my life."

Eric cleared his throat. "Ask it, Matty. It will fester if you don't."

"You know, that's really annoying," Matty complained. "I keep thinking back over all the private thoughts I've had around you throughout our friendship, and I'm super pissed you were listening in."

"Oh, please. Your private thoughts weren't interesting until you met Jake. Private thoughts related to Peter were boring as fuck. I tuned that shit out." Eric grinned.

"Seriously," he continued. "I don't focus and listen often. I am doing it now because I'm worried about you and want to help. I did over Christmas for the same reasons. But, otherwise, nothing is sacred to Ellie. I know everything without barging into your mind. But you should ask it. She's wondering if you're wondering, and you're worried you won't like the answer."

"Are we friends because you wanted to keep me around?" Matty whispered, eyes filling with tears.

"Yup," Ellie choked out. "We are friends because I absolutely wanted to keep you around. You're adorable and hilarious and prudish. You were the best friend I had up until Charlie wandered over to our table, trying to rescue you. But we didn't need to be friends for me to siphon the energy, Matty. If I didn't want you in my life, I could have just spent a few minutes in the dorm room every week or so."

"Okay," Matty said, nodding.

"Okay," Ellie whispered, wiping away tears.

"What the fuck?" Eric bitched. "I don't rate on the BFF scale? Damn vampire."

20

Jake started Monday morning with a new group text thread.

JAKE: You know what I find myself wondering about this beautiful Monday morning?
NOAH: What are you wondering, Jake?
JAKE: I'm wondering how my second youngest brother knows my future wife's little sister? What's up with that?
WILL: Amazingly, I find myself wondering the same thing. What a coincidence!
MATTY: My little sister? Your brother knows my sister and never mentioned it? How could that be?!
MATTHEW: Ugh.
HANK: There must be a misunderstanding. My son doesn't date anyone. Doesn't talk about significant others. He just quietly goes about his life. He would NEVER have a relationship he kept hidden from his loving, adoring family.
DARLA: Not Matthew. Noah, absolutely. Not Matthew. So, there must be some confusion.

ADRIAN: Whoa! Are you suggesting Captain Fucking Chaos had a lady friend? I'm pretty sure he's a monk. You know, like Sam was.
SAM: Sex is good.
HENNESSY: I hope "Captain Chaos" sticks.
MATTHEW: It's Captain Fucking Chaos. Get it right.
JAKE: Spill! What's the story? How quickly can you end that farce of a marriage?
MATTHEW: We knew each other in college. Not much to tell. She was an undergrad in one of the classes I taught.
NOAH: Woo, spicy role-play possibilities.
DARLA: LOL
NOAH: Mom, don't laugh at that!
DARLA: Noah, I had NINE children.
WILL: Eww! Eww! Parental sex!
HANK: Sex is good.
LUKE: We are way off course here.
DARLA: I'm not sorry.
ADRIAN: Lucy can't breathe. She's laughing too hard.
MATTHEW: Let's not kill Lucy. We should stop this now.
LUCY: So, "Randa," huh? I could see that working during sexy time. "Oh, Randa…"
HENNESSY: OMG, Lou! You're becoming one of us.
LUCY: He's so quiet and unassuming. We never get to tease him! This is priceless!
MATTHEW: Are we done?
MATTY: Never. This will be funny forever.
MATTHEW: …
MATTHEW: Jake and Matty had sex on a pool table!
HANK: Meh. That one's getting old. I like the new Miranda twist. We'll stick with this.
MATTHEW: Luke has a girlfriend that hasn't come to Sunday dinner.
DARLA: I'm a little bit salty about that, Luke.
LUKE: …
LUKE: So, when Matthew was teaching English Lit 102, he got into a

philosophical argument with Miranda. She was less timid then, and she has strong opinions on classic romances.
MATTHEW: I take it back. Sorry, Luke.
ADRIAN: SPILL IT, LUKE!
LUKE: Pathetically little to tell. Great friends. The potential for more was destroyed by the Captain Fucking Chaos thing in a way that William and Adrian would understand well.
MATTHEW: It never got that far. Great friends. But just friends.
LUCY: Uh-huh. I'd swear you were thinking about destroying the shit-bag's mind last night.
MATTHEW: I don't deny it. She deserves better than me and definitely better than Larry.
HANK: Where did I go wrong with you boys? Why would you think you don't deserve to be happy?!?
BETH: It's to do with the ethics and morals, Dad. Too much high road, not enough selfishness.
HANK: It was a rhetorical question, Beth. But please be more selfish in love. Stop trying to do the right thing for everyone else and do the right thing for yourselves on the love front, you morons.
DARLA: Ahem.
HANK: ...
HANK: I came around.

"HELLO?" Miranda answered the phone timidly on Monday morning. The same unknown number had called her three times in the last ten minutes.

"I wondered if you were going to answer or if I'd have to call Matty," Sam grumped.

"Sam? Hi. I didn't recognize the number."

"That's because I've never called you before," he teased. "How are you? Is the shit-bag around?"

Miranda smiled at the phone. That had to be Matty's nickname for Lawrence. It just sounded like something she'd say.

"Lawrence is at work this morning," Miranda responded primly, a slight reprimand in her voice.

"There's a zero percent chance I will ever call him by his preferred name. You should let go of that hope right now." Sam laughed.

Miranda sighed.

"Are you trying to kid yourself into thinking you like him more than I do?" Sam asked. "He gave me a splitting headache immediately upon entering the house."

"Huh. He doesn't give me a headache. I wonder if he makes Matty's head hurt. She's never said anything," Miranda wondered aloud.

"Oh. Maybe headaches are a 'me' thing. People don't give you headaches? Make your skin crawl when they touch you?" Sam asked.

"Nope. No idea what you're talking about. Your energy feels different to me, but not bad. Adaline's energy feels...invigorating."

"That's not surprising. How long have you known about energy? Do you know about circles?" Sam asked, curious. "I was so happy when you knew what you were! No one ever knows what I'm talking about when I ask stuff like that!"

"Since I was a little girl. Younger than Ree. My maternal grandmother had strong elemental fire. She explained it. I haven't been in a circle for years and years, though," Miranda admitted. "Not since she passed away when I was twelve."

Sam was quiet for a minute, considering how to respond. "I'm sorry for your loss."

"Me, too. I miss her every day." Miranda's voice was subdued. "I wish I could talk to her now. I don't understand why she didn't tell me about Matilda. I didn't think we had secrets from each other."

"We can look backward if you want to try. I wouldn't bring you with me. It seems to hurt others when I do that. But maybe we could figure out why," Sam offered.

"Look backward?"

"In time. We can look back and see if we can find a reason."

There was a long pause.

"Miranda? Are you still there?"

"I'm here," she whispered. "Sam, do you Walk through time? Is that why you feel different?"

Sam sighed. "Yes, but I swear I'm not an asshole."

"What do you mean?"

"You don't need to be afraid of me. I promise. I won't hurt you. I don't want to hurt anyone. I hate that everyone's afraid of me," Sam blurted.

"I'm not afraid of you," Miranda said, sounding confused. "Why would I be afraid?"

"Everyone else seems to be afraid of the Walker thing. But you don't have to be afraid."

"Oh."

There was a pause as Sam waited for her to continue.

"That's it?" he finally asked.

"I'm not afraid of you. You're Matilda's friend. She loves you. And you're Matthew's brother. I'm predisposed to like you. Plus, you give good hugs."

"That's great!" Sam said, his happiness audible through the phone connection.

"Did you just call to say hi?" Miranda asked after a couple seconds of silence.

"Doh! Sorry. Sidetracked. No, I called to ask if you want to be a part of our circle."

Miranda's voice was full of wonder. "You have a circle? Here? In Chicago?"

"How have you cycled energy without a circle?" Sam asked.

"I talk with the earth. We take care of each other." She shrugged her shoulders as she said it and then laughed at her silliness. Sam couldn't see the shrug.

"Interesting. Maybe you'll show me how to do that one day?"

"Sure," Miranda said, catching herself shrugging again. "But you have a circle?"

"I guess I do. I guess it belongs to Addy and me now. It gathers on Monday nights. We've been meeting at a farm west of the suburbs because my family's energy is still a little wonky. Want to stand the circle?"

"I do!" she said, doing a little happy wiggle in her chair. "I can get a car for tonight—"

"Matty said to tell you that she and Jake will pick you up at five o'clock if you want to ride with them."

"Oh! Good. A circle and Matty time. This is great! I'll text her and let her know."

"Don't bring Larry."

"Wouldn't dream of it," she responded immediately. "He doesn't understand about the energy. He doesn't believe me, says I was too pampered in my 'silly tendencies' as a girl."

"That's because he's a shit-bag. A flaming, smelly shit-bag."

"Not that you're judging." Miranda rolled her eyes.

"Not at all. You know who's not a shit-bag?"

"Who?"

"Matthew," Sam said, tone playful.

"Uh-huh. Preaching to the choir on that one, Sam."

"I don't know what that means in this context."

She grinned. "That's good. I'll see you tonight. Thank you for inviting me!"

BY MONDAY AFTERNOON, Noah had significant control over his energy and was feeling better about life.

Pulling the energy all the way back, away from his mind, was like suddenly losing feeling in his earlobes—not painful or disruptive, but disturbing all the same. He couldn't sense the people around him in the same way. He wasn't as aware of women. It felt awkward.

Leaving the energy in what Will called "neutral" felt more natural but took concentration. He could sense the attraction of people around him. But, unlike before, he could sense attraction directed at other people. A couple sitting together at a restaurant focused on each other. Teenage kids screwing around in a mall parking lot. Running on

Sunday morning, he could even sense attraction between a pair of dogs.

It didn't take any focus at all to pull the energy forward. The power naturally wanted out of his mind. But, after playing with it for a couple days, he noticed when people were reacting to it. Rather than attraction focused elsewhere, it all turned to him. Any age, any sexual orientation, it didn't matter. When he turned the energy up, all eyes turned to him.

Based on the reactions, he figured the energy naturally sat at about a four on a ten-point scale before he learned how to control it. As Jake said, enough to lower inhibitions. Not enough to change someone's nature.

Having made peace with the realization, Noah's relief was evident in both his attitude and outlook. In a few months, this would be hilarious fodder for joking around, but right then, it was still too fresh and sensitive.

So, when he felt a woman eyeing him at the deli across from the office while picking up lunch on Monday, his first response was to check that the energy wasn't leaking out.

It was in neutral.

Thinking he must have made a mistake somewhere along the way, he pulled the energy back, all the way away from his mind.

"This still isn't your phone, right?" a sultry, familiar voice said from behind his right shoulder as he waited for his food.

Noah paused, considering what to do. The energy was tucked away. If she was talking to him now, it was because she was interested in him.

Noah smiled, turning to meet her eyes. "We have to work on your lines."

"You might be the only guy I've ever met that is immune to my charm," she admitted, smiling back. "Still working through things on your own?"

"Oh, I think it's time I got over it, got back out in the world."

"So brave." She smirked.

"I'd ask for your number, but I don't even know your name."

"You can ask for my name, too, you know?"

"I thought I just did." He grinned. "I'm Noah."

"Hi, Noah. I'm Kaylee," she said with a little curtsey.

"I'M RIDING with Will next week. It means sitting in the way-back of the Suburban, but at least I won't get bitched at for the whole fucking ride," Noah declared.

Forty-five minutes into the car ride on Monday night, Noah wished he had opted out of the circle this week in favor of dinner with Kaylee. It had been a toss-up.

While confident he'd be fine without a circle, he didn't want to leave Sam to deal with the judgmental assholes. Sam wasn't good at cracking jokes in tense situations. Like flirting, smart-ass comments were Noah's schtick.

"Would you stop screwing around? I'm serious," Luke snapped. "She's very upset about it."

"I'm *oh* so glad you're worried about your girlfriend's feelings after she kicked me in the crotch for nothing, Luke. Don't worry, I'm fine, man."

"Noah," Matthew started.

"Please shut up about this. I will not bother her. I won't talk to her or look at her. I'll stay the fuck away. I wasn't trying to scare her last week. Didn't even realize she was scared, Luke. I don't want her to be frightened of me. I'm a lover, not a fighter," Noah snarked, before considering the words.

"Noah—"

"Oh. Come on. I say that all the time. I'm joking. You know I'm joking. I will not try to romance your woman, Luke. Let it go."

"You don't understand," Luke said. "She'll feel your anger, Noah. Please, just let it be. Leave her be. She has enough other shit to deal with without you being a baby about a misunderstanding."

Noah sighed, all humor gone. "Luke, I feel terrible that she was so scared last week. I don't want to cause her any pain, discomfort, humiliation, or trouble. I'm not angry about it; I won't bitch about it. She was scared and trying to keep herself safe. I would never fault someone for that, even if it is a misunderstanding.

"For the third time: I will stay away from her. Physically and emotionally. I won't tease or be silly. I will just leave her alone. I won't even speak to her. I promise. Can we please talk about *anything* else? Continuously talking about the time I unintentionally cornered a vulnerable, overwhelmed, frightened woman is extremely depressing. It makes me feel even worse about the whole thing than I did before getting in this fucking car."

The car was silent, with just the background music playing for a solid minute.

"To be fair," Ethan said, "I don't think either of them realized you were upset about scaring her. They expected you to do the smart-ass whining thing you do when you feel you've been wronged."

"Well, two things on that front," Noah began. "First, I told them that I felt terrible about it when this conversation started. I'm not sure how else I could have made that clear.

"Second, it's irritating that my brothers don't understand that something like this would bother me. I don't deny that I bitch and whine like a small child, but never at someone else's expense.

"I'm not so selfish and unaware that I'd verbally attack the empathic woman trying to figure out how to exist in life with a fully functional brain. I'm just not that big of an asshole. I'd piss and moan to you guys, not to her.

"I didn't say a fucking word to her last week after it happened. When she got back with Sam and Addy, I hobbled my sore nut sack outside and sat on the hard porch steps so she wouldn't have to look at me."

The car was silent until they pulled into the grass at the farmhouse.

"You spend so much time being a snarky prick, it's hard to tell when you're serious. I'm sorry," Luke apologized. "Sometimes, your humor stings, Noah. She can't take the burn right now. That's what I was hoping you'd understand before we parked the car. Obviously, you do."

SAM AND ADALINE appeared alongside Noah, Ethan, Luke, and Matthew as they walked toward the house.

"You know, people might be a little less creeped out by you if stopped Walking. Drive a car," Noah bitched.

Adaline frowned, looking at him. "Are you well?"

Noah forced a small smile. "Yeah, Addy. I'm fine. Just cranky. I'm sorry."

At a touch of her hand, Addy's calm, quiet love washed over him, taking the hurt out of the car ride from hell. Without thinking, he grabbed her hand, kissing it before touching it to his chest in what was meant to be a walking hug of thanks. At her smile, he knew she understood.

"I don't want to drive. I suck at driving," Sam muttered.

"Maybe that's better now?" Noah asked, mood lighter. "You're sleeping regularly, right?"

"Mostly." Sam nodded.

That gave Noah pause. "Dreams are back?"

"No," Sam disagreed. "Middle of the night sex is fun."

Noah burst out laughing at Adaline's horrified face.

"Actually, all kinds of sex are fun. I haven't found one I don't like," Sam admitted as Addy's cheeks flamed red. "I'll keep looking, though."

"Please stop talking," she whispered to Sam.

"Eh, he's totally distracted from his foul mood now. You have your way, I have mine." Sam grinned.

Ethan smiled. "I can't think of two people that deserve great sex more."

"Pfft. That's bullshit. I totally deserve great sex," Noah said, still laughing.

"You deserve great sex more than Sam?" Ethan asked, surprised.

"Why does it have to be a competition? Why can't we all have great sex? Great sex isn't pie, Ethan. We can all have great sex without diminishing each other's great sex," Noah said with a straight face.

"I think you could have fit 'great sex' in there one or two more times. Addy's not horrified enough yet," Ethan coached.

"I was told that sex was a life thing. Then they laughed at me when I was uncomfortable. This is payback," Sam teased, squeezing Adaline's hand.

"Laughing about sex with Jess is different than laughing about sex with your brothers, Sam," Addy whispered.

Sam's eyebrows rose. "Not from where I'm standing!"

"They're both terrible prudes. It's so nice they have each other." Ethan laughed with Noah.

"Hey, speaking of great sex, when are you going to see Miranda again?" Noah threw over his shoulder at Matthew.

Matthew sighed.

Ethan snorted. "Don't worry, Matthew, we totally believe that 'college friends' thing."

"I hate you all," Matthew said.

"Boo! She needs out of that terrible marriage," Noah yelled before coming to a stop.

"Oh, shit. Is that her?" Noah whispered, uneasy. "Sorry. I don't think she heard."

Miranda was standing on the porch, talking with Matty and Jake.

Noah turned in time to see Matthew's eyes go wide.

"Yup, totally college friends. We buy that. Don't worry, we won't tease you until she's out of earshot," Noah muttered.

As they walked closer to the house, Noah could feel a woman's interest, focused on Luke, moving closer.

As Luke set foot on the steps, Talise grabbed his hand.

"Hi." Luke laughed, startled.

"Hi," Talise said. "I'm sorry. I thought you heard me."

"Nope, you're stealthy. How are you? No gloves today?" Luke grinned.

"I told you I would try, and I will." She smiled.

"Thank you." Luke smiled back.

Turning to the larger group, Talise's smile became nervous. "Hi, everyone. Noah, I'm so sorry—"

But he was already out of earshot, greeting Matilda and Jake.

"Don't worry about it, Talise. He's fine. Upset that you're upset, more than anything else," Ethan explained. "He'll leave you be."

Her lips turned down at the corners. "I was hoping to apologize."

"Maybe later," Luke said. "How was the rest of your week?"

"Ice cream free." She laughed.

"So wrong," Luke muttered as they walked into the house.

21

Miranda saw Matthew arrive with Noah, Ethan, and Luke. But he disappeared before the circle. She didn't get a chance to say hello. By the time she saw him in the field where the circle stood, it was too late.

She tried to catch his eye to give him a wave. He seemed to be avoiding her gaze.

Is he mad at me? Should I not be here? she wondered. The thought made her stomach squirm with anxiety. Matthew didn't get mad in general and certainly never at her.

When Adaline's foot touched the line to close the circle, it flared, exploded outward, and collapsed, startling everyone.

"It's too out of balance. I can't have both of them in the wrong places," Sam muttered to Adaline.

"Miranda, move where Matty is. Jake and Matty, go stand by Ethan. Matty, you're across from Miranda," Sam directed.

"Talise, what is your name?" Sam called.

Talise looked around at all the eyes focused on her. "Sam, I told you. Talise Marie Ayers. I don't have another name."

Sam's irritation swept across the field, causing gasps and muttering.

"Tone it down, Sam," Noah muttered. "You're going to the scary side."

"Go, Miranda. Go stand where Jake was. You're not where you're supposed to be. Go. It won't hold if you're both out of place," Sam bitched.

She glanced at Matthew. His eyes were forward, pretending like she didn't exist.

Oh, God. He doesn't want me here, she thought, wanting to cry as she changed spots.

"Let's try this again," Sam yelled.

"Sam," Hank called in warning.

Sam's eyes were hot with fury when he turned to his dad. "This is wrong. It's not how it's supposed to be. We're somewhere we shouldn't be. I don't know what to do."

"Calm down. We'll figure it out," Hank soothed.

The circle stood on the second attempt.

Miranda had never been in a circle this large before. There were more people and more power in this circle than she imagined possible.

When it was her turn, she offered her excitement and joy at being included. Then, the circle pulled anxiety, fear, and loneliness from her, against her conscious will.

Well, that just happened, she thought as her cheeks flamed and the circle ripped away her embarrassment.

Matthew offered his calm and caring for others then seemed to fight against the energy. The circle wasn't having it. Miranda winced in sympathy as his jaw popped.

She sucked in a breath of recognition. *That's chaos energy. Pure chaos. Holy shit!*

The circle erupted in fire then the scent of blooming lavender. It snowed for a minute before lightning touched down next to Sam. Every animal within hearing range, from a screeching squirrel to bleating sheep, sang into the nighttime breeze. Then the wind gusted into a sudden, short storm burst of rain.

Sam shot Matthew an inquisitive look.

Matthew's eyebrows lifted. "It wasn't my idea, Sam."

∞

"WHAT THE FUCK?" Noah muttered to himself, running a hand through his damp hair.

"That was crazy!" the woman next to him enthused.

"Indeed."

"You're one of them, right?" she asked. "One of Luke's brothers?"

Noah nodded.

"Are you the sex god one?" Her grin was an invitation. "Talise kicked you last week, right? That's no way to greet newcomers. She's a shit-show. Don't judge us all based on her."

At her turn, Lucy dumped worry and stress into the circle.

Noah sighed. *No breakthrough in Ree's treatment.*

"It was a misunderstanding," Noah replied, not looking at the woman.

"Well, I'm sorry it happened all the same. She's the only one in this circle not interested in knowing you better."

And there's her sleazy lust energy. This was so much more fun when I didn't understand what was happening.

William shared hope and fear when it was his turn.

Noah nodded to himself, realizing he was getting better at understanding the circle energy. *Spot on for Will.*

"Thanks," he finally said, realizing the woman next to him was waiting for a response. "Is that your husband standing on the other side of you? That you walked out here with, hand in hand?"

The smiling invitation appeared again. "It is. He'd like to know you better, too."

"Ah. Thanks."

Fuck my life. These people suck. And not in the fun way. Or not only in the fun way.

The woman's husband shared shyness and excitement with the whole circle as he smiled toward Noah.

At her turn, the woman dumped pure lust into the energy mix, staring at Noah to see his reaction.

Noah's eyes stayed fixed on the ground as he dumped scorn and pity into the circle. When he looked up, he met Talise's eyes on the other side of the field.

She flinched back, obviously upset, as Noah's emotional energy hit her.

Holy hell, Hot Brunette. No wonder you're so twitchy, surrounded by these assholes.

SHE'S A MARRIED WOMAN. *Married woman. Married woman. I'm just going to stay away,* Matthew mentally coached himself as he walked back to the farmhouse after the circle.

He had fought back the urge to gag when the circle spread her loneliness among them. It was none of his business. She hadn't intentionally shared that feeling.

Not unlike my fucking madness, he acknowledged. *Now, these people are afraid of Sam AND me. Hurrah!*

"Matthew?" Miranda said from right behind him, interrupting his mental pity party. She was breathless, jogging to keep up with his long strides.

He immediately slowed down. By the time he realized what he was doing, it would have been rude to speed up again.

"Hi, Randa," he said, tone neutral.

"S-Sam called and asked if I would come here tonight," she blurted, anxiously chewing on the inside of her lip.

"It's good that you could make it. The circle is interesting, isn't it?" he asked, tone still neutral.

She nodded. "I haven't had a circle in a long time. Not since my grandmother died."

"Huh," he said, unsure what to do to end this conversation.

"I didn't realize you were Jake's brother," she said, talking fast. "Small world, right?"

"Please don't be mad at me!"

Matthew came to a full stop, steadying her when she almost fell over from trying to stop too fast.

"I'm not mad. At all. It's great to see you. Why would you think I'm mad?"

"You just don't seem like yourself," she admitted. "I didn't know you had energy. When we were in school? I didn't know."

No fucking kidding, Miranda. I kept it away from you.

"It's not something I talk about. I don't exactly make the earth bloom with health," he muttered.

"But usually, I can tell. I couldn't tell," she said. "You had it then?"

He nodded.

"Would it have mattered?" she asked, voice quiet.

His eyebrows shot up.

"If you knew I had it, too?"

She just had a brilliant display of my energy. Why is she even asking this? Married. Married. Married. Married to Larry the shit-bag, he mentally chanted.

"Miranda." He sighed in frustration. "You are without question the sweetest, gentlest person I have ever known. I would not choose to involve you with the shit-show that is my energy. I stand by what I said to you then. I want better for you."

She nodded, staring at his chest.

"Speaking of shit-shows, he's fucking awful, Randa. Why? Why would you choose that?"

Miranda shook her head, still not meeting his eyes. "It's a long story. Things got away from me. By the time I realized it, I was stuck."

"Get unstuck," Matthew suggested, tone flat.

She blew out a frustrated sigh of her own. "Easier said than done."

"Bullshit!" he barked. "File for a divorce and get out of there!"

She gave a cynical little laugh.

"You love him?"

"No."

"Did you love him?"

There was a long pause as she considered how to answer. "I loved the idea of him. My family liked him, my dad approved, and he treated me well at first."

"And now?"

Her shrug was somehow sad.

"What does that mean?"

"We should go inside. Jake and Matty probably want to hit the road. I came here with them."

"Please get out of there, Miranda," Matthew pleaded. "I can't stand the thought of you miserable with him."

"I don't have anywhere to go, Matthew. And you don't get to guilt-trip me." She stalked off toward the farmhouse, angry.

"Miranda?" Matthew called as she walked away.

She turned to look at him. When he didn't speak, she walked back to him. "What?"

"You know what my energy is?"

She nodded.

"I'll end it if you want me to," he whispered, cringing at his own words.

She laughed.

Matthew's eyes darted to meet hers.

"If I get desperate, I'll ditch him in a sinkhole in the backyard. No need to get exotic. I'm holding out hope he knocks his girlfriend up before it gets that far."

Matthew laughed, startled. "I don't believe for a second that you're capable of that."

She made a so-so gesture with her hand. "If it gets bad enough. Or the incentive to leave is good enough. Maybe."

TALISE AND LUKE were walking toward the farmhouse when Adaline caught up to them.

"Hi," Addy said, falling into step with Talise.

Talise bowed her head in respect. "Mistress Life."

Adaline frowned.

"Are you all right, Sam?" Luke asked, laughing as Sam caught up.

"Why were we running? And why do you move so damn fast?" Sam complained at Adaline. "Holy shit."

Addy grinned at him.

"I am not out of shape," Sam said.

She kept grinning.

"I'm not! I feel great!"

She didn't respond.

"Maybe some cardio would be good?" Luke asked. "You were wasting away for a while."

Sam frowned at his youngest brother. "I'm not out of shape! She's fast!"

Adaline rolled her eyes.

"I wondered if I could help you with shielding emotions," Addy said to Talise, suddenly shy. "I know how to do that."

Sam's forehead creased with concern. He caught meaning in her words that the others didn't.

Luke raised his eyebrows but let it drop at Sam's minute head shake.

"I would be very grateful for your assistance, Mistress," Talise murmured respectfully, eyes downcast.

Adaline sighed as she reached for Talise's hand. At the touch, Adaline did nothing to hide her feelings of being lost and somewhat lonely.

Talise stopped walking, startled. The emotions were not overwhelming, but they were apparent, along with joy, love, peace, bravery, and fear.

"May I share a binding with you? So that we can speak in thoughts and I can find you to visit? Shielding will take time and practice to learn. I will come to see you when Sam works, if that's okay?" Adaline asked.

"Please," Talise said, still trying to process the wave of Addy's emotions as they entered the house.

∞

NOAH STOOD ALONE in the front yard, waiting for his brothers.

The circle is over. How long does it take to wander outside and get in the fucking car? he mentally complained, shrugging off the people staring at him.

The sound of Luke's laughter rolled out through the front windows.

Since when is Luke a social butterfly?

"You're Noah, right?" a girl's voice said from behind him as her interest pinged off his brain.

Noah suppressed his eye-roll as he turned to her. "Hi."

Fuck my life, she can't be more than fourteen.

"Hiya. I'm Jamie," she bounced.

Was that supposed to be a boob bounce?

Noah stared at her.

"Are you waiting for someone? Want some company?" she asked, touching his arm.

"Go away. Please," Noah said with no inflection.

"Huh?"

"Go away."

"Are you grumpy?" she asked with a flirty smile. "I can make you—"

He snorted, interrupting her. "Uh-huh. Go away. You're like twelve."

"I'm seventeen!" She was trying for outraged but looked more petulant.

"You're fourteen," a voice said from behind him.

"Like you know anything, Talise. Gonna kick him again, bitch? You were more fun to be around when you couldn't remember shit. At least we got a good chuckle at your stupidity," Jamie sneered.

Noah's temper flared. "Jamie, you look like a little girl playing dress-up in mommy's role-playing hooker outfit. Save the boob bounce for after the girls grow in, hun. Fuck off."

Jamie's mouth dropped open in shock as her eyes filled with tears.

Noah's stomach dropped. *Holy shit. When did I start verbally attacking little girls? I gotta get out of here.*

He stomped away without a backward glance.

"Noah! Please wait!" Talise called.

His steps sped up.

22

The next morning, Talise was sitting at the kitchen table in her pajamas while her parents got ready for their day.

Without warning, Adaline's voice was in her head. The words came through as if Addy was sitting right next to Talise, sharing her overnight oats.

"Good morning, Talise. Sam goes to work today. May I visit you?" Adaline asked.

Talise almost fell out of her chair.

"What's wrong?" Monica's eyes were huge, terrified that some new tragedy would befall the family.

"Um, the Mistress spoke to me. In my head."

Mike was on his feet, sharing his wife's sense of ill-boding. "I can call Greggory. Maybe something is just—"

"No. I'm fine, Dad. She told me she would visit to help me work on shielding emotions from others. She told me she'd reach out like this. I just didn't think it'd be so…sudden. Startling," Talise explained. "Sorry to freak you out."

"She's going to come here?" Monica's panic was transferring to house chores.

"Well, I think she would, but I don't know how to answer her," Talise admitted.

There was a knock on the front door, making everyone jump.

"Um," Mike said, getting up. "I'll get it? I guess?"

It was seven-fifteen a.m. Very few people would be visiting at this time.

"Good morning." Sam's voice was cheery as it drifted back to the kitchen from the front door.

"W-walker. Good morning. Mistress," Mike stammered out.

"We're not very smart," Sam admitted. "Addy made the binding to talk to Tali, but neither of us explained how to answer. I was going to call Luke to get a phone number for you, but he's cranky when he doesn't get his beauty rest."

That made Talise grin as she walked to the front door.

"Hi, Talise!" Sam called as she approached the door.

It wasn't until she was at the door with her dad that she realized Sam's smile and cheer were brittle. He was nervous. Nervous and ashamed.

"Why a—?" she started to ask.

"He dislikes that you are afraid of him. It hurts him. Please don't ask him about it," Adaline shared.

"Why are you here so early?" Talise asked instead, earning a smile of thanks from Addy.

"Mostly because I keep forgetting that it's an hour later at the lake house in Michigan. I'm terrible with time zones," Sam said.

Talise grinned before she thought better of it. "Oh, fearsome *Time* Walker."

Sam laughed, smiling for real as some of the tension left his shoulders.

"Tali, do you want to work on shields this morning? Do you have time?" Adaline asked, a little smile shining in her eyes.

"I have nothing but time, Mistress. No life at all, other than dancing and music. Please come in," Talise said, ignoring her mother's squeak from behind her.

"Walker, Mistress, welcome," Monica murmured, head bowed. "May I bring you breakfast? Coffee? Anything?"

"Anything?" Sam asked.

Monica looked up, surprised. "You are welcome to anything I have."

Sam sighed. "Then I would have your friendship, Mrs. Ayers. I mean no harm to you or yours. The titles and formality make me sad, in the same way that people pandering for money make me sad. I am socially awkward at the best of times; this new wrinkle has made it more profound. Please. I am just Sam. She is Adaline."

Unsure what to say, Monica nodded. "Call me Monica, please."

"I can come back later today," Addy offered. Her voice faltered into resigned tones as she continued. "I don't have anything at all to do. Not even dancing or music. So when you—"

"No!" Talise exclaimed, already moving toward her bedroom. "I want to do this. It'll just take me a minute to get dressed if you don't mind waiting."

"I'm going to go bother Hank," Sam said, grinning at Adaline. "I'll ride into work with him."

"Tell him I say hi," Adaline said, laughing. "I'll bring Glinda over this afternoon."

Sam rolled his eyes. "You don't have to humor him. She'll be moving in before he knows it."

"I told him I would, so I will," she replied. "Have fun at work!"

Sam pulled a face, startling a laugh out of Monica and Mike both. "Work was only fun when *I* didn't have better things to do. Now it's just silly."

"Amen to that," Mike agreed, laughing.

"What do you do for a living?" Sam asked, trying to make small talk while waiting for Talise to come back. Adaline was more nervous than she appeared about this visit.

"Medical billing," Monica said. "I work from home."

"I'm a construction foreman," Mike responded.

Sam's eyes lit up. "What—?"

"No, Sam," Adaline said.

"But—"

"No."

"I wasn't going to ask him to teach me things! I was going to ask him to build me things!" Sam objected.

"No. Not right now," Adaline disagreed. "That will just make them more uncomfortable."

Sam frowned, disappointed. "Maybe later, then."

"I'm fine, love. Go bother Hank. Maybe Darla will make you waffles."

"She's making waffles?" Sam said, perking up.

"I imagine she would if you asked," Adaline said, smiling.

"Hmm. It is early yet."

Adaline nodded.

"I love you. Have fun shielding." Sam grinned, bending to give her a quick kiss.

"Bye, Talise!" Sam yelled, and then he was gone.

"Holy crap! He's gone!" Mike exclaimed.

Adaline grinned at him.

"No noise or fade or anything. If you blink, you miss it," he continued. "That's really neat."

"Mis—" Monica stopped herself at Adaline's sigh. "Adaline, would you like some breakfast? Something to drink?"

"Thank you, but Sam made omelets this morning," Addy said, fidgeting as she looked around.

Monica blinked. "Why was he looking for waffles, then?"

"He's a boy," Adaline said with a small smile, making Mike laugh.

"Fair point." Mike laughed. "Plus, they're waffles."

"I'm ready!" Talise called, leaping back into the room.

Adaline raised her eyebrows.

"Force of habit," Talise admitted. "I like to jump and spin. Where should we do this?"

"Somewhere quiet to start," Adaline suggested.

"THERE IS JOYFUL ENERGY IN HERE," Adaline said, her smile speaking volumes.

Talise nodded. "It is my favorite place. I spend a lot of time in this garage. My parents converted it not long after we moved. Even when my mind didn't work, my body knew dancing, and my soul knew music."

Addy walked the perimeter of the space. One whole side of the garage was mirrored with a ballet barre. Another wall was full of family pictures, awards, and high school playbills. She paused to look at the pictures. A younger Talise leaped through the air in one collection. In another section, she was singing on a stage. There was a painting of Talise at about the same age as Jess's Mia, lacing up ballet slippers.

"Who paints?" Adaline asked.

"My mom used to paint," Talise said, tone flat.

Adaline could feel the pain in Talise's words, so she changed topics. "You went to school?"

Talise nodded.

"What was it like?" Adaline asked, thinking back to Sam's description.

"Miserable," Talise said, surprised and a bit annoyed when Adaline burst out laughing.

"Samuel says the same thing in exactly the same way," she explained, grinning. "I hoped you could give me a different perspective, but no. It makes sense."

"You didn't go to school?"

"No," Adaline said simply.

"Why?"

"I was dying. Until Sam finally came, the power was killing me a little more each day. Even as a small child, there was too much energy."

Talise could feel the sadness and loneliness rolling off Adaline. "I'm sorry."

"Me, too. But it is done now." Addy said the words with a lightness that didn't align with her feelings.

Talise stared at her.

"Your emotional awareness is excellent. I think maybe even better than it was last week. Shields will come easily once you know how," Adaline said with a small smile.

"So much sadness, Mistress?" Talise asked, undeterred.

"I'm lost. I don't know what to do now," Adaline admitted. "I think maybe you understand that feeling better than anyone else."

Talise nodded. "I do."

"We will find our way together," Addy declared.

"WE NEED JOBS," Talise declared, sitting on the garage floor, eating lunch.

Adaline's face was a question mark.

They had spent the morning practicing emotional shielding from each other before taking a break so Adaline could return to the lake house to let the puppies outside.

"Purpose. Independence," Talise added. "No?"

"You cannot tolerate people. And unless it involves channeling the energies of the universe, I'm completely useless. What jobs do you think would suit us?" Adaline asked.

"I don't know. I didn't get that far," Talise admitted. "But I don't want to sit in my parents' garage forever."

Adaline nodded in agreement.

"The only things I've ever liked to do are dancing and singing, but I haven't really tried doing anything else. What would you do if you could do anything?" Talise asked.

Adaline smiled. *"I would go to school. I would know things and meet people."*

"Well, you can absolutely do that," Talise agreed. "Though I think you're overestimating the wonders of the classroom."

"I cannot go to school," Adaline disagreed.

"Why not?" Talise frowned.

LATER THAT AFTERNOON, Monica answered a knock at the front door.

"Where's my wife?" Sam laughed. "I thought she'd be home long before now!"

"Your wife? I didn't realize you were married," Monica said, startled.

Sam shrugged. "Well, 'soul-bound lover' sounds awfully dramatic. 'Wife' is better shorthand."

"She's in the garage with my daughter, being ridiculous," Monica said, grinning. "Maybe get married so 'wife' is accurate?"

"Bah. Jake and Matilda are getting married first. Then probably Hennessy and Beth. Maybe then, if Adrian and Lucy aren't ready. With my luck, I'd ask, and she'd say no," Sam said, grinning in return. "They're having fun?"

"Thick as thieves, giggling in the garage. I have no idea what they're doing out there, but I heard Tali shriek, 'He did not!' a few minutes ago." She laughed, leading him through the house.

After a knock on the door, Monica opened the garage door to find both women sitting on the floor, facing each other in silence.

"Boo!" Sam teased, walking into the garage behind Monica. "Don't let her do that, Talise! She needs to practice words."

Talise took one look at Sam and burst out laughing.

"What'd I do?" he asked her.

She kept laughing, actually tipping over as she tried to catch her breath.

"What'd I do?" Sam asked Addy.

She beamed at him. "I love you."

"I love you, too." He smiled. "What'd I do?"

Addy just grinned.

"It was probably an accident, Tali," he said.

Talise gave another shout of laughter, wiping away tears of mirth.

"Whatever you told her, can you tell the rest of the circle? This is so much better than fear," Sam admitted.

"No, Sam. It's not a story to be shared," Adaline said, laughing.

Sam turned to look at Monica then back to the women on the floor. "What'd I do?"

"Oh, that's a great idea!" Talise teased.

"Oh," Sam said, turning to Monica. "They're talking about sex. They're laughing about me having sex."

Monica shook with silent laughter. "I didn't doubt it for a second, Sam."

Sam looked around at the laughing women. "Oh well."

"We will go to school, Sam," Adaline said suddenly, gesturing between Talise and herself. "Tali will practice shields, and I will practice reading and writing, and then we will go to school."

Sam's eyebrows lifted.

"We will do things," Adaline said, resolved. "Talise will not live in this garage for the rest of her life, and I will not spend my days ignorant. I am better now. I will get better at being in crowded areas. Then, I will do things."

"Good." Sam nodded.

23

"So, what do you do for a living, Noah?" Kaylee asked over pizza on Wednesday night.

"Ah," Noah murmured, dropping his eyes. *I hate answering this question.*

"Uh oh." She smiled. "Unemployed? Living in your parents' basement?" she teased.

"Ha! No. Hank and Darla would kick my ass out. They were done living with me by the time I went to college."

"Hmm." She kept smiling. "Good. I'd hate to get stuck with the check."

"What do you do, Kaylee?"

"I'm a restaurant manager," she said, seeming to brace for some sort of reaction.

"Good restaurant?"

"Yep, very hipster. Very trendy. I hate it, but it pays the rent. Are you dodging my question?"

"I am." Noah grinned. "It's awkward."

"Oh, boy. Are you a gynecologist?" She grinned. "It could be worse. At least you'd know your way around."

Noah burst out laughing. "I am not a doctor of any sort, but I pride myself on being a lady bits specialist."

"Lady bits?" Her eyebrows hiked up, mocking.

He grinned. "No, I work with my brother."

"And what do you do?" she asked, taking the bait he offered.

"I oversee the development of new products in the electronics and technology sphere, primarily online shopping."

"You build online shopping?"

"I manage people that build online shopping," he corrected.

"Woo, a *manager*." She laughed with a little head swagger. "How big is your team?"

And here we go…

"Three thousand, six hundred fifty-four people."

She froze.

"My brother's company is Trellis Industries. I'm Noah Trellis."

After a charged silence, she chuckled.

"You're rich?"

He nodded, not meeting her eyes.

"A billionaire, right?"

Noah nodded again.

"Why are we eating pizza?"

Noah's eyebrows hiked up, meeting her eyes. "Because pizza is good. You don't like pizza?"

"I do like pizza. I like two thousand-dollar bottles of wine more, though." She grinned.

"But if you get stuck with the check…" he teased.

"Noah, you're wearing jeans and a t-shirt. It's a designer t-shirt, but still."

"And? What do you imagine billionaires wear while eating pizza?"

"Armani?"

"I think you overestimate the comfort of suits. Ick."

She rolled her eyes, quiet for a moment, processing things.

"Are we headed to your place or mine after dinner?" Kaylee asked, her flirty smirk back in place.

It was Noah's turn to pause.

Is she interested in me? In the money? Or in the energy? Do I care? It never occurred to me before, but I'm curious now.

"I have to work tomorrow. Maybe dinner on Friday?" he suggested.

Kaylee's head tipped to the side in surprise.

Noah grinned. "I haven't taken things slow before. Let's give it a try."

"Bummer," she said with a little laugh. "There will be good wine on Friday, Noah."

"So be it." He smiled.

"NOAH, THIS PLACE IS NOT FANCY," Kaylee observed Friday night.

"It's true."

"Why are we eating at a hole-in-the-wall restaurant?"

"It's not a hole-in-the-wall. It's incredibly clean and well-organized," Noah said primly. "We're eating here because the food is amazing. It's the best Mediterranean food I've found outside of the actual Mediterranean."

"Noah, we ordered at a counter, and then you picked our food up from the kitchen. There's not even a waitstaff here."

"Well, there is. They take the dishes and clean the tables and booths. Don't judge. It's a family place. Do you like the food?" he asked, eyebrows raised.

"I do."

"Are you complaining about the wine?" he asked, smiling.

"No, I'm just surprised that you brought the wine here. They didn't serve it. It's bring-your-own-bottle, for crying out loud. Are you a penny-pinching billionaire?" she teased.

"Is it good wine?"

She grinned. "I already told you it's the best wine I've ever had."

"The date requirement was 'good wine.' I chose to accompany it with delicious eats in an atypical venue." Noah smiled, raising a challenging eyebrow, daring her to disagree.

"I can't decide if you're trolling me or not. Are you obtuse on purpose?"

His smile fell a bit. "I'm not trolling you, Kaylee. I eat here because the food is great and the family that runs the restaurant is wonderful. I am happy to give them my business. We're drinking a seven-thousand-dollar bottle of wine because it accompanies the meal well. Look around you. The restaurant is spotless, crowded, and efficient. There are generations of family pictures on the walls, live plants as decorations, and comfortable seating. We could sit here for hours, drinking our beverage of choice, and no one would bother us."

He shrugged after a short pause. "This is the kind of place I like to frequent when I'm on my own. I haven't brought a date here in the past. We can do a fancier date at a trendier restaurant where the food isn't as good, and the decor isn't as charming. But you work in a place like that. I thought you might enjoy the change of pace. If this doesn't work for you, though, we'll do something more ordinary the next time around."

"Wow," she replied. "That was surprisingly thoughtful, Noah. Touching, really."

He nodded.

"Thank you for sharing this place with me. The food is great, the wine is awesome. Both pale in comparison to the company." She smiled, squeezing his hand on the table.

"I'm not a penny-pincher, Kaylee. I don't have any problem with spending money. But the money isn't ingrained into who I am. My family was upper-middle class until Sam started raking it in. I've been known to frequent a high-end restaurant in a fancy suit. I can do that. We can do that if it's really what you want. I'm not opposed to it. But I'm also a beer and pizza kind of guy when the mood strikes. If that's not your scene, so be it."

"Well, here's the real question, Noah: What are you making me for breakfast in the morning?" The smirk was back.

Noah huffed out a little laugh. "Here's a better question: What are you doing for dinner on Sunday night?"

∞

"SEE, ICE CREAM IS GREAT!" Luke cheered on Saturday afternoon.

Talise smiled.

"Oh, come on! You did awesomely! In short sleeves, no less."

She nodded. "It's true. No one touched me, so that made it easier."

"I didn't have to help at all." He grinned.

"Adaline came over earlier this week," Talise explained. "She's teaching me. It's not as hard as I thought it would be."

"Adaline has a gift for making complex topics simple. I think it is why she and Sam fit together so well. Sam has a habit of overcomplicating everything. Most of the time, we understand what Adaline is saying. That's not as true with Sam."

"She's wonderful," Talise agreed.

"She's awesome. But that awesomeness pales in comparison to you making it through ice cream!"

"You're relatively easy to please. You know that, right?" She laughed.

"Gotta count the little victories," Luke said. "I'm so proud of you."

She flushed a lovely pink color. "It's ice cream, Luke. I have a long way to go."

"I know, but this is a big step. Last week, you were so scared to leave the house, you were all but frozen in place."

"I have to practice with more people than just my parents. So, I will actually go for ice cream when you ask." Talise smiled at him.

"Want to cash in the Sunday dinner raincheck? You can practice with my family." Luke grinned.

"Will that be awkward?"

"No, it will be ridiculous. My family is absurd. I get shit about not bringing you to dinner daily. Come to dinner!"

Talise pressed her lips together. "If I screw up the shielding—"

"Addy and I will both be there, Talise. We'll help if you need it."

She was silent for a moment.

"Why the hesitation? My family won't judge. They know you're adjusting to a lot."

"Ugh. I kicked your brother. I'm still mortified by that. I tried to talk to him on Monday. He just walked away from me."

Luke's expression went flat. "Tali, Noah is fine. He won't give you any grief."

"I'm not worried about him giving me grief. I'm worried that he hates me because I freaked out."

"Shush and eat your dipped cone! You're coming to dinner tomorrow. I'll pick you up at six o'clock sharp."

"Did you have to get large cones? This is unwieldy."

Luke grinned again. "Eat it quick. Things get out of hand if the ice cream melts before you eat the chocolate."

"WELL, IT'S ABOUT DAMN TIME!" Darla cheered, walking to meet Luke and Talise as they came in the front door on Sunday. "More chairs, Luke. More chairs!"

Darla blew Tali a kiss without touching her.

Luke grinned, kissing the top of Darla's head. "What's for dinner?"

Darla glared. "I don't want any lip about it. Your brothers have been bitching since they got here."

"Why?" Luke asked.

"We're grilling. Burgers, chicken, hot dogs, brats, corn on the cob, baked potatoes, coleslaw, and three-bean salad."

Luke's lips twitched as he tried to fight off a smile. "No lasagna?"

"Well, if you had told me Talise was coming, I absolutely would have made it," Darla complained. "We'll have to test her next week."

Talise's eyebrows shot up.

"I make lasagna when new people come to dinner. If the new person refuses to eat it, we get to take a family vote on whether they get to stay in our combined lives," Darla explained.

Talise frowned. "Dietary restrictions aside, who refuses lasagna?"

"Exactly," Luke and Darla said together.

"We're just missing Sam and Addy. Noah brought a date, too. Don't quote me on this, but I think he's known her longer than three days," Darla quietly murmured as they walked toward the big room.

"Date? Is this a date?" Talise whispered, slightly confused.

Luke grinned at her. "Don't ruin Darla's fun. There are worse things than going on a date, Tali."

She smirked at him.

"What does that smirk mean?" Luke laughed.

"No convincing necessary when it comes to dating you, Lucas. Get with the program," she whispered as they turned the corner into the big room.

"Why do you look confused?" Matthew asked Luke.

"Never mind. Hi, everyone. I think most of you know Talise."

"Kaylee, this is my youngest brother, Luke, and his friend, Talise. Don't touch her. She freaks out," Noah said before he returned to talking with Jake and Matty.

It was as close as he'd come to talking with Talise since the day she kicked him. While Noah's tone was indifferent, Talise caught a spike of fear from him.

She winced. *Is he afraid I'm going to kick him again? I don't know how to make this better.*

From beside her, Talise could sense Luke's annoyance.

"Noah, don't be a jerk—" Luke paused when Talise squeezed his hand.

"Don't," she whispered to Luke. "It's my fault."

Before he could respond, Sam and Adaline arrived with the pack of puppies.

Sam glanced at Talise, then Luke, then Noah and Kaylee. His forehead creased as the air vibrated with his anger.

"This is not right," he complained. "We are somewhere we shouldn't be. Why are we still here?"

The room went still.

"Sam, we have guests," Hank said, pointedly looking at Kaylee.

"I don't give a flying fuck, Dad. I don't know who she is," Sam yelled, eyes starting to glow with energy. "This isn't right. I have no idea where we are. I can't find us. Talise is not where she's supposed to be. Miranda's married to the shit-bag. This is wrong. It just keeps getting more off course. I don't know what to do. I don't know how to fix it."

"Samuel," Darla growled. "Get yourself together. You are being excessively rude to our guests, and there are little ears present. If you can't be nice, sit down and shut up."

Sam threw himself into a wingback chair on the opposite end of the big room without another word. Adaline's gaze traveled from Sam to her family, to Hank and Darla, then to Noah. She frowned then turned to sit with Sam.

The room was awkward and silent for a half dozen heartbeats.

"So, that's my brother, Sam. He's nuts. And that's Adaline. She's awesome. They found a box of puppies a couple of weeks ago. Addy is taking care of them until they're old enough to go to their forever homes, but the puppies come for dinner, too," Noah explained. "Hope you don't mind the dog hair. That's everyone."

"There are a lot of you people." Kaylee grinned, nervous.

"Don't sweat it. I won't quiz you until after your third family dinner," Noah teased.

"Onward!" Matty cheered. "Now that everyone's here. We have exciting news! Ahem."

She paused, shooting Beth a look.

"The engagement party is booked for the second to last Saturday in September. Save the date!"

All heads swiveled to Hennessy, though Talise and Kaylee looked confused.

"I thought she was with Jake?" Kaylee whispered.

Noah grinned. "She is. But booking the party was a prerequisite."

Hennessy glanced at Beth, eyebrows raised.

"N-no. Not now. Not in front of everyone. No," she stuttered.

"Boo!" Hank bellowed.

"Daddy," Beth muttered.

The room exploded in laughter.

"Oh, no. Don't you 'Daddy' me, Bethany Rose! Your mother told me about the proposed elopement. No. Absolutely not," Hank said, serious.

"Get on your knees and start begging like all good Trellis men!" Will yelled, slapping Hennessy on the shoulder.

"Nonononononono," Beth panicked. "No! Jessup! Get up!"

"Bethany," Hennessy said, on bent knee in front of her.

"No! NO! Not like this! Yikes! NO!" Beth squealed.

Hennessy paused, his expression downtrodden as he looked at her. "Really, no? Like the answer is 'no?'"

Beth's eyes went wide. "What? No. Stop it. You know that's not what I mean."

"Do I?" he asked.

The room fell into a heavy silence.

"I love you more than I have loved anything. Anyone. Ever. I want to get married and have a family together. That scares the shit out of me, Beth. I don't know how to do that. The only model I've ever had for how a family should behave is here, in this room.

"So, tell me. Are you just not ready for this? More time? That's fine. You don't need to come up with another delay. You can just say that."

Beth's mouth opened and closed without words coming out. She shook her head.

"You don't want this with me? I would understand. I swear to God, I would. I'm damaged goods, babe. I've never pretended otherwise."

"Hennessy, no! I meant not here, not in front of everyone," Beth choked out, breathing hard.

"Why?" he asked, baffled. "You people share *everything* anyway. Why not this?"

"They're going to make fun of me for crying like a girl!" she wailed, bursting into tears.

Hennessy was dumbstruck.

Will and Emma started shaking with silent laughter.

Hennessy looked around the room. "I don't know what's happening right now. Are these happy tears? Sad tears? Confused tears? What do I do?"

"This is the part where you ask her to marry you," Hank stage-whispered.

"While she's crying? Shouldn't that stop first?"

Hank winced, swallowing back laughter. "It's not going to stop for a while. There will be snot involved."

"DAD!" Beth screeched. "Don't ruin this!"

"Oh, yeah, because I'm the problem right now," Hank snarked as choked giggles broke out throughout the room.

Hennessy turned to his best friend.

"Go for gold, man. You got it in the bag." William grinned.

A deep breath in and out, then Jessup spoke again. "Please marry me, Beth. Teach me what happily-ever-after is all about."

"Oh, man. So cheesy. So great!" Emma exclaimed, wiping tears away.

Even through her emotional shields, the family's overwhelming love and acceptance rolled into Talise's mind. Louder than all the emotions in the room, Noah radiated positivity and excitement, joy and love for his sister.

It must be something to be loved that much, Talise thought with a touch of envy for Beth. *So much hope and passion for life in this room.*

Glancing over, Noah met Talise's eyes briefly before dropping his eyes again.

By the time the ring slid on Beth's finger, the only dry eyes left in the room had belonged to Noah's girlfriend.

"Sam! You fail!" Noah yelled.

"What? Why?" Sam asked, sounding insulted. "This is the *only* thing that's on track."

"You're supposed to warn us so we can lock down the man tears!" Noah bitched, smiling.

"Boo!" yelled the Trellis men in unison, startling a loud snort of laughter out of Talise.

"Yeah, I deserved that." Noah laughed. "But I triggered a real snort out of the ballerina. Score!"

Talise blushed as she laughed.

Maybe we can move past the kick, Talise thought, hopeful.

"Gee, thanks, Noah. Don't worry, I won't tell anyone about your panicked search for tissue," she teased.

He didn't respond. If she hadn't been sitting three feet away from him, she'd assume he hadn't heard her.

Or maybe not.

"Champagne!" Hank cheered, hopping off the couch. "Who's next?"

24

"So the engagement party is essentially six weeks from now," Matty explained to Miranda. They were standing with Talise in the field behind Nora's farmhouse the following Monday, waiting for the circle to start.

"Darla wants to dress shop next week. Are you up for it?" Matilda asked Talise. "It'd be great if you could come with us."

Talise nodded. "We'll try it. I should be fine. Luke is helping me practice the shields. I'm getting better at them. It sounds like fun. I can't wait to meet your friends."

Miranda smiled. "They're fun. Lawrence is going to be out of town next week, so it shouldn't be a problem for me. So exciting!"

"Meh," Matilda said. "Everyone's going to stare at me."

Miranda pulled a face, making both women laugh. "You need to let go of that stage fright."

Matty grinned. "Easier said than done. Anyway, Beth and Lucy are already onboard with the shopping plans. Emma won't go because she doesn't want to get spotted. We just need to ask Addy now. I am, admittedly, more excited about shopping for the party than I am for the party itself."

Talise pulled an affronted look across her face. "Matty! Music and dancing? Come on! It's going to be great."

"Um, maybe for you, Ms. Ballerina. It's not my scene." Matilda laughed.

"But you even have someone to dance with!" Talise objected. "Boo!"

"Talise," Matty said with a completely straight face, "there are eight Trellis boys. I'm certain you'll never want for a partner, even if Luke lets go of your hand for a few minutes."

Talise blushed, looking around the circle. Luke was in the house. Noah and Ethan were directly across the field from her. Noah's face was lit with laughter, dark chocolate eyes dancing, as he and Ethan talked.

I fucked that up. We're not friends because I freaked out. She sighed, again regretting her snap reaction on the day she kicked him.

She waved. Noah turned around, pretending like he didn't see the gesture.

"Wow," Matty said.

"Yeah. He hates me." Talise said. "I've tried to talk to him at least a half dozen times to apologize. He just walks away like I'm not even there."

Matilda frowned. "I don't think Noah does 'hate,' Talise. Maybe he didn't see you."

Talise shot Matty a look.

"Still, seven Trellis boys. Seven out of eight is good enough. You won't want for a dance partner," Matilda assured her.

Hot brunette is absolutely beautiful. I wonder what Kaylee's doing after work tonight, Noah thought.

"Talise can probably feel you staring at her, Noah," Ethan said, joining his brother in the field behind Nora's farmhouse. They were standing directly opposite of Matilda, Miranda, and Talise.

Noah had been staring off into space for several minutes, mind wandering as he watched the women laugh.

"I wasn't really staring at her," he lied. "More just wool-gathering. How are you, Ethan? I haven't talked to you all week."

"Why are you standing here, staring at Luke's girlfriend?" Ethan asked.

Noah started a bit at that. "I wasn't really staring at her, just admiring the view: beautiful women and all that. Luke's with her now? I haven't talked with him, either."

"I don't think officially yet, but it's going to happen. They're perfect together."

Noah nodded, somehow sad. *I'm glad Sam made his head explode. Luke sucks.*

Then he gave his head a violent shake. *What the fuck?*

"You okay?" Ethan asked.

"Yeah, I'm fine. Just out of sorts."

"Well, I mean, you've been seeing the same woman for more than a week and haven't slept with her yet, right? That's gotta be a record. Honestly never thought I'd see this day."

Noah snorted. "Just a week, but yeah. A couple of dates. No sex yet. Probably a record."

"Are you in love?" Ethan asked, drawing the word out.

Noah laughed again. "She's fun. It's a little early for love, though."

When his eyes drifted back across the field, Talise was looking at them.

She waved to Ethan.

Fuck you, too, Ethan, he thought, knowing his irritation was misplaced.

Rather than get annoyed, he turned his back to the women.

"Are we doing suits or tuxedos for the engagement party?" Noah asked.

"Mom says tux. Jake says jeans. Probably suits." Ethan laughed, completely missing Talise's wave.

"ICE CREAM DAY AGAIN ALREADY?" Talise laughed, opening the front door as Luke walked up the sidewalk on Wednesday afternoon.

He grinned. "More like, 'Check on Tali' day. How is shielding going? Obviously better. You didn't tackle me in the front yard."

"Did you want me to tackle you? I'm willing to do it, just for the fun of it."

He grinned again. "How are shields?"

She smiled, greeting him with a hug and a shrug. "Good. I'm not getting as much random noise from the neighbors."

"Have you been out and about?"

"Nope," she admitted with a sheepish little smile.

"Challenge mode! Let's go to the mall and walk around with a bunch of hormonal teenagers."

She laughed like it was a joke.

"I'm not kidding. Go put on shoes. Let's do it!"

Talise's expression turned flat. "I'm not going to the mall, Lucas. Online shopping is my friend."

He clapped his hands. "Mall! Mall and buttery pretzels! Given the lack of ice cream in your life, I'm nearly certain you're also missing out on the junk food binge that is mall soft pretzels."

Her face flickered with uncertainty.

"We'll leave if it's too much, Tali," Luke soothed. "But I know you can do this. Sam told me you're going to go to school with Addy in the spring. That's amazing. I want to see that happen. So let's push the boundaries. No more hiding."

"You won't be upset if I want to leave?" Talise asked.

Luke sighed. "Tali, am I ever upset with you? We've been friends for most of a decade. Have I *ever* been angry with you?"

She shook her head. "No, but until the mental tie was removed, your feelings toward me were more like pity. Your emotions haven't leveled off in this new reality yet."

That gave Lucas pause. "Pity? I hated that you were tied and trapped in your mind. We had so much fun with music together, I hoped for better for you. More for you. I don't think pity is the right word for that."

They were quiet, walking into the house together.

"There's an opportunity for better now. For more now. I want to see what you do with it." He smiled. "But it's your life. I'll nudge and push, but I can't make you do it."

Looking up into his eyes, Talise sighed. "I told you I would try. I am working on it. We can attempt the mall. I'll be right back. I need to change."

Standing on tiptoe, she kissed Luke's cheek before heading out of the room.

"HOLY SHIT," Kaylee muttered against Noah's mouth late Friday night. "I wondered if you were going to continue with the monk routine forever."

Her mouth drifted up his jaw to his ear as he chuckled.

"You have no idea how funny that is." Noah laughed. "It's just two weeks since you tried giving me your phone the first time, Kaylee. Not exactly forever."

"Feels longer, Noah. Feels like I've known you forever," she said, reaching for his belt as his hands wandered under her shirt, making her gasp.

"Impatient?" Noah teased.

"Fuck, yes." She grinned. "Work sucked tonight. Take my mind off it."

"Aww," Noah breathed. "Rude restaurant patrons?"

"Hipster idiots," she murmured. "No respect for the working woman at all."

"Poor you," Noah teased.

"Poor me," Kaylee agreed. "Stupid work."

Noah had been careful about keeping the energy tucked away around her. Confident this attraction was natural on both their parts, he slowly shifted his power to neutral while lifting her shirt away.

Kaylee's lust and excitement roared into his mind, distracting him as he tossed her shirt toward the couch so it wouldn't end up a ball on the floor. Her fingers dug into his back as she ground her hips against him, breathing hard.

As he bent to nibble the sensitive skin on her neck, she moaned. "Noah, hurry up. Holy fuck, hurry up. Fast now, slow later."

She ripped his shirt in her haste to get it off, tugging at his pants as she dropped to her knees in front of him.

LATER THAT NIGHT, as Kaylee slept tucked in beside him, Noah ran a hand down her bare back, listening to her steady breathing.

"Noah," she mumbled in her sleep, snuggling further under the covers next to him.

This is new. Noah smiled to himself, feeling her desire in his mind, even while she slept.

"WE'RE DOING Labor Day at the lake house in Michigan. You're welcome to join us if you want," Matilda said into her wireless headset later that week.

Miranda considered how to respond, adjusting her cellphone to her other ear. "I would love to, Matty, but I know Lawrence won't go for it, and he'll be unhappy if I go without him."

"God forbid Larry be unhappy," Matilda said before her brain caught up with her mouth. "Sorry. I shouldn't have said that."

"No, it's a fair point. He doesn't seem to mind making me unhappy. I'd just rather push that particular argument off for a little bit longer," Miranda said thoughtfully.

"Wow," Matty said, surprised that Miranda would be so calm about things. "Are you okay?"

"I'm good. Just a lot to think about. Sam called yesterday."

"Oh?"

"He told me that he'd help me leave if I want to part ways with

Larry. Lawrence. Lawrence. Holy cow, I've called him Larry three times in the last week. He lost his shit." Miranda laughed.

Matilda was silent for a few seconds.

"Sam is good people," Miranda whispered.

"The very best," Matilda agreed, swallowing tears.

"He wasn't trying to white-knight me or push me in any direction at all. He just wanted me to know he had my back if I needed it," Miranda said, her own tears in her voice.

"He means that. You know that, right? He...he helped me a lot. Helped me find my way when I was so confused about Jake," Matty said.

"I know he means it. I still can't imagine you being confused about Jake," Miranda admitted. "I've never seen two people more in love. You're so confident about your life and career. How could you question that?"

Matty took a deep breath, nodding even though no one could see her. The words came out slowly. "It was not one of my better choices in life. Career success can be measured. Quantified. Analyzed. My craft can be refined to be better on the next big project. It's easy to have confidence when there are metrics that point to awesomeness.

"Relationships were the opposite for me. All signs pointed to me being unworthy of this type of love with the kind of person that Jake is. A lifetime of shitty relationships with terrible, selfish people, Mom included, leaves a mark.

"We can't always be our best selves. He was too good, too perfect, to be true. Things that seem too good to be true are usually a pile of shit in disguise."

Miranda snorted a tiny, ladylike snort of laughter. "Sister, I feel that truth down to the marrow of my bones."

Matty laughed. "I thought you might. There's a world of difference between confidence and trust. I had plenty of confidence in my ability to live a happy, successful life. My definition of 'happy and successful' just didn't include Jake. I didn't trust that he'd want to be a part of it, long term.

"Before you and Jake and his family, I had precisely three friends in this world and no remaining family. They're amazing friends, and my life is better because they're a part of it. But I'm so bad at relationships that I don't even have coworkers. I'm an independent contractor. I have clients.

"All that to say, I don't trust easily. I'm working on it," Matilda finished, wiping tears from her cheeks.

"I wish I was there to hug you right now," Miranda whispered. "That had to hurt to admit out loud."

"I've been thinking it through. I hurt him. I owe him an explanation one day. Figured I might as well vent the first draft to you."

Miranda burst out in what sounded like teary laughter.

"We would help you, too, Miranda. You could come here. I hope you know that," Matty said.

"I do know that, but it's nice to hear all the same. Love you, Matty."

"Love you, little sister."

25

Luke was walking up Talise's front sidewalk right on time at two o'clock on the Friday afternoon before Labor Day.

Monica opened the door, grinning at him. "She's wearing *shorts,* Luke. Like, actual shorts. No tights or leggings under them."

Luke smiled. "Brave."

Monica nodded. "Please thank the Mistress for her help and instruction. There's been more progress in the last month than the last ten years."

Luke's smile morphed into a full grin. "I'm glad."

Monica hugged him then, standing on the front door stoop. "Thank you for bringing her back to us, Luke. You. Your brother. Your family. Saved us. All of us, not just her. There were days I only got out of bed because I knew she would need me."

Lucas hugged her back, sharing his peace. "Monica, are you okay?"

Talise's mom pulled away from him, wiping tears off her cheeks. "I'm good, Luke. Better than good. Sentimental and grateful and maybe a bit lost, but happy. She's not been away from us for more than two or three hours at a time since she was thirteen. And most of those outings have been with you, especially in the last month."

"We don't have to go this weekend. She doesn't have to go. I just thought she'd enjoy the lake house. It's pretty. Isolated. A lot of open land around it. Addy and Sam have been staying there while their house is being built. It sleeps a lot of people. Do you and Mike want to come with us? I didn't even think to ask. The main house has ten bedrooms and a kid's bunk room. The guest house has four more bedrooms," Luke offered.

"What in the world is a kid's bunk room?" Monica laughed, leading Luke through the house and into the kitchen. "She's just finishing packing."

"The lake house was the first house Sam ever built. Or, more accurately, the first house he *had* built, because Sam ain't building any kind of house on his own. Darla told him to plan for thirty-five grandkids. So there's fourteen bedrooms on the property and a bunk room that sleeps twenty kids. He jokes that we'll build more guest houses when we run out of space."

"Good Lord, I can't even imagine that kind of wealth. I forget about you being that rich." She laughed.

"Me, too." Luke grinned again. "The kid's bunk room is awesome. There are no hard surfaces, and the floor bounces like a trampoline. This is the first time there will be actual children in it. Usually, it's just Matthew, Noah, and me being idiots."

"I'm going to need a video of her flinging herself around in that room. You know it's going to happen." Monica grinned.

"I'll be disappointed if it doesn't," Luke agreed. "Do you want to come? We can wait for Mike to get home."

"No, Luke. We're good here. She needs her own life, and she can have it now. Mike and me, too. You'll be there. Your family. The Mistress. She'll be fine."

"YOU READY FOR THIS?" Luke asked, teasing, as they walked out the front door to his Audi. "Four days with my crazy family?"

Talise smiled, not meeting his eyes. "Four days with you."

"That, too," Luke said, trying to not blush. "Did you eat? Want to grab a bite before we're on the road? It's probably going to be a lot of traffic, and there's nothing once you get thirty minutes into Indiana until we cross over to Michigan."

"Are you hungry? I just had lunch about an hour ago, but I'll eat if you haven't."

"I'm fine," he said, tossing her suitcase in the trunk while she got in the car.

Talise smiled. "Would you still be fine if I suggested ice cream?"

"You know my feelings on ice cream," he said stoically, meeting her gaze as he turned the car on.

Holy hell, he thought, watching as the smile reflected in her amber eyes. *So beautiful. Even more stunning, shining with happiness.*

"Are we going to go?" she asked, a crease in her forehead. "What's wrong?"

Ah, shit. Stop staring, self. He shook his head to clear his thoughts then put the car in drive.

"How long is the drive?" she asked.

"About three and a half hours," he said. "Music? Audiobook? I don't care, whatever you want to listen to is fine."

She was quiet for a minute. "Whatever I want?"

"Sure." He nodded.

"Great. Tell me I'm beautiful," she said quickly, almost spitting the words out before her cheeks flushed.

Luke hit the curb.

"Holy shit! Sorry!" he yelled.

He tried to reverse the car off the curb. It didn't move. So he threw the car in park. "Are you hurt?"

"Nope," she said, eyes forward, face flaming red. "Sorry. I didn't think you'd react like that. I thought you'd laugh."

There was a decided tilt to the car. *I wonder if the tire is flat or if I broke the axle.* He considered it for a minute. *Maybe both.*

He put his head down on the steering wheel, laughing.

"Sorry," she muttered again, eyes downcast, humiliation on full display.

Luke's stressed laughter fell away at the sight of her embarrassment.

"You are more beautiful today than I thought possible. Glowing with happiness and health. Your eyes blend with your tan and your dark hair to create a striking, breath-taking monotone sort of beauty that I don't think I've ever seen before."

It was Luke's turn to be embarrassed, staring out the front windshield, turning red around the ears.

"That was pretty good." She laughed.

"Thanks." He grinned, meeting her eyes. "I was thinking along those lines as I was starting the car. I got distracted by your loveliness. Did you have to bust me right away?"

"Yup." She grinned.

Luke started laughing in earnest.

"What is this, Luke? Are we friends? Will we be more than friends at some point?" she asked, voice tight with anxiety.

"We will always be friends, Talise. I will always want you in my life, no matter what. Whatever else comes is up to you. I won't rush you and don't want you to feel like there needs to be anything more. I'll be happy if you're happy."

She took a deep breath, exhaling through her nose. When she touched the side of his face, Luke turned to look at her. His surprise came through her emotional shields loud and clear when she pressed her lips to his.

This is nice, he thought, touching her face, pulling her closer to deepen the kiss.

Tali pulled away a second later, looking relaxed enough to nap.

"Too much peace." She laughed.

"I think I broke the front axle," Luke admitted as they both cracked up.

"WHAT HAPPENED that you're so late? What does 'unexpectedly delayed' mean? You didn't answer my call or my texts," Darla complained when Luke and Talise finally arrived at the lake house shortly after nine o'clock that night. "I saw the headlights as you pulled up. The kids are asleep, and everyone else is outside drinking beer around the fire pit."

"I hit a curb, broke my car axle, and had to get a new car. How are you, Mom?" Luke said, babbling as if saying it fast would make it sound less idiotic.

Darla blinked. "Are either of you injured?"

"Nope," Luke said.

Darla's laughter rang through the room. "Are you taking driving lessons from Sam? What happened?"

"I got startled."

"Was there an animal in the road?" Darla asked.

"Yeah. That sounds good. Let's go with that," Luke suggested, pressing his lips together to control his embarrassed laughter.

Darla looked at Luke, then she looked at Talise.

"This is great!" she said at last.

"Do we have to tell them about the axle?" Luke winced.

"You don't think they'll notice the new car?" Darla asked.

"Not right away."

"Sorry, honey. It's too funny to hide. Drink more beer to take the sting out," Darla said, leading the way out of the French doors and across the patio to the fire pit.

"You're finally here! What happened?" Hank asked.

"I had a mishap," Luke replied with a straight face, looking around the fire at his family. Will and Emma shared a bench with Adrian and Lucy. Jake and Matty sat with Sam and Adaline. Ava, Jess, Clyde, and Blake shared a bench. Beth sat between Hennessy and Ethan. Matthew sat alone. Noah shared a bench with Kaylee.

Everyone was staring at Luke and Talise except for Noah, who seemed more interested in the sole of the shoe resting on his knee.

Holy crap! It's been a couple of weeks. Kaylee's still around! Luke thought, laughing to himself. *Is Noah finally done screwing around? Is he embarrassed by this new commitment? Possible distraction fodder?*

"What kind of mishap?" Hank asked, brow furrowed, looking between Luke and Talise for any signs of injury.

"The front axle of my car broke," Luke muttered.

"Holy shit!" Matthew exclaimed.

"Luke! Did you get hit? Have you gotten checked out? Are you hurt?" Hank sounded a bit panicked. "How fast were you going? Some of those potholes are serious business, but holy cow!"

Darla shook her head.

"We're fine, Dad. Everything's fine. I just had to get a new car."

"Well, what happened?" Will asked, eyebrows raised. "Axles don't just break."

"I drove up onto a curb," Luke said lightly, not meeting any eyes.

No one responded.

"I was startled," he continued, staring off across the water.

"I'm a better driver than that," Sam said to Adaline. "I hate driving, but I'm not that bad."

After another pause of disbelief, the laughter started.

"Poor Puking Peace. What the fuck, Luke? What startled you?" Jess asked, laughing.

"No, Talise. You don't get to laugh at this one!" Luke bitched, not answering Jess.

Talise's giggles continued unabated.

Luke groaned. "It's going to be a long weekend. Where's the beer? Talise, want a beer?"

Noah having a girlfriend isn't going to help me. I'm kidding myself, he thought, digging for beer in the outdoor fridge.

26

Noah startled awake on Saturday morning as the sun was rising. Kaylee was tucked in next to him, gurgling a bit in her sleep.

Noah smiled, watching her steady breathing for a minute before he slid out of bed and headed for the bathroom.

He and Kaylee had been seeing each other for almost a month. Fun time was very fun, indeed, when you knew exactly what the other person liked.

Done in the bathroom, Noah considered what to do. He'd only slept for a handful of hours but felt awake. He could climb back into bed and shuffle around until Kaylee woke up. Morning fun time didn't sound like a bad idea, but she tended toward grumpiness in the morning.

He heard a puppy squeak from the living room. Deciding someone else must be awake, he went to pilfer coffee from the pot someone else had undoubtedly started.

"Bah!" he teased quietly. "You're the only person in the house that would be up and not start the coffee, Adaline."

She turned, a small smile on her drawn face.

"Maybe you need coffee more than me," Noah acknowledged. "You look exhausted."

"I didn't sleep well," she shared with him.

Noah frowned. "What's wrong? No words this morning? Can I help somehow?"

"This is easier. Do you mind it?" she asked.

"Not at all," he responded, starting the coffee machine and heading over to sit by her on the couch. "How are you holding up?"

Adaline's eyebrows raised.

Noah shrugged. "We ripped you out of isolation and dumped you into our crazy way of life. You've known Sam forever, but the rest of us are probably overwhelming at times."

"I'm well. Adjusting. Overwhelmed sometimes. But not by you. So much love in this family. Acceptance. You must think I'm bizarre, though."

Noah gave a shocked gasp. "I grew up with Sam. You're amazingly well-balanced and normal by comparison."

She grinned then, a genuine smile of amusement.

"My poor Sam. All those years searching. He finally found me only to realize he'd been cast as the villain."

"Villain?" Noah asked.

"Relatively speaking, at least," Adaline acknowledged with a nod.

"I'm not envious of his lot in life." Noah smiled.

"Nor I. But I cannot imagine a better person for the job. Gentle and kind until there's a reason not to be."

Noah nodded, quiet for a moment.

"You two seem to fit together well. Does the 'fated to be together' thing bug you? Do you secretly wish you could go hunt for love on your terms?"

"Fated? No, I think not. We chose it in the end. If I did not want to be with him, I would not be here. When I was young, I was terrified of him. It took years for me to see him for what he is. The dreams gave us that time. I'm not as confident I would have accepted the role without it. I would not stand beside a monster, nor would I stand behind anyone. We are partners."

Noah watched as sadness settled over her face. When she met his eyes, he lifted an eyebrow.

"I hurt him. Hurt us. When we took the names."

Noah sat quietly, watching her, waiting for more information.

She shook her head. *"Let's talk of something else. He will be upset if he hears us talking of this."*

"I'm the only one that can hear you, Addy. You can tell me. I won't judge. You've helped me. I would be glad to listen if it's bothering you."

"I have not told anyone, Noah. Mama and Jess would be upset. Disappointed."

Noah shrugged. "I won't talk about it."

Addy took a deep breath, causing Noah to laugh.

"You're not talking, Addy. You don't need breath for this." He grinned.

She tried to smile, but the tears swimming in her eyes gave her away.

"Adaline," Noah murmured, taking her hand. "Whatever happened, it's over. He loves you more than life itself. It will be fine."

Her face crumpled as she started to explain.

"The power called to me when we took the names. I would have taken it from him if he didn't help me. I might have killed him. Destroyed us. Destroyed more than us.

"I don't think we're fated to do anything, Noah. I don't think fated acts would turn so terrible. But now I wonder. If we are to walk this path together, am I to be the monster? The darkness to his light? He's shown resistance and control where I have failed."

Tears dripped from her eyes.

Noah started laughing. He took a deep breath, trying to gather himself, then met her eyes and laughed again in earnest.

"What's so funny?" Adaline asked, hurt.

"Why are you upset? You should not be upset about this. Ask Darla. She'll applaud you for immediately making your ability to knock him on his ass known. You have a lot of years ahead of you. Can't let his ego get out of control."

After a pause, Noah continued, more serious.

"I'm glad you tried to take it from him. I'm glad you have that instinct in you, Addy. I would not see you become subservient to anyone, even Sam. So it's good you have the strength to fight. And it's good he has the power to balance things when needed."

They sat quietly for a few minutes, listening to the coffee maker. "I don't think anyone is all darkness or all light. It's good you and Sam stand together. You're each powerful in your own right and scrappy enough to survive when others have failed. Together, maybe you'll take turns walking in the light. I think that'd be good for the planet. Good for life."

"Sam has said much the same to me. 'We will take turns reminding each other.' It's hard knowing I hurt him, though. I carry that guilt. I'm ready for my turn to steer him to rights."

"Well, I have a suggestion," Noah said.

Adaline's eyebrows hiked up.

"Just hear me out on this: wardrobe."

Adaline burst out laughing.

"The man refuses to wear patterns. And nothing yellow. What's wrong with yellow? And why is he so fond of the color brown? It's the color of poop. It should not be the color of an entire suit. No fashion sense at all. He wears plain, solid ties, Adaline. Do you have any idea how stupid that looks? You could really save him a lot of embarrassment."

Her giggles continued.

"That's probably not a fair trade. I mean, your thing was just a night or whatever. Probably not that long. Dressing him properly is a serious commitment. But it could be your gift to me."

Noah got up to make himself a cup of coffee as she continued to laugh, only then looking at the time. "I'm awake before seven on the weekend with a beautiful woman still sleeping in my bed. Sam is right. The world is off-course."

Adaline grinned as Noah sat back down. *"He's very upset about that."*

"Oh, I'm aware. I know what he's like when he's stuck on something. What does he insist is so wrong with our current path? I wish he'd stop dismissing Kaylee. She's the first woman I've dated for any length of time. He could try to be a little pleasant."

"He believes Talise is out of place."

"Where does he think she should be?"

"He won't tell me, and I cannot read it from him, though your Kaylee upsets him almost as much. Are you in love, Noah?"

Noah shot Adaline a mock-glare.

"I am, in fact, hopelessly in love. With you. And Sam. Together. I love seeing you both happy. I'm glad you chose this."

She nodded, smiling, obviously waiting for him to continue.

Noah gave a half-smile. "I like her. I like being around her. She's funny and assertive and smart. We've not been together long, but I could see us having fifteen kids and growing old together."

A crease appeared in Adaline's forehead.

"Wrong answer?" Noah asked.

"No. Just surprising. She is not empowered. What does she think of the energy? How does it react to her?"

"What do you mean? I haven't told her."

Adaline looked confused. *"But what does she think is happening when it cycles? When it's shared?"*

Noah shook his head, not understanding. "She thinks we're going to have sex. Because that's what my energy is."

"No, Noah. That's not what I mean. Not exactly. When the energy cycles and balances between you. When you and your energy are aligned and in agreement. In accordance. What does she think is happening?"

"She likes the lusty stuff, but who doesn't?" Noah grinned, shrugging.

Adaline shook her head. *"Maybe it will come with time."*

"I'll pay attention. Maybe I just haven't noticed. I walked around for all of my post-puberty years, not realizing the lust thing."

Adaline was still out of sorts. *"She does not try to interact with your family. She doesn't seem to care what they think."*

"She recognizes it's going to take a while for them to get used to her. She knows many a women have come home to family dinner with me, never to be seen again."

After a moment, he considered his words again. "In a non-creepy way. I've broken up with a lot of women. They've all been seen again. Just not by my family."

Adaline's chuckle was audible. *"There is very little darkness in you, Noah. You're a lover, not a fighter."*

"That's what I keep saying!" He laughed.

"What does Kaylee want? Where does her heart rest?" Adaline asked, returning to the original topic.

Noah grinned. "It's in my bed with the rest of her bits and pieces."

Adaline laughed out loud, grinning as she hugged him.

"Will you show me how to make coffee? I would like to know how to do that."

TALISE WOKE at the feeling of someone walking past her door on Saturday morning.

Ugh, that's going to be annoying, she realized, rolling over out of a dead sleep.

Her water senses meant that she'd feel all movement around her, including people walking in the hallway outside her door. At home, her room was off the opposite side of the house. It provided her parents some notion of privacy, however fleeting.

Luke said there are a bunch of rooms. Maybe I can switch to one that's more out of the way.

Talise laid in bed, considering the day ahead. There were no plans other than relaxing and hanging out.

Maybe I can bully Luke into an "ice cream" trip later. She laughed to herself, thinking about him hitting the curb the day before. *Poor Luke. So sweet. So calm. Seemingly innocent. He needs to get over that.*

Someone in the room next door rolled over, waking up. There was a moment of confusion, then interest.

What the hell is Noah's girlfriend doing? Is she looking through his luggage? Talise shook with suppressed laughter. *I guess poor Noah, too!*

Addy's emotions drifted by from the direction of the living room. She was sad, shameful, remorseful... *What happened?!*

Then the sadness was gone, replaced with laughter and joy, acceptance, and tolerance.

Noah. Adaline was talking with Noah. It was Noah that had made her laugh, made her feel better. Addy and Noah were laughing in earnest now, sharing a familial love that made Talise…sad.

He won't even look at me. Won't talk to me. Won't accept my apology.

Talise sighed.

She could sense the good humor and cheer radiating off him when he talked with other people. She could *feel* the hilarious, snarky attitude, the desire to make others happy, and the love of life that was all part of Noah.

But they weren't friends. He wouldn't overlook her error in judgment. Wouldn't let go of her over-reaction. Somehow, knowing he was a genuinely good person with a great sense of humor made his indifference and dislike that much more upsetting.

I messed that up. That's on me.

Once again wishing she could take it back, Talise got up and started to get ready to face the day.

"WHY HAVE a pool right next to a giant lake?" Talise asked Sam as they sat together with Adaline on the patio later that day. Most of the Trellis siblings were playing flag football while Hank and Darla were inside making lunch.

Sam smiled at her. "Why not? Are you complaining that there's too much water around?"

"Ha! No. There's water everywhere." Talise smiled back. "In the middle of the driest desert, I could still find water!"

"I know."

"Someone told me last week that you're supposed to have not only time and space but also the elements. Is that right? Do you feel water like I do?" Talise asked, curious. She had never known another elemental water user.

Sam gave a firm nod. "I think it's similar but maybe not the same. I can work with water and fire easier than air and earth, though."

As a demonstration, Sam stretched his hand out, pulling an orb of water from the pool to rest in his palm.

"I've been practicing. I'm not very good yet," he admitted. "Addy's better with it. Air, too. She can call lightning on purpose. I just get it by accident right now."

"Wow, that's amazing! It's more than I can do," Talise said, appreciating the control it took to hold the sphere of water with enough tension for it to stay in shape.

Sam's concentration wavered, causing the water to drench his hand. "It's completely useless but cool. Have you tried to do it? I bet you can."

"I don't think I can, Sam."

"Well, not with that attitude," he chided. "You have as much or more water energy than me."

"Nah, too much life intertwined with it. It makes a big mess."

Sam frowned at her, shaking his head.

"Not yet, then," he muttered, sounding resigned.

Talise understood his implication, even if she disagreed with his assessment. They sat in awkward silence for a minute.

"I carried Addy's life energy with me for years. It was difficult," he said eventually.

Talise's eyebrows shot up.

"I could taste emotions in food: animal suffering, the drama of the cook's life. Before there was balance, eating was hard. Do other people sometimes make you feel ill? Miranda doesn't have that. I wondered if it's a water-life thing."

"You mean like being around too many people?" Talise asked.

Sam shook his head then paused. "Well, that, too. Sometimes crowds are still hard. But I mean when you meet a bad person, someone that would hurt others without remorse."

Talise nodded. "Two people that I can think of recently. I don't meet many people, though."

"Was I one of them? When I touched you?" Sam asked, voice quiet and loaded with shame.

"No," Talise answered quickly. "You didn't make me ill, just overwhelmed. Everything was raw and fresh then, Sam. I'd still be hopelessly lost if Addy didn't start showing me how to make it better."

Sam smiled at Addy, reading her book in the lounge chair next to Talise. "She's glorious."

Adaline ignored them, but her lips twitched up just a bit.

Talise laughed. "She really is. I never expect humor from her, so it catches me by surprise."

"Me, too. I'm glad you see her humor. I think most people miss it."

Talise made a so-so gesture. "I think she chooses not to share it with everyone. I feel fortunate."

With a glance and a wink, Addy grinned at them both.

"What happened with the two people that made you sick?" Sam asked.

"What do you mean?"

"Who were they? Why did they feel bad?"

"Oh. One is not bad. I just avoided him. It's easier now that he's left the circle."

Sam's eyebrows shot up. "Jared?"

Talise nodded. "I know he's not bad. He just made me feel…not right."

Sam's expression turned thoughtful. "And the other?"

"She doesn't feel evil or anything. Just not…happy. Genuine."

His face went blank. His words came out in a whisper. "Kaylee feels wrong to me as well."

Talise rocked back, surprised.

Adaline sighed. "Sam."

Sam frowned at Talise. "We are not where we should be. You are not where you should be."

"Where am I supposed to be?"

Sam pressed his lips together, shaking his head.

"Try the water orb, just for fun. Let's see if you can do it!" he suggested.

After twenty minutes of failed attempts and a lot of laughter, Sam outright tossed Tali into the pool, fully clothed, still in her lounge chair.

"Do it now! Toss it at me like a water balloon!" he goaded her.

Talise was wiping water from her eyes, trying to pull off an outraged expression.

"I'll keep tossing your ass back in there until you do it! No easy escape for you!" Sam threatened.

"I'm telling Luke that you were mean to me!" Tali bitched. "Your baby brother's going to be mad at you again, Sam. Don't pout too hard!"

Sam threw his head back, laughing.

Tali smacked him in the face with an orb of water.

Sam cheered as he dumped a spout of water on top of her head. "Luke would only be mad if I overloaded you again! I didn't touch you —you went into the pool with the whole chair!"

Five minutes later, they were both in the pool, throwing waves at each other as Adaline laughed, still trying to read her book.

"What the hell are you two doing?" Hank yelled.

Sam hit him in the side of the head with an orb.

"I didn't do it," he said, all innocence, pointing at Tali.

Talise gave an outraged gasp. "I did not! Don't tell him that!" She flung water at Sam's face using her hands rather than her energy.

"Leave the water in the pool, children," Hank said, monotone.

Sam turned a sheepish smile on his dad. "Sorry. It seemed like a good idea at the time."

"And now?" Hank asked.

"Now it's mostly funny," Sam admitted.

Hank glared at his middle child. "Go change. Your mother is about done with her smorgasbord preparations."

"Lunch in five," Hank yelled to the football players.

Talise hopped quickly out of the pool. Running over, she shoved Sam in the t-shirt covered chest, pushing him back into the water when he was almost out. She blew a raspberry at him.

"Oh, that's mature." He laughed after he resurfaced, pulling a face at her.

"Now we're even."

"What's your name, Talise?" he asked, suddenly serious.

"Sam—"

"Nope, we're not even yet. Still off-balance."

"DON'T DRIP ON THE FLOOR," Sam complained as he and Talise went into the house laughing together. "You're making a mess. I just know I'm going to get stuck cleaning it up!"

"What the hell happened to you two?" Darla laughed.

"We bonded." Sam shrugged.

Darla rolled her eyes. "Clean up the water, Sam, before someone slips."

"I knew it!" he shouted at Talise as she walked down the hall to her bedroom, cackling.

As she pulled her wet clothes off, she heard a chuckle and murmuring voice from the next room. Shaking her head, she pulled on a clean, dry sundress and hung her wet things over the shower stall door in the bathroom attached to her room.

Without warning, a wave of raw lust and sweet affection crashed through her emotional shields, almost knocking her to the floor. The emotions were followed immediately by a feeling of…boredom. Indifference. Then greed. Avarice and some sense of urgency.

This is none of my business. I have to get out of here, Talise thought, heading to her door with her comb in hand.

Neither Noah nor Kaylee surfaced for lunch.

"What's wrong?" Luke asked as they cleaned up the kitchen together after everyone was done eating.

Talise didn't meet his eyes. "Nothing."

"Are you upset about Sam tossing you in the pool? Did you get whomped with his emotions again?"

Her lips turned up into a small smile. "No, I'm not mad. We had fun. He didn't touch me."

"He's rarely friendly with anyone outside of our family. I hope you know that he's fond of you," Luke offered.

"I do. Me, too. He taught me to make water orbs." She smiled for real, still not meeting his eyes.

Luke sighed. "You really won't tell me? It's just me."

"It's really not my business, Luke. Talking with you about it is ugly. Spreading gossip."

"Well, now I really want to know." He laughed.

When she stepped close, Luke immediately wrapped her in a hug. She quietly explained, making sure no one else was around to hear her.

Luke frowned. "Noah's probably just done being with her, Tali. He does this. A lot. It's amazing she's lasted as long as she has."

"I think that's backward, Luke."

Luke shrugged. "He'll be fine. He does this all the time. Don't worry about it."

Well, easy for you to say. She doesn't turn your stomach, Talise thought, wondering if she should talk to Sam. *This is really not my business. The man already hates me.*

Still, she watched Kaylee, flirting with Noah, throughout dinner. She couldn't get a read on anything. Talise realized that she'd spent all her time and energy learning how to block other emotions out. She didn't practice reading them at all.

Maybe I should give that a go with Addy during the next visit.

NOAH ROLLED OVER IN BED, wide awake. It was still dark out. A quick glance at his phone told him it was 3:13 on Sunday morning.

Ugh. Why am I awake again?

He shifted around in bed, attempting to wake Kaylee without actually shaking her awake. She didn't stir.

Damn. No middle of the night fun time.

There had been no bedtime fun, either. Kaylee objected to sexy time when the house was packed with his family. Understandable. But he knew for a fact that the walls were well insulated and soundproofed. There had been other guests that didn't share her discretion.

Probably not a good thing to point out, Noah thought. *But still.*

They'd had an afternoon interlude while everyone else was outside or in the kitchen. But it ended quickly, before it began in earnest. Kaylee wasn't into it. When he realized she was just going along with it, he backed off. If she wasn't into sexy time here, they'd have time when they got back to the city.

I think there's leftover chicken in the fridge—midnight snack for the win.

He quietly snuck out of bed then tiptoed out of the room and down the hall. When the great room came into sight, he almost yelped in surprise.

Talise was dancing. Spinning. Continuously spinning.

Holy fuck! This is the coolest thing I've ever seen!

She kept extending her non-balance leg out then swinging it back around to provide momentum. Her arms whipped through motions, keeping her centered. She extended her spine, arching, so her chest was seemingly parallel with the ceiling as her spinning slowed to a stop.

"Did I wake you?" she asked, her back facing Noah. "I'm sorry. There's no room for this in the bedroom. I couldn't sleep."

"No, you didn't wake me. I didn't mean to startle you."

"You didn't." She shrugged, turning back to him.

"Ah. What's the range on the water sense?" he asked, curious.

She shrugged again. "I've never measured."

"Another difference between men and women. It'd be the first thing I did," Noah said, cracking the joke before he thought better of it.

The hot brunette does not need my shit. I scared the fuck out of this woman. Turn around, self. Back to bed. Turn around. Turn around. Turn around.

Noah didn't move.

"Why are you up?" she asked.

"Same as you."

"You couldn't sleep and decided to frolic around the living room?" She smiled a little bit.

"Pfft. You should be so lucky to witness my graceful dance moves.

They are so elegant and powerful, I keep them to myself. Jealousy is an ugly emotion."

Ah, fuck. Should have thought that one through. No jokes about emotions, self. She's sensitive. Now she just looks overwhelmed again.

"Anyway, I couldn't sleep and came out to raid the fridge. Hungry?"

"No, thanks," she whispered. "I'm going to go back to bed."

"You don't have to go, Talise. I won't stay out here. Keep dancing. I won't bother you."

I'm still a giant asshole. She's still afraid of me. Noah wanted to smack himself in the forehead. *I shouldn't have come out here. I should have just gone back to bed when I saw her dancing. Spinning. Awesome spinning.*

She shook her head. "Good night. Thanks for talking to me."

She headed down the hallway to her room.

Noah frowned. "Good night."

"Thanks for talking to me?" I'm sure I've talked to her. I just don't talk to her often. I don't want to upset her. But I'm sure I've spoken to her.

He thought about it for a moment.

Actually, I guess I haven't talked to her. That makes me a jackass of epic proportions as well as a giant asshole.

Remembering back to the way he introduced her at Sunday dinner a couple weeks ago, Noah almost groaned as he smacked himself in the forehead.

I'll apologize. No wonder she seems so out of sorts.

As he turned the corner to enter the hall, he ran full into Talise, knocking them both to the floor.

"Holy shit, I'm sorry, Talise! Are you all right?" Noah asked, his whisper urgent with concern as his heart raced and skin tingled.

FUCK! I should have just gone back to bed!

She didn't respond. She was breathing deep, lying on the floor.

"I'll go get Luke. I'm sorry, Tali." Noah was on his feet, heading toward Luke's room, when her voice reached him.

"I'm fine," she whispered to him. "Don't wake Luke. I'm getting better at this on my own. I'm sorry. It's my fault. I felt you coming toward the hall and thought you knew I was coming back."

Talise pushed herself to sit upright, leaning on the wall, as Noah walked back to her.

"Why were you coming back out? Did you need something?" he asked, losing track of why he was headed down the hallway.

She closed her eyes as her cheeks flushed. "Uh, I wanted to ask you something."

"What?"

"Um. Sorry. I'm a little jumbled right now," she muttered. "I was going to ask how well you know Kaylee."

Noah shook his head. "Pretty well. We've been together for about a month. Why?"

"It's not important," Talise said quickly, chickening out.

He frowned. "You've gone this far, no turning back now."

"It's just...she feels bad. Sam thinks so, too—"

"Sam once had a meltdown because the person that made his turkey sandwich hated their mother. We did not know the person that made the sandwich, or their mother, but he was offended all the same. He's maybe not the best judge of character." Noah laughed, but the sound was tense.

Fucking Sam, starting this shit. He hasn't even had a real conversation with Kaylee.

"Earlier, Sam and I got into a water fight, and I came in to change clothes. You were in your room with Kaylee. I got whomped with some emotions. I don't think she's entirely sincere, Noah. She was... indifferent. And then her greed bled through," Talise said, head hanging.

Noah blinked. *What the ever-living fuck?* He shook his head.

"She's never asked me for a damn thing," Noah objected.

"Okay," Talise muttered, eyes down, shoulders hunched, looking pitiful at his feet.

What the fuck? It's like I attacked her. Why is she fucking cowering?

"Talise, Kaylee is fine. Don't worry about it," he snapped.

"Sorry," she whispered.

Why is this woman so afraid of me?

"This is so not your business," he quietly scolded. "You don't know what you're talking about. Again, she's never asked me for a damn thing. You really need to work on those controls more. And stop cowering. I'm not going to hurt you."

She nodded meekly.

"You know what? I know her a fuckton better than I know you. Stay out of my business," Noah said, angry.

Talise nodded again, standing up. She didn't meet his eyes or say another word before she turned to go back to her room.

When Noah heard her door close, he threw himself down on the couch, annoyed and frustrated.

27

"Mom," a little voice said into Jess's ear on Sunday morning. "Mom, we're awake."

"Urgh. Go say hi to Grandma."

"I tried that. She told me to come to say hi to you," Mia whispered.

"Go say hi to your aunt," Jess tried again.

"She's not here."

"Wake up Uncle Sam. He likes you."

"He's not here, either."

Jess smacked Blake's arm.

"Your children are awake," she muttered to Blake.

"Urgh. Too many shots. Too much beer," he whispered.

"Uh-huh," Jess agreed. "Your children are awake."

"I got up yesterday," he muttered, rolling away from her.

"Ugh."

"Sometimes the truth hurts," he murmured.

Can I send my kids to Darla? She likes kids, right? She's the textbook definition of "Grandma." She'd probably get up and make cookies with them. Mmm. Fresh cookies, Jess thought.

She opened her mouth.

"Jessica, do not send our children to Darla," Blake warned. "The woman has cancer. Let her sleep."

She glared at him. He didn't notice.

She rolled out of bed.

I will not puke in front of my children. I will not puke in front of my children. I will not puke in front of my children, Jess chanted in her head.

Oh no. I'm going to puke in front of my children.

"I'm up, Mia. I'll be right out. Go keep Meg company, please."

"Don't get back in bed. Yesterday you got back in bed," Mia complained.

"I won't get back in bed. I'm going to the bathroom," Jess lied.

Blake laughed as she flopped back in bed.

"Just for a sec. I just need a second to get myself together."

"We cannot drink with Will and Hennessy. Remind me of this tonight when we try drinking with Will and Hennessy again," Blake muttered.

"No shit. I don't think they were even drunk last night," Jess complained. "I grew up in a bar! I'm ashamed of my lousy tolerance."

"Babe, Will is a full foot taller than you and weighs at least a hundred pounds more than you. You probably shouldn't challenge He-Man to a drinking game."

"You're right, I was totally wrong," Jess agreed. "Now, get up with your children."

"I love you, but I am not getting my ass out of this bed for at least another half hour," Blake disagreed.

"Do you think they'd notice if we stole this bed? Holy fuck, it's the nicest bed I've ever slept in," Jess rambled.

Blake scratched his head, groaning at her. "You're ruining my lazy wakeup with words. Not fair. I got up quietly yesterday and let you sleep."

"Fine," Jess said.

She intended to roll and then sit up in the bed, but she was closer to the edge than she thought. She rolled right out of bed onto the floor.

Blake's snorts of laughter were muffled by the pillow he pulled over his head.

"I dislike today," she bitched, heading for the bathroom.

By the time she wandered into the great room, all three kids were sitting on the couch, staring down the hallway.

"What?" Jess asked.

Mia scowled at her. "You got back into bed!"

"I did not!" Jess pulled an affronted face.

"I heard you!"

"Fine, but I only got back into bed for a minute. I'm awake. What do you want on TV this morning?"

"Princesses!" Meg cheered.

"Objections?" Jess asked, looking at Mia and Ree.

"We can watch her show first," Mia agreed magnanimously.

"Ree?"

"I don't mind," he agreed.

He's so easy. Such a good kid. Poor Ree. No kid deserves to be sick, but it kills me to see such a sweetheart go through so much pain.

Maybe it was the thoughts that pulled it forward. Maybe it was the unfocused nature of Jess's mind with a hangover. Either way, as she bent to pick up the TV remote, she saw it. Out of the corner of her eye, she saw the flicker. Just for a second. Only in her peripheral vision. But it was there. Like when Ben touched a mind.

Jess got a chill down her spine, standing straight quickly, looking around for help.

"Uh, Mia, did you see Uncle Sam or Aunt Addy before they left? Do you know where they went?" Jess asked, fully awake and entirely focused.

"No, I didn't see them."

"Would you please go tell Grandma that I need her?"

"What's wrong?" Mia asked, confused.

"I just need Grandma, sweetheart. I feel sick. Go get her for me."

"JESSICA. You are an adult. You can get up in the morning with your children. This is ridiculous. I half expected you to send them to Darla," Ava griped.

"Mom," Jess said, holding out her hand. "Please help. I feel sick."

Ava frowned. Jess didn't look ill. At least, not sick enough to need help. She looked...scared.

"What—?"

"Shh," Jess murmured quietly. "Everything's fine, Mia. Watch your show. I just need Grandma to help me feel better. I stayed up too late last night."

"Look with me, Mom. Don't speak about this. I don't know who's listening or watching us," Jess broadcast as Ava took her hand. Jess didn't have Adaline's or Ava's raw power. She needed physical contact to share her thoughts.

Ava nodded. "Okay, Jess. I'll help. But maybe not so many shots tonight, please?"

"I wholeheartedly agree."

"What are we looking at?" Ava asked.

Jess shivered again, terrified. Ava's eyebrows shot up. Jess didn't scare easily.

"It's faint. I caught it out of the corner of my eye when I stumbled out here to turn on the TV."

Jess began filtering out the bindings that were irrelevant, leaving the love shared between a mother and her child. The binding from Ava to Jess shone with a blue-violet maternal love that included respect and appreciation for the woman that Jess had grown to become.

Jess's links to her girls were brighter, tinged with yellow hope and the soft orchid color of love that was particularly for little girls.

"Do you see our bonds? Do you understand them?" Jess asked.

Ava nodded.

Jess filtered the visible maternal bonds away as well.

"I couldn't have done this two months ago," Jess admitted.

Closing her eyes, she pulled more power into her sight while holding her mental filters in place. She knew it was visible when Ava gasped.

Upon opening her eyes, the maternal bond to Henry was faintly visible with the deep indigo color of a grieving mother. Overlaying the bond was the putrid khaki color of malice and the pea soup green of envy. Worse, the bond was vibrating with activity, indicating that someone was using it to access Ree's mind.

"Kids, are you hungry?" Ava mumbled, sounding ill.

"Pancakes?" Meg asked.

Ava nodded. "Ree, do you want pancakes?"

"No, thank you. I'm so tired, Grandma Ava. Not hungry."

"I bet you are," Ava responded, meeting Jess's eyes and then hugging her tight.

"We need Sam and Adaline," Ava shared before letting go of Jess's hand.

"IT'S COMPLETELY GONE NOW. I can't even see the maternal bond anymore. It's gone like it's been cut," Jess said, watching the kids in the living room through the patio door.

"And we're sure the bond wasn't tied to Lucy?" Sam asked.

He and Adaline had returned from getting fresh beignets from the New Orleans French Quarter for the family to find Jess and Ava near panic.

Jess shook her head. "No. Lucy's bond is different. More silver than blue-violet. Ree is family to her, but not her child."

"She calls Ree her child," Sam disagreed.

"She does, but she also acknowledges that Ree is not hers. She'll fight for him and gladly die to keep him safe. But she knows, deep down, she is not his mother. Ree does not call her 'Mom.' She is 'Aunt Lucy.' That distinction has meaning to both of them," Ava explained.

Addy shook her head. "I do not see it, either. I see his body fighting for strength as if battling a disease. But I don't see the disease itself. I agree, Mom. I don't think he has cancer. It's different than Darla. I think his body is attacking an enemy that is not always there."

"I don't know what to do," Ava admitted. "Adrian got upset when I suggested there was more to Ree's illness."

Sam frowned. "If he doesn't have cancer, don't you think we should stop torturing him with chemo? Why is there indecision on this?"

"We can't prove it's not cancer, Sam. We can't show them. What Jess and I saw is gone now," Ava replied.

"I'll talk to him. We need to be careful about what we say and do in front of Ree from now on," Sam decided.

Ava nodded. "We should have Ben look at Ree's mind. He might be able to tell us which memories have been touched."

"I don't understand," Adaline said.

They waited for her to continue.

"He has been sick for much longer than he has been around us. If someone is using that binding to gather information, what information are they seeking? It's not related to us."

Sam winced.

"What?" Jess asked.

"Stalkers. She has stalkers that have been chasing them for years. Tormenting Lucy. We should see Ben as soon as possible. I'll go talk to Adrian and Lucy now."

AFTER FURTHER DISCUSSION, Will decided they would not rush home to see one of the most skilled and recognized mental energy wielders in the country. If someone was using Ree to spy, it was best to avoid tipping them off that Jess noticed anything. If they ran to Ben, and Ben started rooting around in Ree's mind, the spy would know they had been spotted.

Instead, Ben came to them.

"Oh! The gang's all here," Nora exclaimed cheerfully, walking onto the back patio of the lake house. "Thanks for letting us join you so late in the weekend! I didn't think we'd finish the things we needed to get done at home, but we did. How is everyone? Have the kids left the pool at all? Everyone's so tan!"

"You made it!" Darla cheered, almost tackling Nora with a desperately strong hug.

It had been a rough morning of waiting. Darla felt they should do something immediately to help Ree. No one disagreed, but no one knew how to help. So they had to wait.

"Kids, it's past lunchtime. Let's take a swim break, please," Adrian said, his voice calm even if his shoulders were rigid with anxiety.

Jess slipped inside the house while the kids were distracted, heading down a hallway to the walkway that connected to the guest house. Ben, Gregg, Lucy, and William were waiting.

"Sit, quickly," Ben commanded. "It was this morning?"

"Yep," Jess said, sitting on the bed.

"I'm going to walk back in your memory to then and see if your mind retained the image of the links you perceived. If it is still in your short-term memory, I'll find it. If it has transitioned to your long-term memory, it's less likely I'll find it. This will go faster and easier if you don't fight me. By my power and on my very life, I swear I will do nothing other than I have described in the last two minutes."

"Just do it," Jess agreed.

Ben gently touched her forehead.

Jess's stomach flipped as her memories from the morning rolled back in her mind. It was like living her day in reverse within a virtual reality game. Ben stopped moving backward when Jess fell out of bed.

"It was after this, correct?" he said, voice quiet and soothing. If her mind jumped, he'd lose the place.

"Mmhmm," Jess agreed, not wanting to open her mouth for fear of being ill.

"We'll move forward now, more slowly."

He paused, gasping, at Jess's first glance of the binding.

"Go forward a little more," Jess said, moving her lips as little as possible. "It's clearer when I look with Mom."

Doing as instructed, he paused again at Ava's gasp.

"William," Ben murmured, "would you share your energy with

me? I would like to try projecting this to your minds."

Will grabbed Ben's forearm.

"Patience, please. I have not tried this before," Ben said. "I have thought about it since Jess projected her vision out, but I have not tried it."

"Fine," Lucy said, tension radiating off her as Adrian slid into the room.

"I saw that flicker, Ben," Will said.

"Thank you. That helps," Ben responded.

About thirty seconds later, everyone in the room could see the image of the poisoned binding attacking Ree's mind.

"That is a natural binding, taken by force, and actively attacking his mind. I won't be able to tell for sure until I look at his mind, but I don't think anyone has taken control of him. I think they are reviewing his memories, maybe seeing through his eyes. Possibly draining his life force, not unlike a hunter would do," Ben explained.

"How do we stop it?" Adrian asked, voice just short of a growl as his rage rolled through the room.

"When the opportunity arises, when it appears again, we follow this binding to the source and attack the source. We cannot do anything to prevent it from this side. The fact that the binding is gone now tells me the mother is cutting it as soon as she has control of herself again."

"How is it reappearing, then?" Will asked.

Jess laughed, breaking the mental bookmark and removing the image from the minds in the room.

"William. You know the answer to that better than anyone else on the planet," Jess reprimanded. "It's the same way your binding to Emma kept reforming over and over."

Will frowned. "I don't understand."

"Ree rebuilds the link with his love for his mom, his memory of his mom. He reaches for her mind and pulls her binding back to himself over time. He's holding onto her," Ben explained.

"Linda is doing this to him?" Lucy asked, tears dripping down her face.

Ben shook his head. "Someone is using her, attacking her, taking her mind by force, and doing this."

"How do you know it's by force?" Lucy asked.

"Lucy, the binding does not cut itself. The deep blue, almost black color of the binding indicates her grief and fear for her child. She does not do this willingly. Of that I am sure."

Lucy nodded, her words a vow. "I'm going to free him from this."

"What now?" Adrian asked.

"Now, we wait. The Walker should be informed. He can Walk to the source easily when the binding is present."

"He needs to practice Walking with more than one person," Adrian said. "He and Lucy aren't going alone."

William nodded in agreement.

"Are we certain there is no cancer?" Adrian asked.

Lucy's eyes snapped to Adrian. He looked ill.

"No," Ben said. "I am not certain. Ava thinks there is no cancer. Addy does not see cancer. But I don't think we're certain."

"I'll talk to Gretta about options," Adrian said, looking at Lucy. "I'll tell her we're concerned that there is no change and think it might be time to slow down and look for more information. She'll agree. She danced around, suggesting as much when I saw her in the cafeteria last week."

SUNDAY WRAPPED UP QUIETLY, with most of the adults tense and the children confused. They would head home early on Monday. When the kids objected to the early departure, as expected, Lucy and Adrian agreed to spend a few days at Jess and Blake's house.

Jess would watch for the binding, looking for a pattern.

"Yeesh, everyone's so boring tonight. I can't believe we're going to bed at ten o'clock. What's wrong, Noah?" Kaylee asked as he brushed his teeth.

Rinsing his mouth, he shrugged. "I haven't slept well. How are you? Did you enjoy the weekend? You've been very quiet."

"The house is gorgeous." Kaylee smiled.

That's not what I asked, Noah thought.

"Is my family too much? I don't think you've said much to anyone but me."

"Too much? No." Kaylee shrugged. "They just seem to ignore me, so I'm returning the favor."

"They don't ignore you. Hank tried talking to you like six times tonight," Noah disagreed.

She rolled her eyes. "Fine, not your entire family. But your billionaire brother won't even look at me. I never did a damn thing to him. What's with his girlfriend and her bizarre contact lenses, anyway?"

Why is she talking about Sam's money?

"Addy doesn't wear contacts. Her eyes are violet. Genetic oddity."

"She's definitely odd. Do you think your brother actually likes her? I saw them sitting around the pool today, completely ignoring each other."

Noah paused to consider their conversation. "Sam has loved her for most of his life. They will spend eternity together. But that's not what I was asking about. I asked how you felt around my family, not what you thought of Sam's relationship."

"I don't know, Noah. They're fine. I want to punch the ballerina, though. She kept glancing over at us all day and then looking away like we're disgusting or something. Could she be any more jealous? How does she fit in, anyway? I thought she was dating Luke, but they're in separate rooms."

Noah shook his head, temper flaring. "She's not jealous. For all intents and purposes, she's dating Luke. It's a long story. But you're still avoiding the original topic. Why not talk with Hank and Darla or my sister?"

"I don't want to talk," she said, wrapping her arms around his neck and tugging him down for a kiss. "I want to do something else."

Noah sat on the bed when she backed him into it.

Oh well, he thought as she straddled his legs. *We'll talk about it later. I shouldn't be worried about this, anyway. Talise doesn't know what she's doing, and Sam doesn't know Kaylee. It's fine.*

SEPTEMBER

28

Talise met Luke at her front door the following Thursday evening.

He smiled as she walked toward him. Her long hair was up in a tight bun, as usual. She wore a light pink sweater over a simple knee-length silver-grey A-line dress with ballet flats.

So pretty. But different. What's different? Luke wondered.

"You're wearing makeup."

She lifted her eyebrows. "Should I not be wearing makeup?"

"I've just never seen you wear makeup unless you were performing."

She stared at him.

"What?" he asked.

"Should I wash it off?"

"No! It just surprised me. You look beautiful. A more dressed up, made-up version of your already beautiful loveliness," he babbled, cheeks turning red.

"Did I find good words?" he asked with a grin when she didn't respond right away. "I could keep going."

She grinned back, shaking her head. "At least you didn't hit a curb this time. Improvement."

"Ha. Ha. Ha," he said flatly.

"They only made fun of you a little bit each day. It wasn't that bad."

Lucas rolled his eyes. "Correction: they only made fun of me a little bit each day when you were around. They laughed extensively at my expense when you were not around. And they will continue to do so for years. It's like the pool table."

"What's the pool table?" Talise asked. "I heard references to that a couple times, but I never heard the underlying story."

Luke flushed red. "Um, I'll tell you later. Should we say bye to your parents?"

"They went out to dinner," she said. "Where are we going on our first official date?"

Luke smiled. "It involves Thai food and music."

"I like both of those things!" Talise grinned.

"I know, right?"

Conversation and laughter flowed smoothly over an early dinner and an outdoor concert. Longtime friends with shared interests, Luke and Talise didn't struggle with their transition into a couple until the evening was ending.

They walked back to the car side by side, but not holding hands.

Should I take her hand? Luke debated. *We would typically hold hands right now. But it's not just holding hands now. What if she doesn't want to hold my hand* like that? *Ugh. We'll just walk. We're almost to the car.*

Luke opened the car door for Talise, stepping back out of the way so she could get in. She stepped back close to him, a slight tilt to her head, inviting a kiss.

Is that a sign for a kiss? That would be a sign for a kiss from anyone else. Holy fuck, what am I doing?

After a hesitant, pregnant pause, Luke accepted the invitation, gently and carefully teasing her lips. It fell apart when Talise stumbled backward drunkenly, almost asleep.

"Too much peace." She chuckled. "We should figure that out."

"Damn, it doesn't go any further into the background than I have it. I'll work on it," he promised.

"Sorry," she muttered, sliding into the car.

Fuck! What do I do now? Why is this so fucking strange? She's perfect.

"Maybe a movie tomorrow?" Luke asked before closing her door.

She nodded in agreement, eyes closed in a light doze.

BY THE TIME Sunday dinner rolled around, Luke and Talise figured out how to hold hands as more than friends. However, they had not yet mastered kissing without getting embarrassed or sleepy.

"Hi, Roscoe," Luke said, rubbing the dog's chest. "You're all spunky! Is Glinda coming to stay soon? Are you excited? I'm excited for you."

"Hi!" Darla called from the big room.

Talise's presence at Sunday dinner was expected, though Luke wasn't sure if his family knew their relationship dynamic had changed. Walking into the big room, he realized that they were nearly the last to arrive, with only Noah, Sam, and Adaline still missing. Sam and Addy would appear before the food. But Noah was usually present by this time.

"No Noah?" he asked.

"He didn't say he wasn't coming." Darla shrugged. "Probably just running late."

Luke shrugged back, noticing Jess staring at him. When he looked at her, her face split into a giant grin.

"Shuddup," Luke grunted.

"Aww! Puking Peace has a girlfriend!" Jess laughed.

"Good grief, it's about time," Beth complained. "I wondered if we were going to go in circles again for a year like we did with Jake and Matty."

"There were complications!" Jake objected.

Hank glared at him.

"I do not deserve that glare, Dad!" Jake bitched.

"You absolutely deserve this glare, Jacob."

"Complications!" Jake said again.

"There were complications of your own making," Hank disagreed.

"I didn't claim otherwise," Jake agreed. "Complications all the same."

At Talise's glance, Luke shook his head. "I'll tell you the story later."

"You still owe me the pool table story," she reminded him.

"No! No pool table story!" Matilda disagreed.

Luke blushed, grabbing chairs from the other end of the room. "It's kind of the same story."

"Sorry, Carrots, but she needs to hear the story. Otherwise, half our jokes won't be funny," Will said.

"Can I hear the story?" Mia asked.

"Absolutely not. It's not your kind of story," Blake said quickly.

"Oh. Are there monsters?" Mia frowned.

"Yup," Jess said. "Great big horned monsters."

All the adults in the room immediately dropped their eyes, avoiding looking at each other as they swallowed laughter.

"Horny monsters?" Mia asked. "That's terrible."

Emma squeaked, trying to cover her laughter with a cough.

"Definitely not a kid's story," Jess agreed.

Darla glared at Jess.

Jess ignored her.

"Kids," Darla said, "there's still thirty minutes till dinner. Want the TV on in the playroom?"

As soon as the kids were out of earshot, walking with Darla, the room erupted with laughter.

"I can't believe you did that." Blake laughed. "How did you keep a straight face?"

"I have a gift for bullshit." Jess laughed. "You know this!"

"I think I might understand the pool table story now," Talise muttered to Luke.

When Noah walked in with Kaylee a few minutes later, his eyes landed on Talise immediately. After she'd been so afraid of him at the lake house, Noah had made a point of avoiding her for the remainder of the weekend, thinking that some space would help.

As soon as she noticed him entering the room, Talise's shoulders dropped, her gaze fixed on the floor.

Something like anger crossed Noah's face. He smirked, leading Kaylee to the other end of the big room and pulling her down onto the couch with him.

"Feeling anti-social?" Matthew called.

"Eh, it's crowded over there. No privacy at all. We'll stay over here until dinner's done."

Talise flinched.

Watching her, Luke frowned. "Noah?"

"Lucas?"

"Are we going to have a problem?"

Talise put her hand on Luke's arm, shaking her head slightly, but not meeting his eyes.

"*I* don't have a problem, little brother. I mind my own damn business," Noah said, sneering, somehow irrationally pissed off at his entire family.

Matthew shook his head. "Snide isn't a good look on you, man."

"I'm over here out of the way, leaving everyone alone—lots of space. Plenty of room to be peaceful. I was told, repeatedly, that space was imperative. Remember that? Why am I getting the snark?" Noah asked, the chip on his shoulder all but visible.

"I'm going to see if Mom needs help," Ethan said, standing up from the floor. He walked over to Noah on his way out, quietly saying something that made Noah flush red and drop his eyes.

Not long after Ethan left, Sam wandered into the room with Addy and the puppies.

He saw Kaylee first, then Noah. His gaze swiveled to the other end of the room, where Talise and Luke were sitting together, fingers intertwined.

"Wrong. Still wrong. Really wrong. I'm going to be sick," he groaned before bolting out of the room.

"He is so fucking weird." Kaylee laughed.

"You have no idea." Noah laughed with her, unwilling to meet Adaline's scowl.

∞

THE FOLLOWING SATURDAY, three innocent dates later, Talise was at Luke's apartment, helping him work on a song. After lunch, they camped out on the couch to watch a movie together.

About a quarter of the way through the movie, she began feeling the anxiety seeping off of Luke.

"What's wrong?"

"Nothing. Why?" he asked.

"Luke." She rolled her eyes at him. "Really?"

"Oh. Yeah."

"So what's wrong?"

He shook his head. "Nothing. I just wish we had chosen a different movie."

"Why?" she asked, confused. He had suggested the movie.

His cheeks turned pink. "I didn't think about it is all. Love scenes are coming up. We can change it."

Talise raised her eyebrows.

"I don't want you to be uncomfortable."

"I'm not uncomfortable. You're uncomfortable."

"I know," he admitted, running a nervous hand through his hair.

"Luke?"

"Hmm?"

"I don't think we should date anymore," she said lightly.

He frowned at her. "Why?"

She stared at him.

"Yeah," he agreed, acknowledging defeat. "I know. I keep thinking it'll change. It might change, Tali."

She bumped him with her shoulder. "Love you. You are my very best friend. The only friend I had for a long time. But we're friends, Luke."

He stared straight ahead, not responding for a moment.

"Love you, too, Tali. You're absolutely perfect. Honestly. Perfect for me."

She snorted. "We're absolutely perfect for each other, except for the complete lack of physical attraction."

"Except for that."

After another pause, he sighed with relief.

She smacked herself in the forehead. "Luke, why? Why put yourself through this? You could have just told me!"

Luke frowned. "I didn't really think about it before now. And, again, you're perfect—gorgeous and smart, and we like all the same things. I thought it would change."

Talise scrunched up her face. "I don't have any siblings."

"It was like making out with Beth." Luke nodded as he scrubbed his hands down his face. "It seemed like such a good idea. I say again: you are perfect—my ideal woman in every way. I had no trouble recognizing that. It might change."

"It's not going to change, Luke."

"It might change."

She shook her head. "Not for me, I don't think."

Luke frowned, hurt. "You don't like me?"

"I love you, but it wouldn't work, Luke."

"Why?"

"Because I have slept *really* well since Labor Day." Talise chuckled.

That caught Luke off-guard. He broke into a grin. "That whole falling asleep thing should have been a clue."

"Minor detail."

"Gah!" Luke winced. "Darla's going to freak. You'll still go to the engagement party with me, right?"

"My stipulation remains. I will attend if you will dance."

Luke nodded. "As previously agreed, I will dance if you will sing."

"That is acceptable," Talise said primly before breaking out in a grin.

"I'm sorry, Tali."

She shrugged. "I'm not. We tried it. It didn't work. We're fine. Still us. You know, I still haven't seen *Spaceballs*."

Luke's mouth dropped open in faux-horror as he reached for the remote. "We should rectify that."

∞

TALISE OPTED out of Sunday dinner, leaving Luke to explain things. Darla frowned immediately when he turned the corner into the big room alone.

"Where's Talise?"

"Yeah," he said, rubbing his hand through his hair. "About that."

"What about that?" Hank was frowning, too.

"We're just going to be friends. We're not—"

"What did you do? Go say you're sorry!" Darla yelled.

Sam exhaled a gasping sigh of relief. "Better. Okay. Better. Maybe we'll get back on track."

"This is not better!" Darla yelled.

"This is better, Mom! She wasn't going to end up where she belongs if it stayed the way it was!" Sam yelled back.

"Sam! That doesn't make any damn sense, and you know it! They are *perfect* together!" Darla kept yelling, looking like she was going to cry.

"Mom," Luke said, touching her hand to share a bit of calm. "Really. He's right."

"So you dumped the recluse? That's out of character for you, Lucas," Noah observed, obscenely happy for reasons he couldn't identify.

Luke shook his head. "She ended it, not me. And she was right. It stung in the moment, but she was absolutely right."

"Well, why not try to work it out? I don't understand!" Darla was distraught, almost hyperventilating.

"Mom, she's great. One of my closest friends. I love her. Love her to bits. But she's a friend," Luke said, trying to put the conversation to bed.

Matthew sighed, meeting Luke's eyes with a shrug. They had strategized how to break this news to the family and decided it was better to not share details.

"Well, don't worry, Luke," Kaylee chimed in. "You can do better.

She was so quiet and aloof anyway. One of my closest friends is single, and she's super cute. Maybe we could do a double date one night?"

William started laughing.

"What?" Kaylee asked.

"I think that's actually the first thing you said as part of a family conversation, and it was to criticize a close friend for being too quiet. She says more to us than you do. Butt out."

Kaylee frowned at Will. "I was just trying to tell him not to worry about it."

"Will is not known for his kind and gentle manners," Noah soothed. "Ignore him."

Will shook his head. "Whatever, Noah. Pipe down, or we'll start talking about what you're known for."

Noah glared at his older brother.

"You really want to do this?" Will asked, serious. "I'm not taking the piss-poor attitude from you, Noah. I'm not impressed."

Will looked at Darla.

"I'll allow it." She nodded. "Don't push your luck. Watch your mouth. But I agree on the attitude."

Noah shook his head in annoyance, trying to change the subject. "So the engagement party is next week! Hurrah!"

"I'm not excited," Matty said.

"Is Talise even going to come to the party now?" Darla asked. "She has a jaw-dropping fancy dress for it! It's upstairs. We were going to do hair and makeup and everything!"

"Yes." Luke nodded. "She'll be here Saturday afternoon to get ready. She will stay at the hotel with us Saturday night. Again. We are still friends. We are just not a couple. The couple angle didn't work out. Rewind your view of our relationship a few weeks, and you'll be great. Things aren't even awkward now."

Sam was nodding excitedly. "Yep, this is great. Fucking great."

Darla glared.

"The swearing pass is over?" Sam asked, instantly contrite.

Darla nodded.

"Kids, don't talk like Uncle Sam," Sam coached as little heads nodded.

Luke glared at Sam. "Really, Sam? So gleeful?"

"Uh-huh!" Sam grinned.

"Where does Talise belong, Sam? Will you finally fess up to why you've been so angsty about things?" Luke asked.

Sam glanced around the room, eyes landing on Kaylee, who had no context for Sam's strange behavior.

Sam grinned. "Let's go into the dining room. I'll bet you ten bucks!"

Luke rolled his eyes. "No bets. I never bet against you."

"Just come on! You're not going to believe me. You'll take this bet."

Three minutes later, Luke yelled, "NO FUCKING WAY!"

"Lucas!" Darla yelled back.

"Yeah, yeah, I'll start scrubbing. But there's no fucking way! He got this wrong!"

"LUCAS!"

NOAH GOT up and went to work on Tuesday morning. But by the time he got there, he realized he had no desire to be there and nothing to do. His family was pissed off at him about nothing—no point in sitting through the day, getting glared at. After a short meeting with Jake and Hank, he left the office, intent on pastries and a leisurely day with the girlfriend he left in his bed that morning.

Kaylee worked Monday night. She'd still be sleeping when he got back to the apartment. Noah could climb back into bed with her and pretend like he never left.

He was quiet while unlocking the apartment door, trying not to wake her. As he gently closed the door behind himself, he heard the sound of Kaylee talking from the bedroom.

She's up! Morning sex! he thought.

Before he called out to her, he heard some of what she was saying. Curious, he moved closer.

"—so fucking stupid. He just goes along with it," Kaylee said.

Maybe talking to the friend for Luke? Talise was indeed so fucking stupid, and Luke did just go along with it.

"No," Kaylee sighed, sounding frustrated. "I mean, he has no problems leaving me in his place but doesn't seem in a hurry to move things along."

Not Luke. Decidedly not Luke. Noah closed his eyes, wincing as she continued to talk.

"No, no bank accounts. Can you believe it? Almost two months of fucking like rabbits and nothing to show for it. I'm never going to get out of that fucking job. Girl, I'm seriously considering a birth control whoopsie at this point. The rubbers are right here. A few teeny tiny holes, problem solved! Even if we didn't stay together, could you imagine the fucking child support check? I'll take it!"

Another pause. Noah could hear the murmur of someone else talking on the other end of the line.

"Don't get me wrong, the sex is amazing. Seriously. Holy fuck. Really lights my fire. But he has this crazy family, and they're all up in his shit. I just about punched his asshole brother on Sunday.

"Yeah, seven brothers. Mostly taken. But his younger brother is absolutely adorable. Total hottie. Super sweet, too. His shrew girlfriend just dumped him. I'll hook you up when the opportunity arises."

Wow. Kaylee and I have very different ideas of what constitutes being a shrew.

Then Noah was thinking back to snapping at Talise over the holiday weekend. She had tried to warn him, tried to tell him.

Fuck, he thought with a heaving sigh. *I need to apologize to her. For this and for scaring her. Maybe we can start fresh.*

"Hello?" Kaylee called.

"Hang on a sec," she said into the phone. "I thought I just heard something. Maybe the maid is here. Yeah, a fucking maid. I love it! Be right back.

"Hey, please be sure to scrub the tub," she lectured, coming around the corner. "I saw some soap scum in there—"

She stopped short at the sight of Noah.

"Yeah. Pack your shit. I'll order you a car. You can make a grand exit in a fucking limo," he said, voice cold.

LATER THAT DAY, Noah was sitting in Jake and Matty's apartment, telling the story.

"Ethan and I were at her restaurant right before all the shit went down in Dallas. Apparently, I was flirting with her, joking around while paying our bill with the AmEx. I don't even remember.

"She saw the name and had been looking for me around the office, stalker style. She eventually found me. It never occurred to me to ask her why she was in the Loop so early in the morning when she works afternoons and nights," Noah admitted.

"I'm sorry, Noah," Matty said.

"You all right?" Jake asked.

"Yeah, surprisingly fine. She was fun." Noah shrugged. "There was no reason to end things before now. With the energy under control, I'm less flighty. I was thoroughly entertained by sleeping with the same woman for more than three nights, so maybe Will has a point with the whole 'relationship' thing."

"You know what's even better?" Jake asked, smiling.

"What's that?" Noah asked, smiling back.

"Love. Seriously, next-level stuff."

Noah snorted. "Eh, maybe I did love her. I don't know."

Matilda shook her head. "I don't think so, Noah. You'd know it if you did."

"Would I? Let's be honest, Matty. My view of relationships is a bit whacky. I'm not sure love is something I'll ever share with someone outside our family."

"It's just not right yet, Noah. It'll be right eventually," she counseled. "And then when it is, there's no escaping it."

Jake snorted.

"Shuddup." Matty smiled at him.

"Nope," Noah said, shaking his head. "You left my heart in tiny shriveled pieces, Carrots. There's no one for me now that you're with the pool goober."

Noah grinned at her as she threw a coaster at his head.

"Do me a favor?" he asked, hesitant.

"What?" Matty asked back.

Noah smiled again. "I appreciate that you didn't immediately agree."

"I know better these days." Matty grinned.

"I'll tell Dad at work tomorrow, but would you tell Mom to just leave it alone on Saturday? I'm not all that upset about it, but I don't want to listen to her rag about Kaylee being perfect and all that crap like she did to Luke on Sunday."

Jake snorted.

"What?" Noah asked.

Jake shrugged. "She's never admitted it, but I don't think Mom liked her. Not dislike, but just 'meh.' Kaylee ate the lasagna, though, so we didn't vote."

"Well, fuck. Mom should have told me that. I would have ended things," Noah griped.

"Really?" Jake asked, surprised.

"Um, yeah. I'm a terrible judge of character. You people gotta tell me this shit!"

They sat quiet, weeding through loose thoughts for a moment.

"It's one of the few bad breakups I've had," Noah admitted, face scrunched up. "She was crying and carrying on about how she started off wanting the money but had grown to care, yada yada yada. I'm not sure what she thought was going to happen."

"Did you really call her a limo?" Jake asked with a grin.

"Yup." Noah laughed. "Made her carry her own shit out to the car, too. It wasn't quite as satisfying as Stephanie-Bella, but I enjoyed it. Took that page right out of your book!"

29

Talise was sitting in Luke's car in his parents' driveway.

"I should just get ready at home," she said for the fifteenth time. "Please? Can I just get ready at home?"

"Tali, they're expecting you. It was one of the first questions Darla asked," Luke said. Again.

"Do they hate me?"

"Absolutely not."

"Well, tell me what you told them."

"I've already told you. Twice. I didn't give them any details. No embarrassing questions are waiting for you. Maybe just a little bit of Darla nagging, but only because she correctly believes you're perfect."

"Please stop saying that," Talise said, lip quivering.

"Are you about to cry?" Luke asked, trying not to laugh.

"They're going to hate me now!" she wailed, wiping tears away. "Let's be a couple again for tonight, and then we can stop!"

"Talise. They are not going to hate you. They don't hate you. I promise."

She frowned. "Noah hates me. Everyone's going to agree with him now."

"Noah's a jackass. And he just broke up with the bitchy girlfriend, so he's probably too distracted to give you a hard time."

"What happened?" she asked, sidetracked. "He seemed to like her."

"I forgot to tell you. You called that. One hundred percent. Spot on. He went home from work early on Tuesday and heard her bitching to a friend about how he wasn't giving her cash."

"Ugh. That's horrible."

"Yes, it is," Luke agreed, seeing an opportunity. "They hate her now. They're going to spend the entire afternoon girl-talk-bitching about her. We're old news; they've moved on to the Noah drama. So we can get out of the car now."

She didn't move.

"Seriously," Luke cajoled. "I saw Darla watching us through the upstairs window. We should get out of the car before she comes down to check on us."

Talise begrudgingly got out of the car and walked with Luke toward the house. Darla threw open the door just as they were stepping onto the porch.

"Oh! Good. I was coming down to check on you," Darla said.

Talise burst out laughing.

"Hi, Mom," Luke said, giving Talise a smug smile.

"Hi, sweetheart," Darla said, accepting the obligatory kiss. "Everyone okay?"

Talise nodded.

Darla let out a sigh of frustration. "Talise, I absolutely hate this."

Talise froze, eyes going wide.

"Tell me again why I can't hug you? This is so awkward for me! I'm a hugger. Luke! Why can't I hug?"

"Oh," Talise exclaimed, surprised. "Hugs are probably fine now. I'm getting good at controlling things. The emotions don't destroy me quite as much. I can sort them now. It's just a little harder when I'm not expecting it."

Darla face lit up. "I can hug?"

Luke rolled his eyes. "Warning before hugging is probably a good idea."

Darla seized Talise, pulling her into a full hug. "Oh, sweetheart. I'm so glad you're doing better."

Looking on, Luke tried not to laugh but failed miserably. Darla was five foot two inches on her best days. Talise had to be five feet, nine inches in flats. Darla's forceful hug looked ridiculous.

Luke's mirth died suddenly when he realized Talise was crying again.

"Tali?" he asked as he offered his hand. "Was the hug a bad idea?"

She shook her head, declining his help.

"What happened?" Luke asked.

"She doesn't hate me," Talise wailed.

Luke sighed. Darla looked confused.

"She worried you wouldn't want her here because we aren't dating," Luke explained.

Darla laughed. "People get back together, Talise. And I have other sons. We're a long way from me giving up on the romance angle. But you'll always be welcome here."

Talise gave a sniff of snotty laughter.

"Come on, the girls are upstairs," Darla said, pulling Tali into the house.

"Hey, wanna date Matthew? I think he's in love with Matty's little sister, but you never know," Luke offered.

Talise smacked him in the back of the head. "You've ruined me for all Trellis men."

"YAY! LOOK HOW PRETTY WE ARE!" Ellie clapped.

"I cannot believe you're wearing a wedding dress." Matty laughed.

"It looks like a white evening gown. No one will know it's a wedding dress! Besides, Darla's wearing one, too."

"Yes, but Darla's rich and known for being eccentric," Matty pointed out. "No one would dare laugh at her."

"Damn straight," Darla muttered, admiring herself in her white beaded gown. "Besides, we look amazing! Deo did a good job."

Matilda ran her hands down her silver floor-length gown. Fitted over her curves, it fell loose from mid-thigh, making it easy for her to move. While it was backless, the neckline was modest. "I love this dress. I'm so happy it covers my boobs this time."

"You look amazing, Matty." Emma grinned.

"Shut up about the mermaid dress! I love that dress on you," Ellie complained. "How come no wedding dress, Emma?"

Emma sighed. "I'm sad to be missing out on the wedding dress theme. I didn't have one, either. But I had no good way to judge what the baby bump would look like."

"It's tiny, though!" Ellie objected. "If I didn't know the most beautiful woman in the world and He-man were having babies, I'd never notice."

"Shuddup about that," Emma said, turning red as Beth started giggling.

"She hates the 'most beautiful woman in the world' cracks. They make me so happy," Beth admitted.

"Seriously, the lesser mortals are going to be drooling over us tonight. Glowing bride to be. Gorgeous mother of the groom. Breathtaking bestie." Ellie paused to raise her hand. "The most beautiful woman in the world, literally. Lucy, the Barbie. Beth the princess-next-bride. And the fucking ballerina back there, trying to hide. TALISE! Come here so we can fawn over you!"

"Look. It's like her damn feet don't even touch the ground!" Darla laughed. "Perfect posture."

The entire upper half of Talise's body was flushed with a deep, embarrassed blush.

"You've seen. Can I go back to hiding?" she whimpered. "I know this seemed like a good idea at the time we bought dresses, but I can't walk around like this!"

"I'm going to drag you, kicking and screaming, out of your shell," Ellie threatened.

"My shell is so cozy, though. This dress has bare arms and an open back. People are going to touch me," she said, breathing through her panic.

"Talise!" Ellie barked. "You will do as you are told. Now smile. I think there's lipstick on your teeth."

NOAH WAS PACING AROUND HIS PARENTS' kitchen in a fancy suit. It should have been obvious that Darla didn't like Kaylee; Kaylee was not included in the dress shopping.

So, there he was: pacing around the kitchen alone, without a date, because he didn't catch on that his girlfriend was an asshole. It was going to be a long night.

"You all right?" Jake asked.

"Fine," Noah replied, dismissive.

"Because you seem tense," Jake continued.

"Meh."

"Why no date?" Jake asked.

Noah glared at him.

"Noah, I have seen you make a date three minutes after meeting a woman. Why no date? Secretly pining for the gold-digger?"

"No, I just don't want to deal with the bullshit. Maybe I'll make a friend tonight." He shrugged. "Where's Sam?"

"With Addy at Jess's house. They'll meet us there."

"Think anyone would notice if I bailed?" Noah asked, curious.

"Yup. You wouldn't even make it out of the driveway before Hank chased you down, and you know it."

"They're coming downstairs," Adrian called. "Come admire appropriately."

Noah rolled his eyes, moving into the foyer with Jake. "Great, let's get the show on the road."

"We're doing this in order! You damn well better 'ohh' and 'ahh' on cue, boys, or we will have words!" Ellie yelled down.

Hank grinned at Charlie and Eric, laughing.

Charlie shook his head. "Never a dull moment. Never."

Darla came down the stairs first, doing a little spin for the gathered gentlemen to admire.

"You really did buy a wedding dress," Hank said, chuckling.

"Ellie said I could!" Darla laughed. "I'm eccentric. Not weird."

"You look beautiful, wife." Hank grinned.

She looked around the foyer. "No tuxedos?"

"We compromised on suits," Jake said flatly. "Take what you can get."

"Killjoy," Darla muttered as Emma came down the stairs in her pale green evening gown.

After pausing to do a cheeky little camera pose, despite the absence of cameras, she walked over and straightened Will's tie.

"You clean up good." She grinned. "You ready for this? We're going public tonight."

"You are gorgeous as always, Pip, and if anyone tries to touch you, I'll break their hand."

"Behave," she warned, quasi-serious.

Lucy came downstairs next, eliciting actual gasps from the menfolk.

She paused halfway down. "I'm not sure if I should be offended by the shocked looks!"

"You never wear anything but jeans and t-shirts! We knew you were cute, Lou, but I missed the Barbie doll aspects!" Hennessy objected.

She smacked him as she walked over to Adrian, grinning.

"You clean up good." He laughed, borrowing Emma's words as he dodged a smack. "Amazing. You're amazing."

"Better," she agreed.

Beth came downstairs in a dress of such pale yellow, it could be mistaken for cream. Her light brown hair was up in a twist, skin glowing.

"Holy hell," Hennessy breathed.

"I'll take it!" Beth clapped.

There was a long pause as they waited for the next woman to descend the stairs.

"Hello?" Hank yelled.

"GET YOUR ASS DOWN THOSE STAIRS AND BE ADMIRED!" Ellie roared.

Hank snorted with surprised laughter, triggering Charlie and Eric. Luke scrubbed his hands down his face, shaking with laughter.

A second later, Talise appeared.

Oh my God. Noah's brain got stuck trying to process thoughts as she moved down the stairs, head held high, back straight. *She is absolutely glorious.*

Talise's evening gown was a pale rose-tan silk that glided with her movements. It slid down her slender curves, accenting the slight flare from waist to hips. Her hair hung loose and curled, her amber-colored eyes accented by evening makeup.

A wave of raw, possessive lust hit Noah without warning. He exhaled as if he'd been kicked in the gut.

Holy fuck. Get it together, self. The hot brunette is still hot. Fine. She also has a swift kick reflex, the logical part of Noah's brain thought as he tried, and failed, to pull his energy back.

Mine. Mine. Mine. Mine, the energy chanted. *She belongs to me. Mine. My bed. Mine.*

Noah shook his head in disgust at his own cave-man thoughts. *Holy shit, Darla's head would explode if she caught me thinking like that. So wrong.*

The logical thoughts were at the forefront again. *I'll stay away from her. Space. She needs space and peace.*

Wrapped up in his own thoughts, he missed the opportunity to pay her a compliment. Ellie was already coming down the stairs, radiant in her white evening gown.

Is that a wedding dress?

Matilda finally headed down the stairs but lost a shoe halfway. In the time it took her to turn around and stare, horrified, at the wayward shoe, Jake ran up the stairs and grabbed it.

"Are these…house slippers? I love you so much." Jake laughed.

"No one can see them anyway!" Matilda said, turning bright red.

"I wasn't objecting, Cinderella. I think it's great; you won't have sore feet! Step into your house slipper, and let's hit the road before shit gets real. You look amazing. Breathtaking. Radiant. Beautiful. All the words." He grinned, getting a laugh out of her.

"THERE ARE CAMERAS OUT THERE, Matty. Please don't freak out," Luke teased. "Do you need help?"

She shook her head. "Over it."

Luke beamed at her.

"You should be the last ones out of this car," Darla instructed. "Hank and I will go, then Luke and Talise, then you two. Ethan, Noah, and Matthew will probably go together out of their car, followed by Beth and Hennessy and then Adrian and Lucy. Charlie, Ellie, and Eric can go whenever they want. But I'm guessing no one wants to be stuck behind Will and Emma."

Hank's brow furrowed. "Sam and Adaline are in the car behind Will and Emma. Do you think Sam should go before Will?"

Darla paused. "I don't know. They're all going to cause a scene no matter what. It's up to him."

"I can't say that to him," Hank said, voice flat.

"Why?" Darla asked, confused.

"He'll leave."

"He wouldn't ditch my party," Matilda said, eyes narrowed. "We would have words. If he gets to escape, we do, too!"

"Hush!" Darla scolded, glaring at her. "It's five hours. You can stand five hours of being admired, Matilda. Then you can run away to your hotel room upstairs, be done with it, and put the whole thing behind you."

"Mom, there are like five hundred people at this thing. No one would notice..." Jake stopped talking after Darla gave him a look.

"You will do this, Jacob," Darla declared.

"Obviously," Jake muttered under his breath.

"This is the price of getting engaged first." Hank grinned.

Jake shook his head. "William went first! This is bullshit."

"Still, I'm not giving you the room keys until after dinner. We put all the overnight bags in the rooms this afternoon, so you can be cozy after you're a good sport about your party," Hank teased as someone opened the car door.

"Four hours instead of five?" Jake tried to negotiate.

The Trellis family matriarch was glowering when she got out of the car.

"Ready?" Luke asked Talise, grinning.

"Sure." She shrugged.

Luke climbed out of the car and paused, reaching back for Talise's hand.

There was a slight pause from the cameras and reporters.

"Lucas, who's your date?"

"Luke, is this your—"

"What's your name—"

The shouts changed tone when Jake and Matty appeared.

"Matilda, who designed your dress?"

"Jake have you talked with—"

"Are you both ready to—"

Questions continued as each family member arrived. The cameras went crazy when someone noticed Beth's engagement ring.

Ellie was so excited, she almost danced her way into the hotel with Charlie on one arm and Eric on the other.

"Here we go," Hank murmured, watching the car with Adrian, Lucy, Will, and Emma pull up.

Cameras flashed, and questions rang out to Adrian and Lucy. But it wasn't unusual for Adrian to have a date for a social gathering.

When William reached back into the car to take Emma's hand, there was a loaded pause from onlookers, as if they could sense juicy gossip in the making. Emma emerged from behind Will, giving him a little grin.

The crowd was absolutely still for three full heartbeats.

"Emma!"

"Emma Gracen, are—"

"William, how long have you known—"

"Are you two dating?"

She reached up to pull Will down into a kiss, her wedding ring shining on her hand.

All hell broke loose as cameras swiveled between family members. People yelled questions over each other. The crowd was breaking through the line of security when Sam climbed out of his limo. He shared a look with his tense oldest brother before helping Addy out of the car.

Like hitting a mute button, everything went silent. The crowd backed away as Sam strolled up the entryway to his family with Adaline on his arm. No one shouted questions. The cameras didn't flash.

"That was fun," Sam said with a small smile. "Let's go inside. They're not going to stay this way."

"What did you do?" Emma asked, impressed.

"I showed up." Sam grinned.

MIRANDA WATCHED her older sister walk into the ballroom on Jake's arm and sighed.

So perfect together. So right, she cheered internally.

"She's positively glowing with happiness," Megan murmured, looking in the same direction with a smile.

"Don't ruin it," Miranda chided her mother.

Megan winced. "I swear I wasn't trying to hurt her, Miranda. I want my girls to be happy."

Miranda gave a tiny snort. "You'd be batting five hundred on that, Mom, if you just stayed out of her way."

"Noted." Megan nodded. "I have no intention of commenting on her relationships again."

"Woo, how do I get on that list of cast-offs? Can you write me off in a similar manner?" Miranda grinned.

"Hush," Megan said, showing a sad smile. "I know I'm a terrible mother. Leave..."

Megan's words trailed off as she watched the remainder of the Trellis family enter the ballroom.

"I should have told you," Miranda admitted, watching Matthew. "I didn't want to talk about him."

Megan's eyebrows climbed up to her hairline.

"Trellis, Mom. Matthew Trellis. He's Jake's brother. I didn't put it together, either, until I was standing in the middle of Darla's living room."

Megan stared at her younger daughter, unblinking.

"I'm fine," Miranda said.

Megan didn't move.

"Just friends," Miranda continued. "Please stop staring at me."

"Miranda," Megan breathed.

"I know."

Megan's eyes lit with fire. "Divorce him. Get out of there. Matthew would help you. He has the means to help you get out of that."

Miranda shook her head. "Sam offered me the means to get out a month ago. Jake and Matty have offered repeatedly. I wouldn't take Matthew's help. I don't need to add knight-in-shining-armor to his list of fine qualities. Stop now. Darla's coming over with Hank."

"Oh God," Megan muttered, voice tight with anxiety. "This woman is going to hate me. Judge me and hate me."

"Absolutely," Miranda agreed.

NOAH STOOD ALONE in the crowded ballroom. There were interested women around him. He could feel their eyes. But it just didn't seem worth it. All the trouble he went through to ensure he didn't influence Kaylee was for naught. The money had already corrupted her view of things. There was likely no way out of this bachelor situation with his dignity intact.

The thought caught him by surprise. *Am I trying to get out of this bachelor's situation? When did that happen?*

As he watched, Will and Emma were laughing together, talking to

Ava and Clyde. Adrian and Lucy were at the table in front of him, whispering, so close their foreheads almost touched. And, off to the right, almost out of the line of sight, Luke and Talise danced.

Luke kept spinning her, making Talise giggle. Noah couldn't hear the laughter, but he could see it in her expression and posture.

No smiles or giggles with me. The hot brunette is terrified of me, he thought, suddenly angry. His energy exploded outward as heads turned to stare at him.

The song finished. The crowd clapped as Noah pulled his energy back to himself.

The maestro invited Luke on stage to play the piano.

Here we go—time to put on a show. I dislike Luke. Fucking Peace. It must be nice.

When Talise followed Luke on stage, though, Noah stood up straighter. *Luke said she was musical, didn't he? I'm pretty sure I remember that.*

After introducing Talise, Luke hit a chord and then grinned at her.

Her eyebrows winged up.

"That's not much of an engagement party love song, Luke." She laughed into the microphone.

"That's crap! Matty will love it." He played a series of keys that were somehow teasing and mocking.

"Fine." She grinned at him.

Hot brunette, you're killing me right now. Where's my smile?

Luke hit the chord again.

Talise's voice echoed through the silent room.

"Holy fuck," Emma breathed, startling Noah. He hadn't realized she and Will were standing there. "I love Andra Day's 'Rise Up.'"

"Wow," Noah breathed, transfixed.

When the song finished, Talise sang Adele, then Norah Jones, then Luke's new song. By the time she stopped singing, Noah was headed for the door, sick to his stomach as Luke and Talise took their bows.

"Where are you going?" Hank asked, grabbing Noah's arm.

Noah shook his head. "I'm going to peace out, Dad. No one will miss me. Enjoy the party."

Hank sighed. "Noah, I'm sorry things didn't end well with Kaylee, but don't do this to your brother. Don't do this to Matty."

"Do what? *They* don't even want to be here!"

"Really? Look at them. They look pretty damn happy to me."

And they did look happy, standing together, Jake's arm around Matty's waist, talking to her stepdad.

"They won't miss me," Noah said. "I don't feel well, Dad. I'm going to go up to my room. Maybe I'll come back down."

Hank sighed again, frustrated. "Don't let your mother see you leaving."

Noah nodded.

Knowing she had a sixth sense when it came to her children defying her orders, Noah was paranoid as he made his way to a side door, walking backward so he could watch for her.

"I CANNOT BELIEVE we just did that, Lucas," Talise squealed, following Luke out of the ballroom, into the hallway, in search of fresh air.

"You killed it!" Luke cheered.

"You owe me like six hundred dances now."

"Bah! You loved it. Admit it." He grinned.

Talise bit back her own grin. "It was fine."

"You are so full of shit!" Luke laughed.

"I know. It was great." She grinned, doing a silly little pirouette in place.

Backing out of a secondary door without looking, Noah slammed into her before her spin was done.

"Noah!" Luke yelled, startled, looking at Talise and his brother on their asses in front of him. "What the fuck?"

Fuck! This can't be happening. Please, I can't do this right now. This can't be happening, he chanted internally.

The world slowed down. Noah could feel the heart beating in his chest and the air cycling through his lungs. Turning his head, he knew Talise would be on the ground with him. He knew it.

When his eyes met hers, Noah's energy exploded out of him, uncontrolled.

Oh, God. I hate everything about the energy. I hate this. I hate everything about this. I hate that this is going to be my eternity—women pandering to the money or the energy without giving an actual flying fuck about me.

Talise's eyes glazed over then went glassy.

Noah's stomach flipped in revulsion as he pushed himself back to his feet.

"Are you okay, Tali?" Luke asked, panicked.

TALISE COULDN'T HEAR LUKE, didn't register anything except Noah's deafeningly loud emotions as they washed against her mind.

Surprise. Concern, she identified.

Then, as his eyes met hers, energy exploded from him.

Hatred. He hates me. Actual hate.

Talise couldn't breathe as her body began to shake.

NOAH AND LUKE both extended hands to help Talise up at the same time.

She took Luke's hand.

I hate him. I hate my brother, Noah realized.

"What were you doing?" Luke demanded.

Noah didn't respond, afraid of what would come out of his mouth.

Talise was facing him now.

"N-Noah," she said, eyes filling with tears. "I-I-I'm so sorry about Kaylee. I—"

"What?" Noah interrupted, shaking his head.

Tears? She's so fucking afraid of me she's shaking. Now tears, too?

"Forget about it. It doesn't matter. Sorry. I wasn't looking where I was going," Noah ground out.

He turned to walk toward the elevators. There was a room upstairs with his overnight bag in it. He could be out of this suit in ninety seconds, maybe less.

There was a hand on his arm, stopping him. It was a woman's hand. It was Tali's hand. She was touching Noah's arm, still standing there, holding Luke's hand.

I hate him. She's so terrified of me, she's shaking. Crying. But fucking Luke is golden. He has no fucking clue what to do or how to be with her. I hate him. I hate her. I hate her. I hate the sight of her with him.

His vision went red with rage.

"Don't touch me, Talise," he said, voice low. "Stand there with Luke and keep your damn hands to yourself, you pathetic wretch of a woman. Don't say a fucking word. I don't understand what's happening. Everything is fucked up. This is absurd. Ridiculous. Not unlike that fucking dress. It looks like goddam skin. You might as well be walking around naked. Was that the effect you were going for?"

Talise's spine straightened, shoulders level, chin high. Without a word, she turned and went back into the ballroom.

30

What is happening? Luke wondered, staring at his usually carefree, jovial brother in shock. *He is out of control. Like Adrian was out of control. Did Kaylee fuck up his energy?*

After Talise walked away, Noah turned to go. Luke grabbed his arm.

Somehow, Luke was expecting the punch that Noah threw at his head. He blocked it quickly.

"What is wrong with you?" Luke whispered. "Noah, this isn't you."

Grabbing his brother's hand, Luke pushed calm and peace until the anger left his brother's posture. Noah's gaze dropped to the floor.

"Can you hear me?" Luke muttered. "You're conscious, right?"

Noah gave a small nod.

"You are acting like a child. The next time you want to be self-righteous about how courteous you are of other people's feelings, remember this moment. Remember that you are, in fact, the selfish prick that Matthew and I mistook you for that day in the car.

"She kicked you because she was afraid. She told you about Kaylee because she didn't want you to get hurt. She's done nothing to deserve your scorn, Noah. Nothing at all. You've wavered between an intimidating jackass and a full-on asshole since you met her. Have you ever had a non-confrontational conversation with her?" Luke breathed, his anger and disappointment worse for the quiet of his voice.

"I'm sorry I hurt your feelings when I told you off in the car that day. That's on me, not her. But every last time you're dismissive or rude to her, you're just proving my point. You overreact to everything. Get your shit together. She doesn't deserve this."

Noah didn't move, but Luke knew he heard every word.

After a few seconds, Luke walked calmly back into the ballroom, looking for Talise. She was heading out a door to the balcony attached to the ballroom. He made his way through the crowd, trying not to draw attention to the drama.

"I don't think he's right in the head, Talise. I think his energy is screwed up after Kaylee," Luke explained as the balcony door closed behind him.

The night air had turned cold. A storm was moving toward them, thunder flashing in the distance.

"It's fine," she murmured. "It's just when I said he hated me, I didn't think he *actually* hated me."

Luke tried to turn her into a hug. She didn't move.

"I thought he disliked me. Not hate. Not real hate. But there's hate there. Stomach-churning, active hate. I'm not sure anyone has truly hated me before. I am not used to hate, you know?" she rambled quietly.

"He's not right, Tali. He's not. He took a swing at me. Noah's a lover, not a fighter. He doesn't do that. I don't think any of us realized how tore up he was about Kaylee."

She nodded.

"I pumped him full of calm just now. He was so ashamed, he couldn't even look at me."

She nodded again.

"Tali, please don't do this. It's not worth it."

"Luke, I'm fine. I just need to get myself together. I'll be inside in a few minutes, okay?" she choked out through tears.

I'll never forgive him for this, Luke thought, silently loathing his brother.

"Tali," Luke soothed, offering his hand and his energy.

She didn't take it.

"Just a few minutes, okay? I can do this on my own."

"Do you want to go upstairs?" Luke asked. "I'll walk you up to your room if you just want to be done with tonight. Or I'll take you home. My car is here in the garage. I dropped it off this afternoon when we came down to check into the rooms."

She gave a little snort. "Nice try. You still owe me six hundred dances. It's waterproof mascara. You're not getting out of dancing that easily."

Luke could hear the smile in her voice.

"I'm fine, Luke. I just need a breather. Few minutes, okay? I'm trying to rein things in without help. I wasn't expecting that. I need a few minutes."

"I'll be at the bar," he said, kissing the back of her head.

NOAH STOOD in the hallway alone, chewing on his lip. Things had gotten out of hand. He had been rude. Intentionally hurtful. It didn't sit well. His stomach rolled again at the memory of pain on Talise's face.

He'd apologize when he next saw her. The next circle, he'd apologize and try to start over. Luke was right. Noah was a petulant child. He'd been an idiot since Luke and Matthew gave him grief in the car that day, holding it against Talise.

Letting out a sigh, he knew waiting wouldn't work. The guilt would eat at him.

NOAH: I need Talise's number.
LUKE: ?
NOAH: You're right. I'm wrong. Very wrong. I was an asshole.
LUKE: I'm guessing she doesn't want to talk to you. Leave her alone.

NOAH: Just give me her number. I'll apologize.
LUKE: She's freezing her ass off on the balcony outside the ballroom, watching the storm roll in. Be an adult. Go apologize in person.

Weaving his way through the crowded ballroom, Noah could feel the hungry eyes tracking him, could sense the women (and men) who wanted in his bed. He was too distracted to care. It was white noise in his brain.

Slamming out of the balcony door, he didn't see her. *Maybe she went inside?*

Around the corner of the building, at the other end of the balcony, there was a small sniffling sound.

Fuck. She's still crying.

Noah dragged his feet a little bit so she'd hear him coming, then he realized how ridiculous that was. She knew he was there. There was no sneaking up on her.

"Please go away," Talise said, voice chilled, resigned.

"I'm sorry, Talise. That was beyond rude and wrong. I'm sorry," Noah apologized, hoping she could hear his sincerity.

Her head dropped as she wiped at her eyes. "Just go, Noah. We aren't friends and won't be friends. I understand; I'll leave you alone. So go, please?"

"Talise, I am sorry. I was out of line. Mad about a lot of things, none of which are your fault."

She shivered as lightning streaked across the sky.

Moving closer, he dropped his coat over her narrow, bare shoulders, careful not to touch her. "I'm fond of this suit. Don't do that girl thing where you keep my clothes forever, okay?"

Her shoulders dropped immediately as she started shrugging out of it.

"No. Talise, I was joking. Don't," Noah said as he wrapped the suit coat back around her shoulders. "I'm sorry, really. It's fine. It's a suit. Bleh. Impossible to be fond of it."

There was teary snort of laughter.

"You're all leaky and snotty anyway. I don't want it back. Eww," he tried to tease, wrapping her in a quick hug, still careful not to touch her skin. He let her go and turned to leave.

"Noah?" she called.

"Hmm?"

"I'm sorry I kneed you. I...wasn't well. Scared. Didn't know you," Tali choked out.

He nodded. "I know."

"I don't want you to hate me," she blurted.

Brow furrowed, Noah shook his head. "I don't hate you."

Even in the darkness, he could see Talise's eyes swimming with tears.

"Noah, I felt it."

"Talise, I don't hate you. I'm trying to respect your need for space. I'm trying to leave you be, at peace. I don't hate you. If that's what you think you're getting from me, you're wrong."

She swallowed hard, fighting off more tears.

Noah sighed. "How do I make this better, Talise? I don't know how to behave around you, how to make you comfortable. I can't joke, tease, or make an ass of myself flirting with you because that scares you. I hate that you're afraid of me. It drives me up a fucking wall. So I'm trying to leave you alone."

Talise's mouth opened and closed a few times, but no words came out.

"I don't hate you. I think you're a beautiful person despite traveling a hard road in life. I'm sensitive to that and don't want to make it harder. What exactly can I do or say to make things easier for you?"

She took the coat off as his frustration rolled into her mind. She moved closer to hand him the coat. "Thank you."

Noah blew out a sigh as she wrapped her arms around herself. "Are you coming back inside? It's freezing out here."

"In a few minutes."

"Then keep the coat. Don't stand out here shivering like this." Noah stretched to wrap the coat around her.

HE DIDN'T STRETCH QUITE FAR ENOUGH to avoid touching Talise. As Noah's thumb brushed the back of her shoulder, his emotions slammed through her again.

Shame. Sorrow. Defeated resignation. Then, quieter, desire.

Desire for what? she wondered.

He was telling the truth; there was no hatred. But the emotional mix didn't make sense.

"Did I touch you?" Noah muttered. "I'm sorry. I try not to do that."

Talise was staring at the hand that had touched her, trying to weed his emotions out from her own. It was a confusing jumble, hard to sort through with just a glancing touch.

"Are you okay?" he asked, stepping further back.

His fear washed against her mind.

Tali's lifted her gaze to meet his eyes.

"I'm fine," she replied. "I just don't understand you. I don't understand what you're afraid of right now. I don't understand your emotional shit pile!"

Noah's eyebrows lifted. "You could ask."

"Why are you afraid of me?" Talise almost yelled the question in her frustration. "I don't understand. I'm not going to kick you again!"

Noah gave a little chuckle. "I'm not afraid of being kicked. I mean, I don't want to be kicked. Please don't. But I'm not worried about it."

Talise threw her arms out to the sides in an angry shrug. "What then?"

Noah paused, trying to decide where to go with this. He owed her a little bit of honesty.

"I'm not afraid of you, Talise. I'm worried I'm going to scare you again. I scared the crap out of you that first day without realizing it. You were utterly freaked out. I was too busy trying to give Luke a hard time. I hate that. I hate that anyone would be scared of me, especially you. You've got enough shit to deal with.

"I hate that I snapped at you about Kaylee at the lake house. I hate that you curled yourself in a ball because you were so afraid of my anger."

She stared at him, mouth hanging open in surprise.

"Contrary to my recent behavior, I'm generally not an asshole. I don't want to do anything that causes you pain or makes things worse. I'm afraid I'm going to fuck up and cause you pain again without realizing it. I'm not afraid of you. I'm afraid I'm going to do something that hurts you," he admitted.

"Oh," Talise muttered, taken aback. "I-I wasn't afraid. At the lake house, I wasn't afraid. I was ashamed. Luke told me to leave it alone, and I didn't. I was ashamed for butting into your business. I knew it was wrong. I'm not afraid of you, either."

He didn't acknowledge her words at all.

"Sorrow?" she asked a few heartbeats later.

Noah blew out his own frustrated sigh. "Tali, you're standing out here crying because I was an asshole. That's not something to be proud of, particularly because I'd rather not cause you pain. I just explained that, and yet, here we are. It's like I'm destined to be a dick to you, even when trying my damnedest to leave you alone."

"Desire?" she asked, gaze still on Noah's face in the darkness.

His lips tipped up a bit at the corners. It wasn't the smile he shared with family and friends; it didn't touch his eyes.

The real smile is not for me. We're not friends, she reminded herself. Her own sorrow flowed through her mind.

Noah shrugged. "I don't think that one's mine."

"Your what?" she asked, confused.

"My emotion. I don't think that's mine. Everything with Luke...no. I'm careful with the energy now. If I was lusting after you, you'd know it," Noah promised, half-smile still lurking.

Talise frowned. *That's not mine. He's full of shit!*

She rolled her eyes at him.

"Fine, don't own it. Whatever." Talise handed him back his jacket.

Noah shook his head at her. He put his coat back on and extended his hand to her. "I'll own it if it's mine."

Talise glared at him and didn't take the offered hand, assuming he'd drop it. He didn't.

"Who's scared now?" he taunted, chuckling again at her expression. "You're falling for my charms after all. Poor Luke."

"I am not," she scolded him. "And shut up about Luke. You don't know what you're talking about."

Noah made chicken noises at her.

"Shut up!" Talise bitched, turning red.

"Tali's got a crush on me!" Noah teased.

"Noah, stop it! I do not! Lust is your thing, not mine."

I think, Talise admitted to herself, watching his chocolate eyes dance with laughter.

"It's not my fault you won't own it," she continued.

Noah made chicken noises and flapping motions with his arms.

"Shut. Up," Talise growled. "You're such a jackass!"

"I'm a jackass that you have a crush on!" Noah crowed.

"You are such a pig! I do not have a crush on you!" She paused. "At least not a big one."

Noah threw his head back, really laughing now.

BACK IN THE BALLROOM, Sam was looking for his youngest brother. He finally found him, tucked away by the bar, talking with Claire.

"Hi, Claire," Sam said quickly before turning to Luke. "You know what's fun?"

Luke blinked. "I am so scared of what's going to come out of your mouth right now."

The joy left Sam's face. "Hey."

Luke rolled his eyes. "Fine, Sam. What's fun?"

"Losing ten bucks to me! Right now," Sam replied, his grin smug.

It took Luke a couple of seconds to catch up. Then his lips twitched as he bit back a smile. "You're lying. You've got that wrong."

"I do not. Come on!" Sam was gleefully bouncing.

"What's going on?" Claire asked.

Luke shook his head. "I can't imagine how that could possibly be a thing right now, Sam. Seriously. I told him off not even ten minutes ago for being an asshole."

"It's totally a thing!"

Luke's eyebrows hiked up. "Were you spying?"

"No! Not like that, at least. Come on!"

"Where are we going?" Luke asked.

"The balcony," Sam said, pleased with himself.

"What's on the balcony?" Claire asked.

Luke's smile dipped a bit.

Noah and Talise? Luke thought, not having taken Sam's premonition seriously until that moment.

"You're serious?"

"I am!" Sam said, still bouncing.

"Sam, she can't do the weekend love affair thing. It'll kill her."

Luke's stomach filled with dread. Talise did not need a temporary bed partner. She didn't need the heartache of being dumped and then the stress of seeing Noah regularly.

Luke glanced at Sam, bouncing on the balls of his feet. *Why's he so excited about this? He wouldn't want her to get hurt, either.*

"Would you just come on? He's going to wig out if we don't go!" Sam demanded.

"What? Why is he going to wig out?" Luke asked, confused.

"We have to go. Please? Otherwise, it's going to take them forever. Come on," Sam said, dragging Luke toward the door to the balcony.

"I guess we were done with our conversation, Luke!" Claire called after him, laughing, knowing she missed most of the conversation.

"STOP LAUGHING," Talise muttered.

"I can laugh if I want to. This is hilarious. Apparently, you like jerks." Noah grinned.

"I'm not crushing on you! Stop it," she objected again.

"That wasn't my lust, Tali," Noah said, still laughing.

She glared at him. "I didn't say 'lust.'"

"No, you said 'desire,' which is even better!" Noah teased.

"I don't think that was mine, Noah." She was getting annoyed.

Noah lifted his eyebrows, offering his hand again.

When she didn't take it, he opened his mouth to bait her further.

Before he could get another word out, she grabbed his hand.

As a blush climbed her neck to her cheeks, he realized she was shocked. He choked back his laughter.

"Not mine." Noah grinned.

Talise nodded, embarrassed.

Noah held her hand tight when she tried to let go. Looking at her flushed face, amber eyes glowing, he thought of her coming down the stairs that night at Hank and Darla's house. He thought of the first circle after the tie was broken and the pull of her beauty. Then spinning in the living room at the lake house, singing with Luke, laughing with Adaline at Sunday dinner, and channeling energy in the circle on Monday nights.

Noah released his energy to neutral, laying his own attraction bare for her to sense.

She just admitted her interest. Why not? he thought with an inner shrug.

But, once free, the energy was unwilling to behave. It jumped from neutral to a previously unidentified level, ratcheting up his own desire and lowering his inhibitions.

One good tug later, Talise was in Noah's arms as his head dipped to kiss her. Free hand dusting the side of her face and down her arm, Noah savored the feel of her soft skin as her body leaned into him.

Fuck! Nope. Stop. No more, Noah told his libido. *There's a whole room full of available women willing to frolic naked. Leave her alone.*

No, really, self. Stop.

This isn't right. Stop.

Stop. Step back. Stop.

Noah's smug smile gave way to a pensive expression when he finally stepped back from her. Breathing hard, he pulled the energy under control. "That's mine."

TALISE WAS GOBSMACKED, unsure what to do or say as Noah let go of her hand. His emotional tidal wave was powerful and loud, but something other than lust rose to the surface.

A question finally found its way out of her mouth. "You're ashamed?"

"Huh?" Noah asked, lost in his own thoughts.

"Shame? You're ashamed to like me?"

Noah's lips quirked. "This conversation has been truly bizarre. We've covered a lot of ground in ten minutes."

"I know," she mumbled, dropping her eyes. "Sorry."

He's ashamed to like me. That might be worse than hating me, she thought.

"You're great at picking up the emotions. Terrible at determining the sources. I'm not ashamed of *you.* I'm ashamed of me. You and Luke... This is not something brothers do to each other," Noah said, words quiet and soothing. "This is not a thing, Talise."

"It looks like a thing. Just from right here. It looks like a thing. So you know, it does definitely look like a thing." Sam was grinning from ear to ear.

"Tend to agree," Luke admitted. "I never take your bets, Sam. I never bet against you. Why did I take that bet?"

Sam was shaking with laughter. "I don't know, but you totally owe me ten bucks! Sign it. I'm framing it."

"Fuck," Luke muttered, turning to go back inside. "Come on, freak show. You can buy me a beer."

"Hey," Sam said, offended again.

"It's an open bar, Sam," Luke teased.

"Luke, wait!" Noah called, starting to chase after them.

Luke shook his head, turning around to face Noah while still walking backward with Sam. "It felt like I was trying to make out with Beth, Noah. It wasn't right with us. Just...think about what you're doing, okay?"

After Sam and Luke were gone, Noah turned around to face Talise.

"Um," he said. No words followed.

Talise could feel his confusion and indecision from ten feet away. She waited to see what would come out of his mouth.

"I thought you broke up with him," Noah mumbled, looking lost.

Talise nodded. "I did. It wasn't right. I kept falling asleep—"

Noah's laughter burst out in surprise.

"And he was embarrassed to kiss me. He felt affection and obligation, like he was waiting for something to change. Nothing was going to change."

"Oh. Oh, shit. Yeah. No faking it with you," Noah said, smacking his own forehead, still laughing.

Her eyebrows shot up.

"That's not what I meant," Noah said, flushing red.

Aww, she laughed to herself, feeling his embarrassment.

She continued to watch him in silence. It had worked well for her so far.

"You're just going to let me continue bumbling through this on my own, aren't you?" he asked, laughing.

"Yeah." Talise grinned. "You said my pretty princess dress looked like underwear. You're on your own, Lord Lust."

"I did not say it looked like underwear!" Noah objected. "I said it looked like skin."

"That's not better."

"I know, but at least get my dumb fuckery right!" Noah bitched.

"I stand corrected," Talise agreed, smiling at his overblown, outraged expression.

He grinned at her. "I don't hate you."

She nodded.

"Good," Noah said, grin falling to a sad smile. "G'night, Talise."

"Wait!" Talise yelled as Noah started walking away. "What—? What's happening? Where are you going?"

"I'm going inside," Noah replied, surprised. "It's cold. You should come inside, too."

"You're going to do a lame-ass kiss and run?" she asked. "You moron."

Noah dropped his gaze, not making eye contact. The humor was gone from his voice. "You wouldn't enjoy the turnstile nature of my bed partners, Talise. We're better off as friends."

"Hmm. Do you enjoy the turnstile nature of your bed partners, Noah? There's an awful lot of self-loathing and loneliness coming from you right now."

Noah let out a cynical chuckle. "Don't do this. Five minutes ago, you didn't recognize your own feelings. Don't try to call bullshit on mine."

Talise blinked fast, trying to swallow the tears that instantly surfaced. She nodded. He was right.

"Are you crying again?" he asked.

"I'm fine," she mumbled.

"Talise," Noah groaned in frustration. "I don't know how we keep ending up here! I'm really not an asshole."

"I'm sorry! I don't know why I'm crying! I can't help it. I'm not normally like this," she explained, defensive.

"Is it the water thing? The tears? Do they happen because of the water? Can't you tell them to go away?" Noah asked.

"What?"

"The tears. They're water. Tell them to go away!" Noah suggested, happy to offer a solution.

"What the fuck are you talking about?" Tali asked, choking out laughter. "That's not how it works, Noah."

"Don't laugh like it's dumb! Try it," he demanded. "Tell the water to go away."

"Noah, I'd be willing away a tiny amount of water from a surface that is made up of like sixty percent water. It's not that precise. I can't will a couple of specific drops away from the relatively large mass of water that is my body. I'd be better off calling the rain to us, so it hides the tears. Calling a large volume of water is not a problem. Calling a tiny, specific amount of water is near impossible."

"Oh." He stood there, hands in pockets, unsure of how to help.

"Just go, Noah. We've come full circle. I'm fine," Talise offered.

"You're not fine. You're standing here, crying again, because I'm an asshole."

"Nope, not your fault this time," she disagreed. "You rightly called bullshit. My bad. I'm fine. Just go."

"I don't want to leave you out here like this," Noah said, teasing. "If Darla finds out, she'll murder me in my sleep."

Talise gave a snort of surprised laughter. "Great. You're standing out here with me because you're afraid of Darla."

The humor fell from his voice again. "You know that was a joke."

And she did. She could feel his concern for her, his sadness and admiration. The lust, caring, concern, and admiration combined to something scarily close to, but not quite, love.

"I'm sorry," she whispered.

"Goodnight, Talise."

Long after Noah left the balcony, Talise stood alone thinking.

"STILL STANDING OUT HERE BY YOURSELF?" Sam asked. "Noah came inside almost an hour ago. The party's wrapping up."

"I'm contemplating my five-year plan," Talise murmured, lips turned up.

"Hopefully, the first step in the plan is leaving this balcony and getting warm," he said, offering his suit coat.

Talise took the coat.

"Oh, sure, you'll take *my* coat." Sam smiled.

Talise's voice came out as a whisper. "I thought he hated me. He wouldn't let me apologize, wouldn't talk to me, seemed to get mad… I thought he hated me."

Sam nodded.

"But he doesn't," Talise said, eyes filling with tears again. "He turned around and walked away tonight, though. Doesn't hate me but not interested in me? I'm not sure what that means."

Sam's eyebrows shot up. "Forget about him—"

"I'm not—" she interrupted, immediately irritated.

"Let me finish," Sam chided, smiling.

Talise sighed.

"Forget about him for a minute. What do *you* want, Talise?"

She blinked at him.

"Do you know?" Sam asked.

She gave a little huff of laughter. "I was actually standing here, thinking about how 'calm' is not a necessity anymore. For so long, I needed everything to be calm. I couldn't process the waves of information that came into my mind when the tie was in place. Those days are gone, though."

"So, you want not-calm?"

Talise sighed again. "I was trapped, Sam. Not intentionally isolated like Addy. But stuck all the same. I like calm. It's easy and familiar."

"But?"

"Some fun and adventure would be most welcome." She smiled.

"Is that scary?" he asked, curious.

"A little bit, I guess. But that's the point, right?"

"Probably. So why are you tearing up about Noah walking away? Do you believe he's the only person to go adventuring with?"

She smiled. "No, I know it's not Noah or bust."

"Then what's with the tears?"

"I don't know. I like him, I guess. Despite everything, he feels like a louder, funnier, less polished version of Luke."

Sam nodded. "I don't think he knows what he wants, Tali. He's not prone to anger, resentment, or self-doubt. The last couple of months have been rife with all three feelings for him. So, want my advice?"

"Hmm?"

"Decide what you want, and then answer the door when he knocks."

"You think he's going to knock?"

Sam grinned. "I'll bet you ten bucks."

31

Noah was waiting for the elevator when Adaline took his arm.

"Oh, hello," he said, giving her a small smile.

"Walk with me, Noah." Adaline's voice boomed in his head, not to be ignored.

"Addy, what's wrong? Why—?"

"Shh," she breathed. *"We must Walk. Come. Let me help."*

"Adaline," Noah started again.

"Look at me, Noah," she commanded as she stopped walking and turned to him.

After meeting her gaze, Noah bowed his head.

"Mistress Life," he murmured, seeing the energy that mirrored Spooky Sam in her countenance.

"Correct. We will Walk. Now."

Between one step and the next, they were in the field behind Nora's farmhouse.

"That was freaking awesome. I didn't feel a damn thing! I didn't realize you could do that, too!"

She nodded. *"We must balance your energy, Noah. You will go mad fighting it. Why are you fighting it?"*

"I'm not fighting it," he said, startled.

Adaline glared at him.

"Adaline, I'm not fighting it. I don't know what you're talking about."

"May I look into your mind?"

"Do you need my permission?"

"No, but Ava raised me to be polite," she responded without a hint of humor.

Noah bit back a smile as he nodded.

Adaline met his eyes as she touched his hand. Then they fell back through Noah's memories together.

"Here, Noah. This feeling. This is what I'm talking about," Adaline said, voice echoing in Noah's mind.

In his memory, Talise approached the circle, walking with Luke, after the tie was removed. It was the same day she kicked him. The memory of her beauty at that moment rose to the surface. Her graceful movements and the intelligence in her eyes, calling to him, washed over him again.

"She's beautiful. Alluring. I don't deny that. I'm not fighting that."

Adaline smacked him in the forehead. "Stop it."

The words vibrated with power. "I'm sorry. I didn't mean to do that."

"Are you channeling Sam or what?" Noah asked, grinning.

"It's not funny. You're hurting me," she said.

Noah's smile dropped. "What?"

"Your energy belongs to me, Noah, just as William and Adrian belong to me. Just as Matilda, Lucy, and Miranda belong to Sam. You are out of balance, pulling attraction toward obsession. I'll not cross that line with you," she declared.

"I'm not obsessed," he objected.

Rifling through his mind again, she pulled forward the memory of Noah taking a rage-induced, hate-filled swing at Luke.

"Um," he said, rapidly reflecting on the last few months.

"You found your way to each other tonight. I felt the connection. Why did you walk away from it?"

"Are you saying that Talise and I are fated to be together? Because you didn't believe in the whole fated thing, remember?"

She smacked him upside the head again.

"Stop that!" he bitched.

She glared at him.

"What do you want me to say? I walked away because she's part of the family, and dating her would end badly. She's also extremely innocent, and in case you missed it, I'm not. I don't typically stoop to seducing virgins, Addy. She's better off with Luke."

Adaline reached over and pinched his upper arm through his suit coat, twisting the skin she grabbed.

"Gah! That hurts!" he yelled. "I'm telling Sam! Worse! I'm telling my mom; she's gonna be pissed. That's going to bruise."

For just a second, the energy that made Adaline the Mistress Life dropped from her face as she laughed.

"I'm not a sissy," Noah said, laughing at himself.

"Not fated, Noah. Life is too complex for fate to drive everything. But compatible. Connected. Attracted. Your energies mesh well," Adaline answered his earlier question. *"You don't have to be with her. Walk away if you'd like. But do it now and let her go in truth. Do not push it further."*

"What do you mean our energies mesh well? She'd spend her days wandering around constantly horny if she meshed with my energy." He laughed.

Adaline stared at him.

"What?" he asked.

"What name did you take, Noah?" Adaline asked aloud.

"Lord Lust!" he said.

"That is the name you spoke," she agreed. "What name did you take, though?"

Noah deflated, humor gone. "Caught that? I wasn't sure it mattered. I didn't think anyone would notice."

"I felt it shift. It was a shift for the better. I was delighted with you."

"I didn't know," he muttered, head hanging as he kicked the dried grass at their feet. "Before Jess told me, I didn't know or notice what I was doing with the energy. When I found out, I freaked out that I was affecting people's choices. It's not what I wanted for eternity."

"What is the name?" she asked again.

"You don't know?"

"I suspect."

He smiled. "Passion. Don't tell Sam I wussed out on the Lust thing."

She nodded, unsurprised. "And you believe that Talise would be negatively impacted by that energy? Talise, who sings and dances? Did you know she leaps down the hallway into her bedroom, just because she can? Her life would be worse with more passion?"

"No, not at all. I just don't understand how constant passion would be her ideal state. Luke has that peace thing going on. That seems better," Noah said.

Adaline gave her head a disbelieving shake. "I can't believe you just said that."

"What? Why?"

She laughed. "Noah, your emotions are loud. Everything about you screams. Passion is more than lust and sex. When you're happy, you're ecstatic. When you're mad, you're enraged. There's not a whole lot in-between with you. You are rarely sad or pensive. In the waves of Talise's energy, your emotions would shout down anything that broke through her barriers. Luke makes her calm and sleepy. You can make her everything else."

"Hmm. And you think I should?" Noah asked, eyebrows raised.

"I think you should do as Hank asked and be selfish in love."

Noah stared at her.

She shrugged. "I will not let you go down the path of self-destruction chosen by William and Adrian. They tried to both choose love and let it go. It doesn't work well like that. I don't recommend it."

After a pause, she continued. "Think about what you want, how you feel, and why you feel that way. Walk away if that is what you want. I won't stop you. But walk away in truth. No more admiring from a distance and hating others for holding her attention. Decide what you want and stick with the decision."

They were silent for a moment.

"And what does Tali want?" Noah asked.

Adaline was back to herself, a little grin around the corners of her mouth. "Noah, you'll need to ask her. I'm not gossiping about my friend."

BY THE TIME Noah and Adaline returned to the hotel, the engagement party was over. The lobby was empty of everyone but employees.

"Adaline, do you know—" Noah started.

"Room forty-three-thirteen."

"Thank you," he said, hugging her.

"I'm calling it. Sam says it's too early to call it, but I'm doing it. I'll change it later if I regret it. You're my favorite brother."

Noah gave a surprised laugh. "I love you, you angel-woman-girl-goddess."

"That title got longer," she noticed.

Noah nodded, hitting the elevator button. "It was time for a promotion."

She laughed as he stepped on the elevator.

"Aren't you going upstairs?" Noah asked when she didn't step on.

Adaline shook her head. "We're going to the lake house. Too many people here, even with shielding."

Sam stepped out of nowhere, taking her hand.

"Where were you?" Noah asked.

"Don't worry about it, Captain Passion." Sam laughed.

"ADALINE!" Noah roared. "Passion Pillar. Pillar of Passion! I have a Pillar of Passion!"

The elevator door closed over Addy's grin as she shook with laughter.

NOAH STOOD outside Talise's hotel room door for a couple of minutes, practicing facial expressions and considering words. He wasn't sure if he should go for downtrodden, heart-on-his-sleeve mushy, cocky, flirty, or something in between.

When he finally knocked, she opened the door immediately.

The facial expression he delivered was "surprised."

"Hi," he said.

"Hi," she replied.

There was a pause.

"Were you standing at the door?"

She nodded.

"Have you been standing there all night?"

She bit back a smile. "It's good you're pretty."

"You think I'm pretty?"

She opened her mouth to respond, laughing, when he got it.

"Hey, wait a second!" He pasted on an outraged look before he grinned. "How'd you know I was coming to see you?"

Talise smiled. "I felt you step off the elevator. Then Addy told me."

"Oh, man. Are you two BFFs? Because that might impact my decision," he said, still grinning.

"Your decision! What about my decision?" she asked, taking her turn at being outraged.

"Pfft, you've already made your decision. You opened the door."

"You knocked on it," she retorted.

"I did," he admitted.

"Do the sad face!"

Noah winced. "You were standing there, watching me through the peephole, the whole time?"

"Um, no. There's no peephole in the door, Noah. There are cameras on all the doors. I got the faces in high definition. Sam owns this hotel. You should know this." She grinned.

"Of course. Okay. I'm leaving now, thoroughly humiliated."

"Uh oh, it's a sad Pillar of Passion."

"Gah! You can't make that joke! Too innocent! No!"

"You are such a jackass."

"No Pillar jokes from you! I wasn't sure if you knew where babies came from."

"What?" She burst out laughing in a new fit of giggles.

Noah shrugged. "I assumed there was no boyfriend before Luke."

"You assumed correctly. But Noah, I'm an *empath.* Until recently, emotions from everyone around me flowed directly into my brain, along with all the physical motions that went with those emotions. My short-term memory was hosed, but that just meant I got to relive it later."

The door next to Talise's room opened.

"Holy fuck, dumb ass. Go into her room and get it on already! She needs a good lay. I've already had my nighttime fuck; I'm trying to sleep!" Ellie bitched then immediately slammed the door.

Charlie's laughter was still audible in the hallway.

Noah looked from the doorway where Ellie had been standing back to Talise. "No pressure."

"I'm having a hard time taking you seriously right now," Talise admitted.

"I am flummoxed," Noah admitted in return.

"Woo, good word," Talise whispered, trying to be mindful of the neighbors.

"I got it from Matty!" Noah yelled.

Talise's eyebrows lifted.

"Sam owns the hotel. They ain't kicking me out." Noah grinned. "May I enter your hotel room?"

Talise's eyebrows lifted higher.

"I was going to say, 'Can I come inside?' but that just sounds wrong in this circumstance."

"Noah," she laughed, "how did we get so far off course from the start?"

"I'm not sure. You should let me in so we can discuss this topic further in private."

"You think so?"

"I do." He smiled, covering her lips with his as she stepped back into the hotel room.

"Wait! Wait," he said. "Did you go to bed with Luke? It's not a disqualifier in my decision-making process. I am exactly that selfish. But I'm going to need you to compare and contrast if applicable."

"Not applicable," she said, closing the door behind him.

"I'M SO SORRY, Noah. I'm so sorry about kicking you," Talise gasped as he kissed down her neck. His excitement and hunger danced through her brain with her own eagerness and joy.

"Sam had touched me earlier that night without realizing what it'd do to me. I was already messed up, just getting free of the tie. Then all of his shit mixed with all of my shit. I thought you were going to do the same thing. I freaked out."

He stepped back. "I know, Tali. I understood it, even then. Once I could stand up straight, at least. You have a mean kick."

She tried to smile, knowing that he meant it to be a joke.

"Don't," Noah whispered, wiping away the tear dripping down her cheek. "Talise, don't. I wasn't mad about the kick. At all. I'd never fault someone for protecting themselves. I should have realized you were scared. I didn't. That's my fault."

"Then, why?" she asked. "Why wouldn't you talk to me? I tried to apologize over and over. You just walked away."

Noah sighed. "It bothered me—bothers me, present tense—that you'd be afraid of me. When I saw you that day, when you walked out to the circle holding hands with Luke, I was blown away. I had teased Luke all through the previous Sunday dinner about hitting on his hot brunette. But when you walked into the circle, I almost forgot to breathe. I wanted to know you. Be friends, at least. Then I scared you. No one's scared of me. I had no idea what to do.

"Ashamed of myself, I was going to apologize before the next circle. But Luke and Matthew spent the entire fucking car ride to the farm telling me, over and over, what a dick I was for scaring you and that I needed to leave you alone."

He paused, thinking for a minute before he continued. "I had met

Kaylee earlier that day. By the time we finally got to the farm, I decided they were right. You were Luke's hot brunette anyway, not mine.

"It spiraled from there. When you told me about Kaylee at the lake house and then curled into a ball on the floor in front of me, I was so angry that you were afraid again. I was mad that I hadn't talked with you to make things easier, upset over what you said about Kaylee.

His hand brushed the side of her face.

"I was so fucking jealous of Luke tonight, I was physically ill. I was leaving the party to puke in private when I ran into you in the hallway."

"What changed?" she asked.

Noah shrugged. "I think you know the rest. Luke pumped me full of peace then rightly told me I was an asshole. Even after making out on the balcony, you were still lumped into the do-not-touch pile. For all my teasing, I'd never hurt Luke like that. But then Luke was there, essentially laughing it off. I was still processing things when Adaline took me for a Walk and told me to shit or get off the pot."

"The romance is dead," Talise said with a straight face. "You can go now."

Noah grinned. "Why did you open the door? I don't deserve the chance; I won't pretend otherwise."

Talise fidgeted before scrunching up her face. "It was a *really* good kiss. I figured it'd be worth hearing you out."

Noah threw his head back, laughing as he pulled her close again.

"You will stop thinking of me as 'hot brunette.' That's pigheaded."

"I don't deny it. It bugged the shit out of Luke, though," he said, nodding in agreement.

She stretched her arms up around his neck, pulling him into a kiss. When he seemed to respond in kind, she pulled her mouth away, intentionally teasing him.

"You will not give Luke crap about this," Talise declared.

Noah shook his head. "I cannot make that promise. Sorry, too fun to resist."

She stepped out of his arms.

"Really?" Noah whined. "How about if I agree that sharing details would be in poor taste and only tease about his shortcomings rather than what he's missing?"

Talise glared at him.

"I'm not sure you understand how brothers work," Noah tried to explain. "I can't not tease him. It would throw our whole relationship out of whack."

She continued to glare at him.

"Tali..." he whined.

Her eyes narrowed.

"Can I make jokes about you refusing to smoke his peace pillar?"

She closed her eyes, shaking with laughter.

G*LORIOUS*, *absolutely fucking glorious,* Noah thought, watching her shoulders shake with laughter at his bad joke. Her hair was damp from a shower, hanging in a braid down her back. Face scrubbed clean of the evening makeup, she stood before him in a pajama tank and shorts that showed off her long legs.

Stepping forward, he brushed his lips against hers.

She smiled, eyes still closed. "Do you feel the energy when you do that?"

"Mmhmm," he murmured, tipping her head back to kiss her jawline. At each touch of her skin, energy cycled between them, making everything tingle.

"Always like that?" she asked, voice raspy.

He explored her neck, back up to her jaw, then to her earlobe before answering.

"No, Tali," he whispered, directly into her ear.

It's never like that, he thought, unwilling to admit the words out loud.

"Um," she breathed.

Noah stopped. "What's wrong?"

"Nothing." She blushed.

He stepped back.

She sighed in frustration. "Nothing's wrong. Just a little…nervous? I guess?"

"We don't have to do this," he reminded her.

FUCK! he mentally cursed.

"What? No! That's not what I'm saying. Not what I mean."

"Talise," he began.

"Noah, if you turn to leave right now, I'm going to kick you in the crotch again."

That startled a laugh out of him.

"I haven't done this. Don't judge. I'm a quick learner."

"Oh my God, Talise."

She glowered at him.

"Now I'm cheating," he told her, letting go of a tiny amount of energy.

"What?" she groaned.

"That's better," he muttered, kissing her again. "Okay?"

"Mmmm," Talise purred, stepping closer to him to deepen the kiss. She pulled his suit coat away.

"Holy fuck, Tali," Noah said, gasping from the feel of her teeth nibbling his earlobe as he pulled off his tie.

She tugged at his dress shirt, freeing it from his pants.

Talise started unbuttoning from the collar of the shirt while Noah started unbuttoning from the bottom, their hands meeting in the middle. His fingers teased her nipples through her tank as she tugged the shirt down.

"Too many layers," she muttered after finally getting the dress shirt all the way off of him. She was trying to pull the undershirt over Noah's head.

"Tali, does the amount of skin contact matter? We've been rubbing faces together with much success. Is rubbing naked bodies together going to be an overload?"

"Don't know," she murmured, still tugging at the undershirt. "Let's try it and find out. It's only cheating if you get caught."

Noah grinned as he gave up the t-shirt. "Like that?"

"Feel so good," she whimpered as another little wave of energy hit her.

Keep it together, keep it together, keep it— Holy fuck, he thought as Talise twisted her body against him at just the right place. *Time to move this along before I embarrass myself.*

Noah kicked off his shoes as he yanked her tank top off and scooted her toward the bed.

His teeth closed over her left nipple while nimble fingers teased the right. Kissing his way back to standing, his hands explored the soft skin of her torso while she kissed his neck and collarbone.

Noah's mischievous hands continued wandering around to her back. They slid down into her shorts to grab her bare ass. Pulling her tight to his body, he flicked the shorts down her legs.

"Ugh, Tali, don't," Noah groaned as her hand moved against him through his pants.

She froze. "It doesn't feel good?"

He smiled, pushing her down on the bed before following her down, lying beside her.

"Too good," he admitted, shifting so that he was resting on his side, looking at her.

When a little crease of concern appeared on her forehead, he slipped a hand between her legs.

The first touches were gentle, testing, teasing. After the initial surprise fell away, her hips and legs shifted, giving him access.

"Um," she muttered, running a hand up his chest, looking for mischief.

"Shh," he murmured back, trying to soothe away her nerves. "Just enjoy it."

Fingers circling and caressing, Noah watched as her breathing increased and her body tensed. As she neared an orgasm, he stopped then almost laughed at her glare.

"And don't be impatient," he teased, slipping a finger inside to gently massage inside while his thumb stroked outside. His mouth dipped to her breasts while her body tensed again.

"No!" She scowled at him when he stopped just shy of the goal line again.

Noah did laugh that time.

"You still have your pants on. Don't laugh at me!"

Noah kissed her, still chuckling at her outrage.

"Maybe I'm giving you too much credit for knowing what you're doing?" she asked.

He grinned down at her. "It's so much worse than that. I know *exactly* what I'm doing."

"Great! Get to it," she suggested, starting to laugh at her own impatience.

At that moment, with her eyes shining and a smile playing around the corners of her mouth, Noah dove head-first into love with Talise.

Mine! Noah's energy broke free.

"GREAT! GET TO IT," Talise suggested, heavy on the snark.

Don't stop this time! she thought, smiling up at him as she started to laugh at the situation.

Where Noah's concern and affection once rested in her awareness, love suddenly burned, shocking the breath out of Talise's chest. Then thought disappeared as his unfiltered energy slammed into her.

The first orgasm took her body before Talise knew what was happening.

"N-Noah, too mmm-much," she stuttered, moaning and gasping as the second orgasm rolled by, just in time for the third to begin. Her back arched entirely off the mattress as she tried to catch her breath and force her body to calm down.

His energy was fading as he regained control of it. Closing her eyes, Talise focused on rebuilding her own control for a moment.

"Tali?" Noah breathed, concern washing against her mind.

Opening her eyes, she pulled him down into a kiss.

"You should probably lose the pants, Noah," she panted, still coming down from the orgasms.

Gone and back, sans pants, in a matter of seconds, he was grinning. "When you speak of me, speak well. I am, apparently, an orgasm god."

"Shut up, Noah." She chuckled, pulling him in for another kiss, squirming under him as the energy cycled with the touch.

"You keep wiggling in all the right ways," he gasped, wiggling in kind then chuckling at her return gasp. "Please stop doing that. You're going to ruin my reputation."

Tipping her head, she kissed down the line of his neck to his chest, eliciting a groan from him. When her hand closed over him, moving up and down, he exhaled hard, closing his eyes.

"Don't fall asleep," she teased. "It'd be bad for my confidence."

Noah's hands slid under her, rolling her on top of him.

"Slow," he whispered, jaw clenched as he positioned himself and rocked her gently backward. He let another shot of energy loose.

In response, her body arched with tension and need. Fighting to keep control, she eased back, joining their bodies.

The energy-induced orgasm started slowly, an undulating wave, as the walls of her sex stretched, taking more of him. Panting, she paused in her movement when there was resistance until eventually, he was fully sheathed in her.

Noah grabbed Talise's hips, flipping them back over so he was on top. Weighing her down at the hips, he sent her overboard again with another dollop of sexy energy.

"Hear me?" he asked, breathing deep and trying to be still as she returned to reality.

She nodded, still gasping.

"Shhh," he soothed again. "Tali. Breathe."

She kissed the line of his neck. "Intense," she whimpered.

"Too much?"

She smirked at him, startling a laugh.

He wiped tears from her eyes, kissing her slowly, still chuckling. "Tali."

Just like that, her energy snapped to the forefront, escaping her control and opening the floodgates of her empathic power.

Noah moved then, eyes unfocused as their combined power knitted between them, making an echo of every sensation and feeling.

The pace quickened as they lost the ability to think, rushing toward the finish, flying apart at the same time.

HOURS LATER, Talise stirred to wakefulness when Noah shifted out of and then back into bed.

"Hi," she muttered, half asleep.

"Hi," he whispered back. "Didn't mean to wake you."

"Where'd you go?"

"Bathroom. How are you? How do you feel?"

"I'm trying to think of a pithy comment about having a new barre, but it's just not coming to me."

Surprised laughter whooshed out of Noah. "Hurt?"

"Absolutely," she admitted, face buried in her pillow. "But in the best way imaginable."

"No regrets?"

"None," she said. "You?"

"No," he breathed, kissing the side of her face.

Talise could still feel his love washing against her mind. She wasn't sure if he realized it yet.

"How are you? How do you feel?" she asked in return.

He didn't respond.

"Noah?" she asked, trying to stay calm as she sensed his anxiety ratcheting up.

In the darkness, she thought she saw a glimmer of his white smile.

"You tell me," he challenged.

After a pause, she made chicken sounds at him.

"That's sexy." He laughed.

She made the sounds again.

"Bah! Luke has terrible taste in women!"

"I know, right?" she murmured. "Dude kept telling me I was perfect but then couldn't watch an R-rated movie with me."

Noah laughed. "Are you serious? He's such a Pollyanna."

Talise sighed.

"Huh. Frustrated about something, Tali? Something you want to say?"

She rolled away from him. "Go back to sleep, jackass."

"Tali?"

"Hmm?"

"Are you going to laugh if I say it?"

"Probably."

"Are you going to say it back?"

She sighed.

"Tali!"

"Remember earlier when you laughed in my face about crushing on you?"

"This is not the same."

"It's similar, Noah."

"Well, it's not fair! You know exactly how I feel."

"No, I don't," she disagreed. "To your earlier point, I'm often wrong in the interpretation."

"Interpretation of what?"

"Your feelings."

"What feeling is that?"

"Jackass."

Noah sighed.

"Tali?"

"Hmm?"

"It's Sunday."

"So?"

"Will you go to dinner with me?"

"No."

"No?" he asked, slightly hurt.

"No."

"Why?"

"They're going to make fun of us. You can face that on your own. I'll avoid it until Monday night."

"You're going to make me go by myself?"

"Mmmhmm."

"Would you go with me if I say it?"

"Say what?"

Noah sighed again.

32

"What is *that* doing there, Noah?" Jess squealed when Noah walked into the big room later that day.

Noah frowned. "Shuddup."

"What the fuck happened?" Jess yelled. "Who is this person?"

"Jessica," Darla scolded.

"He's in love, Darla! Real, actual *gold binding* love!"

Darla turned narrowed eyes on her sixth child. "How? When? Who? Where is this person?"

"I don't want to talk about it right now!" Noah yelled to shout out Sam and Luke, who both started talking at once.

The room fell quiet.

"Stop staring at me!" Noah bitched, his ears turning red.

"Come sit down, Noah," Hank encouraged, grinning. "Tell me about your night, son."

"No."

"Why?" Hank asked.

"You're going to laugh at me."

"Son, I'm already laughing at you."

∞

THE CONVERSATION WAS STILTED as the family sat down to dinner. Everyone kept pausing to stare at Noah.

"I have no idea what to do with this," Jake admitted. "Sam, what do you know?"

"Woo!" Jess clapped. "I didn't think to ask."

Sam pressed his lips together, shaking with laughter.

"Addy!" Ava yelled, equally excited. "Spill it. This is too good."

Adaline grinned, shaking her head.

Noah sighed.

"So on a related note," Luke said, voice clipped, "your girlfriend called me after I dropped her off at home, you fucking coward. She said she failed to get your number and also to give you her number."

He paused for dramatic flair.

"Oops. Was I not supposed to mention that?" Luke asked with a completely straight face.

"Fucking priceless," Sam choked out.

The table was absolutely still and silent. Darla's mouth was hanging open.

"I can't tell if you're mad or not," Noah admitted to Luke.

"Me, neither," Luke responded. "Should have said the words, man. Real men say the words."

"But she knows!"

"No, she doesn't," Luke snapped. "We had an awkward couple of minutes in which she tried to ask me if you are often in and out of love. I dodged like six times."

"Ah, shit!" Noah smacked himself in the forehead.

"Stop staring at me," Luke said to the table full of eyes focused on him.

"Stop staring at me, too!" Noah bitched when the eyes turned to him.

Jake jumped up. "I'm going to make popcorn. Be right back. Don't start without me."

Unidentified chortles of laughter broke out around the table.

"I hate you so much right now, Jake," Noah said, cheeks flaming red.

"I don't know where to start." Darla was all but dancing in her chair. "When I told her I had other sons yesterday, I didn't expect her to call another one to heel so quickly! She has a gift!"

Ethan lost his cool at that point, taking Emma and Lucy with him. The table was bedlam for several minutes as everyone absorbed this new twist.

"I need to understand something," William started after a deep breath, looking between Noah and Luke. "Have you both—"

"NO! Nope. No," Luke said. "Please don't ask it."

Will blinked. "No, as in 'don't ask?' Or 'no' is the answer?"

"Both," Luke and Noah said at the same time.

"Stop laughing, Sam," Noah growled.

"She's finally where she belongs!" Sam yelled.

"You are shitting me!" Hank slapped the table, laughing.

"No more lopsided circle. Tell her to take the damn name, Noah!" Sam cheered.

"I can't do that," Noah replied. "That's her thing to do. I have no say in it."

"He's tits on a bull, Sam. Can't even cough out the 'I love you's,'" Luke objected.

"BOOO!" the Trellis men yelled in unison.

"DID YOU CALL HER?" Luke asked.

"Like eight times. She didn't answer," Noah said from the backseat of Luke's car. "I should have gotten a ride with William this week. This is going to suck for the next hour and a half."

"Did you leave a message?" Luke asked.

"Pullover. I'll walk," Noah said, serious.

"Don't be—" Luke started.

"LUKE, SHUT UP!" Noah snapped, startling everyone to silence. "For fuck's sake, man. You heard Jess last night. You heard Sam last night. You lost the fucking bet. You know I'm not screwing around. Don't do this to me for the next ninety minutes."

"Don't fuck it up!" Luke snapped back.

"I'm trying to not fuck it up!"

"TRY HARDER!"

Noah sighed into the heavy silence.

"What do you want me to do, Luke? I was pushing her away on Saturday when you sauntered onto the fucking balcony, laughing with Sam."

Luke veered the car onto the shoulder of the expressway and stared out the windshield. "I want you to avoid fucking this up, Noah."

"Me, too," Noah said, flippant.

"I'm going to punch you in the head if you keep up like this," Luke warned.

"Wanna throw down on the side of the expressway?" Noah asked, inviting the conflict.

Three seconds later, Noah was asleep.

"Luke!" Ethan yelled.

"I win."

"Are you kidding me with this?" Matthew asked.

"I waited until no cars were passing. No risk."

Matthew glared at his favorite brother.

"I'm not listening to him for the next hour. I'll kill him."

"This is bullshit, Luke," Matthew muttered. "And you know it."

"I have no idea what I'm going to do if he hurts her."

"Fine. What are you going to do if she hurts him?"

TALISE WAS WAITING on the porch when Luke, Matthew, and Ethan arrived at the farmhouse.

"Hi," she said, frowning at Luke's expression. "What's wrong?"

"He's in the car, asleep," Luke said, tone flat as he walked into the house.

The frown deepened. "What happened?"

"They had words," Ethan said. "Luke's struggling a bit because Noah's an idiot."

Talise shrugged, nodding.

Matthew grinned.

"I'm not claiming otherwise." Talise grinned back, headed for the porch stairs and then Luke's car.

Noah was zonked out, mouth hanging open and drool on his chin.

Talise walked around to the passenger side, getting into the car beside him.

"Noah, wake up."

No response.

She shook him.

No response.

She shook him harder.

No response.

She clapped her hands loudly in front of his face.

No response.

Fishing his phone out of his pocket, she called Luke.

"What, asshole?"

"Yeesh."

"Tali? Sorry. What's wrong?"

"How do I wake him up? If this is a Sleeping Beauty thing, he's staying asleep. Dude's drooling. I'm not kissing him like this."

"Oh. Sorry. Give it a minute. He'll come around."

Luke's voice was tense, lacking his normal warm tones.

"Luke?"

There was a heavy sigh. "He's not my favorite brother."

Talise was silent.

"Matthew's a great guy. Are you sure—"

"Luke," Talise interrupted.

"Yeah. Figured. I should have known when Sam… Anyway. He'll come around."

The line went dead.

"Noah," she said, shaking him again.

Noah's eyelids flickered.

"Good morning, Sleeping Beauty," she said, monotone. "What'd you do to Luke?"

"Huh?" Noah looked around, bleary-eyed.

"Tali," he muttered.

"Talise!" he yelled, sitting bolt upright, wide awake. "Hi. Hi. How are you? Hi. I…I love you. I do. I love you. I'm sorry I didn't say it. I'm a chicken shit. But I do. I love you. And I hope you love me. Please don't dump me before we really start dating."

She pulled her lips down to hide a smile. "Hi."

"Should I say it again? I practiced."

"You are such a jackass."

"I'm sorry. I really am. I got booed at dinner. Hank glared at me. I didn't even object because I deserved the glare. I'm sorry. Please don't dump me. I would have said it if you said it. I just didn't want to be the only one saying it. And now I'm the only one saying it. I don't say it. Haven't said it. It's not a thing I often do. No. Luke said you asked. The answer is no. No, I don't say it to women often. Never, actually," Noah babbled.

"I love you, too." She let go of her smile.

"Oh, good. That's good." He heaved a sigh, the tension going out of his shoulders as he kissed her. "I thought I really fucked it up when you wouldn't take my call. I thought we were mostly teasing each other yesterday morning and that you knew. But then it turned out that you didn't. I'm sorry."

"You can stop apologizing." She smiled at him. "I did know. I wasn't sure you knew. When you wouldn't say it, I thought we might do a couple of rounds of dumb fuckery before we got to a place where you admitted it. I wasn't sure if falling in and out of love was something you often do."

"No. It's not. I don't. I haven't," Noah said, a frown forming. "If you're not mad at me, why didn't you answer your phone? Also, I love you."

"I was in the bath. I dropped my phone into the tub on accident when you called after dinner last night."

Noah scrunched up his face. "I had a very angst-riddled day."

"I'm sorry," she said, trying not to laugh. "I didn't have your phone number written down. Luke was not happy the first time I asked for your number. I didn't want to call him again. I figured I would see you tonight."

"For future reference, all my siblings, including Sam, have my phone number. You could have asked Adaline."

"I honestly didn't think of it. I'm sorry. I didn't think you'd be upset," she admitted. "You were very blasé sneaking out of the hotel room yesterday morning."

Noah blew out a sigh. "I love you."

"I love you." She laughed. "I can feel that little spark of joy that runs through you when you say that, you know?"

"I do know. That's why I keep saying it." He grinned.

"Why is Luke unhappy? He was fine."

"He's worried that I'm going to fuck it up. Because I almost fucked it up."

"Noah, we'll argue before you get to really fuck it up."

"Promise?"

"Promise."

There was a pause.

"Luke is scary. We were bitching at each other. I asked if he wanted to throw down on the side of the expressway. Then I'm pretty sure he sent me to night-night land." Noah laughed. "He won that fight by default."

Talise's smile was sad. "I'll talk to him."

TALISE FOUND Luke standing alone in the farmhouse kitchen. Neither of them said anything as she walked up and hugged him. When the silence persisted, she took his hand, leading him outside.

"Let's walk. We have almost an hour before the circle," she said quietly, feeling his inner turmoil. Fear, anger, love. Jealousy.

"It's not that I dislike him or that he's a bad guy. He's annoying, Talise. He needles people," he started. "He's going to use you to push my buttons just because he can. I know it. He knows it. He knows I know it. He's still going to do it."

"I asked him not to bug you. Did he bug you?"

Luke frowned. "No. Not yet. But he will."

"I'll remind him not to bug you, Luke." She looked at him with raised eyebrows, knowing this wasn't the root of his issue.

"I just wasn't ready for this," he exploded. "When I showed up to dinner without you last Sunday, Sam was relieved. I asked him where he thought you belonged. He said next to Noah. I didn't believe him. I still don't believe him. I clearly lost the fucking bet, but I don't know what to do with this."

"You seemed fine on Saturday."

"I was!"

"And now?" she asked.

Luke fell silent as they reached the field where the circle would be held. No one was around. Talise sat in the grass, pulling Luke down with her.

"Luke?"

"I know."

"What do you know? Because I don't know. I'm having trouble reading between the lines," Talise admitted.

"I know that I'm jealous. And no, I don't know why. I'm pissed off that he gets to have this with you, though. I wanted this," Luke bitched.

Talise smiled.

"It was fine in the abstract. It was fine on the balcony. I just didn't think you'd actually go through with it! And then we had that awkward conversation yesterday about him falling in and out of love. I thought he was playing you. Or maybe that he was infatuated. It's Noah! You could fill Soldier Field with all the women that have gone starry-eyed over him.

"I was so pissed off going to dinner last night. Cruising for a fight, honestly. He wasn't even all the way into the big room when Jess started screaming about the gold fucking binding. Somehow, Noah gets to be with my perfect woman."

Unsure what to do or say, Talise squeezed his hand.

"Hear me out on this," Luke said, already laughing. "We could just avoid sex. We'd be that BFF perfect couple that everyone loves and just not have sex."

"There's a problem with that plan."

"Is the problem that sex is good?" Luke asked.

"That is the problem!" Talise laughed. "Part of the problem, at least."

"Is the other part of the problem that you love him?" Luke asked, suddenly serious.

"It is," Talise whispered.

"I don't understand how that happened!"

Talise scrunched up her face. "Me, neither. One minute I was crying. Then he was making chicken sounds at me. We were kissing. He was making faces outside my hotel room. Then he was making bad jokes about a passion pillar."

Luke winced. "I don't want the details, Tali."

She grinned. "He is your gentleness in a more obnoxious, annoying, hilarious wrapper."

Luke pulled a face.

"He's very loud. His emotions are very loud. He inspires intense emotions. Addy thinks that he'll drown out all the emotional noise that gets through my shields."

"He's a jackass. He whines about everything," Luke warned.

Her smile was sad again.

"I'm going to have a hard time if he hurts you," Luke admitted.

"Love you, Luke."

"Yeah. Yeah."

"You okay?"

"No," he grumped.

They were quiet for a few minutes, watching night fall over the field.

"Tali, call Ethan when you want to talk about him. I don't want to be the relationship go-between." Luke's voice was sad in the darkness.

"I'm sorry, Luke."

"I'm not. I want you to be happy. If that's with Noah, so be it. But we're going to have issues if he hurts you."

TALISE AND LUKE climbed to their feet as people began filling out the circle.

"Hee hee hee," Jess giggled, walking by. "This is fucking epic."

Talise dropped her head, her cheeks going scarlet.

Noah paused on his way by.

"Fuck off, Noah," Luke warned.

"But—"

"No. Go away. Go to your spot," Luke directed.

Talise didn't look up, but she felt Noah's gaze shift between her and Luke.

"I had no idea you were this possessive. I thought possessiveness was strictly a Sam thing," Noah commented.

Luke didn't respond.

"Did she tell you about—"

"Go, Noah!" Talise yelled over him, laughing.

"Whatever. I'll stand over here by the swinger couple. Maybe I can make new friends for us." He chuckled, knowing he was irritating Luke.

"For fuck's sake," Luke muttered, rubbing his eyes.

Talise shook with silent laughter.

"You have terrible taste in men."

"I have excellent taste in men," she disagreed, turning to grin at him.

"Hear me out on Matthew..." Luke tried again.

Talise smacked him lightly on the back of his head.

Rubbing his head, he tossed her a mock-scowl. "You've spent too much time with Darla."

"There is no such thing!" Darla disagreed, coming up behind them. "I'm going to be honest. I didn't see this coming. I thought Noah would be single long after I was gone."

"He might die before you if he keeps fucking with me," Luke muttered.

Darla grinned. "This is so good for you, Luke."

"What!"

"It gives you something to write songs about. You're too mellow." Darla pinched his cheek. "Get over it. Jealousy is not a good look on you, son."

"I'm aware," Luke mumbled.

Darla rolled her eyes, walking away. "Of course, you are. Entirely too well balanced and self-aware, Luke."

Sam and Adaline made their way to the field with Gregg, Nora, and Ben, chatting about puppies.

Sam stopped in mid-sentence when he saw her. "No! Enough of this. You go where you belong. No more lopsided circle!"

Talise's cheeks turned pink again as everyone turned to stare at her. "Shh. Not right now, Sam. Maybe next week."

"No! Right now! I am so over this. Go!" He was trying to smile to soothe the sting.

She didn't move. "Sam, shh—"

"Talise." Sam's voice turned serious. "I need you to be in the right spot."

"Okay, but not this week. Not right now," she tried again.

"What's going on?" Nora asked, confused.

Talise sighed, looking at Nora, then her parents. "Nothing's going on. It's fine."

Sam's good humor dropped, dragging the entire field into an uncomfortable silence. "Go."

"Sam," she whispered again. "Stop it. I haven't said anything to my parents. You're making this very awkward."

"Talise," Samuel growled, his voice echoing with anger and power. "We are done with this. Go."

Adaline pinched his arm.

"Ouch!" Sam bitched, back to himself. "No, Addy! She has to go. It's lopsided and makes me feel gross."

Adaline lifted her eyebrows, glaring at him.

Sam sighed. “Talise, would you please go where you belong, so the circle doesn’t make me queasy?”

Adaline turned her glare on Talise.

“Shit,” Talise muttered, knowing she lost.

“What’s happening?” Talise’s dad, Mike, called. “Do you know what’s happening, Monica?”

Her mom shook her head.

“What’s going on?” Greggory asked Luke.

Luke sighed as Talise avoided eye contact and moved to stand by Noah.

There was a moment of shocked silence.

“Not that one! That’s the sex one!” Mike yelled. “Go back by Luke! No, Talise. I said no!”

Laughter broke out across the field.

“What happened?” Nora asked, shocked. “How? What the hell?”

“She has terrible taste in men!” Luke yelled, laughing as he turned red.

“Whatever, man! You’re just pissed she wouldn’t—” Noah started.

“Stop talking,” Talise bellowed over him.

Noah frowned. “It was going to be funny.”

“My dad is fifteen feet away,” she said, causing more laughter.

“Oh,” Noah muttered.

“No survival instincts at all,” Will cheered. “I love everything about this.”

“You’re walking home, Noah,” Luke yelled as Sam and Adaline made their way around the perimeter of the circle.

“I got to Walk on Saturday!” Noah responded. “I forgot to rub that in with all the stealing of your girlfriend and everything.”

TALISE WAS TRYING to avoid all eye contact from every direction. People were staring, many envious and judgmental.

She could feel her parents’ hurt and confusion from the other side of the circle.

It's going to be fine. They'll adjust, she repeated in her mind. She hadn't expected Sam to out them immediately. She should have told her parents that things had changed with Luke. And with Noah.

The circle would be standing soon, releasing much of the emotional energy in the field. After that, Talise would feel better. Once it was closed, there would be less noise knocking against her mind.

But as Adaline approached the closing point of the circle, Talise's vision turned dark around the edges. Hit with a wave of vertigo, she sank down to the ground, sitting before she could fall.

"Tali?" Noah asked from beside her. It sounded like he was calling to her through a tunnel.

She wobbled, barely sitting upright.

"Talise?" he asked, squatting down next to her, taking her hand. "What's wrong?"

Love and concern washed over her.

Huh. Addy's totally right about that. He drowns out the noise. Maybe better than Lucas.

"Oh, good," Sam said from somewhere far away.

"Noah, I don't feel right," she muttered as the world went black.

THE DARKNESS WAS COMPLETE.

No light. No sound. No sensation.

Am I dead? Is this death? Talise wondered. *Of course, this would happen right after finding great sex.*

Amusement washed against her with that other, empathic ability that she worked so hard to contain. As her own emotion registered, the world flickered around her with brief glimpses of sight and sound.

"Tali!" Noah's voice rang through the darkness before fading again.

Without thinking, she sought his emotions, wondering if she could find them here.

Terror. Love. Rage.

Fine. Probably not dead. Did I just faint, damsel-in-distress style? I didn't think tonight could get more humiliating.

"—fine!" she heard Sam yell.

Where's Sam? He's an emotional mess. His turmoil will turn the lights back on.

As she reached out with her senses, she could feel the water in the world around her. There was an immeasurably large body of water in one direction, with other smaller masses of water sprinkled over the top of it.

The big one's Earth. Great.

Her senses drifted to the closest dollop of water as she focused.

Wow, Noah's freaking out.

The next closest puddle was Adaline, bent next to Noah, trying to calm him. Adaline's own fear sparked for a moment in Talise's darkness but then faded.

The next blob of water had no sign of life. No emotions. The pool of water was still. Stagnant.

Is that me? No. I don't think so. What the hell?

"Drop the mental block, Talise," Sam's voice rang through her mind. *"I can't tear that one down for you."*

"Sam? Can you hear me?" she asked, in the same way she occasionally shared thoughts with Adaline.

No response.

I guess not. What mental block?

She poked the stagnant pool of water again.

"Knock it off. You're going to give me a headache. Drop your mental block, Talise. Let the power out. Let it free. No more keeping it locked away. Time to use it. The circle is waiting for you. Also, Noah's going to start crying if you don't wake up soon. He's a sissy," Sam responded.

Poor Noah, she thought, amused again. *No respect from anyone.*

For lack of a better option, taking Sam's advice literally, Talise cast her energy out around her.

I wonder how far I can push this. I never did measure it.

She let the energy drift of its own accord, making a natural radius around her. Shock settled in when she felt the farmhouse. *That has to be two hundred yards away, maybe more.*

Still, the energy spread with no sign of slowing down. Talise could feel the expressway, a dozen miles away, as clearly as she could sense Noah's breathing next to her. Thousands upon thousands of tiny pockets of water hit her awareness and then smoothed away, like raindrops under a windshield wiper.

The energy was moving faster now, raging toward the Chicago Loop. Millions of stinging pellets of water rushed against her senses, quicker than she could process, only to fade as the energy drifted further afield.

Then everything stopped.

What the fuck? I can't feel anything now. Did I break it?

She prodded the mental space where her water energy lived. Sensation flickered again as the world tried to come into focus. She prodded it again, harder.

Ouch! Fuck!

Talise tried to pull the energy back to herself. She couldn't find it, couldn't sense it.

Well, shit. Now what?

She slammed the tiny mental compartment where she allowed the energy to live with the full force of her consciousness. Quick, like ripping off a bandage.

Something in her mind gave way as she heard screaming around her.

"STOP WITH THE YELLING," Nora yelled. "It's just mud!"

Talise's eyelids flickered.

"Talise, pull the energy back," Sam said from beside her. "You're done with it. Pull it back to you before the field turns into a swamp."

"Huh?" she muttered.

"Pull your energy back," Sam said again. "You're calling too much water here."

"It's broken."

"Talise, pull your energy back," he snapped.

She sighed, resigned, as she focused her eyes. "You're awfully fucking temperamental. You know that, right?"

There was a snort of laughter from the other side of her.

"Don't ever do that again!" Noah yelled. "Holy fuck, I thought you were dead."

"I'm not dead. Just fainted like a ninny."

"She didn't even turn blue, man. Suck it up," Jake coached from the sea of faces behind Noah, which included her parents and Luke.

"Hi, Mom. I'm fine," Talise muttered, bemused.

"Talise," Sam barked. "Pull the energy back to you."

"I can't," she snapped back. "I broke it. You pull it back, Sam. You have elemental power, right?"

"Talise, how about we sit up?" Adrian asked, trying not to laugh.

"Woo, Adrian, I can't see you," she said, looking around.

He appeared in her field of vision from above her head. "Can you sit up?"

"Sure, let's do that," she said, already pushing herself upright. "Holy shit, what happened to the field?"

"Yeah," Sam said, snarky. "It's like someone's calling Lake Michigan here. Pull your energy back, Talise!"

"I can't. I broke— Oh. Wait. I can," she said, feeling her energy settle back into its newly renovated mental space.

"Sorry. Sorry about the flooding, Nora," Talise called. "Didn't mean to do that."

"Talise, what is your name?" Sam asked.

"Yeah. Okay. I get it," she said, nodding.

"Say it."

"What?"

"Say it. You have to take the name," Sam explained.

"Oh. I am, in fact, Water," she said, laying back in the muddy grass. "Ugh. Dizzy again."

"That's it?" someone asked. "No epic earth-shaking or thunder booms or anything?"

"The giant fucking puddle wasn't enough for you?" Noah snapped.

Talise smiled at him. "I'm fine, Noah. Just woozy."

"Let's not do that again." He smiled back. "That sucked for me. How was it for you?"

"It turns out I have great range on the water senses," she said, lightheaded and laughing.

33

"Linda," the voice whispered. "Linda, wake up. We don't have much time. Can you hear me?"

She did her best not to move. Sometimes, if they thought she was still unconscious, they left her alone to finish healing.

"Linda, please." The whisper was urgent. "They're not going to be gone long. Wake up! I'm going to get you out of here, but we have to hurry."

That caught her attention. If this was a ploy to enter her mind quickly, it was going to work. She'd take the bait. Her eyes snapped open.

John started.

"Holy shit," he exhaled, "you startled me. I was starting to wonder if you were dead."

She stared up at him.

"Can you move?"

Linda sat up, still staring at him.

"They left the key. I don't think they realize they left the key. They're gone to Dallas. We don't have long, especially after you cross the wards. But it's probably long enough to get gone." John unlocked the door. "We have to hurry."

Linda stepped out of the six-foot-by-six-foot cage that had been her home for the last two years. This was the first time she'd be free, under her own control, since the day after she dropped Ree off at Lucy's apartment.

"I know you're a mess. I'm sorry. We don't have time. We have to go now," he said again.

She nodded. "Why are you doing this?"

John hesitated. "I can't watch this anymore. I can't be a part of it. They'll track me down and kill me, but I can't. No more. We have to go."

Grabbing her hand, he moved for the stairs that led out of the basement, out of her dungeon.

They made it as far as the backyard.

At Linda's first glance of the evening sky, a noose slipped around her neck like a dog collar.

"Whoa, not so fast, kids."

There was a moment of silence as reality settled in.

"You didn't leave," John said, resigned.

"No, son. No, I did not."

Linda heard John's body drop to the ground after the sound of his neck snapping.

"Shame, shame, Linda. Look what you made me do," Jared admonished, tugging on the rope wrapped around her neck.

34

Noah's phone buzzed with a text message.

TALISE: Are you practicing facial expressions again?
NOAH: Huh?
TALISE: You have been parked down the block for fifteen minutes. Are you going to pick me up or what?
NOAH: Do I really have to walk to the front door?
TALISE: Be brave. Be bold.
NOAH: I think your dad might shoot me.
TALISE: My mom wouldn't let him pull out the gun. It'll be fine.
NOAH: Do they know I've been parked down here for a while?
TALISE: Man up, Noah.
NOAH: I did not adequately consider the fact that you still live with your parents before this afternoon.
TALISE: I'm wearing a short skirt without much underneath it.
NOAH: Don't tell me that when I have to talk to your dad in like three minutes!
TALISE: I'm going to tell Luke you hid down the block.
NOAH: Sacrilege! You can't play us against each other.

TALISE: I'm not. Just against you. Luke hangs out with my parents all the time.
NOAH: Yeah, but we've already established he's a Pollyanna.
TALISE: You'd do this if you loved me.
NOAH: ...
NOAH: That's not funny.
TALISE: Yes, it is. I can feel you laughing, Noah.

"H-Hi, Mrs. Ayers," Noah stammered as Talise's mom opened the door.

"Hi, Noah," Monica said, obviously trying not to laugh. "Come in."

Noah pursed his lips. "You're laughing at me, right?"

"Absolutely."

"But not in an 'I hate this guy and am going to make things miserable' way, right?"

"Correct," she confirmed. "I'm outright laughing at you being nervous."

"Sounds great. I can work with that." He grinned.

"Come in," she said again.

Noah didn't move from the doorstep. "Is your husband going to kill me?"

"Only a little bit."

"Does it help that I brought you flowers?"

"Those are for me?" Monica grinned.

Noah nodded.

"Noah, you're supposed to bring Tali flowers, not me."

"I got her a different gift. It's an upgrade from flowers."

"I think you might be discounting how much women like flowers when being wooed," Monica disagreed.

"Nope, I'm not. I got this one right," Noah said, confident.

"I feel like I have to tell Mike to behave since you brought me pretty flowers," she admitted, taking the bouquet from him. "Well done."

"Thanks!" he said, finally entering the house.

"I have access to construction equipment," Mike growled as Noah turned into the living room. "They'd never find the body."

"That's an interesting ax you have there, sir," Noah said. "And that's a very fetching flannel shirt you're wearing. You look like Paul Bunyan."

Monica snorted with suppressed laughter.

Mike's face went blank.

Noah glanced between Talise's parents. "I'm just going to be straight with you. It came out of my mouth before my brain considered the ramifications. I'm very fond of all my limbs, sir."

"There. He's said something stupid. Can I come out now?" Talise yelled from the hallway.

"Why this one?" Mike yelled back. "Tell me again!"

"The other one made me sleepy," Talise explained, coming into the living room.

"Sleepy's not bad! There's less risk of unplanned pregnancy and diseases," Mike argued.

"Shut up, Noah. Close your mouth," Talise muttered.

Noah's teeth clicked as his jaw closed.

"Are you done? Can we go now?" Talise asked her dad.

"Be home before the streetlights come on," Mike responded, straight-faced.

"They're already on, Dad."

"You missed the window of opportunity. Maybe tomorrow," Mike said, glowering at Noah.

"Where are we going, anyway?" Talise asked.

Noah smiled.

"Don't look at her like that!" Mike yelled. "I hate this!"

"Oh, shut up!" Monica laughed. "He brought me flowers. It's adorable."

"I signed us up for ballroom dancing," Noah said with a grin for Talise. "Every Wednesday at seven."

A smile of excitement spread across Talise's face.

"That's better than flowers," Monica acknowledged.

"G'night!" Talise yelled, pulling Noah toward the door.

"Ten-thirty! Ten-thirty curfew!" Mike yelled after her.

"See you in the morning," Talise yelled back.

"Tali!" her dad roared.

"I think your dad might want to kill me," Noah muttered as they made their way to the car.

"Nope, he was working hard to not laugh at the Paul Bunyan thing," she disagreed. "He'll adjust."

BY SUNDAY AFTERNOON, Noah was merely uncomfortable walking up to Talise's front door. This was a significant improvement over Wednesday night's outright fear.

"You didn't even sit in the car for ten minutes, giving yourself a pep talk." Talise laughed, opening the door.

"I'm growing as a person," Noah agreed. "Your dad only threatened to kill me a little bit yesterday. I feel like we're starting to find our way."

"It's true. You are. You would have done better yesterday if you didn't make jokes about me being Lady Moist."

"It's not a dirty word!"

"I know, but it sounds naughty."

Noah sighed. "I know."

"It was hilarious, though." Talise laughed.

He grinned.

"My parents are out to dinner. We can go," Talise said, smiling.

"Oh! Yay!" Noah cheered, walking back to the car with her. "Now, let's talk about you moving out of your parents' house."

"No."

"Why?"

"Because this is fun."

"I beg to differ, miss. This is not fun for me," he said, pulling the car away from the curb.

"It's great fun for me. And my mom. And my dad, too, though he won't admit it yet."

"Maybe in like two weeks?"

"Seems unlikely, Noah."

"Why?" he whined.

"Because."

"Because why?"

She glared at him.

"I can't look at that glare right now. I'm driving," he said, smiling.

"How'd you know I was glaring?"

"I can feel it. Is this how Luke hit the curb?"

"Nope, I told him to tell me I was pretty."

Noah snorted. "You're gorgeous. Glorious. Amazing. And pretty, too."

"Thanks!"

"Move in with me."

"Nope."

"Why?"

"Because."

"Because why?"

"We've been on three dates, Noah. Cohabitation seems premature."

"Boo."

"Don't 'boo' me."

"You deserve the boo," Noah said, turning into his parents' driveway.

"I do not!" she disagreed, walking around the car to meet him.

Darla threw open the front door as they walked up the sidewalk.

"Mom, Tali won't live with me," Noah snitched.

"Shut up and get in here, both of you," Darla snapped, voice low. "Tali, they need you in the big room. Hurry. Don't say anything you don't have to say."

"Mom?"

"It's Ree," Darla breathed.

35

"Lady Loch." The Walker's voice echoed with controlled power. "You will tell me what waits."

At that moment, Talise understood why people feared the Walker. Samuel was glowing with rage, his anger a beacon to loose energy everywhere. It gathered within him, waiting for a purpose, waiting for action. Waiting for the catastrophe that would follow. Standing in that living room, the thought of Sam exploding an entire continent, ending millions of lives, did not seem so farfetched.

"Holy hell," she breathed, looking around the room, panicked. Noah squeezed her hand, his own eyes wide with fear.

Ree lay in Adaline's lap, asleep.

"Do not speak," Adaline, Mistress Life, boomed in Talise's mind. *"The child is in danger. He will not tolerate losing this life. Do you understand?"*

Talise nodded.

"There is a binding from the mother that is forcefully taken and poisoned. It is intentionally, viciously, painfully draining the child's life away. It is torture. Someone is intentionally torturing this child. I hold him with me in life. You will follow the binding to the source, without making your presence known, and identify what is waiting on the other side."

"I don't know if I can do that, Addy," Talise broadcast. *"I will try."*

"You will succeed. There will be no failure in this, Talise Marie Ayers, Lady Water, Lady Loch, as the Walker deems. Daughter of Monica, daughter of Michael, beloved of Noah, friend, and confidant. You will do this. Now."

The words thundered through Talise's mind, reverberating on the word "friend." Heavy with command and expectation, there was no option to disobey.

As she sunk to her knees next to Adaline, Talise accepted why the Mistress Life stood with the Walker. Head bowed, she touched Henry's little boy hand.

She fell over, vomiting on the floor, retching in time with the pulses of Henry's pain and fear.

"Tali!" Noah yelled, diving for her.

"Stop," Adaline breathed. "Do not touch."

Talise retook Henry's hand, prepared for the worst. Closing her eyes, she began sorting through the emotions, isolating the pain. She gently hunted for the source.

At her mental touch, the poisoned binding vibrated.

"The binding is trying to shake me loose. I don't know if it's a typical reaction or if the other side knows I'm touching it," Talise shared with Adaline.

"Is there fear on the other side?" Mistress Life asked.

"No. Rage. Hatred. Vengeance. Punishment. Excited, lustful sickness. Envy. Greed. There is no fear on the other end."

"Then they do not yet know what's coming," Adaline shared with a glance at Samuel. *"How many?"*

Focusing her energy again, Talise searched for water and life at the source of the poisoned binding.

After a moment, Talise stood, letting go of Ree's hand and walking out of the room.

AT THE DINING ROOM TABLE, Talise worked with pen and paper as Lucy, William, Adrian, and Hennessy watched.

Absolutely silent, she drew a rectangular box then made notes:

- *Underground, probably a basement.*
- *Stairs here.*
- *Structure above has no life in it. Barren.*
- *Neighbors close. Small houses. Small lots. Probably in a city. Lots of lives in the other houses.*
- *Hot-water heater. Something next to it that's probably a furnace.*
- *Water hoses here, probably a washing machine.*

The notations got scarier:

- *Dead body here—severely decayed.*
- *Unconscious person—Ree's mom? Not dead yet, but almost.*
- *Sick man standing here. Likes hurting others. Gleeful to be torturing a child.*

"That one is mine," Lucy whispered.

"Not if I get there first," Will quietly disagreed.

There was one more note.

Talise drew a bold dark X in the middle of her box.

- *Jared is waiting here.*

"I hope he's waiting for me," the Walker said, peeking over her shoulder.

"Let's go. Jessup, stay here," Samuel instructed.

"Sam—" Hennessy started to argue.

Glowing eyes turned to face him.

Hennessy didn't flinch. "Adrian stays to protect. I go. William and me. This is what we do. This is why we exist."

"Hennessy," Adrian began.

"Jessup, you will—" Samuel growled.

"Sam, go as Spooky as you want," Hennessy interrupted quietly. "Unless you tell me there's a reason I stay and Adrian goes, I'm going. Understand? You and Adrian don't have the stomach for death. Lou goes; she has a lot invested in this. You'll play taxi. Will and I...we're equipped for the fight."

The Walker took a deep breath, searching through time.

"I can't find it," Samuel admitted at last. "I don't know where we are. We are still lost. Adrian?"

"We'll all go."

"No," Samuel, William, and Hennessy said together.

"Someone that can fight has to stay," William insisted. "Matilda is here. Matthew and Luke will be here soon. But one of us that can fight must stay."

Adrian pressed his mouth into a thin line then nodded.

LUCY WENT from Darla's dining room to an unknown kitchen in an eye blink. A glance around confirmed Talise's information. There was no one around but Hennessy, Will, and Sam.

"The stairs are behind you, the door on the right," Adaline broadcast in Lucy's mind. She shot Sam a startled glance.

"We share," Adaline said without words, somehow amused by Lucy's surprise. *"I am with Ree, but also with Sam. Careful, Lucy. Please. He is enraged for you. For Ree. Tread carefully."*

William was already moving toward the stairs, gun in hand, with Sam following.

Hennessy gestured for her to precede him down the stairs.

"Ah, there they are," Jared's voice called in welcome. "Come in, gentlemen. And lady! Lucinda, I didn't expect you to come along for the ride. This is wonderful!

"I mean you no harm. It's time for a chat. The gun will do you no good here, William. You might as well put it away."

Jared grinned, watching Lucy stare at the man hovering over her sister. They were in a cage, but the door was open.

"Sloppy, sloppy, Walker," he continued talking to Sam while watching Lucy. "Leaving that forest clearing for just anyone to come along and take. Don't worry, I took care of it for you. A thousand years of energy just sitting there. Silly children. No idea what to do with your power."

"The child is mine," the Walker said without emotion.

"Yes, yes, of course, Sam. No permanent damage was done. David, you will release the binding now. Lucinda, you may go to your sister if you'd like. We are done with her."

Lucy didn't move, still staring at the man in the cage.

"You cannot kill him, my dear. Too much energy," Jared said, smiling. "Maybe later."

"Stalker?" William asked, eyes still on Jared.

"No," Jared said, grinning. "Well, yes. That, too. But he also tried to cut her in half when they were children. Raped her a couple times. Her power had not yet manifested, but it called to him. Tore his brain to pieces! It was amazing. He was never really stable, but still."

Several things happened in quick succession.

The room vibrated with energy, creating a vortex that sucked the air from Lucy's chest, making it impossible to breathe.

Samuel's eyes focused with cold, glowing intensity. "Jared—" he began, the word echoing through time.

Jared's fear screamed through the room, a look of terror on his face, before he disappeared.

Hennessy fired six gunshots at the man hovering over Linda in the corner. Then he toppled over, dying, as a shot rebounded off of David, directly back at Hennessy.

"Shame, shame." David laughed. "Jared told you the gun was useless."

ADALINE SHRIEKED in terror and pain from the chair in the living room.

"Addy! Is he worse?" Adrian yelled, running for her as Adaline slid Ree out of her lap onto the floor.

"JESSUP!" William roared, diving for his best friend as he appeared in Darla's big room.

"What happened?" Darla screamed, already crying at the sight of the blood pouring from Hennessy's torso and mouth.

"MOVE, WILLIAM! OUT OF THE WAY," Adrian bellowed, dropping to his knees next to his adopted brother.

"He is mine," Adaline breathed with power and intensity as she bent to grab Hennessy's hand.

At her touch, Hennessy's body went into convulsions.

"Rage, pull out the projectiles. Now."

Adrian's eyes snapped to Adaline before he fell backward in surprise. Her skin and hair danced with iridescent white fire, eyes burning with righteous anger and fear.

Adrian would forever envision the angels of Heaven as Adaline looked at that moment.

"Remove them, now," she repeated. "Then help the woman."

With another quick glance around, he realized a battered, beaten, broken, filthy woman was sobbing, trying to drag herself to Ree. "Linda."

"Where are Sam and Lucy?" Hank yelled, holding his sobbing daughter back, out of the way.

WHEN SAM REAPPEARED in the basement, David was on top of Lucy, punching wildly and screaming incoherently. Before he could get there to help, Lucy slugged her attacker in the face and flipped him off of her.

"TIME IS UP, you fucking monster! My sister! My Ree! MY LIFE!" she roared, slamming her fist into his head repeatedly.

He cackled with manic laughter, blood spurting from his nose as his face continued to heal after each contact.

Lucy didn't seem to care. She continued venting most of a decade of rage and terror by pulverizing her tormentor's head. "MY CHILD! YOU TORTURED MY CHILD! HENNESSY!"

"Keep swinging," David taunted as she pounded on him.

"Too much energy," he choked out. "Can't take me down."

Lucy didn't seem to hear him, didn't care as her knuckles ripped open.

"I'll catch up when you're exhausted...just like Linda. She doesn't scream like you do, though."

"MY SISTER! YEARS WITHOUT MY SISTER!" she hollered, ripping at his eyes.

"Getting tired?" David grinned through his wrecked mouth. "You haven't put a dent in the energy, honey. Keep going... Then I'll take my turn, lover."

Shifting a knee over his chest, pinning him with her body weight, she paused, breathing hard, ignoring the stench from the body in the corner.

"Yeah?" she asked. "Can you heal from this?"

Digging her fingers into his eye sockets, Lucy intentionally pulled her energy all the way forward for the first time in her life. Lightning tore down from the sky, ripping through the house, directly into his head.

Panting with exhaustion and revulsion, she fell over, off the shriveled, burned remains as the house started on fire.

"Lucy," Sam murmured.

She didn't respond.

"Lucinda," Sam said, touching her hand.

She flinched back from him, lost in her power.

"Time to finish this."

Lucy stared at Sam, uncomprehending.

"Sweetheart, come back from it now."

No response.

"Lucy, it's done."

She didn't even blink.

"Adrian and Ree are waiting for you. Linda is waiting for you."

The words were gentle, but they hit Lucy like a fist to the gut.

She gagged, wiping at the sweat and blood splatter on her face before she started vomiting.

Out of the corner of his eye, Sam saw David's charred body move.

Wrapping his arms around Lucy, he bodily dragged her away before she noticed the movement.

Then Sam took three steps back to David. Three steps back to the man that tormented and raped an at-risk teenager—short steps back to Lucy's attacker and stalker, the man that tortured and would have killed an innocent child. The man who might have killed his brother. Then he waited.

When David's torn, torched eyelids flicked open, he met the gaze of the enraged Walker.

Pulling forward all his power, Samuel opened Time again, focused on the man at his feet.

"**Go to Hell,**" Sam's quiet voice boomed through time, echoing in the room, ripping eternity from one who found joy in hurting others.

The Walker did not look away, did not flinch, and did not blink as the energy drained from the body before him. He watched the life leak out of a monster, unrepentant for his actions.

When it was done, his gaze lifted to Lucy. She stared, eyes wide.

"It's done."

She nodded, finally breaking down in sobs.

Sam pulled her to standing, kissed her forehead, and then wrapped her in a hug. "No more. You are no one's victim, Lucinda. It's done."

Holding on for dear life, she sobbed into his chest.

"We have to call it again," Sam murmured. "We can't leave it like this. Can you call the energy again? I'll bring fire, Lucy. You must bring the lightning and storms. Understand?"

She nodded into his chest, calling forth her own power, gathering clouds overhead. They could hear sirens in the distance, likely headed toward the gunshots, screaming, and lightning.

Flames exploded around them as the lightning touched down four more times, destroying the house and everything in it.

"Home," Sam soothed. "It's over."

SAM APPEARED in the big room, arms wrapped around a sobbing, shaking Lucy.

"Lucy!" Adrian yelled from the floor where he was helping Linda. "Where are you hurt?"

"She's fine, Adrian. Mostly fine," Sam said, smoothing her hair back as she continued to sob into his chest. "It's done. It's over. Hennessy? Was I fast enough?"

"Fast enough," Hennessy croaked from the other end of the room where he was propped up against the living room table, holding Beth. "Healing."

"Why are her clothes scorched? Why do you smell like burnt hair? What the fuck happened?" Will yelled.

No one answered him.

Heaving great sobs, Lucy continued to cling to Sam until Lucas touched her arm, dropping her into a deep sleep.

"Adrian, we should clean her up before putting her to bed," Sam murmured. "She doesn't need to wake up covered in the gore of a monster. Linda, how are you?"

"I DON'T UNDERSTAND," Nora said again, sitting at Darla's dining room table with the family later that night. "I wouldn't think Jared capable of this."

"I didn't see him until recently," Linda explained. "I don't know how recent. There wasn't a good way to measure days down there. I thought he was new. Some people cycled in and out. I just thought he was another one. It took me a while to figure out that he was in charge, Aunt Nora."

Nora nodded, squeezing her niece's hand.

"I know he was John's father. John told me that along the way. I don't know how David fit in."

Freshly showered and well-fed for the first time in years, Linda was exhausted. But she agreed to answer questions before going to sleep.

"John and David were foster brothers," Hennessy answered, head resting back against the wall behind his chair.

"What were they looking for?" Ben asked. "Do you recall anything they were searching for in the binding?"

"I thought they were spying on Lucy, but then things changed when Jared surfaced. I kept trying to kill the binding to Ree. I didn't want them to get to Lucy or Ree. I thought they'd screw up eventually. They'd push too far, and I'd be broken beyond repair. But they just kept pushing. Then Jared showed up, babbling something about a name, made me say a word."

"What is your name, Linda?" Sam asked.

"Huh?"

"What word did he make you say?" Nora asked, knowing what was to come. "What name did you take?"

Linda blinked a few times, looking lost. "Perseverance."

Greggory shook his head in disbelief. "He was a son to me. How did I miss this?"

"No," Ben disagreed. "I don't think you missed it, Gregg. I spent a lot of time with him. There's no way he could have hidden this from me. Something has changed."

After a pause, Will sighed. "How did he Walk, Sam? I thought you were the only one that could do that. How and why did he disappear like that? He was about to go off on a cheesy villain monologue then just disappeared."

"I don't know how he did it," Sam admitted, scratching his head. "But I'm certain he ran because he felt me opening Time."

The room went still.

"Like high school?" Jake whispered.

Sam nodded.

"What did you do?" Adaline asked. "I felt it, but I don't know what it was."

The emotion dropped from Sam's face. "I took eternity from the man that tormented her. Tormented both of them."

No one replied.

"I'm not sorry, Addy. I knew you wouldn't want me to do it. But he deserves to rot in hell."

"Sam," Ava breathed. "Judging life?"

He met her gaze without flinching. "I know."

"The compass?"

Sighing, Sam lifted his shirt. The compass marking pointed closer to the north-east position, rather than true north. "I felt it moving when I made the decision to do it. I did it anyway."

The room was quiet for a moment.

"Flowers?" Sam eventually asked Addy.

"Three fell, but I don't think they're lost. More like someone stepped on them. I don't know what to expect now."

He nodded. "I'm sorry to have caused you pain. But he intentionally harmed those who are mine."

She nodded, tears dripping down her face. "I would have taken his life if you did not. It would have caused me great pain."

"Adaline!" Ava gasped, shocked.

"Jessup is mine, Mama. Part of me. What happened was wrong."

"I fired the gun," Hennessy said. "My fault. Jared said the gun would do no good. But fuck if I was going to stand there with the man that did that to Lou."

Will and Sam nodded in agreement.

"Beat me to it," Will admitted. "I would have spat the bullets out and had a steak, though, asshole. Don't ever fucking do that again."

"You wanted me to stay here," Hennessy murmured to Sam.

Sam nodded. "I didn't want you to go, but I didn't know why. I couldn't see where we were headed. And you are right. You and William know what battle is."

Hennessy sighed. "Maybe not this kind of battle."

There was a pounding on the front door. After a survey of the baffled faces around the table, William got up to answer it.

Expecting trouble, he unholstered the gun at his side before looking through the window next to the double door.

"What the fuck?" he exclaimed, throwing the door open. "What are you doing here?"

"Obviously, I'm interrupting dinner," Micah said. His grin was conspicuous in its absence.

"That gun would do you no good against me. The best you could hope for is a bit of a distraction. You people need to learn how to use your energy. Playtime is over."

"Micah!" Sam called, relieved. "Please, we need help. Will you take—"

"Samuel," Micah interrupted, "I need you to find James. I must speak to James and Evelyn. Now. They have failed in one of their primary responsibilities. We are far out of balance."

"I know we're lost, but I don't know why," Sam sighed. "Come in."

Thank you for reading!

The Trellis family's adventure continues in The Pillars, Building the Circle - Book 5, available now.

For alerts on new releases and other book news, join my email list at https://maggielilybooks.com/sign-up.

Finally, your Amazon review of this novel would be much appreciated. Reviews are critical to the success of brand new authors (like me!)

ALSO BY MAGGIE M LILY

BUILDING THE CIRCLE SERIES

Building the Circle - Volume 1

The Call

The Power

The Center

Building the Circle - Volume 2

The Corners

The Pillars

The Close

Becoming Hank - A Trellis Family Novella

PEACEKEEPER'S HARMONY SERIES

Ransom

Reaping

Rise

Made in the USA
Coppell, TX
16 April 2022

76609972R00207